The Way I See It

Logan Capesius

Copyright

(*Pending*)

Like the Cover?

The artwork was conceptualized and executed by Mindy Licther! Find more wonderful artwork on her Facebook page and Instagram:

@MLICHTERart

To my forever home as a Hawkeye: The University of Iowa.

To friends and family who have supported me through what is only the beginning of this journey.

To Professor Kevin Smith, who has aided me greatly not only in my progression as a writer, but also in the completion of this manuscript.

To Greg Ahlers, who demonstrated consistent enthusiastic support for my dream, fueling my desire for discipline and excellence.

To Dave Wieland, who established a strong foundation in the art of writing with both encouragement and steady support.

To Mom, the rock upon which I lean.

Finally, to the memory of Gerald A. Berte.

I

The suburban streets tend to remain silent, but I hear the unbearable sound that filters through the avenues and bounces around the culverts. It's not the bustling trees standing like hardened soldiers at the perimeter of the complex. Nor is it the slight *ting* that results when someone closes the community mailbox at the gated entrance. It's not even the lifted Duramax with thirty-eight inch tires that rolls by at a quarter 'til seven every morning, shaking the windows of every house on our street. It's the ambition within the mansion that has four garage doors just a minute's walk down the perfectly-leveled sidewalk. It's the bark of the dog playing with three children in a neighboring backyard. Maybe it's the fulfillment within the two-story blue house with a white top across the street, planted in such a way that it stares at me through a four-paned window when I make my morning coffee. That noise is deafening.

I pour a new Costa Rican blend into a black mug and take a sip too hot to drink. I can tolerate the slight burn on my tongue because it's real. Rounding the granite countertop that weighs down the island, I take a seat on the middle chair. Its brown leather folds underneath where four spindly legs plant themselves into the bottom of the cushion that supports me.

A whistle bends down the staircase followed by the *tha-thump* of feet.

"Good morning, Liam," Alexandra says as she stumbles into the kitchen wearing a slim gray suit, one of the four different suits she wears to work. She deals with money and investing. As a musician, I don't have much experience with those.

"Hey, sis." I take another slurp.

Alexandra opens the cabinet near the fridge. She runs her finger along the shelf until she finds her travel mug. She sets it in front of her, then pauses. I already know what she's about to say.

"Dinner tonight, remember?"

"How could I forget?" I stare back at the house across the street.

Filling her mug to the brim, Alexandra turns to me with a look of understanding. She plants one hand on the edge of the counter and sighs. "If you don't want to be here when they arrive … I get it. If you do decide to stay here with us, please promise me you'll be cordial this time." She purses her lips and ushers a cool breath over her coffee, swirling the rising steam. "Oh, and clean yourself up a bit. Your hair looks like a mop, and your beard makes you look homeless."

"'Course." I slide my mug off the edge of the counter and into my palm and start for the basement stairs. The bottom of the mug is warm against my hand. I don't mind the burn.

"I mean it," Alexandra says indignantly.

"I perform tonight, Alex," I say. "So I won't be here."

"Oh. Play well, then. We'll miss you." Alexandra tries to sound upset, but she and I both know the sadness in her voice is no more genuine than half the country folks in country music. I saunter into the basement, and the front door opens and quietly shuts once I make it to the bottom step. She'll be back by 5:00.

I know why she doesn't want me here. Alexandra fears I'd cause a scene if I were to stick around for dinner. She is inviting the neighbors–my ex-wife Rachel and her new husband Marcus–after all. The last time she invited them over, I may have stumbled in late, slightly intoxicated, and it's possible I said some things I shouldn't have. I'm not really sure. I've found my memory never serves me too well in general, but I'll never forget Rachel's reaction to my drunken rage as she watched me helplessly with a horror-stricken face. That night, I only caught her eye for a second. At first she acted as though my

7

contempt for her was completely unwarranted, but her look of confusion transformed into what I guessed to be empathy. Before I could make matters worse, Alexandra practically threw me down the stairs cussing, later apologizing repeatedly to her guests.

I yelled back, "It blows my mind that you insist on keeping her around!"

To which, Alexandra responded, "You can't expect best friends to just … cut it off."

I said, "You'd be surprised how easy some people make it."

Our basement opens up to a bar on the left that hides in the corner. Some would say an in-home bar is a modern necessity in 2031. I'd be one of those people. Against the far wall sits a black leather couch large enough to seat eight people comfortably, ten if you feel like pushing it, not that we'll ever need that much space. We hardly ever have company. The sofa faces a 92-inch theater screen which Alexandra and I use frequently, streaming sports, Netflix, and Nat Geo Wild.

To the right of the staircase is a large storage room I like to call "The Cave". The door always remains shut, hiding little more inside than an old treadmill, a PC with a racecar steering wheel mounted on a small office desk, Alexandra's firearms, and way too much empty floor space. Everything that's old, out of use, or unworthy of being seen is banished to this chamber of solitude.

Propped up against the far wall of the Cave is a miniature stage, my acoustic and electric guitars hanging in the background. My sister wouldn't allow me to practice my routine when sports were on or when people were over, so we compromised by building a stage in a secluded area where no one would ever see or hear me. It was her idea, but I don't mind. It's honestly good practice since most of the stages in Nashville aren't any bigger than a kiddie pool.

Since big sis isn't home, however, I can bring an acoustic out of The Cave and write music while reclining comfortably on the couch and simultaneously watching Australian dudes catch snakes on TV. I might even mix myself a drink.

Heading over to the bar, I pull out a small whisky glass from one of the drawers and begin filling it with a shot of bourbon. If you tip the glass at *just* the right angle, the liquor won't even make a sound as it hypnotically swirls to the bottom.

Suddenly the pitter patter of little feet thumping down stairs breaks the silence. I hear the footsteps coming closer until they quickly stop. I wait a moment or two, looking expectantly near the bottom of the staircase. I stand relaxed with my drink in hand, when a head of boyish bleach-blond hair rapidly pops out around the corner, bearing a smile that's missing a couple teeth.

"Whoah!" I falter back convincingly.

"Gotchu, Daddy!" Casey runs around the edge of the bar in his blue pajamas to give my legs a bear hug.

"You did." I brush his hair with my hand.

"What are we doing today?" he stares up at me with those little blue eyes.

"I think Daddy's gonna play some music again today."

"Okay." Casey looks down.

I pat his head softly. "Let me grab my guitar. You run up to your room and play for a while. I'll come get you when I'm done."

"Okay." Casey unwraps his little arms from around my legs and trots up the stairs.

I open the door to The Cave, pull my guitar with a caramel-colored mahogany finish off its hook, and come back out to see Casey sitting upright on the couch, his sockless feet bouncing up and down.

"I wanna listen to you play, Daddy."

"Fair enough." I give a smile that quickly fades. Stumbling over to the couch, I take a seat beside my son. He looks intensely into my eyes, expecting something amazing. For a moment, I stare through him with somber thoughts

9

racking my brain. *These songs I've created through pain I'll play for you, so you never have to feel it.*

Resting the guitar on my leg, I begin strumming.

Sometimes I get *lost*. No, that's not the right word. *Found* isn't particularly accurate, either. *Taken*. That's closer. It only happens when I play music. A couple chords can pull me toward the beaches of Florida, the mountains of the West, the hills of the heartland, or home. I'm not the same when I play. With every scale, the hours pass like minutes, and I begin to see the world for what it is: a place full of sin and greed and lust and heartbreak. It's clarity. Progressions force me to confront loneliness. Each note, every pluck of a new string is a solemn reminder of reality. Every now and again I trade my pick for a pen. The pen wills itself into loops and swirls on a small notepad that morph into something far from calligraphy but reminiscent of art.

I'm helplessly drawn to this hypnotic state of being, in the same way a mosquito is drawn toward light. I think I enjoy being at the mercy of its desires. It feels good to no longer be in control. The blame is no longer on me.

I strum ballads from Johnny Cash, the king George Strait, Travis Tritt, and Hank Jr. Occasionally, I throw in a few of my own, but I'll readily admit they don't compare. I don't know for how long I play, but I sing and sing and strum until...

The aroma of sautéed onions and peppers pulls me away from the *taken* world. It's coming from upstairs. I shake my head and rub my eyes. The projector in front of me is off, the bar lights are making the basement bright, and the door to The Cave is shut. Everything in the room is the same as I left it, but Casey is no longer here. He must have gone up to his room while I was playing.

I look down at my watch to discover it's half past five. Alexandra is already home. I'm supposed to perform at Legends downtown in half an hour.

10

Quickly, I run into The Cave and get my things together. I don't need all too much. Gently laying my acoustic into its case, I snap it shut and scurry up the stairs. I can hear small conversation as I approach the main level. When I reach the top of the stairs, I stop to listen, just for a moment.

"Oh, and I could never forget the time when you dropped that pint of ice cream right into your cleavage–" Alexandra's voice is hysterical, comforting me. It's been a while since I've heard her laugh like that.

"We were so drunk–makes me miss college." That voice I hear in my dreams … it both haunts and paralyzes me, followed by the deep, haughty laugh of her replacement.

Reaching the top, I see Alexandra leaning over the stove, no longer in her work attire. She is rather dressed up: navy pants and a white button-up shirt. With her brunette hair curled to her shoulders, she looks very pretty.

I turn the corner and glimpse a woman with curly blonde hair and a man with a dark complexion and glasses sitting at our dining room table, both dressed in similar attire. The man is shuffling a deck of cards, but he stops once he feels my presence behind him. He turns slightly in his chair toward me. Both he and the woman pause to give me forced grins.

I nod to each of them. "Marcus. Rachel."

To be honest, I have nothing against Marcus. He's a good man. I'll even admit he looks sharp tonight. A muscular guy, his clothes fit over him tightly, accentuating his athletic build. Swept up by Rachel's charm after she left me, he married her almost immediately after Rachel declared for divorce. I'd have probably done the same in his shoes.

But Rachel … how can I not hold her in contempt? After everything she's done, after everything I did for her…I'd be lying if I said the pain has gone away. It is still ever-present, making for long-lasting heartaches, constant anxiety, and the best country songs I've ever written.

"Liam!" Alexandra checks her wrist. "Aren't you going to be late to Tootsie's?"

11

"It's Legends tonight … but yeah, I've got to get going."

Alexandra's mouth hangs open slightly. "Right."

Before I go, I should say goodbye to a special someone. Turning around, I saunter up the second set of stairs where I find Casey's room. Inside, my small and fragile son runs silently in a circle, holding his arms out at either side. With spaceship noises, he teeters left and right. When I crack open the door, he pretends not to notice me.

"Hey there, junior."

Bop, bop, bop. Casey's lips pop. Maybe he's switched to a helicopter. Or his spaceship is now armed with an artillery gun. No matter, as his aircraft comes to a somersaulting halt–a smooth landing, nonetheless.

"Daddy's got to leave, okay?"

"Okay,' he says, chest heaving, the fabric of his blue pajamas wearing tight against his little chest.

"Love you, kiddo."

"I love you too, Daddy."

I shut the door, stand outside for a moment, and head back down to the kitchen.

The three of them are once again making small talk at the dining table. They watch me. Rachel watches me, too.

"Case is up in his room," I say, avoiding Rachel's eyes. "You can talk to him if you'd like."

She shares a glimpse with Alexandra, then nods solemnly.

Being in her presence calls to mind many memories. They begin washing over me all at once. Not all memories are bad. In fact, I'd say the opposite is true. Most memories I had with Rachel were great, maybe even perfect. That's why they're so heavy. I feel myself frozen in front of them. It's too much for me to take in right now. I need to get out.

Lending a wry smile to Alexandra, I rush out the door without another word. It's better that our exchanges are left short.

12

Heaving my guitar case into the back of my old blue Ford, I tap my hand twice on a rust patch along the edge of the bucket as if to plead with the vehicle. *Take me away.* I jump in the driver's seat. With a few turns of the engine, the truck growls into gear.

I place the truck in reverse, backing out of the driveway without glancing at the rearview mirror.

On the verge is where I'm at. I turn the radio dial to the right. Hard as I may try to escape, the road is a catalyst. The gates of my head that held back the flood give way. Tightening my grip on the wheel, I give in.

***

"I appreciate it, but I don't think now is the right time to get distracted, sis. You know, just starting college and all." I sighed and took a sip out of the to-go cup I was given, pressing the cell phone tightly against my ear.

It was the beginning of October, the first autumn leaves beginning to fall in Southeast Iowa. On windy days like this one, they would bounce through the streets and alleys like children playing hopscotch. Birds cried from rooftops, blessing ears with their last beautiful songs before they disappeared for months on end. The sun still had enough energy to peek through the clouds and make the state bright, but only for a while longer.

"At least agree to meet this girl, Liam."

"I *have* already met her!"

"Yeah, but she was drunk that time."

I remained silent, unimpressed.

"Give her some grace, little bro. She was just a freshman at the time. Don't act as though *you* haven't been drunk yet." After a bit of silence, Alexandra's voice comes in rather sincerely. "Look, we both know you've been struggling a bit to make friends … and that's nothing to be ashamed of! College is a tough place. All I'm saying is I thought it'd be a good idea to offer

13

you someone who would like to be your friend. In fact, Rachel is the one who thought of it."

I looked to my left to see a young college couple, about the same age as me, happily enjoying a meal together under the shade of an umbrella. The girl was sipping her drink, trying not to laugh while the guy was playing with his food.

Exhaling, I replied. "Fair enough."

"Is that a yes?" Alexandra didn't give me the time to respond. "Oh my gosh, Liam, you won't regret this! I promise you're going to love her."

~

"Hey, a trail!"

"Rach, we probably shouldn't–" but she was already several yards into the light wooded area. The tail of Rachel's red dress bounced behind her and then vanished into a thicket of trees and bushes.

"Of course," I sighed and reluctantly followed.

I didn't have to walk all too far to get to her. The weaving trail led me through twigs and branches, and I had to duck under a few large tree limbs just to get near the edge of the rolling Iowa River. That's where I found her staring up at the sky in awe. Usually city lights hide the stars, but the recent storm left many areas out of power, including ours. The city had a foreign silence to it, only the rapid flow of river water making a sound. Rocks crunched under my feet as I moved to Rachel's side. For a while we said nothing. She kept her gaze on the stars, and I tried to as well.

Out of the corner of my eye, I saw a wisp of Rachel's curly blond hair whipping in the wind at her shoulders. At first, I ignored it, but I felt as though it was trying to tell me something. I followed the strand up to Rachel's blue eyes illuminated by the balls of light an immeasurable distance away. My eyes were then drawn to her bottom lip hanging just below her top. Her mouth

14

quivered. The air was warm. I wondered if Rachel could hear the drums beating. My hand gently caressed her cheek, and she turned her head toward me. Her inviting eyes evaluated me. She smiled as if to say, "I'm here."

~

The sounds of shattered glass woke me. Bright sunlight beamed through the windowpane revealing floating dust particles hanging near the bed post by my warm covered feet. The ceiling fan was rotating violently above me. To my left, where Rachel usually slept, there were crumpled sheets that filled the space of her absence. I was used to her being gone before waking. I forgot she had the day off.

"Darnit, you stupid son of a –" a voice came from the kitchen. Rachel must have been cooking.

Slowly lifting the soft comforter off my chest, I stretched my arms above my head, spots of black clouding my eyes until I exhaled and let my arms fall back to my side. I wiped the weariness from my eyes. On the night-stand to my right sat a smartphone with the charger plugged in, a watch, and a ring. I lightly grabbed the ring with my index finger and thumb, twisting it onto my left hand. Placing my feet at the edge of the bed, I stood up and walked out the bedroom door to a scene that even Hollywood couldn't script.

A cream-colored batter was plastered everywhere. It was as if a massive bomb had gone off, and the epicenter was the large plastic bowl on the counter. It contained a whisk jutting outward at a slight angle. Small white droplets were artistically streaked across the navy-colored cabinets hanging up on the walls, mounds of goo and broken glass sitting like fallen soldiers starkly contrasting the smooth wooden floors. Last but not least, an obscene amount of batter stained Rachel's black pajama shirt that fit her snuggly. The room was still and silent. Rachel bowed over the counter in defeat, supporting

15

herself with one hand pressed against the granite while the other hand was scratching at the back of her head.

"Hey there." From the opposite end of the room, I moved slowly toward Rachel with my palms up. As I moved closer, I noticed bits of batter that were now stuck in her otherwise beautifully braided hair falling over her shoulder. She gradually rose until her blue eyes met mine and began penetrating my soul.

"What happened?" I gave a wry smile.

"I was trying to make pancakes," she said sternly.

I nodded. "For an entire tribe or ...?"

"Very funny." She scowled. With both of her palms she gestured toward the bowl filled with batter. "I was mixing this, so I wrapped my arm around the bowl, and in doing so I managed to bump one of the glasses I had sitting on the counter here. It fell to the ground and broke, so then I was pissed, right?" I nodded. "So I smacked my hand against the counter. Well guess what? My hand hit the darn bowl instead and made a darn mess everywhere in our gosh darn kitchen." She was fuming at this point, breathing heavily like she does when she has a fit.

While attempting to force the grin off my face, my eyes fell upon the desperate scene in front of me once again. Some of these stains would be a pain in the rear to clean. Beside my toes was a particularly large glob of batter that would have made a nice pancake had the ground heated up to a few hundred degrees. I reached down, folding both hands around the glob like it was a baby bird. Rachel eyed me curiously.

Standing up, I said, "Tag." I lobbed the batter toward Rachel. It held together surprisingly well and hit her square in the chest. "You're it."

Backing up with a gasp, Rachel looked at her chest in shock. "What the hell's the matter with you?" I was practically on the floor laughing at this point when she decided to fire back. Bent to the ground, I wasn't able to see the barrage of batter that pelted my side. I got up, and goo was steadily dripping off my white t-shirt. Rachel expressed her satisfaction with a wink.

Holding my arms out on either side of me as I was soaked in pancake batter, I took a step in Rachel's direction. "How about a hug?"

She held one finger up at me. "Don't you dare. Liam–" she yelped as I chased her around the counter, playing cat and mouse until I caught up. I grabbed her by the shoulder, and we both fell to the ground. Rachel landed on top of me giggling, her perfect smile just inches away. Time slowed down. Her heartbeat thumped in unison with mine. Suddenly Rachel was all I saw, all I felt. Leaning her head to the right, she left the goose bumps on her neck vulnerable, enticing my lips. We were close now. Everything was silent save for those scattered breaths and moans that were unique to Rachel grazing my ear.

I loved her.

***

I park the truck about a block away from Legends, quickly grabbing my equipment from the tailgate and scurrying inside an old-fashioned bar with a small stage to the left of the entrance. It peeks out the window so street goers and passersby can take a quick look at the performing act before deciding to enter. Checking my watch, I notice I'm a few minutes late, but the bartenders don't seem to mind. One is mixing a martini while the other counts their tips. They pay no attention to me as I walk through the door. The bar is particularly empty, only a group of three sitting at a small table in the back. I guess I'll be playing for the smiling faces plastered on the record wall tonight.

It takes me a couple of minutes to tune my guitar and set up the amp. Once I plug the microphone in, I flip the switch and lift my head to the audience. For my opening melody, I play an original: "Mourning Cowboy".

Performing for me is a strange departure from normality. Not because of the nerves. I don't get nervous when I play for strangers. It doesn't even have to do with the sudden demand for perfection, knowing that one mess-up can be the difference between making or breaking it. That's irrelevant to me. No, performing is abnormal because I am present for it. I can feel and hear the music I play. It is the only time I have control over where I'm *taken*.

I start by closing my eyes. I take one, two deep breaths. Strumming a few notes, I open my eyes. The people vanish. The bar disappears. Suddenly I find myself back home in The Cave performing for nobody but myself and the large empty space in front of me. I'm free in this moment. For years I have been doing this, perfecting my ability to control my environment.

After every song, however, the noises of applause and endless cheering become more and more deafening. I assume the bar is inevitably filling until it's packed to the corners. The noise almost has the power to pull me out of my *taken* world. The Cave fades in and out of view as reality attempts to snag my focus. I try to ignore the people in the crowd. I focus on me. Again I close my eyes, taking a deep breath to silence the world around me. My ears ring, but a couple licks of the guitar take me right back to The Cave. When I told Alexandra of this trick I rely on, she didn't believe me at first. But many musicians before me have detailed similar experiences.

Angus Yung attributes his crazy on-stage behavior to a "guitar demon" who allegedly "possesses" him while he shreds for sell-out crowds. John Lennon described feelings of possession when writing music. Even Kanye West who now writes lots of Christian music has used the term "possession" when detailing his past writing affairs. What I do is no different, except in the fact that I don't feel as though an outside presence possesses me. Though I do call it my *taken* world, it feels more like freedom. A weight lifted off my shoulders.

Ending the performance with my own rendition of "The Devil Went Down to Georgia", I strum my last chord, the music fades, and the bar pops back into view. The place is completely full. Icy buckets of beer sit on every other table with groups of people circled around them, holding their bottles to the sky. People are clapping and laughing and drunk. Standing near the stage is an older woman in a black leather jacket and blue jeans, clapping politely like one would at a golf tournament. I meet her eyes.

"Spectacular as usual," she says with a smile.

Over the past few years, I have attracted one loyal fan who stops and talks to me after every performance. She's an elderly woman named Josephine who really enjoys the party life, I suppose, showing up at some point in the middle of my act and staying until the end.

I pull the guitar strap from around my neck, setting it in its case behind me. Hopping off the stage, I give Josephine a warm hug. "Thank you. I'm glad you came."

"You know I wouldn't miss it."

Though her face is pale and worn from the trials of life, her smile is so warm, her eyes so inviting that it almost hurts. A few patches of ginger remain in her white curly hair. I wonder what her secret is. She always seems to be so full of life. Little does she know, I'd die for a chance to feel like her, happy and fulfilled. Just like I used to be.

Glasses clink together in a toast near the bar. It gives me a good excuse to focus on something else. I look to see a man and his wife enjoying one last round. My gaze falls, obviously enough for Josephine to notice.

She places a finger under my chin. "What's the matter?"

"Nothing." I try for a smile, but she stares expectantly back into my eyes. She might as well put her hands on her hips. "Fine," I say, "I've been dealing with a couple of things at home. That's all."

"You're fooling nobody, Liam."

Sighing, I take a seat on the edge of the stage. Josephine moves closer. For extra comfort, I fiddle with my fingers while I talk. "Rachel was over again tonight. With Marcus."

19

"And?"

I frown. "And that bothers me?"

Josephine rests a hand on my shoulder. "Please, the two of you have been split for two years now—"

"Three."

"At some point, the past can no longer own you, Liam. Surely you've learned that by now."

Placing my hands on my legs, I look up in her direction again. Those same wise, joyful eyes see right through me. I can't hide anything from her. "Clearly I'm doing a poor job of that."

"Yes, you are." She chuckles for a moment. Then she sits beside me on the stage, examining the ceiling in contemplation. "I used to tell my grandson two very important phrases, Liam. One was that you cannot change the past, but you *can* change the future. The other was to always believe in yourself."

"I wish wise words were more proactive."

"Words may not do much, but they can spur you into action." Josephine paused. "You can make it through this. I promise."

"What if I can't?"

"You can." I scratch the back of my head while Josephine stands in front of me, ready to leave. She pulls at the flaps of her leather jacket. "Keep plugging away, and keep writing that wonderful music."

"Will you help me?" I meet her eyes. "Make it through this, I mean."

Josephine nearly cracks up. "Help. Ha! Only *you* have the power to help yourself. An … experienced woman like me might only be able to provide you with a few tips and tricks."

"I'd settle for a tip."

Fumbling with her pocket, Josephine pulls out a crumpled and discolored ten, gently laying it in my palm—not the kind of tip I was looking for, but it'll have to do. "As I said," she starts, "keep plugging away."

I stand and give her another embrace. "Thank you, Josephine."

20

"When will I see you next?"

"Tomorrow. Honkytonk Central."

Slowly making her way to the exit, Josephine waves her fingers at me. The stage lights reflect a glimmer in her eye that almost looks like a tear. "Bye, bye." She turns and walks out the door.

I'm alone by the stage. A few strangers dressed in flannel shirts, cowboy hats, and boots come up to me. They pat me on the back, saying things like "Great show, man!" or "How can I buy your music?" I sign phone cases, peoples' skin when they have nothing else for me to sign, and some souvenirs that tourists picked up from the store a couple doors down. Every once in a while, I agree to pictures.

When they leave, I walk behind the bar, tracing my hand along the wooden countertop. I feel the bumps and nooks in what was once a perfect seal, smooth and clear, protecting crafted oak underneath. After decades of use, the seal has been worn, but it is still there nonetheless. This seal doesn't allow anyone to feel what's really underneath. You may ask a man to touch the counter, and he'll tell you it feels like wood, but the man doesn't know what wood feels like. He only recognizes the bumps and the patterns, unable to acknowledge the fact that he's touching a coat of seal. It doesn't make the wood underneath any less real. Some things just need a layer of protection in order to withstand time.

I pull a bottle of Jameson off the wall while pretending the bartenders aren't furious, and I grab my own glass. Men at the bar must recognize me. They stare as I pour my shot.

"Cheers," I say to no one in particular.

I wake to find myself lying sideways on dark leather without a blanket, unable to recall much of the previous night. My head pounds, and my breathing is ragged. The lights aren't on. Beside my face is a small patch of drool. At least I hope it's drool and not the tiniest amount of vomit. Wiping a

21

bit of sweat off my forehead, I turn my body over so that I'm lying on my back. I take a deep breath.

The shower soaks my body once I find the strength to make it there, steam rising and clinging to the clear glass door. Resting my hand against the wall, nausea continues to broil inside. I step out and grab the soft brown towel hanging on the wall. It brushes against my face to dry warm tears the showerhead cried onto me. After drying myself, I use the towel to wipe the mirror down. I stare at the reflection. Perhaps Alexandra was right. I do look like a homeless man. My beard has grown a couple inches out in all directions, and my dirty blond hair, even after just being washed, maintains a greasy look.

Once dressed, I walk out to find Alexandra sitting at the dining room table in a robe. Through a pair of glasses she stares intensely at her phone, likely reading CNBC's most recent take on the markets.

"Hey, sis," I grumble.

Her eyes glance up. "Sounds like you had yourself a night."

"Something like that." I pull out a chair across from her.

"You sounded great last night," Alexandra says. She looks at me with a smile, but it fades as her eyes dart left and right. Quickly pointing to her phone, she says, "Social media was buzzing."

My palms cover my eyes, and my fingers wipe my temple as I attempt to eradicate the migraine. I pull my cell phone out and slap it onto the table.

"Who posted a video? I want to look."

Reaching over, Alexandra snags my phone away from me.

"The last thing you need is some screen time right now. That'll make your migraine worse, dummy. You need an aspirin and some breakfast." She hops out of her chair. Floating over to the kitchen, she pulls some pans out of the cabinets and several items from the refrigerator. "Bacon and eggs alright?"

"Um–"

"Here." She places a glass of water and a couple pills on the island near the left barstool.

22

Slowly I get up and stumble into the kitchen area. Sitting at the edge of the island, I wrap my hand around the cold glass. In a sip I knock back the pills. "Everything alright?"

With a straight face and the slightest hint of a smile, Alexandra says, "Yeah, why?"

"Never mind."

In a few minutes, she whips up a quick plate of eggs, bacon, and toast, placing it on the counter in front of me. "Eat up."

I oblige.

Alexandra goes back to her phone, leaning against the island on her elbows. I finish, and with my thumb I slide the plate closer to the center of the island, peeking up at my sister in the process. "How was your little date with Marcus and Lucy last night?"

"Lucy?"

"Yeah. Lucifer, Satan, Rachel. Whichever name you prefer."

Rolling her eyes, Alexandra says, "We enjoyed ourselves … and don't call her that, Liam. Rachel isn't a bad person. Grow up a little."

"I'm only kidding." *Sort of*, I think to myself.

A silence falls upon the room. Alexandra turns her head toward the sliding glass door that leads out to the porch. Outside, the sun shines on everything, giving life to the day lilies Alexandra planted in the spring. The grass looks a bit long since I haven't cut it in a week, but it glistens with that beautiful lush green color.

"I won't be home tonight," Alexandra says.

"Okay."

"I have a date."

"What's his name?"

Alexandra flips me off. "*Her* name is Grace."

"How'd you meet her?"

"The internet."

I scoff. "Nothing good has ever come from the internet."

Taking my plate from the center of the island, Alexandra tosses it into the bottom rack of the dishwasher with a bit of excessive force. Then she storms off toward the stairwell. "You're a real jackass sometimes, Liam."

As she trundles away up the stairs, I call out, "I was kidding again, sis."

A door slams.

"Happy for you," I mumble.

I'm left alone in the kitchen, bending over the countertop. I begin to wonder why I'm drawn to conflict. Maybe it's because I struggle with control. My middle school teachers used to tell us we have to "let go, and let God". In other words, let "Jesus Take the Wheel" if you prefer the powerful voice of Carrie Underwood. Half the time, I wonder if it's someone else grabbing at the proverbial wheel that drives my life forward.

I feel Jesus when I pray. At least, I'd like to think I do, and I know Jesus isn't the one who takes control of my actions. Something more sinister does. That's not to say that something wholly evil is responsible for the things I do, the words I say. No, but I think a perfect entity like Jesus would allow me to "take the wheel" back every once in a while.

A smaller pair of feet start tumbling down the stairs. Lifting my head, I turn to see a little boy with blue eyes and gnarled blonde hair that's longer on top than it is on the sides wearing a white shirt with blue pajama pants. Casey stares up at me innocently.

"You must've just woken up," I say.

He gives an over-exaggerated nod.

I look back out the window. My eye catches an old tire swing hanging from a massive limb. I set it up for Casey when I moved in with Alexandra just after the divorce. Looking back at my son, I see a smirk has crept across his face. He must have read my mind.

"Swing?" I ask to confirm.

In a burst of giggles, he runs to the glass door and waits there, staring out into the yard like an eager soul standing at the gates of Heaven. Since he can't reach the handle yet, I have to do it for him. Casey bolts for the swing the moment I slide the door open. Leaping off the edge of the porch, his hair is buffeted by the wind until he finds himself resting on a fat old tire. He wraps his small hands around the ropes. Casey waves at me to come push the swing.

I take a step off the porch. Surrounding our yard is a dark wooden fence. Alexandra put it up. I guess she likes her privacy. I don't mind it, either.

"Hurry!" Casey says.

"I'm coming." I smile.

Circling the tire, I put my hands on the rough, beaten leather. I give a push, and Casey delightedly screams. Another push. The enjoyment he must find from the mundane act of swinging back and forth like a pendulum could never match the pride I have in being Casey's father. I'd do anything to see him smile, and to my death I'll fight for the life he deserves. That's what fathers do–or what they're supposed to do. Suddenly, he starts to sing.

"*Row, row, row your boat ...*"

I begin twirling the tire now so that he's spinning in a circle.

" *... gently down the stream.*"

My vision falters for a second. "Case."

"*Merrily, merrily, merrily, merrily ...*"

The world around me begins to spin, green grass, the weathered bark of the tree, the peaceful porch all melding into one pool of an image. "Casey."

"*...life is but a dream.*"

***

Methodically I tapped my index finger on the dining table, calloused over at the tip after the past eight years of guitar-playing. The overhead light swayed above me. It was the only light I left on. The darkness of the night

25

crept in through the windows leaving me alone in my own lit circle that fended off demons. Or maybe it welcomed them. Staring into a clear glass of brandy, I heard the choppy laughter of a woman emanating from within. The sound wove its way into my brain to produce a vivid series of images.

The sight of an old unfamiliar dive took over. Billiards balls cracked to my left as middle-aged men circled the two pool tables that had been placed too close to the walls. A lonesome woman launched darts into the cork-style board in the far corner. Orange lights were hanging from old nails pounded into the ceiling trim, signaling the spooky season. The bartender stood below a couple flickering lights next to the liquor selection, having the same conversation he's had a hundred times before with an old man and the annoyed woman to his left who I presumed to be his wife. I saw it all perfectly … except for the outline of a woman standing on the far end of the room. She was blurred completely from my vision, but I could tell she was wearing something black and that she had fair skin. This woman contrasted the man next to her who was wearing a white undershirt below his plaid short-sleeve, jeans with a big belt buckle, and a John Deere cap on his head. He had dark skin, darker than any tan could ever give, and a bright smile that appeared with every haughty laugh.

I could tell this man had a connection with the mystery woman, but I didn't understand the unease I felt, possibly due to that fact that I couldn't tell if the woman was comfortable. Was she smiling with him? Did she want the drink he bought her? Was she willingly clinging to him, or was I supposed to step in? I didn't want to cause a scene. I couldn't even if I did want to. This was not my experience; I was not in the driver's seat.

For what felt like hours, I sat watching the two of them interact with each other. Not once had they acknowledged my presence, so I began to wonder if I was even there at all. I didn't mind. In fact, I preferred it that way. Everyone wants to be a fly on the wall at some point … at least until things begin to spiral out of hand.

26

Closing his eyes, the man leaned his head to the right, moving closer to the blurred woman. Then I zeroed in on his left hand. The ring he was wearing was too big to deny. In an instant, an inexplicable wave of anger washed over me. Hopping out of my chair and approaching the man, I balled my hands into fists. As I cocked one back, he froze and opened his eyes.

This vision was suddenly interrupted by a small click at the front door, pulling me back into the dining room. Heels tapped the hardwood with a sound like that of a judge's gavel until a figure entered the circle of light in which I was sitting. Wearing a darker gown, Rachel stumbled over to the table, her blonde hair in a mess as it fell out of her headband. I hadn't realized my finger was still tapping lightly on the hardwood of the table, so I stopped.

"Where have you been?" I asked.

Rachel wiped at her hair, losing her balance in the process, but regaining it in a few steps. "I was out," she said. "Just downtown with the guurrls."

"Was Alexandra there?"

"Yes." Rachel smiled for a second.

I took a swig of brandy.

"Babe, if you don't mind, I'm going to go to bed. My feet are killing me." Rachel leaned against the wall and began rubbing at her calf.

"You walked back?"

"It wasn't that far."

"Rachel, what were you thinking? I could have picked you up and taken you home." I raised my voice a bit higher than I meant to, taking Rachel by surprise.

She stood up straight and flipped her hair over her shoulder. Placing one foot firmly in front of the other and doing it again, Rachel rounded the dining room table, inching closer to me by the second. Her heels *click, click, click*-ed against the floor. I sat still with my head down and only my peripheral vision acknowledging my wife. She laid a hand on my shoulder as she crept directly

27

behind me. Her hands caressed my neck, soon falling down my chest. She wrapped her arms around me as I felt her face rub up against mine.

"You're right," Rachel whispered in my ear. Her lips grazed my neck once, then twice. "Maybe I can make it up to you."

It was nearly impossible for me not to fall under her spell. She had power over me that I could not deny. The touch of her skin made me crumble. But now it was different. This wasn't the first time she had come stumbling in late with a poor excuse, but this was the first time I would say something I never had before.

"No."

I felt Rachel freeze. It was as if the ring she wore on her left hand had suddenly gained weight. She was stuck. Then, without a word, she slowly removed her arms from around me. I could feel her standing in confusion at my back. She gave an uncomfortable laugh.

"What?"

"You heard me," I said. "No."

"Baby–"

"Don't 'baby' me." I stood up out of my chair and spun around so she would no longer be talking down to me. "You've been doing this for far too long ... going out and then coming back late thinking you can place a band aid on my trust by making love. I've had it."

Rachel's face showed nothing but shock and disbelief. Her eyes tested me, pondering the validity of my tone. I held my stern gaze. Her eyes widened, and her mouth hung slightly open. She said nothing. Turning her head, she crossed her arms. I could tell her mind was spinning. Rachel took a couple steps away from me, twisting her body so that I could no longer see her face. After standing in silence, Rachel murmured something barely audible and walked back into the darkness from which she had come. She took more steps than were necessary to get to the bedroom. I cocked my head when I heard the handle on the front door turn slowly.

28

"Rach, where are you going?"

"I'm leaving."

"Rachel." I moved closer to the door. I had been sitting in the light for so long that I couldn't see my wife through the darkness, but I had the feeling that she could see me. "Where are you going?"

I stood awaiting her response for what felt like forever. I began to wonder if she had already left. Had I been talking to nobody the entire time? Then the silence was broken with Rachel's deafening reply.

"Home." The door slammed, separating the two of us.

~

Keys rattled as I pulled them from my jeans pocket and stuck one into the door. Turning the key counterclockwise, I was shocked when there was no click. I was just getting back from the gym, and it was mid-afternoon. Surely I hadn't forgotten to lock it when I left. I never forgot to lock the door. I had my guitars resting on the wall just inside. I'd never risk allowing them to be stolen.

The door creaked open as I peeked around the corner. Immediately my heart sank. I couldn't believe what I saw. Standing at the door as if he had been expecting me was a little boy with messy blonde hair wearing blue pajamas. Behind him were a couple suitcases and several bags lying in the corner next to folded clothes and essentials.

I walked past my son toward the counter. I examined the clothes that were lying there. On top of one of the piles was a regular white t-shirt. I rubbed the soft cotton with my fingertips to see if it was real. My hands moved to a flannel that I had outgrown and later given to Rachel. All the clothes lying before me were unmistakably my wife's. Then I knelt closer to the bags lying on the floor below me, bulging as if they couldn't have been packed any fuller.

29

They were also hers. I did a one-eighty to find my son looking up at me with innocent eyes.

"Casey … what's going on?"

"Daddy, thank God you're here. Momma, she–"

I heard the sound of rapid footsteps coming from the bedroom. Rachel was putting an earring in as she turned the corner. She nearly gasped. Apparently she hadn't been expecting to see me in our apartment.

"Rach," I looked around and held my hands out at my side, "what's the meaning of all this?"

She stood there biting her lips while Casey rested against the wall, observing us.

Rachel's face grew red. Tears were forming in the wells of her eyes. "I can't do this anymore."

Letting out a sigh, I rolled my eyes back into my temple and scratched at my forehead. I was standing between her and her things as I said, "We talked about this already. You don't have to go anywhere; we're better off together than we'll ever be apart. Remember?"

The sob Rachel had been holding back burst out of her like river water through a broken dam. "Liam, I'm so sorry."

I was so taken aback, too paralyzed with shock to say anything. I tried to speak, but nothing came out. It was all happening too quickly. I wondered if it was real. Tears were streaming down Rachel's face, but I couldn't cry. Not because I was too manly; I simply couldn't find the emotion within me. I had no idea what I was experiencing.

The last words she spoke to me that day were also the last she spoke as Mrs. Crawford. She looked me dead in the heart when she said, "I'll come back later for all this, but I have to go. I can't keep pretending." Before I could say a word, she dashed out the front door, leaving Casey and I behind.

My feet were glued to the hardwood floor. I couldn't tell if my heart was racing or if it had stopped. Either way, there was a sudden pain in my chest I had never felt before. My breathing became erratic. I could hardly even swallow.

Casey, his face as somber as mine, waddled closer to me with open arms. "I'm sorry, Daddy."

I bent down and pulled him in close to my chest. I rubbed his back, laying my head on his tiny shoulder, and I said, "Me too."

***

I find myself rocking back and forth. The last rays of sunshine are illuminating half of a square yard while the other half is darkened by the fence's shadow. My hands are clutching a rough rope while my legs sit atop a black leather tire. Whipping my head and fluttering my eyes, I attempt to bring myself back into reality. Casey is out of sight. I groan.

Hopping off the tire, I wipe my eyes with my index finger and thumb. I begin walking toward the porch and become irritated when I see that the glass door has been left open, only a tattered black screen door blocking out the moths, flies, and mosquitoes while also letting out the cool air from inside. A few birds chirp at me from high in the trees as I take a step onto the porch.

I stop abruptly near the small outdoor table when I hear voices coming from inside. Familiar voices. At first it sounds as though the chatter is coming from the dining room table, making its way outside, just loud enough for me to hear. Standing as still as possible, I lean to my right, hoping to grab a peek through one of the kitchen windows, but the blinds are shut just enough to block my view, which means I can't see who's talking … and they can't see me.

"I think we've let this go on for far too long, Alexandra," a grumbly voice booms. "At this point, we have only one option."

31

"This isn't your problem, Dad," a voice I assume to be Alexandra's responds indignantly. "I love having him around. Besides, I don't know why you're so concerned. You never were when he needed you to be."

"Alexandra–" a petite voice begins but is instantly interrupted.

"The same goes for you, Mom. We wouldn't be here if you'd have supported him instead of treating him like a castaway ... both of us for that matter. Grandma is the only one who ever seemed to care, and she's gone."

A silence results, strong enough for me to feel its weight from outside. I consider leaving my spot on the porch to run inside, greet my parents whom I haven't seen in a few months, and hopefully turn this conversation into something better, something more productive. But I'm stuck. I feel frozen in place while the evening breeze brushes against my facial hair.

A grunt that I've heard from Dad hundreds of times breaks the silence. "He thinks he's a big-time musician. These dreams–fantasies of his ... they're nothing more than that."

"If you bothered to listen to him play once, just once, you might discover he has a talent."

"A talent that will serve him no good, dear," Mom says, her voice loud. Then it softens. "Aren't you tired of living with your brother? You'll go bankrupt if you continue to support him."

Support me? I make plenty of tips on the weekends to pay my half of the rent, thank you very much.

"I've spoken with Rachel recently," comes Dad's accusatory tone.

"And?"

A slap on the table. "For God's sake, Alexandra, don't you see? She says he mopes around all day, has nothing to live for anymore, except *Casey* ..." he says the name with an almost sarcastic emphasis. Knowing my own father had never been there for me, knowing he considered me a point of ridicule to all his "buddies" ... it hurts. But it plagues me significantly more to know he has no desire to be there for his grandchild, either. Dad says something quiet that I

32

can't hear, then, "–and if he does … you could get hurt. Do you want him to end up like your grandfather?"

Alexandra growls. "Is it me you care about? Is it him? Or is it your spotless view of society you believe to be under attack?"

At this point, I've had enough of the conversation. As I make my way toward the screen door, I stop yet again to hear Dad say, "I won't stand for this. You and I both know Liam is going nowhere but down, down into the ground. I won't let you go down with him. Your mother and I are resorting to Plan B whether you like it or not."

Chairs slide against wooden flooring. Mom and Dad are about to leave. Why so soon? Surely they haven't been here for that long. My heart conflicts with my mind. I feel insulted they still refer to me as though I'm a child or some kind of disease. The hurt that curls within me plants my feet to the ground. My fingertips slide against the screen door. My throat begins to close.

Men don't cry, Liam. I've told myself that phrase a few too many times over the course of a lifetime to believe it anymore.

Peering through the screen door, I watch as a burly man in a gray button-up t-shirt and a small round woman in a teal shirt storm out the front door. I stand outside, helpless. I've had this feeling before. I'm reminded of the time I watched Rachel walk out the door for the very last time. My chest gets tight in these situations. A knot always forces itself into my throat. A few minutes are necessary for me to gain composure.

Brushing away a few tears, I finally step inside.

Alexandra perks up from her chair to hide the fact that she had been leaning over the dining room table with her head in her hands.

"Liam, hey!" She isn't fooling anyone, not even herself.

I try to force a smile, but I avert my gaze and head for the stairs. Alexandra makes a peep for a moment, but whatever she means to say gets stuck in her throat.

33

The truth is that Mom and Dad feel as though I'm a waste of space, for lack of a better term. They believe I'm wasting my time as an aspiring musician and that my time would be much better spent in some type of trade. I know it by the disapproving way they look at me, or rather the way in which they *don't* look at me when they're around. I can still hear my Dad scolding me after I announced I'd be pursuing a career in Nashville. *Become a plumber, an electrician ... anything other than a musician.*

Mom and Dad were always incredibly hard on me. They believed it would help me out in the long run. Maybe they had a point all along. What if I am nothing more than a waste?

Making my way to the stairs, I feel Alexandra's eyes boring into my back. I imagine compassion must fill her gaze. For a moment, I turn around just briefly enough to confirm my suspicions. When our eyes meet, she quickly lowers her head to perhaps admire the shape of the dining table. Up the stairs I go.

The top step creaks with a small sound like it always does when I reach it. It's dark upstairs. All bedroom doors are closed. However, a small one-inch by three-foot strip of carpet is illuminated below a white door with a decorative blue racecar on it, giving me just enough light to see.

I find Casey playing with his action figures after turning the knob. He ignores me as per usual when I tell him I have to leave for my performance.

"Love you." I quietly shut the door.

I make my way down to The Cave to grab my things. When passing through the kitchen, I notice Alexandra has vanished. She must have left for work.

My guitar cases snap shut, and I place all my cables, capos, and other miscellaneous items in a small black duffel bag. I'm only missing one thing.

Shelves holding a few clear totes and a couple hard cases stare at me from my left. They call me over.

My hand rubs the outside of a small rectangular box. It's smooth and inviting. It's what I need. Flipping it over, I snap each of its latches open to feel what's inside. A custom Smith and Wesson M&P 2.0 subcompact pistol that has been asleep for years lays on its side atop soft gray foam. Two loaded magazines accompany the firearm. I'm not sure why Alexandra thinks it's necessary to have two. One will be enough.

Driving down the highway I head toward downtown. Honkytonk Central is the bar tonight. My left hand grips the wheel tightly. My right is still, with my index finger pressed softly against the radio dial while the other fingers clutch a handle that morphs into a trigger and barrel. A little pressure is all it will take. The radio turns on.

I breathe, staring into the darkness of my eyelids. I see Casey in his pajamas, holding his arms out for a hug. I see Mom, Dad, and Alexandra gathered around a table. Rachel and Marcus are in the distance watching them. I see Josephine. She looks upset. But she holds my gaze, unwilling to let go. Josephine tilts her head slightly and grins. My heart begins to race, I don't feel welcome anymore. I want to open my eyes. It's something I've been meaning to do for a while now. She can't stop me. I don't want her to stop me. Now is the time.

I feel myself pause. My heart quiets, and I feel a calm wash over me. With the slightest jerk of my finger, I pull and feel nothing more than recoil.

Josephine's voice rings in my head. "You can change the future, Liam. Believe in yourself."

35

II

I shoot upright, a plain white t-shirt clinging to my heaving chest. I rub a hand against the shirt to feel how soft it is, abruptly retracting. Something doesn't feel right.

A thin trail of light creeps through a window just past my feet, barely illuminating a small rectangle of a room. I peer over the edge of the twin-sized bunk I find myself lying on. With a blanket covering my feet, I shift on the bed. It's soft and comfortable.

The room looks familiar, though it's small, with no more space than a jail cell. I notice a quilt decorated like the Australian flag spread over another twin bed pressed against the opposite wall. Near the window bordered by an ugly gray curtain, I see an uncomfortable-looking plastic office chair tucked into a small wooden desk. Atop this desk is an unlit lamp, a stack of books, and a coffee mug with letters that I'm too far from to read.

I pull the quilt that is covering my legs closer to my face, fumbling with the fabric. The quilt looks familiar, too. Running my hands across the stitching, I feel the square pattern, sewn together with incredible precision.

Hmm, strange.

I scan the room again, but it's too dark for me to see. I'll have to look for a light switch.

Cautiously I climb over the rail and out of the bunk, wondering why I feel so rejuvenated as my feet land lightly on the floor below. I press my right hand near my clavicle and run it down the length of my torso.

Why do I feel ... skinny?

36

I lean to my left. The two bunk beds form an alleyway to a wall of darkness. I blink a few times, hoping my eyes will adjust enough for me to see a few feet further. Surely a light switch must be somewhere over there, at least I hope.

Eventually as I creep alongside my bunk, I see the outline of what appears to be a desk tucked in a corner. It is identical to the one by the window. A sliver of light cast through the glass of the windowpane shines upon this new desk, on top of which a small cylindrical prism faces me. I reach my hand out to grab it. It feels cold, like it's been sitting there for a while. My thumb finds a rubber bottom. I press down on it.

In an instant, a beam of light shoots out the other side. Now I can see.

Shining the light on the new desk, I let out a gasp as my heart stops for a second. A miniature lamp, a spherical stress ball made to look like Earth, a white mug filled to the brim with pens, and a square marble coaster are placed from left to right on the opposite side of the desk.

They can't be the same ones ...

I feel trapped, panicked, and maybe a bit nauseous. For the first time, I begin to question my own sanity, but I don't dwell on the thought for long, as curiosity wills the flashlight in my hand toward new discoveries. Ducking, I whip the light under the bunk I had been lying in, shocked to find exactly what I hoped I wouldn't.

A small black circle chair with dented fabric sits beneath one end of the bed. Pointing the flashlight in the other direction, I move the light slowly up and down to reveal a small flat-screen TV on an old wooden dresser beneath the opposite side of the bed.

I press the rubber button once again, allowing darkness to consume me. I don't want to see any more. My head is spinning. I feel a twitch in my neck as my hands begin to shake. I figure I must be dreaming, but the pain I feel after slapping myself firmly on the cheek is too real to deny.

Maybe I'm in my *taken* state, and I just haven't gotten out of it yet ...

37

I look to my left and to my right, trapped within the confines of a small room–a room that replicates one I hadn't seen since I was just a teen.

Suddenly, a rattling noise comes from the far side of the room. I stand and stare as the sound continues for a few long and unbearable seconds.

Where's my gun?

Turning the flashlight back on, I look all throughout the room. I hop on my knees and bend to look beneath the circle chair. Nothing. The rattling noise continues, seemingly growing with intensity. Frantically, I open and close the desk drawers, hoping to find something with which I can defend myself.

When the rattling stops, so do I. I feel my chest pounding as my breath becomes more ragged. With no time to react, I feel a panic wash over me.

"What do you want from me?" I shout in a voice much higher than I anticipated.

From within the darkness, a door opens to reveal a rosy-eyed boy in his late teens stumbling through the threshold, the light at his back making him into a silhouette. He flips a light switch to reveal a smirk on his face. He stands rather tall. His dark hair is tossed up and to the side. His cheek bones are prominent, along with his dark and bushy eyebrows. Unease floods my nervous system as he stares at me from the other side of the room.

"Go' a bih uh whiskay?" he mumbles, a slight Australian accent coming through the slur.

I am frozen in place.

"What in God's name–" I try saying to myself, but the boy hears me and giggles.

"Ha! Tweakin' are we?"

Standing before me is someone who looks like a younger version of a man I used to know, but it's not him. It can't be, I don't think. It's weird because he's even got the same accent.

Instead of answering him, I ask, "What's your name?"

38

My hearing must be altered because my voice still sounds far too high-pitched.

For a moment he regards my question with curiosity, then he bursts out in laughter and starts my way. "Definitely tweakin'! You know, mate, I din't peg you as a guy who touched the stuff, Liam. I guess you can't ever really know someone."

My brow furrows when I hear my name. How could he know my name? With slight and sudden concern for my personal safety, I cautiously take a step backward, which this boy also finds amusing as he can't help but chuckle to himself, shaking his head at the ground.

"How do you know me?" I ask.

"Ugghh." The boy stretches his neck and rubs a hand across his temple, apparently no longer entertained by the situation. "And I thought I was messed up. But a jolly guy like you won't remember much come tomorrow morning. Neither will I. So I *suppose* I'll play along with your lit'le charade … just for my enjoyment." He pauses, and I realize I hadn't heard much of what he said, far too invested in his appearance to care. It's uncanny.

Then, the boy says, "I'm the foreign student whom you decided to pair yourself wit before ma'ing the long and miserable trek to university!" He cups his hands around his mouth, like someone in theatre seats after a big reveal, imitating the *ooo's* and *ahh's* of the imaginary crowd watching us. Then he walks over to me and nudges my shoulder with his elbow, lending a wink in the process. "What a mindbender, eh?" he says, in a hushed tone. "And now you say …"

"What's your name?" I ask again, except this time with stern conviction, hoping beyond hope he doesn't say the name I'm thinking of.

"I was searching for a mo' adventurous response … but tha'll do." The boy gets back into character, heaving his chest outward.

Don't say the name. Don't say the name. Don't you even think about saying his name.

39

clouds that dotted a baby blue sky, the black and gold flag billowing on a pole that protruded from it.

It was a day filled with a multitude of emotions: joy, reminiscence, a sense of accomplishment, and not least of all fear. I feared for the future and what it might hold, but more than a fear for the uncertainties of life, I feared for the past. I remember being afraid that the best days and years of my life had surpassed me. Little did I know that I would become a musician in none other than "Music City" in Nashville, Tennessee. It's crazy how quickly life can change.

I begin pacing the small enclosed room, suddenly feeling the urge to splash my face with a handful of water. Maybe it will wake me up. At this point, I've guessed that I'm in a deep sleep or simply knocked unconscious, though I've never before been able to acknowledge when I'm dreaming, and whatever dream this may be feels much more vivid than usual. More likely than a dream is the possibility that I've been *taken* here. However, this setting would be an abnormality, considering nobody else typically travels through my *taken* world with me. Whatever this is, I want to escape it right now.

"I have to go to the bathroom," I say.

Todd gives an irritated look as he lolls his head to the side in order to face me. "Then use i'."

"Where is it?"

"Liam, you're get'ing at my nerves now, lad."

"I'm serious."

Todd sighs and lazily points a finger toward the door. "They're ou'side. You know, 'cause this is a dorm."

I turn to the door, and as I move closer to it, a sudden anxiety almost paralyzes me. I don't know where the thumping of my heart or the twitching of my hands came from or why panic chooses to come at this moment. Perhaps my subconscious knows what lies behind that door. Part of me expects a white abyss to be on the other side, where I become lost forever in

42

an endless void. Another part of me wonders if Heaven awaits me … or its alternate. I do my best not to let my mind wander to an image of the prince of evil readily anticipating the arrival of another one of God's children so that he can feast on the misery of a soul for the rest of eternity. It's always good to be optimistic in times of trial.

I remember stepping into the driver's seat of my truck, blaring the radio music, and holding a Smith and Wesson in my hands at the beginning of the night. The next thing I know, I'm waking up in an exact replica of my old dorm room with my drunk Australian college roommate there to greet me. However, something tells me the peculiarities have only just begun.

I jump at a strange sound that cracks the silence in the room. When I come to realize the noise had come from the bed, my shoulders release tension. Todd is already snoring, out just like that. I forgot about the high-pitched noise he made in his sleep, kind of like the trumpeting sound you hear at a ball game before the crowd yells, "CHARGE!" I always found it odd that his non-sentient self could emit such a specific sound, and it's one that, even crazier yet, is giving me the slightest bit of courage, pushing me to "charge" the door.

One confident step after the other, I ball my fists, ready to face whatever awaits me on the other side. I continue forward.

As I rip the door open like a band-aid off an uncured wound, a sense of anxiety conjures itself within me yet again, quickly welling up in my chest. It terrifies me to look any further. Sticking my head out the door, I lean against the frame with one hand, looking left and then right. I do a double take. Then a triple take for good measure.

All right. This can end now.

A hallway lined with doors similar to the one I'm poking my head out of extends thirty feet to my left and about twenty feet to my right until the hallway opens up into a common space. On my side of the hall, doors are spaced tightly, about every ten feet or so, whereas the opposite side of the hall contains just a few doors spaced far apart. Screwed into the walls right outside these doors are small rectangular signs.

"Bathrooms."

Behind me, the snoring momentarily stops. "The hell did you expect?"

I cock my head back a touch, and the snoring continues seconds later, silenced only once the door hinges shut behind me.

Walking in through the closest bathroom door, I come to find a tiled room shaped almost perfectly like a cube, the only exception being a shower outlet to the left. Someone must have taken a midnight shower before I entered, leaving a mist hanging inside.

The sink where I wash my hands is accompanied by a foggy mirror that hangs above it. As if this dreamlike experience weren't vivid enough already, the lukewarm water running through my palms, down my fingers, and swirling into the drain persuades the idea that I am truly in this moment, that I'm not *taken* or dreaming. With the water still running, I steal some by cupping my hands underneath the constant stream and lightly tossing what I can gather into my face. Somewhat mesmerized by the feeling of the water, I do this once more. But when I rub my hands across my temple, down to my cheekbones, and finally stroking my chin, I become confused. The water feels right. The knobs on the sink felt right when I turned them. But why does my face feel so … smooth?

I look up again at the cloudy mirror. With a flat hand, I swipe at it from top to bottom, water beading up in streaks behind each stroke. As I continue this motion back and forth down the mirror, my hair is revealed in the reflection, seemingly more kempt than usual. Another swipe allows me to look into my own eyes, the blue in them more vibrant than I can recall. When I swipe one more time at the mirror, a yelp forces its way out of me. I jump backward from the mirror in an immediate bout of terror.

"WHAT THE–"

Although horrified, I can't look away. Like Narcissus staring into a puddle of water, I'm unable to retract my gaze from the younger, beardless version of myself standing parallel to me. For a moment, I suspect an optical illusion. However, looking down and patting my tighter chest, rubbing my smooth face, and stroking my shorter hair tells me that I'm not in a fun house, where all the mirrors are warped. No, this is a fine, straight piece of glass reflecting a perfect image.

Everything about my reflection says, "I'm here. I'm alive." From the smooth, young features that make up the boy in the mirror to the athletic build which had become foreign to me over the past few years. This is a new me. Well, it's the old me, my eighteen or nineteen year-old self if I had to guess, but I feel so rejuvenated, like I've had fourteen years to rest but instead of waking up fourteen years in the future, I've traveled back to the past.

Caught between emotions of ecstasy and panic, my brain struggles to allow either one to take over. However, as with most highs in life, they begin to fade with time. Eventually, after a few solid minutes of examining this new/old form I've taken, panic becomes my sole operator. I don't know what I'm doing here. Least of all, I don't know why. Determined to discover the true parameters of my circumstance, I exit the restroom, slipping back into the hallway.

I walk by the line of closed wooden doors, concerned that the rooms within are devoid of sound. I don't have a watch or a clock to reference, but my assumptions have told me that it's probably around one, maybe two in the morning. In most areas, rural or urban, you'd expect things to be dead silent at this hour. But not here. Usually, if my memory serves me correctly, you can count on at least one group of teenagers to hoot and holler all throughout the night in direct violation of "quiet hours". They're not always the same people, and the raucous collaborations don't necessarily come from the same rooms, but it's safe to say there were more repeat offenders than not back in the day.

45

There is a very specific room number burned into memory. 623 was located directly across from the study room. This used to be the well-known "spot", where drinking games, smoking, and other more risqué activities took place. It didn't matter whether it was a weekend or a Monday night during finals. Typically, 623 was where the magic happened.

Making my way to that area of the floor, passing the common areas, I count the doors 605, 607 ... until the infamous door appears. I lean close to it. To my dismay, there is no drunk singing, hysterical laughing, or smacking of lips to be heard from inside. Normally, this would delight me. Not tonight. The eerie quiet is a nightmarish setting.

I backtrack to the common area where a few square desk tables are accompanied by four empty gray chairs each. Fall-themed decorations like yellow and orange cut-out leaves hang still on the surrounding walls with not a soul to admire them and a cut-out that says "OCTOBER". Standing in the middle of the area, I envision a time when this was where freshmen in pearl-snap shirts and tank tops would congregate before hitching a ride on a bus downtown. It was where they would gather on a weeknight, setting their homework in front of them, pretending to be productive as they casually conversed with their friends about the latest trends. Now it's a forlorn ghost town.

I rear back and let out a loud cry like a four-legged beast in the woods making an attempt to contact anyone or anything that might be out there. My head does a three-sixty. I wait a few seconds, anticipating a response, one hopefully less barbaric than the call I've put out. Nothing.

Aside from the drunken boy passed out in the room I woke in, I am alone here. It's nothing new for me to be alone. I've taken refuge in it nearly all my life. Isolation is a part of who I am. But something isn't right.

I head for the elevator doors just beyond the floor lobby when suddenly a rattling noise comes from behind me. I turn around rapidly to see a blonde girl with a few purple stripes through her hair leaning against a doorframe. She fashions a couple pink bunny slippers on her feet in addition to some blue-striped pajamas that cover everything else. With bloodshot eyes magnified by the glasses she wears, she scans the scene. When her eyes land on me, she sighs and stumbles in my direction.

"Liam, is everything okay?"

I'm unsure whether to feel relief or terror. It's the same feeling I had when seeing Todd. It is mildly comforting to run into a familiar face, but rather alarming as well.

"Emma?" I say.

"Yes, I'm Emma," she says it like I asked a stupid question.

"You used to be my RA."

"Used to be? Did you move floors or something? As far as I know, you're still my resident, and speaking of ... what are you doing screaming at–" she checks her wrist, "3:43 in the morning?"

"I–"

"It's quiet hours, Liam."

"Yes, I–"

"I'm going to have to write you up for this."

"I–"

"You probably woke up a lot more people than just me."

"I thought I was alone." I manage to get out.

This seems to silence Emma. Her expression shifts from anger to annoyance in about half a second. She squints up at me through her glasses.

"You think you're being funny?" she says.

"What? No, I–"

"Come with me." She grabs my wrist, guiding me toward the elevators.

"Where are you taking me?"

"Downstairs. I told you I was going to write you up, didn't I?"

I don't respond, mostly because my mind is suddenly stuck on the fact that Todd was coming back to the dorms at nearly four in the morning ...

47

alone. Everyone else on the floor was evidently fast asleep at this hour. What would he have been doing alone so late? Then again, Todd always was a night owl. He didn't really need an explanation.

"Emma, please, this is just a misunderstanding. I'm not drunk or anything."

As Emma leads the way into the elevator and pushes the button that takes us to the lobby, she scoffs. "I'd sure hope not with midterms being this week."

Once we reach the bottom floor, the moody RA pulls me onward by grabbing my wrist again perhaps to further display the uneven power dynamic between the two of us. It strikes me as unnecessary, but I don't have the energy to complain. Besides, I've almost entirely forgotten my way around this dorm. Each hallway, corner, and doorway is a rediscovery of what I used to know. It's not all too bad having an unconventional tour guide.

Emma takes me through two large wooden double doors by pressing the circular button sticking out of the wall, automatically swinging them open before us. The miniature hallway we walk through opens into a much larger space where blue, yellow, and red assorted couches sit atop a fluffy brown carpet to the left. They look comfortable while pleasantly contrasting the white walls and tile floors surrounding them. More Fall-themed decorations hang in no particular order from the walls of this area, which I've now concluded to be the main lobby.

Still gripping me rather excessively, my old RA takes me to the right where a white marble fixture twenty-or-so feet in length, a few feet in height, protrudes from the ground, concealing a reception area where only one person sits at the counter. As we come closer to the fixture, a young man with pale skin, freckles, and dark hair pulled back by a headband is slowly revealed. With his legs kicked back next to a keyboard and monitor and a phone stuffed in his face, he pays us no attention as we walk up.

For a minute or so, we stand awkwardly waiting for something, I'm not sure what. Acknowledgment? A tornado to touch down? God?

Out of the corner of my eye, I look at Emma, concerned we might be standing here 'til morning. She must feel my concern.

Emma clears her throat and says, "Jordan."

The emo-looking dude peeks up at us, then looks back down at his phone. "What seems to be the problem, Em-cat?"

"I've got a report to file, *Jor-man*."

"Sorry, chica. No can do."

Jordan's deep voice makes the name-calling exhibit occurring in front of me somewhat amusing when contrasted to Emma's squeaky high voice as she assumes a polite tone in a very obviously impolite way.

"And why is that, J-dog?" Emma says.

"System's down, sweetheart." If Jordan would have had gum in his mouth, this is where he would've blown a bubble and let it pop.

"That's a load. And did you just call me SWEETHEART!"

"Yup."

"That's it."

Finally letting go of me, Emma rounds the marble wall, storms through the mini swinging doors that bar the reception area, and swings the office chair, along with Jordan in it, out of her way. She stands where the chair had been and begins rapping on the keyboard. As if speaking to herself, she says, "System's down. The system is never down."

For a moment I watch Emma furiously navigate her way through the "system", but I become more interested in the lobby surrounding me. For a dorm, the place is nice. Though college is a hectic place, there's something comforting about this environment. It speaks psychologically to students, saying, "We know your life is gonna suck these next few years, but here's a comfy couch, a goofy looking chair, and some kick-ass study rooms for you to power through."

In front of me, Emma and Jordan continue to argue as the RA presses a stubby finger against the monitor. She must be proving a point.

49

Aware that I'm no longer a concern to them, I wander over to the right where a small bulletin board highlighting the "RA of the week" hangs a picture of a young man whose smile does a poor job of hiding the pain associated with his job. A few other announcements and club sign-ups are posted as well. As I'm looking through these, I don't even notice the figure standing to my right. It isn't until I catch a swift movement out of the corner of my eye that my head snaps in that direction.

"Whoah." I lean back to get a better look.

Now near the main entrance to the building, I stand by two rows of glass doors that act as security for the dorm. Outside these doors, in the dark and wind-filled night, someone stands with their palms pressed up against the outer door. A girl. She wears skinny jeans and a rainbow-colored shirt that peeks out of her black leather jacket, along with ruby-red hair curling just in front of her shoulder. As we make eye contact, she gives a wry smile that reveals her youth–in her twenties I'd wager. With a wave of her hand, she signals for me to come to her. Maybe she needs help getting in.

Before I go, I should tell Emma so she doesn't wonder where I'm at, I think to myself.

As I turn around, I can tell my RA and Jordan are in the heat of their argument.

Never mind.

I turn back to the glass, but the girl is gone. She isn't standing outside a different door. She hasn't managed to get in. She's just disappeared.

I start to wonder if something bad could've happened to her. You never know in a town like this what can happen. Without further hesitation, I bolt out the doors and into the brisk night. The short white T I'm wearing doesn't act as much of a barrier to the howling winds as they whip against my chest.

The world opens up once I'm outside with a tall building to my left, one made of dark brick, and an open driveway to my right. At first, I don't see any sign of life around me until a flash of red disappears past the corner at the far end of the building.

"Miss?" I call into the windy night.

I'm compelled to follow, something within me screaming that I have to, I must. What if she's truly in danger? With little regard for my own safety at this point, I dash that way into the strong fighting wind, sprinting head-first like a bull toward the matador's cape. The wind seemingly becomes stronger with every stride, but I continue to fight through it.

I reach the corner. Streetlights just ahead highlight an intersection. In the distance, there are a few trees surrounding small, house-like structures where another road winds up into a hill. To my left is a walk bridge made of concrete that travels up and over the empty road.

There she is. Fifty yards ahead of me is the red-haired girl. To my surprise and relief, she's walking across the concrete bridge by herself, nobody holding her hostage. She might even appear to be going for a late night/early morning stroll to someone who doesn't know any better.

I should stop here, knowing she's safe, but I can't. Compelled now just as much by curiosity as instinct, I follow her up the bridge, jogging now instead of running. I'll be able to catch up with the girl soon enough.

However, as I near the bridge's apex, the girl has once more managed to disappear. I begin wondering whether my head is playing tricks on me. Or maybe she's got tricks of her own.

I stop where I am, wishing I had an owl's neck that would allow me to quickly swivel my wide-eyed gaze 360 degrees while keeping my feet planted. The streetlights in combination with red and green traffic lights hanging over the intersection below illuminate both the road and sidewalk. Because there are no cars or red-haired girls in sight, I'm alone again … or so I thought until a sudden movement attracts my eye another fifty yards ahead.

The girl has just reached the end of the walk bridge, now crossing the much larger bridge structured overtop the river that runs through the middle of campus. Her regular stride hasn't changed. In contrast to the ripping winds and the rolling river below her, she calmly and confidently treks onward. Except, instead of electing to use the sidewalks on either side of the road, she walks right down the middle of the bridge, where oncoming traffic would usually be speeding toward her if it were a busy hour. She is fearless. But how does she move so swiftly?

I stare at the concrete on the walk bridge before me. I watch as the girl and I become farther and farther apart. What was moments before a bright green light shouting from within me to follow this mysterious person has suddenly transformed into a red warning flag just as vibrant and persuasive, yet causing even greater intrigue than before.

Should I continue this curious chase, the path ahead is uncertain, but the thought strikes an adventurous match in my brain, an old flame perhaps being brought back to life–the younger form I've adopted evidently not only reshaping body, but mind as well. For the first time in a long time, I smile. It is no charade. The smile is real. I smile because excitement forces its way past the blockade barrier to emotion I had previously erected. For the first time in a while, I can *feel* something.

As I grasp the feeling tightly, I wonder if this is what it's like to hold a hummingbird. Small, fragile, and majestic. You can watch one flutter outside your window while it feeds on sugar water from a feeder or nectar from a colorful assortment of flowers, and you casually admire its beauty from a distance. But if a hummingbird were to rest in your palm, caressed by five strong fingers, perspective shifts. I think this feeling is comparable. I can let it go or hold it for just a while longer and relish in the awe. I've made my decision.

Bolting across the second half of the walk bridge, I take the curves of the spiral downward at full speed. The girl has managed to maintain the distance between us, now at the next intersection far beyond the bridge waiting for the walk sign to appear before crossing. I'm confused for a moment, because there's nothing stopping her from j-walking. Perhaps this is what finally allows me to catch up to her.

"Miss! Hey!"

I wave a hand in the air as I keep jogging. Surprisingly I'm not out of breath yet. For a second she turns backward in possible acknowledgement. She might have even given a smirk, but I'm still too far away to tell.

In a flash, the light at the intersection changes from an orange hand to a white stick figure mid-stride, and she's off again. And yet again she disappears behind a building just moments after crossing the street. I run after her. Reaching the corner where I last saw her, I come to realize she's still just as far away as before, about to round another corner, then another.

This cycle of cat and mouse continues for much longer than necessary. Before I know it, the sun has started peeking over the horizon in the East. I've been led downtown through the ped mall area, past the business building, then in a large circle to find myself up against a large gray rock that resembles a brain. It's been plopped in the middle of a wide and lengthy walkway that separates a number of lecture buildings. With one hand, I support myself against the rock while wiping the perspiration off my face with the other.

Breathlessly I examine the curves and notches within the large rock. *The brain*, I think to myself. *It's so mysterious.* This multi-ton representation of the mind before me seems incomplete. There's so much more than the brain that goes into one's thought, like the heart for instance. Although heart and mind are two separate entities–thank God they are–they often work together and can be synonymous. Inconclusive decisions arise, and our advice is *listen to your heart*, not your mind. Yet when the forces of heart and mind work together, it's miraculous what can be achieved.

I look to the open spaces on either side of the brain rock, then nod understandingly at its isolation. *Meh, the heart isn't the most appealing object anyway.*

Stepping away, I imagine Casey standing atop the brain with his arms out wide, likely feeling as though he were on top of the world. I smile at the thought.

The sky brightens with each second, creating a beautiful row of shadows that are cast onto the walkway. In between the shadows are streaks of light that managed to sneak through the cracks and crevices of the lecture halls. My eyes follow the light, visually hopscotching from one pointed streak to the next. I know what they lead to. I've been doing this for a while, and just now I'm catching on. I follow and can never seem to come any closer to what I'm chasing.

The red-haired girl stands at the end of the walkway, looking like a tall and skinny pencil hundreds of yards away near the Old Capitol building. It's a captivating sight when the sun's rays reflect off the golden dome in the morning. The girl finally remains still, as if to taunt me. But I'm done. I'm tired. It's time to go home, time to go to bed.

"Run along!" I encourage the girl. "I'm sure you can find other guys to chase you around all night."

I rest my head against the brain rock, allowing myself to recuperate for a moment when something shocks me. It's a voice.

"Don't give up, Liam. You're almost there."

As if jolted by a taser, I stagger backward. "Who said that?"

The way the voice came to me, I could have sworn someone whispered into my ear. But the only other person currently within sight is the girl still standing in the distance. I give her the squinty eyes. What kind of trickery is she pulling? How does she know my name?

Apparently able to read my mind, she yells from across the walkway, "I'm talking to you, Liam. Come." This time the sound of her voice originates from where she stands. She motions for me to follow once more as she makes for the Old Capitol building.

I'm conflicted for more reasons than the obvious. Clearly this girl has been toying with me all night. She's demonstrated her superiority in a convincing fashion. No matter how quickly I run or how hard I try, I'll never catch up with her.

With my doubts in mind, something about the way she encourages me to move on tells me that things might be different this time around. And the flag hanging atop the Old Capitol is somewhat symbolic of a checkered flag, a beacon that signals the end. But why should I keep going? The sense of awe that initially struck me regarding the girl has faded. If anything, resentment has taken over above all, and this quest has become a matter of pride. I've come too far to give up now.

She continues to move farther and farther away, and I can feel time slipping. Her outline gets smaller and smaller, morphing into building. I have to make a decision quick, before she's gone for good.

My knees are slowly aching, and my chest is still heaving. I'm exhausted and frustrated, but with one final push, I jog down the walkway, gaining speed with every step. Finally, I feel as though I'm getting somewhere. I don't know where the extra boost comes from. All I know is my legs seem to be making much longer and fuller strides than before.

All of the sudden, I'm covering more ground and closing the gap. The girl has just rounded the front of the building. She takes the steps up to the main entrance one at a time, proceeding rather slowly. Does she know I'm not as far behind as I was before? Or maybe she's slowing purposefully, giving me hope just to swipe it away once more. Either way, it's time to make a move.

The gap keeps closing. Passing the lecture halls, I estimate only twenty to thirty yards between us. She's only halfway up the steps. This is it. I round the front of the building and hit the first step just as she's at the top. Taking the incline one step at a time won't be quick enough. I'll have to go every other. So I start, skipping over one step, then another. For a moment, I feel like

Rocky climbing the steps to victory. The girl stands at the door with one hand grasping the handle as I leap over two steps to get to the top.

"Hey! Who are y–"

I don't get the chance to finish my question because my foot gets caught, causing me to tumble forward with all my momentum. I completely biff it, face first on the concrete below. Most of the pain instantly strikes, luckily not at my face or chin which both seem to cushion my fall, but rather at my right ankle. I grab for it with both hands, wincing and groaning on the top platform. Just a few feet in front of me, the door opens and shuts.

I hobble up onto my left leg and hop over to the door, attempting to ignore the pain. She must be waiting for me on the other side. I grab at the handle. It makes an odd crunching sound that I ignore, but when I pull at the door, it doesn't budge. Strange. I try again. It remains stuck in place. I shake, scream, and pound at the surface that is inhibiting my entrance for another minute or two–to no avail. It's locked.

With my hand still gripping the door handle, I let out a sigh of defeat, nearly letting out a tear or two in the process. Nearly.

"Who are you?" I say. No response, so I ask again, only to be greeted by the chirping of a nearby robin.

Rearing a fist behind me, I get ready to pound at the door one more time. I swing at it, but midway through, I slow my hand down just enough so that my skin only grazes the smooth wood and stops to rest against it. I remain still. Extreme pressure forces my fingers into my palm. If God hadn't made human skin so thick, my nails might have brought blood forth like spring water. One can only hold tension within them for so long before letting go. I let out a huff, and the pressure in my hand releases like a deflating tire.

I fall toward the door until my forehead rests in the center, and I close my eyes. I came so close.

I turn to rest my back against the building, and as I release my grip from the door handle, something gently falls to the ground with a tiny *crunch*. I

56

squint down at what appears to be a small, bunched-up piece of notebook paper that has come to rest near my foot. One of the punched-out circles stares peculiarly upward, begging my interest. Curiosity bests me, so I reach down for the small paper and unfold it with one hand to reveal a short message written neatly in cursive on one side.

11 S Dubuque @ 11

I look back up at the door.

"What does this mean?" I ask.

Silence is the response.

"What does this mean?" I ask again, louder.

Nothing.

Looking back down at the crumpled up message, I read the short, seemingly meaningless phrase over and over again. This note could have been left for anyone, but I'm certain the girl left it. What does it mean? What is she trying to tell me? A light bulb pops in my head.

Wait a minute.

Suddenly, I think I understand.

IV

The morning sun heats my back and forms a shadow that stretches before me as I walk across the bridge over the river with a limp in my stride. The air grows warmer, and a new day is arriving. The wind from the previous night has died down, leaving in its wake a few autumn leaves scattered across the sidewalk and roads. I look peculiarly upon the colored leaves, wondering why they would have fallen so early. When I had been pushing Casey on the tire swing, the weather had been hot and humid. Now the air outside has cooled drastically, and here I am, with my eyes falling upon orange and yellow.

Sweat stains my previously white t-shirt, and my right ankle throbs with every step. Still, my focus remains on the pen-written note that rests lightly in both my palms. It provides me with hope, if not the slightest bit of contentment knowing that the physical and mental trials of the night have not gone for nothing, even if it's for a few words.

11 S Dubuque @ 11. That's what it says. An address with a time stamp. I'm pretty sure it's an important one.

Placing too much of my concentration on the piece of paper, I don't see the oncoming wave of people rushing toward me. The narrow width of the sidewalk prohibits me from skirting out of their way as they continue forth in a stampede. Bodies carrying backpacks, cell phones, and ear buds all heading to the same place crash into me, an oblivious wanderer. I'm immediately tossed into discomfort, completely out of my element, so I stop. Panic usually finds me in a public crowd. Normally, this is where I become paralyzed, or where I long to escape via my *taken* world. However, while I observe the convoy of people who rush past me, I feel oddly calm.

A tall boy with shaggy hair and headphones bumps past me with a disapproving comment. Another shorter guy simply rolls his eyes at me, as though I'm an annoying traffic cone that he must avoid. Then a petite girl wearing leggings and a regular t-shirt makes eye contact for a second while offering up a shortened smile. The diversity of folks to be found here breeds confidence within me. Because there is no quota, no requirement of appearance nor expectation of action, I feel as though I fit in. Standing alone on a stage makes a man stand out, but here I can blend into the crowd, even if I am moving in the opposite direction. There's no need for a *taken* world here. I smile, and I walk down the middle of the sidewalk, confidently into the fray.

The path winds and takes me right back to the double row of glass doors at the entrance to my dorm. I walk through them to find a mostly empty, mostly quiet lobby, save for the sound of a stern conversation occurring near the reception area.

"…then you can't possibly argue whether the system of oppression even exists!"

"You seem to be doing fine for yourself, miss RA."

"No thanks to someone like you."

I move swiftly to the elevators, paying the arguing couple behind the desk no attention. They seem far too invested in each other to notice me.

Upstairs I find Todd still fast asleep on his bed, that trumpeting snore impossible to ignore. I'm careful not to wake him as I take a change of clothes from the dresser on my side of the room. I should probably be surprised to find an entire wardrobe stuffed within each one of its drawers. I *should* be surprised they're not all empty. After all, I didn't fold the shirts neatly and stack them on top of each other. I didn't toss the socks and other delicates in the top drawer, either. I simply woke to this world, everything perfectly prepared for me when I arrived. I should be flabbergasted by all of this, but I'm not. By now I've accustomed myself to the fact that I'm living in another world, I can't seem to escape it, and accepting circumstance is the quickest way to move on.

After a quick shower, I feel fresh. I discard my yellow-spotted shirt and scratched up jeans into the hamper and replace them with a royal blue hoodie and gray sweat pants. Before heading back out the door, I take a quick look at Todd as he rests peacefully with the morning light shining through the blinds that cover our window. I compare my bed to his, empty and enticing. As much as I'd love to rest my head against a soft pillow and fall into eight full and long hours of restorative sleep and unpredictable dreams, the clock has reached 10:30. I have somewhere else to be.

Before heading out the door, however, I notice a bland calendar hanging from the wall. It's been flipped to October.

Hm. I nod, accept, and move on.

I understand feelings of adoration for Fall. Tailgate season brings an energetic spirit to the cities and streets while the weather holds steady at a cool, comfortable setting, and the trees morph into spectacles of vibrant colors like yellow, orange, and red before going dormant for the winter. It is a wonderful time in the Midwest. Yet looming in the near inescapable future is a frosty and unfriendly environment that sends everyone back to the bleak reality of seclusion indoors. Harsh and severe winds that wreak havoc on those previously beautiful trees rip every ounce of character from them, leaving behind a dim brown shell of something much greater. It is only for a while longer that outdoor festivities can be enjoyed. The multitudes buzzing through the jubilant town, in between aromas of American, Korean, Mexican, and Indian cuisine seemingly ignore, or are content with, this contemporary reality.

Meals and beverages are enjoyed in the calm outdoors with family and friends while the sun grants a bright and natural warmth to dining areas, at least when they aren't covered by the shade of sponsored umbrellas. Longboards, roller skates, and bikes dodge through bustling walkways nearby, and headphones playing opera, hip hop, country, or a true crime podcast provide passersby with a sense of serenity amidst the chaos. Everyone here is a unique individual, present in this city for their own reason, working with the others unknowingly in harmony.

I am one of the few who is perhaps disrupting the harmonious flow of the strangers around me. I stand still as a rooted tree in the middle of the sidewalk, facing a small, insignificant entrance that blends in with the other restaurants bunched up against it. The siding around the threshold is painted in an unflattering gray color that is to be contrasted by the golden letters protruding from the area above. It says: The Pub. Despite its somewhat basic curb appeal, the restaurant is a go-to for many a person. Besides, in this area of town and in a city with tens of thousands of paying customers, presentation is nearly irrelevant. Reputation reigns supreme in terms of importance, and The Pub will forever and always be doing sufficiently well in that category.

I know why I'm here. I know the significance of this restaurant. A legitimate argument could be made that I should leave. I should escape. Yet I have to confirm my belief that I was brought here for a reason. Call it detrimental pride, call it stupidity, call it whatever. I want to stay. I have to.

From my pocket I procure a smartphone that I had earlier found nestled within the clothes I picked out for today. The screen says 10:59. With yet a slight limp, I stumble over to one of the empty tables outside and pull up a chair. Not long after, a young gentleman in a black shirt with a waist apron tied around his black pants greets me.

"Hey."

"Hello."

"What do ya need?"

"Nothing yet, thanks." I give a brief smile.

"Ahh." He stands still, pen and paper in hand with an expectant stone-cold expression, his swooshing black hair listing in the breeze.

"Maybe a water would be nice," I concede.

The waiter disappears and later comes out with a pitcher of ice water and a glass. "Here. Are you ready to order?"

61

"Oh, no."

"Huh?" His mouth hangs slightly open.

"I need a few more minutes." I look back over at the empty chair across from me.

"Okay" he says before disappearing back into the restaurant.

There are five more tables arranged in a circle outside. The three tables with tan umbrellas sticking out of them are full, but the other two are empty. These tables are flipped once, maybe twice before I check my phone again for the time. 11:46. Twice in this span of time the waiter comes back to see if I want to reconsider placing an order. I told him no both times.

The clock ticks. I become bored of sitting alone, so I find creative ways to entertain myself. The best I come up with is watching the folds in my hands bend and stretch as I twiddle my thumbs around each other. It's quite amazing that our fingers are willing to bend so far. Entering a state of hypnosis, I lose track of time rather quickly, to the point that I don't notice the waiter standing next to my table until he speaks up, seemingly annoyed.

"Hey, man. Sorry and all, but I do have to ask you to leave. Nothing personal, just business policy."

Though part of me wants to protest, to ask him for just a bit more time, I'd rather keep the length of our encounter to a minimum. Pushing the chair out from under me, I stand on my feet when suddenly I hear a familiar voice in the distance, confirming my need to be present. My intuition had steered me in the right direction after all.

"Oh, there he is. Come, Rachel. Come. You need to meet my brother."

From the sidewalk come two girls, one a taller girl with brunette hair curled over a formal tan-colored dress who leads a shorter girl with blonde hair tied back in a ponytail. This one wears a more comfortable-looking outfit than the girl she came with, donning a turquoise long-sleeve with gray-white skinny jeans. Both of them look so young and full of life, like the truth of time has not yet ailed them, and I'm not sure what to make of it.

62

"Liam! Hi! This is Rachel. Come say hi." Alexandra wraps me in a hug before holding her arms out in Rachel's direction like a game show host revealing the prize behind door number three.

A flurry of emotions racks my brain. In front of me is the woman who stole my heart, bore my first child, and subsequently shattered my will to survive by leaving my daughter and I for someone else. She's undeniably beautiful, just as I remembered. If a shy, self-aware woman were lying in contradiction below the façade she presents, it'd be nearly impossible to tell. I expected the same apathy and anger to be present, as it has been for so long. I anticipated this moment would be difficult, that the pain and hate I'd harbored would be ever-present.

Yet, as if those years of hurt were nothing more than another autumn leaf being blown from a branch off into the distance by a stiff Fall breeze, Rachel disarms me with an innocent grin.

"Hi. I've heard so much about you already. I'm Rachel."

She sticks out a hand for me to take, but I'm momentarily paralyzed, not by her beauty but rather her tone. Rachel speaks softly and with an openness that tells me she's ready to let anyone in, that either her love for people or her ignorance of betrayal are so great that she knows no other way than to radiate a loving warmth, such a stark contrast to the cold-shouldering nods I'd grown accustomed to receiving from her.

Suddenly I'm forced to acknowledge that this isn't the Rachel I've come to know. The Rachel standing before me has no idea what the next fourteen years have in store—the highs, the lows, and everything in between. Although part of me holds on to anger by a thin string, this Rachel has not yet done me any harm. She doesn't know who I am or the distress she'll cause me. Right now she sees a stranger, and in some sense, so do I.

Snapping out of the momentary trance, I take the hand she offers me.

"Uhm ... Liam, sorry."

"No need to apologize."

While Rachel and I stand in a somewhat awkward visual embrace, Alexandra reaches into the purse she has slung over her shoulder, and after some digging, she pulls out her phone to evidently check the time.

"Oh, but *I* have to apologize, not just for being late–sorry we kept you waiting, Liam–but I have some business school stuff to attend to ... I was thinking you and Rachel could get to know each other while I bounce?"

"That sounds wonderful," Rachel says to Alexandra. "Have fun."

The two girls smile at each other, then Alexandra turns down the sidewalk as swiftly as her high heels will allow her.

"Good to see you too, sis." I give a sarcastic wave.

"Always busy, that one." Rachel, with her hands on her hips, watches Alexandra head off in the opposite direction. Once my sister turns the corner at the next block, Rachel's pony tail flips back behind her, and she slaps her palms on her thighs. "So ..."

My head lowers to the ground, and my foot swipes shyly across the concrete below. I don't know what to say. I'm not sure if I should even speak. Should I turn the other way and run? Tell her that this doesn't work out, so we shouldn't waste our time? I begin questioning my own motives. Why *did* I come?

Maybe my intuition led me here to relive a moment in time. Or perhaps I arrived for a sense of pride and confirmation. If that's the case, I've already received what I came for. I was right. This is where Rachel and I first met. Now that she's here, what am I supposed to do?

"Sorry again for being late. Your sister and I got caught up in our philanthropy assignment for the sorority. Trying to put some meals together for the local homeless shelter."

I press my lips into a quick smile.

"It's okay," I say, then pause. "You really don't have to stay here if you don't want. I'm sure you have plenty of important things to do and important people to do them with."

"Nonsense." Rachel walks around me and settles into the chair on the other side of the table. She raises a finger to call the waiter over. "Hey! Two pints over here, please."

The waiter, now standing near the entrance to The Pub, looks hesitant at first, but then he and I make eye contact. His eyes move from me to Rachel and back again. I try to signal my discomfort with widened eyes that illustrate my desire for an exit, but he must've misinterpreted. With a smirk, he enters the restaurant.

Rachel, now seated, gestures for me to sit with her. I'm afraid it's too late to back out now.

I try to avoid looking at, or even facing the woman opposite of me as I lower awkwardly into the chair. I pretend to be enamored by the birds that are perched atop the buildings and the pigeons scouring the pavement for crumbs. I even watch those who stroll the sidewalk, hoping desperately that one of them will look me in the eye and save me from my predicament.

"How are you liking college so far?" Rachel asks.

I give her a slight acknowledgment out of the corner of my eye. "Uh, yeah it's good."

"That's good," she says.

My knees bounce underneath the table.

"Have you made some good friends yet?"

"Yes." *Not really.*

"That's always fun." Rachel pauses. When she determines that I'm likely going to maintain my silence, she sort of glances down at her fingers. "College is where you meet the people who you'll likely spend time with for the rest of your life. There's so much opportunity. It's a really great place."

My body is still angled away. I grin in artificial agreement.

"I like your hoodie," Rachel says. I have to admit her persistence is admirable.

I look down at the logo on my blue sweatshirt and almost chuckle. I guess I hadn't paid much attention to the clothes I'd put on before I left. The hoodie I'm wearing is adorned with a "Life's a Beach" logo.

"Thanks." I smirk.

"Two Busch Light pints for ya." The waiter sets our drinks in front of us–Rachel first, then me. As he places the beer down before me, he gives me a wink, but I'm not really sure why. "I'll be back," he says to Rachel.

The waiter disappears. I examine the clear glass full of carbonated golden liquid before me. At the top of the glass is a small head of foam from which microscopic bubbles dance, occasionally sending one up like a firework.

Once the waiter navigates his way back to our table, he doesn't even have to ask for our order. Rachel beats him to it.

"We'll take two of the burger baskets."

"Ok." Back into the restaurant he goes.

Rachel attempts to pull conversation from me with pleading eyes that are accompanied by a grin, but I'm obstinate. The awkward silence doesn't bother me all too much anyway, though Rachel is clearly uncomfortable with it as she scratches at her temple. I intend to uphold this statue-like state for as long as possible, at least until we can go our separate ways.

Over the next few minutes, Rachel continues to make more small talk, met by my refusal to cooperate. Part of me empathizes with her, just not enough of me to promote conversation.

Instead, I study her subtly as she looks awkwardly elsewhere. I see the little brown freckle that's always dotted her left cheekbone. Her forehead has no worry lines on it yet, and her blonde hair is so vibrant, not a discolored strand to be found.

Shortly, the waiter brings a couple baskets filled with a mound of fries and a greasy burger in each. He sets Rachel's down first, seemingly unable to take his eyes off her.

"There you are," the young man says politely, a stark change from the way he addressed me. "Anything else I can get you?"

Rachel explains to the waiter that her drink is a bit flat and that if she could get a new one, she would be truly grateful. Yet when the waiter offers to take the flat beer from her, she insists on finishing it just so it doesn't go to waste. The waiter half-nods then stumbles into The Pub.

Without saying much, Rachel digs in. I examine the food set before me. It looks good. And I am hungry. But I fear partaking in this initial peace offering, almost as though I'd be conceding the upper hand to Rachel immediately. This is how she does it. This is how she wins people over. First by forcing you to let down your guard and let her in. Not this time. I'm not falling for it. But as I watched the waiter and Rachel interact, although shortly, there was an obscure spectacle to be observed, piquing my curiosity enough to inquire about it.

"How did you do that?" I ask.

Rachel appears both surprised and immediately elated that I've spoken, so much so that she nearly chokes on the food she was in the middle of chewing on. She dabs a napkin at her lips.

"Do what?"

"You know, get the waiter to serve you, like, like he wanted to. When I showed up, he hardly acknowledged me, but for you..." I gesture at whatever just happened because words can't explain it. "He didn't even card us for the drinks."

"Oh, well it's his job right? He's supposed to do that. Plus, they aren't typically party poopers in this town anyway."

"Ah." I take a sip of my beer.

Rachel glances down at her food. Then, swiftly from the top edge of the building, a pigeon flies down to pick at the crumbs underneath an empty table, landing softly on the concrete. Its purple and blue feathers glimmer when it exits the shade in a natural search of food. The pigeon's head cocks with each minimal step it takes until, directly underneath Rachel's chair, it perks its head up and freezes for just a moment.

I lean over in my chair and watch the bird curiously through the diamond holes of the table. My eyes bounce up to Rachel as she picks at her fries, tossing one down to the little scavenger, perhaps sympathetically. Gladly, the pigeon accepts the charitable offer. Flapping its wings, it rises and glides along the sky until it becomes a small speck in the clouds.

I'm impressed, filled with a bit of wonder even, but I do my best to conceal that impression. At that moment, Rachel eyes me. She appears to debate something in her mind, like there might be something she isn't telling me. Then she leans a little closer. "You know, between you and me, it's pretty easy."

"Pigeons?"

"No, not pigeons. People."

I frown.

"Let me explain," she says, setting her burger down. "That guy." She nods in the direction of the restaurant, keeping her voice down. "He's what we call an 'easy read'. They always say you can't judge a book by its cover, but you learn quickly in life that yes, you absolutely can. How a person chooses to present themselves, how they act with one group versus another, it immediately builds a foundation to their character."

I pretend to understand, nodding. At that moment, the waiter comes out with a fresh pint and sets it on our table.

"Thank you so much," Rachel says endearingly, to which the waiter bows before regretfully moving to his next table. The moment he turns his back, Rachel's eyes get cold. "When your sister and I were approaching, I saw the way he was talking to you. He was rude, short with you. Then I show up: the 'pretty' girl who's going to boost his ego and bat a flirty eye at him. Suddenly, his personality switches, just like that." She snaps her fingers together. "To conclude, my read on him is your basic college frat boy who only has this job because his rich parents forced him to do so in order to add some 'perspective' to his life. But he's still too focused on girls and beer to give a rat's ass about perspective." Finally, she sips her beer. "In other words, he's easy to manipulate–but I suppose most guys are."

"How so?" I ask somewhat defensively.

She shrugs. "I don't know if it's chivalry, stupidity, or lust, but batting the eyes and smiling are practically the key that turns a man's ignition."

"I see."

Rachel laughs. "I don't want to call it bending them to my will, and I know the word *manipulate* comes off as evil, but..." she adjusts the sleeve of her turquoise top. "I guess it's not the worst thing in the world to give a guy like Mr. Waiter a taste of his own medicine. *That* is how you add perspective."

"Yeah, but how do you go about doing that?"

"Hmm." Rachel squints. "We've only just met. Why're you so interested?" Shocked by the slight accusation to be found in her tone, my eyes dart around. "I'm just kidding," she says. "I guess I've just learned a lot in my psych classes over the years. After reading a thousand pages about the 'five personality types', I think I've got a good idea of who most people are within the first few minutes of meeting them."

I sit back in my chair, contemplatively. Letting out a huff of amusement, I notice the nerves have disappeared. The shake in my hands is gone. Perhaps I've found a bit of unanticipated comfort here with Rachel. Only a bit.

I don't want to say anything more, but now I'm curious. "So ... if you were to read me, what would you do?"

Rachel seems more than happy to answer my question. It's like she'd been waiting for me to ask. "Oh, you'd also be easy, just not nearly as easy as him." She says it in a joking manner, but I'm caught between retorting and laughing along with her.

"What makes you say that?"

69

She points a finger at me. "You're a shy guy who, for some reason, is hesitant to say a *word* to anyone. You avoid eye contact, yada yada yada." As she says that, I look away from her. "So, one easy way to win you over is to get you out of your comfort zone, force you to interact with me, kind of like you're beginning to do right now."

"Hmm, and why would that be easy?"

"All it takes is a physical touch." Rachel reaches her hand across the table and sets it on mine, and a shock goes right through my system. I look into her blue eyes, and they warm me. The skin of her neck is smooth, inviting. All I see is her.

"It's not working," I say indignantly, slowly pulling my hand back. "I–it won't work. Not on me."

"That's a shame," Rachel says. "Maybe I've got my read on you all wrong then." She pierces me with a look of confidence. "I'll give it some time."

I keep my head down to avoid looking at her again. I try to deny the tingle of enjoyment within me. Talking to Rachel, being near her again. It's strange, and I'm clearly unsure how to deal with it. I don't know how to cope with the mixed emotions. My brain assures me that she's awful. She left me for dead, left Casey and I as though we were nothing to her. I still hate her. Right?

"Can I ask you a favor?" Rachel says.

"Uh, yeah. Yes, I suppose."

"Will you please eat that burger before it gets cold?"

As I look down at the table, I consider the salted golden fries and the bun. I wasn't planning on indulging, but what's the worst that could happen? I look up at Rachel. To entertain myself, I plaster concern on my face.

"I'm a vegetarian," I say.

"Oh, my. I'm so sorry, I–"

"I'm just kidding."

Rachel looks both defeated and amused at the same time. "You got me."
I chuckle.

"I was this close," Rachel says as she holds her index finger and thumb up to her eye, "to unfriending you."

"We're friends already?"

"Sadly." Rachel sighs. "And I can tell this is going to be a *long* relationship, in every sense of the word." She rolls her eyes in a theatrical manner.

I snicker, but let my eyes fall to the diamond-shaped holes that make up the flat of our table. *You have no idea.*

"Hey," Rachel says softly. "You're gonna have to learn to take a joke if you're going to be around me. Surely with Alexandra as your older sister, you can't be a softy, right?"

I let my hands graze over the holes in the table, feeling the way they glide under my fingers. Suddenly, I wish I could grab hold of this space in time. Though it is but a fleeting moment no more significant than any other, I think I feel joy. I ought to be used to it by now, but it's surreal to *feel* again, and I fear it's only a matter of time before this newfound ability vanishes.

"So tell me about you, Liam."

I wipe my face with a napkin and swallow before speaking. "Hmm?" I ask not because I misheard or misunderstood her but more so because this conversation, this type of small talk, seems unnecessary to me.

"You know … tell me about yourself, since I apparently haven't had the chance to offer a proper read on you." Rachel offers a smile.

"There's not much to tell, I don't think." I glance up, hoping Rachel accepts that as an answer, yet she looks expectantly at me while she continues to munch on her burger. So I try to think of something, anything to say. "I guess I like music."

"Okay. But what about you yourself? Who are you, Liam?"

I'm caught a bit off guard by her question. "Uh, I'm not sure."

71

"Come on, like what makes you tick? What motivates you?"

With such a simple question, Rachel has managed to stump me. What she really wants to know is what wills me to live, to continue forward. At the moment, I don't have an answer for her. At one time, I did. In that time, my answer would have been: *You drive me forward. You and Casey and Alexandra. I live for you.*

"I–I don't know."

Rachel seems slightly displeased with my inability to respond adequately, but her eyes are filled with something like intrigue. Then she works on finishing the last of her meal.

"I'll tell you about me instead," Rachel says. "It might give you a few ideas." As if she'd prepared for this, she begins rattling off her likes and dislikes. "I love football, mostly because of tailgates. I like the outdoors ... usually. I *hate* the color pink. Um, I think it's super important to help people in need. Philanthropy is awesome, and I just really enjoy being the person who can do that ... hence why I'm going to grad school to get my doctorate in Psych." She puts a finger gun up to her head. "It'll be stressful but worth it! At least that's what they tell me."

I consider her words for a moment. There's an opportunity for a subtle jab. "It must be difficult dealing with that stress and not take it out on the ones closest to you." I peer into her blue eyes to see if they can tell me more than her words do.

"Sometimes I think I might be in the wrong profession, that I'd be better suited as a teacher or accountant, anything but a psychiatrist. It's not that I don't like the curriculum. I do. And I know I can help people someday. It's just–"

"Tough to cope with uncertainty," I offer.

"Exactly. Like, there are no guarantees in my field. I suppose there aren't any guarantees in life, either." Rachel places her temple in her palms. "I just wish I had a crystal ball that let me see into the future."

I'm compelled to tell her that everything is going to be okay. I know, after all, that this is partially true. In terms of career, Rachel does just fine in opening her own practice. Her social life, on the other hand, well…

My hands reach over to take Rachel's. She appears less surprised by the intimate gesture than I am. Her hands feel so soft in my own, and though mine aren't worn any longer, the contrast of her touch feels just the way I remembered. She wants a crystal ball, so for the moment, I'll be that for her.

"This is a tough time in life. You're going to experience so many highs and lows in the coming years. Do what you can to savor time. It goes quick." I let go of her hands, as if now realizing I may have overstepped my bounds. However, Rachel didn't seem to mind. In fact, I'd say she *wanted* me to comfort her in a physical, as well as verbal manner. As I slowly retract my hands to myself, I say, "Trust me, you do just fine."

Rachel scans me with a hint of wonder. She smirks. "Are you sure you're just a freshman? You sound like my professors."

I shrug and avert my eyes back to the holes of the table. A figure approaches in my peripheral vision.

"Can I get these out of the way for you?" The waiter points to Rachel's empty basket and mine that holds a small chunk of burger with a few fries.

"Please and thank you," Rachel says. "Oh, and put this all on one."

The waiter stacks the baskets and carries them off, later returning with one check that Rachel places a twenty-dollar bill on. I give her a puzzled look.

"Don't worry," she says. "You can take the next one." Rachel shrugs, offers her eyes for a moment, and leaves me with an inviting grin.

The next one? Taken aback by the insinuation that she could even *want* to see me again, after doing almost everything in my power to ensure that wouldn't happen, I struggle for a moment to respond. I barely talked to her throughout the entire meal. This arrangement might have been just as awkward and uncomfortable for her as it was for me. Yet, inexplicably, she wants to

73

meet again. Granted, I'll never be able to fully escape Rachel. She's almost as close with Alexandra as I am. But I'd be a fool to accept this invitation.

I know where this goes. I know exactly how this story ends. I've told myself over and over that I would do everything differently if given the chance. I'd never get involved with this girl. I would pursue a different life. I'd prevent myself from getting close to anyone, living happily on my own with maybe a dog to provide me company.

But now in this moment as I meet Rachel's eyes, I'm less confident I'd be able to do so. This woman overrules my obstinacy with her charm. Her beauty extends far beyond the physical realm. She might even convince a heart-broken skeptic to believe in love. Although I'm regretful to admit it, she's able to captivate me in all the same ways she used to. Rachel and I are no Hollywood romance. We have nothing close to a happy ending, but sometimes innate desire is as inescapable as fate.

"Give me your phone." Rachel lays a hand on the table with her palm up. Without objecting, I lay the smartphone in her hand. She takes it and taps at the screen for a short while. "There." She sets the phone face up on my side of the table.

"What did you do?"

"You have my number now, dummy. Next week sometime, you'll get a call from me, not a text. I'll never text. We can do something like this again."

I look down at the screen to see her contact information.

Rachel gets up, readjusts her pony tail and says, "And don't be late." With a wink, she's gone. I twist in my seat to watch her strut through the street until she disappears in the distance.

Just like that, I'm alone at the table once again, unable to make sense of what just happened. I heave a sigh and brush a hand through my hair while something like a smile attempts to escape me. Honking car horns and police sirens in the distance do their best to interrupt the sudden calm that I feel, but to no avail. I enjoy the moment only for a second when a vibration in the table disrupts me. She must have texted already.

"That was quick," I say to myself.

The black screen of my phone lights up with a message, but not from Rachel. A different name shows up, indicating the message is from "Sis". It says: "Sorry again for having to leave :(I owe you one. Let's meet up in a couple days, okay?"

I respond with: "Sounds great."

Sliding the phone back into my pocket, I stretch over the back of the chair with my arms spread out in either direction. I stand on my feet and notice that my ankle doesn't seem to hurt quite as much as before. I leave a couple more dollars on the table as a tip to the waiter and then head off down the sidewalk.

It feels good to blend in with the other street-goers, to be part of the harmony.

The route back to my dorm does take a while when walking, close to half an hour if you take your time. Particularly on a day like today when the sidewalks are full of people who are taking in the last of the sun's rays before the world gets bitter, it can be annoying to navigate the city. There aren't any shortcuts for me to take. I'll have to pass the library and cross the bridge.

It isn't until I start walking back that I realize just how weary I am. Using my index finger, I wipe at the corners of my eyes, removing a bit of crust from them. Exhaustion is beginning to take over. I have been up and quite literally running since three in the morning. Even outside in the sun and calm wind, I've hit the point where I can almost feel my head resting against a pillow.

I round the corner of a building constructed with red brick and walk downhill. The slope from downtown to the river can be drastic–a pain to climb and equally as annoying to descend. Typically, I do my best to avoid eye contact with strangers. I find it best to pretend they're not even there sometimes.

However, my eyes are drawn to one specific person climbing toward me. They keep their head and eyes low, hair covered by a ball cap. Their face is hidden from view. It's not as though this person stands out from the crowd in a physically noticeable way. They blend in well, actually. I'm drawn to them for a different reason that I haven't determined yet–maybe spiritual or otherwise. I hate to stare, but this person jumbled in the crowd continues toward me, and this connection I feel suddenly grows. It grows as they approach, grows until they're right beside me. When they walk by, one eye and what appears to be a grin peek out at me from under their hat. Then I notice their hair. Her blazing red hair. I stop in my tracks.

"Hey!" As I flip around, I'm stuck in the middle of the sidewalk with strangers to my left and right who keep me immobile. The girl turns the corner I had just come from. Intuition tells me she's going to disappear again, but I'm already so close. The chase commences.

Pushing my way through unappreciative groans, I reach the corner of the building and halt. Even when standing on my toes, neither the girl nor her vibrant red hair are anywhere to be found. I grumble. She's managed to vanish. Again.

"GAHH!" I slap my forehead forcefully with the palm of my hand several times over. To those nearby, I probably appear to be a frustrated drug addict or psychopath. Or maybe they aren't batting an eye, instead sympathizing with my frustration as they misplace its source to college stress. I think I hear a couple girls walking by say, "Yeah, we've been there."

While I stare in defeat off into the distance, I raise my right arm to place my palm against the rough brick wall to my right. As I do so, I hear a *crunch*, so I retract my hand from the wall and whip my body around to investigate the noise. I think I understand the game being played.

Hanging from a piece of tape is a small folded square of notebook paper. I remove the tape from the wall and unfold the paper to discover its hidden contents. Another message:

Bus W10 tomorrow @ 9

This message, just like the one before it, initially strikes me as gibberish. I understand the time stamp on it, though it'd be helpful if a simple "A.M" or "P.M" could delineate the difference for me, but that'd make things far too easy. At least *"tomorrow"* gives me a day, so I can probably assume it's a morning time. Nobody wants to meet at 9 at night.

Bus W10. Throughout the course of a day, there are at least a hundred buses that go directly through the city. Locating exactly the correct bus would be like finding a moving needle in a haystack. I examine the message once more. *Bus W10.* What if it's code? Could it lead me to a secretive location? Then I think to myself, *Wait a minute. What if this is more of a riddle? Maybe W10 isn't a bus at all. What if it's a building?*

A light comes on in my head. I know exactly *where* to go. But this time, I don't know *why*. A few hours of rest might help.

V

Encapsulated in a cloud of darkness I stand. A low hum persists. Echoes of a woman sobbing. Although they're merely shadows blending in with the absence of light, the walls are closing in. I can feel it. My arms hang at my side, helpless as a man sentenced to death.

Here there is nothing to look at, things can only be felt. I feel a wooden bedpost to my left standing erect, a guard that points into the gloom. I hear *the solid* tick, tick, tick *of a golden-rimmed clock hanging upon the picture-frame walls as they* close, close, close *in. There's an opening a plank's distance away. It's just wide enough for man to walk through, just enough space for demons to crawl out. I feel its gravity, a black hole. Ragged breathing prevails over the hum. I think it's mine.*

"Liam." Rap, rap, rap. *The sound reverberates around the walls that attempt to suffocate.* "Liam, are you in there?"

Then, from the opening comes a steady light with an occasional flicker. It illuminates a trapezoidal path before me that begins at the base of the opening and widens as its borders reach desperately outward like arms longing for embrace. Carpet fibers struck by the light sway back and forth like corn stalks in a storm. A golden line separates them from tile that has been hardened farther ahead. Flowing farther and farther into darkness, the light battles for truth.

Often relief is felt when light replaces obscurity. Not now. This light unsettles me. It commands my attention. It demands *to be seen. Or maybe it attempts to shine upon something even more troubling than itself. I want to look away but the fear of not seeing is greater.*

I look into the opening as though it contains my fate.

"Liam!" Rap, rap, rap. *"Liam, are you in there?"*

My eyes flutter open to the close view of a smooth white surface with small dimples scattered across it. A circular smoke detector with a green light that strobes every ten seconds hangs quietly from the surface, so as not to disturb the silence of the room. I blink a few times to wipe the exhaustion from my eyes and then lift myself so that I'm sitting upright. Near my feet beyond the edge of the bed, the blinds to the window have been left open, allowing solid rays of sunshine through.

I crawl out of the bed, descend the ladder, and make my way to the door, noting as I pass by Todd's bed that it has been left unmade with no one in it. Once I approach the door, I place my palms flat and look through the peep hole with one eye. There's no one on the other side, just a desolate hallway. Maybe I should open the door to be sure. It creeps open just enough so that I can get a good look. Upon peering through the slit, it is confirmed. No one is there. Finally, I pull on the door handle to swing it wide open and lean my head out as I'm sure to check both directions for good measure. Nothing.

Turning back into my room, I let the door automatically swing shut behind me with a *click*. My fingers pass through my hair as I let out a sigh. The clock on the desk tells me that it's 8:00a.m. I must've been asleep forever. I suppose I needed it.

A little bit to the left of the cell phone is an unfolded rectangle of notebook paper, the creases preventing it from lying flat on the hardwood of the desk. My eyes wander over the neatly-written note. I check the clock again. As far as time goes, I've got plenty of it. But it wouldn't hurt to be early.

Bus W10. Bus isn't a reference to a large transportation vehicle, at least not in this instance. Here, Bus is short for Business, the location of my next endeavor. The business building is a large, phenomenally constructed L-shape with large pyramidal pillars rising above each corner and smaller ones evenly spaced elsewhere along the top edges of the building. Each pillar rises toward the sky like beacons attracting knowledge from the heavens above.

I find myself standing outside the entrance to W10, an auditorium, as labeled by the long, rectangular, greenish-colored sign that has been implanted into the side of the building. It's placed just above the three rows of double doors that filter students routinely in and out throughout the course of the day. Naturally, the wind blows on this cool Fall day, creating a wind tunnel over the large walkway between the lecture halls. The breeze blows through my hair and makes the strings on my blue hoodie bounce up and down. A bit of cloud cover overhead hints at rain, so I head inside.

Orange marble flooring squeaks underneath my shoes as a wide entryway opens up into an expansive auditorium with hundreds of gray folding seats that have been bolted to the floor in ascending rows. The room has been dug below ground-level so that the entryway is level with the top row, and the first-row "goody two-shoes" seats can be accessed by using the wide stairways at each end.

As I move closer to a ledge that peeks over the middle of the auditorium, I observe the current lecture taking place and the students who fill only a quarter of the available seats as they attentively copy notes. At the front of the lecture hall, a middle-aged male paces back and forth, his booming voice amplified through the speaker system. This man dressed in black dress pants and a white long-sleeve with a flower-patterned tie is miniscule in size compared to the projector screen in the background. Occasionally, he works his way over to the podium on the left-hand side of the room to change slides as he rapidly covers several topics. I imagine there are only a few more minutes to his lecture, so I'd be smart to move now before this calm setting turns into one of rushed chaos.

Once more I look over the length of the auditorium, admiring its structure while also looking for a place to sit. It's not as though there aren't any empty seats. It's just that I prefer to situate myself as distantly from others as possible.

The back few rows seem to be mostly empty, so I start for those, rounding the corner of the ledge and descending the stair-like platforms that lead to the third-to-last row where I find a lonesome corner seat. I plop down into the chair and pull up the swinging desk built into the armrest. There, I wait.

While the professor describes markets and the ways in which supply and demand react differently to certain events, I begin to wonder why I'm here. Obviously the note I found directed me to this place, "*Bus W10 @ 9*", so I came. There's nothing too difficult about the notes themselves. I find them, and I follow their instructions. It's that simple. But I start to wonder why I'm following in the first place. I'm under no obligation to do so. Sure, being thrown into this world of the past leaves me with few better options, and I kind of enjoy the thrill of pushing my own boundaries. But what if I'm just a mouse following a bread-crumb trail to a cube of cheese that snaps on me?

My guard is up. I know to walk this path carefully, though a certain level of apathy is held toward my own demise.

From my left pocket, I procure the crunched-up note to review it one more time. It's very similar to the one preceding it. The first note took me to the place where Rachel and I first met. Will I see her here, too? If so, then why?

Internally I scold myself for the boyish longing inside me. I know better than to give into it. Still, part of me wouldn't mind seeing her. I know the potential, if not certainty, for harm. I know how foolish it would be to even partially succumb to natural desire, and I could never scold myself enough if I were to allow the woman, who not to mention destroyed my very will to live, into my life for a second time. But occasionally, it's a thrill to tempt fate and knowingly sail through treacherous waters.

In college, there are no bells to indicate the beginning or end of a class period. Students operate either by the time on their watches or by the commands of the professors who will end lecture sessions early on rare occasions. It's somewhat beautiful to watch as an entire group simultaneously rises, collects their belongings, and leaves, only to be replaced by a nearly identical crowd who follows the same routine, all conducted by one professor at the front. The students sit. They remain quiet. They take notes and pay attention. These are all individuals who can make their own individual choices, or so they believe. In some ways, they all know, consciously or otherwise, someone or something higher is really in control.

The newer group filters in, one much greater in number than the last. From bottom to top, seats fill rapidly, a large wave inevitably coming my direction. Eventually, the row before me is occupied, and soon the seats beside me will be the only available options. I lower my head. My leg bounces up and down. The seat beside me squeaks as someone lowers into it. I guess we're in for a packed house.

"Hello, everyone!" A shorter woman hushes the buzz from the front of the auditorium. The projector flashes on. "Your grades are online, and you all did so well on the midterm. Yay! Give yourselves a pat on the back." In an almost cultish manner, the auditorium gently erupts with a three-second bout of finger-snapping. "So," she continues, "without further ado, let's dive right into our next lesson." The professor truly does act "without further ado", as she pulls up a seventy-slide lecture that she plans on completing in probably two sessions.

A feminine voice whispers at me from the seat next to mine. "Let's hope this one isn't as boring as the last one. That stuff made me want to shoot myself in the head." Without facing her, I decline to acknowledge her odd joke and avert my eyes to the wall. "You know, kind of like how you did."

My head snaps to my right. My eyes widen.

"You."

"Hi there." A black leather jacket. A bright smile, long-nailed fingers waving at me. A smooth nose. Bright green eyes. Blazing red hair falling out of a ball cap. I'm frozen, unsure what to say, so I repeat myself.

"You…"

"You said that already." Her voice is low and warming, almost reducing the turmoil occurring in my brain.

"How–" I'm at a loss for words, so that's all I can manage.

"I'm good, how are you?"

"No, how…"

"How's the weather outside? The rain is starting to make my hair frizz up." She grabs at her ponytail.

"No, no. How did you–"

"Ohh! You want to know how *I* knew you played Russian roulette with a *not*-revolver, woke up, and traveled back in time to rediscover your college days and the good times that accompany them, along with the people and places that had previously slipped into the recesses of your mind. Yes, that must be it." I look at her with amazement and slight disturbance. She leans in close to me with an expression that indicates she's rather pleased with herself. "You must have so many questions."

I give her the squinty eyes, unsure of what to say. She is right, though. I do have questions. So I nod.

"Ask away," she says.

"Um," I stutter after being put on the spot so suddenly. This woman knows what I did. She must also know why I'm here. "I don't know … uh, what am I doing here? And how did I get here in the first place?"

"Those aren't the right questions."

"Huh? What do you mean?"

"That's also not the right question."

83

"I don't know what the right question is, then."

"I'll be asking the questions around here."

I stare at her with a look of confusion, her smug face encouraging me to pound my head through a brick wall. Is this really what I've spent all my hours chasing? To say the least, I'm underwhelmed.

"Riddle me this, Liam Crawford. Are you dead, or are you alive? Is this Heaven or is this hell? What *are* you doing here in this world of the past?"

I gesture a hand at her. "I was hoping you'd be the one to tell me."

"No, *you* tell *me*."

I place my index finger and thumb on my temple and groan as though fighting a migraine, which suddenly I think I am. "I have no idea," I say more to myself than to her.

"Sure you do," she offers. "You're smart, Liam Crawford–"

"Please just call me Liam."

"–*and* you're a brilliant musical artist with great taste. What do you think you are doing here?"

"What does my music have to do with this? How do you know everything about me?"

"What makes you think you can change the rules? I'm asking questions. You give me answers."

I look around, surprised by the fact that nobody nearby is paying us any attention. They're locked in on the lesson, I guess.

"I don't *know*!"

"Try."

I spend a moment in solitude, eyes closed, attempting to shut out the world around me. I can feel the girl's eyes boring into my skull, like she's hoping to extract the right words from me, which in all honesty wouldn't be the worst. Clearly she knows the answers for which she is looking. I don't. Even after a solid minute or two in thought, I come up with …

"Nothing. I can't think of anything. I'm lost."

I look into her eyes, half expecting them to become as bright red as her hair, incinerating me to nothing but a mound of dust on this seat. However, she contains her disappointment just enough.

"Let me spell it out for you. Nobody who puts a loaded gun up to their head and pulls the trigger while also driving a truck has lived to tell about it … but you have. What is that called?" Again, I'm shocked by the fact that our conversation has yet to affect anyone around us.

"I'm alive?"

"Answers, Liam. You give me answers."

"Uhh … it's called luck, I guess."

The girl stares at me, evidently not amused in the slightest. "Try again."

I groan. Have we gone back *another* fourteen years? I feel as though I'm being reprimanded by a kindergarten teacher who would like to know what it is that I have done wrong, even though she is fully aware of said wrong-doing. My mind is stuck on her question. Until now, I haven't been forced to confront the truth of my situation so deeply. I suppose you could say I'm a quickly accepting individual. But she's right. I shouldn't be alive right now. Life is a gift, one that I've been given–twice.

"It's a second chance," I say with only half confidence. I almost cower in my seat, awaiting for the girl's head to explode, leaving me covered in a gruesome combination of brains and red hair.

"Yahtzee!" she says gleefully. "You aren't so clueless after all." I'm unappreciative of her passive insult, but also relieved. "So why exactly have *you* been given a second chance?" My mouth hangs open, and as I begin to shake my head, the girl says, "And don't you dare say you don't know."

My mouth closes. I'd like to ask her for a hint, but I know I can't phrase it as a question.

"I need a clue."

The mystery girl appears as though she wants to deny my request but then seems to acknowledge the statement. "Okay. You've followed my notes, correct?"

I nod.

"Where did the first one take you?"

"A restaurant."

"What restaurant?"

"The Pub."

"And who did you see there?"

"My sister."

"Wrong." She makes a buzzer sound. "Who else?"

I sigh. "Rachel." I think I know precisely where she's going with this.

"So you put all the dots together, and what do you get?" The girl slides her palm face-up through the air, as though she has served me the answer on a silver platter. In all practicality, she has.

I sit where I am in silence. I know what she wants me to say. I just don't want to say it. I don't want to admit that what she's hinting at must be true. Surely there's another reason for me to be here. Not this one.

"I've been given a second chance to do things differently with Rachel, to do it right this time," I concede to her in a grumble.

Instead of responding, the red-haired girl gives me a look of satisfaction, a satisfaction that I have regretfully granted to her. She's looking for a smile in return, but I won't give it up.

"What if that's not what I want?" I'm hesitant to ask.

"Oh, please. You believe in some pretty crazy things, Liam, but I'm not sure that even *you* could fool yourself into believing *that*."

I watch my thumbs twiddle over one another as they rest in my lap. "She hurt me pretty bad," I say.

"Ahh." The girl puts a finger up in the air. "Was she the one to hurt you, or were you the one to hurt yourself?"

86

"What do you mean?" Apparently I'm asking the right questions now.

"In your mind, you believe that you have done nothing wrong and therefore don't deserve the pain that has come your direction, a very unhealthy state of mind to be in, if I might add."

Great, so now she can read my mind.

"But what if I told you that everything might not be perfectly as you remember it?"

"Explain," I say.

The girl reclines back in her chair, folds her hands together, and faces the front as she leans over to me in a more hushed tone now, almost like she's suddenly interested in what the professor has to say and would hate to interrupt. But I'm locked in on her. Any other words or sounds that arise in the auditorium are irrelevant.

"All that I'll say," she begins, "is that obviously things didn't work out between the two of you." She makes a heart with her hands and then cracks it down the middle. Then she uses her index and middle finger to illustrate. "You were two individuals–see, here's two–who came together as one. When things fall apart, one is not more at fault than the other, the one whole is at fault, so therefore the two are guilty."

This woman really loves her riddles. "I have no idea what you're saying."

She gives me a gentle slap on the cheek, which is completely unwarranted. "Think, child. *You* messed things up just as much as she did." I don't consider her words to be entirely true, and she must be able to tell by my hesitance. "You did, Liam, so accept it."

Gently rolling my eyes, I say, "Okay, sure. Whatever."

"But!" she offers and quickly grabs my attention, along with each of my hands as she locks me in a visual embrace. "You can change it all this time around. Discover where you went wrong. Don't make the same mistakes as before. This is your chance. If you don't mess it up, then maybe, just *maybe* …

87

you'll experience the lifetime that you've always dreamt of. *That* is the reason you're here … isn't it?"

I retract my hands to myself and ponder her words. The phrases she uses almost act under the assumption that I'm omnipotent and can alter my future to my exact desires with nothing more than the snap of a finger, but her repeated questions and inquisitive tone indicate a knowledge of the truth. I can't. For all I know, things could end up just as badly as they had before, maybe even worse. I don't think I'm ready to experience that kind of pain again. Is the risk really worth it? Maybe this second chance would be better used if I were to move far, far away, purchase a short-hair bird dog, and construct my own cabin in the woods. Sounds like a well-used second chance if you ask me. Above all, how am I to trust this woman? Maybe I don't have a choice.

While I'm stuck in my own head, the girl lets go of my hands, pats her knees, gets up unannounced, and walks toward the center aisle, greeted by a few displeased students in the row who had been taking notes. She is leaving. Why so suddenly? As she climbs the platforms up toward the exit, I whip around in my chair.

"Wait!" I say, loud enough to attract a few heads. The girl's green eyes look me up and down. Quiet words escape me. "What do I do? Where do I go from here?"

The girl continues to take the steps up. "Follow the notes," she says.

I sit with my own thoughts for a moment. Then, as she's right at the exit, I grab her attention for a final time.

"One more thing!" I add. She stops herself with a hand on the pillar that holds an exit sign up above it. I give her a pleading look. "Who are you?"

She gives a bright smile, laughs to herself, says, "Call me Jay,", and then disappears behind the pillar. She's gone. As quickly as she arrived, she has disappeared, leaving me with far too many questions unanswered.

Just when I consider going after her, the lecture ends, and hundreds of students fill the exits and entries. I won't be able to catch her.

My right leg begins to buzz, so I pull out my phone as a text from Alexandra lights up the screen.

"You should come to my place to hang out tonight if you have time ... feels like I haven't seen you in so long :)"

Perhaps this is my next note.

"I'll be there." I reply and then stuff the device back where it was before.

For a second time, a crowded rush of students who walk closely with one another replaces the previous group. But I don't notice them anymore as I remain seated, fixated on the small gray bumps that make up the backrest of the chair in front of me. If you look closely enough and stare at one particular point or bump until the outer edges of your vision become blurry, you can find microscopic craters within the makeup of the chair itself that look like the surface of the moon. Much like the moon hanging in a black starless sky, these craters have a gravitational pull and an implicit beauty that make the area around them disappear. A field of gray takes over my vision.

My eyes fall to my empty lap. I imagine Casey sitting atop my knee as it bounces, the little boy laughing gleefully. I miss him already, wish so badly that I could see him.

A second chance.

What if this girl–Jay–is right? Maybe I need to use this second chance to right my wrongs with Rachel. I think of Casey once again, and the gray that infiltrated my vision becomes slightly less muddled.

VI

Eight multi-colored cards tap on the riveted wooden table as I consider which one to lay upon the center pile. I can either stack a yellow skip or reverse onto the seven lying face-up. I suppose it doesn't really matter.

Laying one after the other, I say, "Skip and ... skip."

"Darn you," Alexandra says with little concern.

Her apartment is decorated neatly, at least for an old, beat-up setting. Faded white cabinets have turned tan but remain smooth, other than a few scuff marks likely imparted by previous tenants. They hang over an oven and a narrow cream-colored countertop that follows the walls of the kitchen to form a small L-shape, stopping just in time for the refrigerator.

"You want anything to drink?" Alexandra asks, nodding toward it.

"Nah." I look absently upon the light fixture hanging from the ceiling.

Its flickering brightness is just enough to dominate the darkness of the night and illuminate the entire space. A small pot of plastic flowers adorns the elevated table on which a not-so-heated game of Uno is taking place, but the pot has been pushed off to the side so as not to impede. I don't like the plastic flowers, so I avoid them and watch as my sister heavily debates which card she should lay next.

Seeing Alexandra as a twenty-something again has really thrown me for a loop, and though I've accustomed myself to every other replication of the past, being in the presence of my sister in her younger form is something that will take a little more time to understand. That's why I've purposely held my cards at eye-level every now and again, to hide the fact that I've been staring. Her face is so much smoother, the wrinkles above her eyes not yet formed, her

90

brunette hair is without the few tiny streaks of gray that will come with age. She's held the same pleasant and oblivious face since we started playing, telling me she either doesn't notice or doesn't care that I've been locked in on her.

After half an hour of being dismantled by a combination of unlucky draws, Alexandra's skill, and my lack of caring, I lay down my final card to win and go one and four on the night.

"One more game," Alexandra demands.

"Nope." I wipe my hands in the air and then hold them up on either side of me as I slide out of the high-top chair. "That's it for me."

The kitchen opens up into a living room of about double the space, where a large bean bag chair and maroon recliner with a few tears face a fireplace and a thirty-five inch flat screen on the mantle above. This is where Alexandra and I later come to rest, me on the recliner and she on the bean bag as we both take from a large gray bowl of popcorn Alexandra laid upon a small wooden desk between us. The fireplace emits a warmth that makes the blankets we have wrapped around ourselves unnecessary. However, they do provide extra comfort and protection from the cool draft seeping in off the right through the sliding door. After flipping the light switch off, the living room remains mostly dark, save for the three separate light sources coming from the candles near the entrance, the fireplace, and the television screen.

Though my memory has turned blurry over the years and I find it difficult to recall much of what I did in this time—nearly a decade and a half in the past–I do remember the day when I helped Alexandra move into this apartment and the agonizing late summer heat and humidity that made the process nearly unbearable, not to mention the fact that she and I were a crew of two that day. Hauling her heavy and awkward bed frame, mattress, and chairs up the tightly compacted stairways and through the door–with me at the bottom struggling to support the brunt of their weight and Alexandra guiding at the top–exhausted every ounce of energy I had, and then some. Mom and

Dad were gone that day. Dad had chores to do back home, and Mom didn't want to leave him alone in case anything were to go wrong with his aging and frail heart.

We spent the entire day walking up and down those stairs. Alex's watch indicated that we had completed about twenty miles of walking each. After several hours, Alexandra and I manually transformed a bare and empty space into an imperfect, yet suitable place to exist. I remember how it looked in the past, and it is exactly the same today as we had left it back then. It may not be anything special, but there's still pride to be had in what we created. We did it together.

I watch as the sharp flames within the fireplace jolt up and down repeatedly and at random in an attempt to escape the clear glass confines in which they are held. They strike at the air above as though they wish to consume the mantle and everything it holds, only to spread, spread, spread across the walls, over to the drapes, down to the floor, and merge with the candlelight to form an inescapable trap that leaves two siblings to a fiery demise.

"Hey, we should shut that off." I point to the fireplace.

Alexandra does a double take and gives me a funny look. "You're kidding, right?"

"Can we please?"

"Is it too hot?"

"No, I just ... wish it were off."

"If you have to, go ahead," she says with a sigh and a subtle head-shake.

The recliner's footrest snaps back into place as I get up and head over to the fireplace. Bending down on my knees, I find the knob that controls the gas. Twisting it slowly to the left, I watch as the flames begin to die out like falling hands hopelessly reaching out for someone to catch them, someone to bring them back to life, until *poof*. They're out.

92

As I come to rest in the recliner once again, I snuggle into the blanket, a necessity now more than a comfort. I grab a couple kernels of popcorn, toss them into my mouth, and focus my attention on the show playing before me.

We've decided to put on the Netflix series "Dexter", where a Miami Metro blood spatter analyst doubles as a serial killer who takes pleasure in "taking out the trash" of society. To everyone around him, Dexter is a moderately normal individual, with a few quirks that aren't significant enough to out him as a stone-cold killing machine. But he knows who he is. He has to live with the monster inside him, constantly battling between the lie he lives, the lie he shows to everyone else, and his true self: a killer. I can't imagine the struggles Dexter would face if he were real, forced to hold this mind-boggling and truly awful secret within him, just so he can pretend to have some semblance of a normal life.

"So," Alexandra interrupts the show. I don't mind. I've seen it all before. "How did lunch go with Rachel?"

My heart starts, and a nervous wave quickly washes over me. It's not as though Alexandra's intent is to interrogate me. She isn't trying to pry some type of loose information from the farthest reaches of my soul. The thought of Rachel is just naturally unsettling to me, let alone the idea of having to talk about her. It's an especially challenging thing to do when I'm unsure of the feelings I have toward her at the moment.

"It went well."

"Good," Alexandra says. She plops a couple more kernels of popcorn in her mouth without letting her eyes stray from the television. "She's such a nice girl, I'm glad you got the chance to meet her."

Outside the window, a crack of lightning turns the outside world bright for a moment, shaking the windows and the floor. The thunderhead must be close. What starts as a sprinkle turns rather quickly into torrential downpour, the streetlamp just outside the window becoming invisible, shielded by a

93

curtain of rain. Water droplets crash hard against the shingles on the roof, sounding off like ocean waves through the ceiling.

Alexandra couldn't be less concerned as she turns the television's volume up a notch with a few clicks of the remote to overrule the harsh sounds of nature. She continues munching on popcorn, unconcerned that the roof of this old apartment building might cave in on top of us if the wind continues to pick up. Whether she's pretending to be brave or not, her impenetrable façade vicariously breeds a confidence that allows me to watch our show with the slightest bit of intent, even with the storm brewing upon us.

Doubling both as a thriller and romance series, Dexter combines his horrific life with a few romantic relationships. Dexter begins the series dating a single mother named Rita. Their relationship becomes … complicated, to say the least. Dexter leaves Rita for someone else, a choice he discovers is a grand mistake. Alexandra and I have reached a moment in the Dexter timeline when he is able to make amends with Rita and recover the life he used to have, one that was far better than any fantasies he might've had with someone else.

Every so often, the series features revealing sexual scenes, which I consider to be somewhat unnecessary … and awkward when watching them with your sister. I consider these to be perfect times to distract from the show.

"Hey, sis," I say.

"What's up?"

"What if Dexter wouldn't have gone back to Rita, or what if she wouldn't have taken him back?" I ask, then pause. "Hypothetically speaking."

"They wouldn't be together," she shrugs.

The rain outside has not let up. If anything, the winds have gained momentum, and we've hit a much darker spot on the radar as lightning continues to strike periodically.

"Well … yeah," I say. Her answer is obvious. Perhaps I need to phrase the question differently. "But what if Dexter had chosen not to go back to

94

Rita? You know, let's say she caused him a lot of pain, and he wasn't sure if a life with her was going to be right for him."

"That's not how the story goes." Alexandra tosses a kernel in her mouth.

The winds howl through the small cracks in the sliding door.

"Okay," I say. "But let's say that it is, just for now."

Alexandra turns her head to me, the rest of her body cocooned in a blanket. She addresses me with what appears to be concern. "Why? What's going on?"

"Oh, nothing." I try to convince her. "Just curious."

Although she doesn't appear to have been persuaded by my tone, Alexandra shakes up her hair and attempts to answer my question. "Well, I suppose that would be his choice, and if he thought it was for the best, then so be it."

Alexandra's words are very matter of fact, which isn't entirely new for her. My sister processes information in a very "Type A" sort of way. A and B go into an equation, and C must therefore result. Not often does she take emotional consequence into account when discussing hypotheticals. The situation must be *real* in order for her to think not only with her brain, but also her heart. However, since Alexandra seems rather invested in the episode, I decide not to press on any further, though I can't say I'm completely satisfied with the answer she gives.

Dexter and Rita finish partaking in passionate love on the screen as candlelight rides up the walls, outlining the smooth silhouettes of two bodies that have joined together as one. They fall back into the sheets side by side, their eyes locking on one another in an obvious display of love. It's supposed to make the viewer feel that love from the place in which they're seated, if not long for it. I'm not sure whether it's working on me or not.

By the end of the episode and as the solid twenty minutes of heavy rainfall recede to a light mist, the empty television screen and the water slowly dripping from the gutters leave the room in silence. That is, until Alexandra clears her throat.

"He'd be a coward," she says.

"Huh?" I ask.

"Dexter," Alexandra says with conviction. "He'd be a coward. Dexter loves Rita. If he didn't chase the woman he loves when given the chance, that would qualify him as a grade A coward. Yeah, he messed up, but he's human, and she gave him a second chance. That's more than anyone usually gets."

"Ahh," I say.

"Plus," she continues, "Rita's well out of Dexter's league. She's gorgeous and sweet and an awesome mom. Dexter would be an idiot not to go after her."

I rub my neck. "Yes," I say. "Dexter would be an idiot."

"And a coward."

"And a coward," I agree.

Alexandra turns the TV off, signaling the end of the night and that it's time for me to leave. Throwing the blanket off herself, she offers to take mine with an extended arm. As I give it to her, the cold air that has infiltrated the room attacks my body.

After tossing the two blankets into a notch between the fireplace and the wall, Alexandra plucks a set of keys from the table on which our game of Uno had earlier taken place. She's going to give me a ride back to my dorm.

"Like I said, that's not how the story goes, is it?" she says.

I meet Alexandra's eyes as she flashes the keys before me. Then the trampled carpet floor draws my attention for a moment, though there's nothing special about it.

Looking back up at her, I give a quick snicker. "No," I say. "It's not how the story goes."

At least it doesn't have to be.

96

On the ride back, I gaze up into the night, perplexed to see a starry sky revealed above. The storm clouds that would have hidden the constellations must have completely passed through. I'm able to spot the Big Dipper, the North Star, and even Orion's Belt along the way. What was previously cloudy and unclear has turned into bright lights like checkpoints guiding me home.

VII

"Of course, here you have the custom mahogany finish of a Gibson. Go ahead and feel the neck." A pause. "Now feel free to pluck a string or two." Again I do as he says. "Pretty awesome, right?"

"Yeah," I say. "Gibson smooth."

"Gibson smooth," the man smiles.

The small guitar shop sits in an outlet that is surrounded by various other businesses: a pizza place, apartments, etc. Lining every wall on the inside are bolted hangers supporting guitars that would otherwise fall to the ground on top of a collection of amps and cords, where they would likely tumble into the racks in the middle of the cramped store. Luckily, the hangers have been fabricated to provide a sturdy, long-lasting support, so such a disaster is improbable.

As the man who I presume to be the store owner guides me through the tight space, he introduces me to every big-name guitar. Usually, you'd expect a salesman to highlight the most expensive guitars as "the best" and "the one you need", but this man is apparently in love with every guitar, every brand, displaying them all with an equal sense of pride, evident in the way in which his rose-colored cheeks crumple when his bearded white face projects a smile.

"And if you'll follow me over here," he gestures with one arm, "I'll show you one of my favorites, a bit of an underdog, if you will: the Mitchell MX430. Now don't be fooled by its price," he says as he quickly covers the tag with four calloused fingers. "Inexpensive guitars aren't always an indication of cheap quality. This one here, for example, is light weight, super rocking with its rich brown color and smooth finish, and it plays with the low strum of a dreadnought, even with its jumbo body style."

"Rocking," I confirm.

The man puts a finger up to his chin. "You know, it is pretty wicked that the jumbo body style is typically smaller than your dreadnought, despite its *jumbo* name ... guitarists, man. We don't make a lot of sense ... or cents." His left hand climbs up to point at his head while his right rubs his index finger and thumb together, as if he were a pirate sliding gold doubloons on top of each other just to hear them *clink*.

I acknowledge his pun with a finger gun.

He continues to guide me through each guitar, each brand, each body style, and the history of them all. Occasionally, he'll lightly pull one off its rack, strum a few common riffs, and place it back just as carefully, forgetting to ask whether his customer would like the opportunity to play them. It's alright; I don't mind.

After each guitar he plays–and there are at least twenty instruments on which he decides to demonstrate his clear skill–he'll hold it in both hands, admire its handiwork, and provide me with a fact about its creation and how it came to be in this exact store. I'm rather impressed with his knowledge, even though most of what he tells is nothing new and somewhat a waste of my time.

Yet I follow him around the store for nearly two hours, more for his enjoyment than mine. The thing is, I don't have anything better to do. Technically, I've already graduated from college, so going through the motions, attending classes, and obtaining a degree all over again would be a waste of my time. I'd much rather be here in this guitar store, surrounded by the world's finest creations. I've discovered that when given a second chance at life, you should live it precisely in the ways you wish you would have beforehand, so I'm doing just that, or at least attempting to do so.

At the end of my guided tour, interrupted only by one young guitarist who made a quick stop to grab a new set of strings, we end up back by the entrance to the store. This is where the owner, whose name I learned to be Travis, pats his palms against the jeans that wear tight around his thighs and says, "So, man. As I've said, no pressure to pick one out today. No, *wait!*" I'm startled as he places his two index fingers in temple formation and presses them to his lips. "That's the wrong way to put it. Your guitar picks *you*. My mistake."

"Not a problem," I assure him.

"If you feel like the right guitar has spoken to you, then you grab it, you take it home, and you strum that thing like there's no tomorrow. There might not be, after all–a tomorrow, I mean. And if one hasn't spoken, you wait until it calls to you, calls like a lone wolf in the wilderness to its pack–"

"The Mitchell," I say. " I'll take the underdog."

Travis is taken aback, perhaps not because I interrupted him in the middle of one of his many inspiring speeches I've heard within the last two hours, but I'd imagine he's surprised a guitar would "speak" to me so quickly. Then his shock quickly transforms into joy as he raises a hand for me to clap.

"Rock *on!*" he clasps my hand for a second before letting go. "Grab your beauty, man ... she's yours." He points to the section with the Mitchell guitars.

The guitar that attracts my eye, reminding me of my first-ever instrument, is a Mitchell with an almost cherry-like finish, yet it contains an appealing darkness that complements the natural tree-ring swirls glossed over with a nitrocellulose seal. Travis had played the one next to it earlier. The sound resembled a guitar I owned back in Nashville, and in that moment, my selection had been reaffirmed.

After purchasing the guitar and enclosing it in a case, I bid Travis farewell and listen to the *ring* of the exit door as I walk outside to a large parking lot.

A cloudy gloom has been cast across the city, and the streets and sidewalks have not yet dried from the previous night's rain. Yellow leaves have been blown into rippling puddles and street corners. Fallen limbs–some much larger than others–have left shattered twigs and branches lying on top of concrete, yellowing grass, and even parked vehicles.

Apparently the storm had been just as bad as I feared. Many buildings–businesses and otherwise–have been left without power, uncertain of when they'll be able to return. Thankfully, the guitar store wasn't hit too badly, perhaps fortunately placed in the path of the storm's eye. Many businesses were not so lucky and will remain closed for an indefinite period. There are even wheeled stop signs that have been planted in the center of a large portion of traffic-light intersections because they aren't functioning. It's scary the damage that can be done by nature.

Dispelling the last of fall and ushering in winter cold, the storm has seemingly altered the city's environment, as if Mother Nature had been riding the thunderheads herself last night in an autumn orange dress, and immediately after passing through, changing into her frosty white-colored garb that foreshadows a Midwestern holiday season. That's how it goes around here. One day you're eating dinner outdoors, and it's sixty degrees. The next you're unable to spend more than an hour outside of a heated environment before you freeze to death.

Although I'm unable to see my own face as I hunker through the cold winds, I can feel the redness in my cheeks. My freezing fingers tighten around the handle of the guitar case. If I don't get back quickly, I could damage the wood of my guitar, as it is extremely sensitive to changes in temperature and pressure. Increasing my pace, I head for the dorm.

Arriving through the glass doors just before being frozen in place outside, I welcome the warmth and comfort of shelter. Every building or home you walk into has a different aroma, sending neurons through your nose, up to your brain, generating an automatic emotional response. Sometimes the smells can be associated with joy, hurt, discomfort, laughter, or some other form of reminiscence altogether. This building is no different. Here, the pleasant scent of fresh air reminds me of home.

I can't help but regard this place with somewhat mournful nostalgia, in the same way that a widow might receive the site of her marriage, whether it be a chapel or a beach. Past memories might have been wonderful, and though they have the power to bring great joy in that time, they also have the power to hurt in the present.

But overshadowing any nostalgia are thoughts of restoration and new beginnings, opportunities to start again. In this exact building where I had woken up just two days ago to a changed, yet familiar world, I had been given this opportunity for a second time. It won't be squandered.

A standard elevator with stainless steel walls takes me to the sixth floor. The doors open with a quiet *ding*.

As I turn the corner to my side of the floor, there is no one to be found in the lobby, except for a taller dark-haired guy and blonde girl pressing their chests closely together in the RA's doorway. The girl wears gym shorts and a pink hoodie, while the guy fashions black pants and a white button-up from which a colored and offset bowtie peeks out. As much as I try not to pay them any attention, the contrast in their outfits is unavoidable, and the girl adjusts the man's bowtie in a flirty way that makes it difficult to look elsewhere. They lock eyes, and as I begin to place the two of them in my memory, I'm struck with utter confusion.

"I don't know what I'll do without my Jor-man today."

"I'll miss my little Em-cat." Jordan, the man who had been working the front desk a couple nights ago, rubs Emma's cheek with a thumb.

Emma, my RA, responds with something that resembles the sound of a feisty baby kitten.

I catch myself in a frozen trance, staring at the couple with befuddlement plastered on my face. The willies course through my entire body.

I walk hurriedly by them with guitar case in hand as though I saw nothing. My presence must have only been alerted to them as I passed by, judging by the change in tone I hear behind me.

"Uh, yeah! I'll be sure to get that report to your desk as soon as possible!" Emma says.

Jordan clears his throat. "Yes! Yeah. Right. The report."

Swiftly, I push my door open, and as it closes too slowly behind me, two faraway groans slip through the crack before it shuts.

Whatever was going on out there is none of my business, and I haven't the energy nor the time to care, but it is peculiar.

I twist the lock shut, and only when I hear a subtle groan from within the room do I realize that I probably should have entered more carefully and quietly.

"Ugh ... mate. What time is i'?" a shirtless Todd says groggily as he places a hand on his forehead, just below his disheveled brown hair that ascends in a flame-like pattern. He had been covered too well by the comforter of his bed for me to notice his presence when I barged in. Then I look at the clock sitting on my desk, and suddenly I feel less guilty.

"It's noon," I say.

"Argh." He plops his head back on the pillow, just to lift it back up swiftly. "Oy, what's tha' you've go' there?"

The case has grown heavy after holding it for the past half hour, but my shoulder had grown numb to the pain about halfway back.

"Just a guitar." I set it on the ground.

By now, Todd has hung his legs over the edge of his bed so that his feet are parallel to the ground. "You play?"

"Yeah."

"Well wha' are you wai'ing fo? Pull tha' thing ou'. Les hear somethin'."

I give Todd an uneasy look. I hadn't exactly been given the chance to play in the store before coming here. It's not as though I'm worried about having to "brush out the cobwebs" or "shake the rust off", so to speak. My concern stems from the fact that I might not even be able to play at all.

103

I remember how long it took to learn a few simple chords on the guitar the *first* time I was eighteen. Will my inability to play revert to the way it was then? Am I going to have to learn all over again? There's only one way to find out.

The thought scares me, almost enough to not even dare opening the case. But it sits there on the floor, waiting to be opened. The guitar seems to call to me from within, the same way it did in the store.

"Alright," I say, giving Todd a weak smile.

Unhooking the latches one-by-one, I open the case to reveal the MX430, its strings and body facing up. I grab it firmly by the neck, extracting it from its case.

Todd awaits his performance eagerly, swinging his feet back and forth like a child on a swing.

I twist the simple gray chair by my desk around so that I can sit and rest the nook, or the curved part of the body, on my knee. As I do so, I pluck each string just lightly enough to be able to tune it. Every now and again, I look up at Todd to see if he's losing patience, but he offers the same, somewhat oblivious grin.

E-A-D-G-B-E. The guitar is primed and ready to go … but I'm not.

I feel a shaking in my fingers, a prominent thumping in my chest, both an otherwise normal occurrence for me–just not when there's a guitar in my hands. I'm not sure why nerves might strike now at an inconsequential time, playing for a roommate who couldn't really care less how I sound.

Placing my left hand on the neck of the guitar, I arrange my fingers to form a C-shape. It feels somewhat awkward at first, and the panic within me grows. I give the guitar an impulsive strum, and the sound that results is nothing short of horrific.

Todd expresses slight perturb, his confidence in me fading quickly … my own confidence doing the same.

So I avoid Todd's eyes and close mine. I'm alone here. I take a few deep breaths. I gaze into the darkness my eyelids have provided until the world around me fades. Suddenly, I see the Cave again. The miniature stage, the computer, my guitars hanging from the walls, a place that exists only in the future–and right now in my head. It allows me the comfort I need, the ability to play. So I strum.

And there it is, the beautiful melodies that had become foreign to my hands over the past two days. They are back and better than ever. Ballads, love songs, classic tunes all coursing through my fingers and into the guitar in a possessed manner. I'm not in control. The music is.

Although this world of the past has granted me the ability to feel once again, it's nothing in comparison to the emotions and feelings that hit me as I play music. I quickly realize what I would be without my guitar–nothing.

In the middle of strumming, a voice interrupts me–but not Todd's.

"Liam!" *Thump, thump, thump.* "Liam, are you in there?"

My vision of the Cave vanishes, and Todd comes back into the picture, looking rather uncomfortable, so I stop playing at once.

"I'm sure you'll ge' i' down eventually," he says. "It'll jus' take some practice."

I can't tell whether he's being sarcastic or not. Truthfully, I don't care.

"*Liam.*" I hear a small, fading and distressed voice coming from beyond the door, a woman's voice. It sounds familiar…

"I should get that," I say to Todd as I set the body of the guitar on the floor and rest the neck against my desk. He doesn't seem to acknowledge my comment.

"Very cool that you've star'ed playing, mate."

I get up from the chair and walk cautiously and curiously over to the only entry and exit to this room. I look through the peephole but see no one. Sometimes they can hide below the peephole's view if they're short.

105

Undoing the lock and twisting the door handle, I open our room up to whomever awaits on the other side. I stand in the open doorway, however, with no one to greet. I peek out into the hallway, both to the left and right. Nobody is there.

"Hmm," I say to myself. I wait a few seconds, holding the door ajar with my foot. Maybe they had to use the restroom. A few seconds turns into a minute. No one shows up.

"You alrigh'?" Todd startles me from a foot or so behind. I almost jump.

"Huh? Oh, yeah … sorry. Thought I heard someone."

Todd's concern transforms into a squinty-eyed smirk. Turning around and pulling a few items of clothing from his drawer, he chuckles to himself. "Yuh really shood stay off the drugs, mate." Pulling a soft gray towel from the rack, Todd slings it over his shoulder, walks through the door that my foot continues to hold open, and crosses the hallway toward one of the bathroom stalls, presumably to take a shower.

A blank stare arrests me as I allow the door to swing slowly, slowly shut until it *clicks* back into place. If someone were watching me, they'd wonder about my infatuation with the pattern of the door as I analyze the few oily handprints that sunlight reveals when shining directly upon them.

But it is not the wooden pattern nor the sets of fingerprints that have attracted my focus. Rather, the desperate voice that had come from beyond them. I know I've heard the voice before, perhaps hundreds of times, maybe thousands. Yet I'm unable to attach the voice to anyone in my memory. It bugs me, like something that's on the tip of your tongue. You know what you're looking for, and you know that you know it, but for whatever reason it escapes you in the moment. Had it not been for the fact that the voice had been muffled, I wouldn't be frustrated with this problem.

Nothing can jog my memory quite yet, so I give up for now and abandon the stare I'd been holding. Turning on the heel of my foot, I pause.

106

From beside my desk, the guitar calls to me once more. It begs to alleviate my mind. Much like a man searching for his purpose, the guitar searches to be played, for without someone to hold it, the guitar has no purpose, and every second or hour that a man and guitar sit likewise without a purpose is another second or hour gone to the abyss of time.

I pick up the instrument and rest it on my knee just as before. Again, I make a C-shape on the strings, wait a moment, take a breath, and strum. After strumming for maybe a second or two, I stop. Something's wrong. The nerves are gone. There's nobody for me to play for, yet the sound emanating from the soundhole isn't right.

It's not a scratchy or buzzing kind of sound as it was beforehand due to improper technique. No, this time it is a more muffled sound that immediately hits my ears and sends signals to my brain, indicating a clear problem.

I try a G chord. The same result. F, B, D minor, A, all producing the same bothersome noise that would plague both a musician's and audience's ear. Heck, even Hellen Keller might have objected to this guitar.

I don't understand. Pulling my hands from the strings, I flip the guitar so that the headstock, steel string posts, and cream-colored nut–where the strings are assembled into rows–all point to the ceiling. After giving them a close examination, I determine that they're all in fine working order.

Next, I trace a finger down the length of each string. I know they're all brand new. Nothing could possibly be wrong with them. After doing a full body check, I find nothing out of the ordinary, which frustrates me almost more than if I had come across a clear issue.

Not often do I let anger take hold of me, but in the same way that joy has made its way back into my life, other feelings and emotions have broken the barrier as well, including the ones that aren't as pleasant.

My grip on the neck of the guitar tightens. I place a tense hand on the low end of the body, and I give the guitar a violent shake, hoping to expel whatever demon has possessed it. In doing so, not only does a grunt of

107

frustration escape me, but another sound manages to catch my attention. It seemingly came from within the instrument itself.

I pause, gaze upon the cherry-wood, and give it another shake, less violent this time. Again, a clinking sound escapes the guitar, coming from the soundhole this time. I don't know why I wouldn't have thought to check the soundhole. Guitarists drop their picks in there frequently. Once they're in, picks are harder to get out than a ship in a bottle.

But there's two problems with that philosophy. One, I don't use a pick, and neither did Travis, the guitar store owner. Two, the sound that results when shaking the guitar is not that of a pick. It sounds like something even lighter in weight.

I bring the guitar up closer to my eyes. I adjust the angle of it this way and that as I peer into the soundhole. Suddenly, a small white object tucked into a nook inside forces me to freeze. It appears to be square ... and folded.

Flipping the MX430 upside down above my head, I look desperately into the hole as I give the guitar a few more violent shakes. I can hear the object slowly coming loose, so I shake and shake, careful not to bump the guitar into the wall or the bed frame nearby, until *plop*.

A folded white piece of notebook paper falls flat against the strings. With the care and precision of a surgeon, I hold the neck with my left hand as my right slowly lets go of the bottom end until my index finger gently pokes through the E and A string in an attempt to push the piece of paper more vertically. It doesn't want to budge at first, but eventually the paper falls through the strings and lands on my lap.

Lightly I set the guitar against the bed frame in an almost apologetic manner. Then I pick up the note, unfold it.

The message is brief this time–too brief. I check both sides of the paper to make sure I'm not missing something. Then I hold it up to the sunlight, wondering if perhaps the riddle-loving mystery girl named Jay, who is

108

undoubtedly the author of this inscription might have inserted a hidden message within.

Nope.

I frown as confusion weaves a migraine in the crevasses of my brain. This is just the third note I've received, but each one has been progressively more difficult to comprehend.

Setting the notebook paper flat on the desk, I read over the message several times. There is no location, no date, just two words:

Listen carefully

I read the words ten, fifteen, twenty times over when a sudden vibration coming from the desk jolts me. A phone screen lights up with a name that frightens me just as much as the initial vibration had. It vibrates again and again as I debate whether I should answer the call.

"This is your chance…" a voice in my head says. *"If you don't mess it up, then maybe, just maybe—"*

"Hello, Rachel," I pick up the phone.

"Liam! Hey, how are you?" a voice filled with excitement rings through my ear. My eyes remain locked on the sheet of notebook paper.

"Confused," I say in a quiet whisper.

"Sorry, I didn't catch that," Rachel says.

"Uh, good. I'm doing well … how are you?"

"Great." I can hear a smile through the phone. "And free. Tonight at 6:30. What will you be up to?"

I peer once more at the clock, noting that it is just after noon now. "Um, not sure. Probably nothing, I don't think. How come? Does Alexandra have something in mind for the three of us?"

"Oh no," Rachel says with a deep and inviting tone. "This is going to be just you and me." My heart rate autonomously doubles. Before giving me time to respond, Rachel continues, "Meet at that outdoor ice cream place on Riverside then, just after dinner."

It takes a moment for me to place the ice cream shop in my head. "Wait a minute. That place is closed by now. It's too cold out. Besides, I'm pretty sure most buildings lost power on Riverside after the storm last night."

"I know," Rachel says confidently. "I'll see you then."

She hangs up.

I slowly lower the phone from my ear to watch Rachel's name disappear from the screen. Just then, Todd barges through the door with wet brown hair, a towel around his waist.

"Ahh, I feel much better now."

I hold the note in my hands, then say to myself, "That makes one of us."

"You should come ou' with us la'er tonight."

"We'll see," I say dismissively.

The sound of Todd shuffling through drawers and tossing clothes in a hamper disappears behind me, overshadowed by my racing heart, which hasn't stopped since the call.

"This is your chance..." the voice rings in my head once more. *"If you don't mess it up, then maybe, just maybe ... you'll experience the lifetime that you've always dreamt of."*

VIII

Misty clouds of vapor leave my nose and mouth with each breath, rising into the cold, black, star-spotted sky. A couple of wooden picnic tables sit atop the aged and pot-hole ridden blacktop to my right. Their seats are empty, their surfaces cracked and beaten after several years of surviving the elements, much like the road beyond this lot.

Between the road and the sidewalk fifteen yards before me, I'm accompanied by a couple of steel poles that protrude from the ground. They support lightless neon signs at their peak, one on each. During late Spring and throughout the Summer, a bright ice cream cone lights up and can be seen from a mile away. It remains unlit tonight, however, as does any other signage lining Riverside, turning the regularly bustling street, along with the businesses around it, into a miniature ghost town struck by an electric virus.

The structure I lean against is made of white brick, infected by the cold night air. From my closet, I had found a dense black hoodie that doesn't seem to fend off the shivers very efficiently. The cold is inescapable tonight, and an annoying on-and-off mist hangs in the air. I suppose it doesn't help that I've been standing alone here for the past ten minutes.

6:35

I'd forgotten about Rachel's severe tendency to be late, combatted by my compulsive desire to do the opposite. I begin to wonder if I misheard Rachel through the phone. She did talk somewhat quietly, after all. Did she say 7:30 and not 6:30? My memory doesn't always serve me to the best of my interests.

A lone car passes by, with a speed far exceeding the limit. It would have delighted Casey to see the speeding vehicle. I'm sure he'd be clapping loudly

111

like he does when watching NASCAR with Aunt Alexandra if he were here right now. Then a white city bus passes by, flinging tiny droplets of water up out of the wheel wells.

At about a quarter 'til seven, I close my eyes. Letting my head fall back on the structure behind me, I take a few breaths.

I start whistling one of my own original songs "Mourning Cowboy", tapping a fist methodically against the white brick, which results in a dull *thud* with every beat. It's one of my more popular tunes, judging by how the crowd used to react to it back in Nashville. Although it's a slower song, I think the lyrics tend to lure an audience in. I start to sing the chorus to the night, the empty tables, and the soon-dormant trees that line the river.

Though the sun may rise upon this town,
A broken man don't feel no joy.
As Conway Twitty, I used to 'Lay You Down',
But without you, girl, I remain…
A Mourning Cowboy.

"Whatcha singin' there, cowboy?" the voice comes from my left, and my head snaps to it.

"Oh … hey, Rachel."

I'm not only surprised at her sudden appearance, but I'm immediately stunned by her look. Her smooth red cheeks support a bright smile, and the pupils of her eyes have expanded so that they look more black than blue, enticing me to become even more lost in them. A fuzzy white hat upon her head steals my focus. Falling out of it are a few long strands of her blonde hair that lay over her shoulders. Rachel has buttoned up a remarkably red cardigan all the way to her neck, so as to protect from as much of the cold air as possible.

112

"I didn't hear much," she says, "but what I did hear sounded … amazing. I didn't know you sang." She sounds genuine in her wonderment.

"I don't." I hide a smirk and look off toward the road. "Not yet."

Rachel responds with a dejected sigh and a moment of silence. When she doesn't speak up, I do.

Looking around us at the powerless street and the empty building, I say, "So what are we doing … here?"

"Nothing," Rachel says in a matter of fact way. Responding to my frown, she continues, "Our *true* destination is just a bit farther down the road."

Heading South on Riverside, there are plenty more businesses and places of interest, though they're also out of power on this night. However, Rachel's stare seems to be off in the other direction, where the road is lined with trees on both sides, and the next useful destination on isn't for another mile or two.

"Uh, you mean that way," I point to the South. "Right?"

"Nope, follow me." Rachel gives a quick three-sixty glance and heads off speed-walking toward the tree-lined sidewalk.

"A–alright. Don't wait up." She manages to get ten or fifteen yards ahead of me before I begin to take her seriously. "I guess we're really going this way." I put my head down and follow.

Fortunately, Rachel doesn't go too far before she says, "Ah, the trail."

Stopped a few feet before me by the thicket of trees lining the river, Rachel peers into a small opening within them.

"Rach, we probably shouldn't–" but she plunges herself into the wooded area, the color of her tan-white boots soon to be doomed by the muddy trail. The tail of her red cardigan bounces with each step and then vanishes into the tree limbs and bushes.

"Of course," I sigh and reluctantly follow.

The weaving trail twists and turns around and below twigs, branches, and tree limbs until I come out on the other side. Rachel stands near the water's

113

edge atop stone and pebble, gazing up into the star-filled sky, only the rapid flow of river water making a sound.

Rocks crunch under my feet as I slowly inch my way to Rachel's side. She remains motionless, evidently stricken with the constellations. My eyes are equally as attracted to her as they are to the river. In the distance to my left is a dam, where immeasurable amounts of water race underneath the car bridge just to crash thirty, forty feet below in a flurry of white caps and foam.

During the day, the water is too brown and murky to see more than a few inches beneath the surface. But right now, in the dark of night, the river is even more so. It causes waves of anxiety to flow through my chest as I wonder at its unknown depths. A man caught in its stream would be guaranteed a watery grave, especially after umpteen amounts of rainfall the previous night.

I take a step back, farther from the river's edge.

Out of the corner of my eye, I see a wisp of Rachel's straight blond hair whipping in the wind at her shoulders. It doesn't mean much to me at first, but suddenly I feel as though it aims to reveal something. Following the strand up to Rachel's starry eyes, I pause.

My heart momentarily stops. The anxiety within me grows, no longer caused by the rolling water.

"You know, when I look up, I wonder…" Rachel begins. "Our God above has created so many beautiful things–the stars for us to look upon with awe, the water that supports life, the trees that produce the oxygen we breathe, the rocks upon which we stand." She bends over, picks up a small pebble, and tosses it from one hand to the next several times over. Finally, she flings the rock out toward the water with a flick of the wrist, watching it hurtle into the raging waves. "Everything he has created is just for us … why?"

At first, I thought she was asking a rhetorical question, but her eyes look over me with clear expectation. I stumble for a response. "Uh–he loves us … and without something to promote our survival, we don't–or can't–live."

114

"Yeah." With the toe of her boot, Rachel moves a pile of rocks this way and that. "That's what I think, too."

I nod. A light gust of wind tunnels through the river channel and swipes the last dying leaves off nearby branches, some twirling through the air until they come to rest on the water. I watch a few specks of orange, yellow, and red float miraculously atop the surface of the still violent waves. I wonder how far they'll go before they submerge.

"It's just that a professor of mine had a crazy thought this week. I can't get it out of my head." Rachel speaks in a slightly broken tone, begging me to ask.

"What did he say?"

"She," Rachel corrects me. "This professor explained to us a philosophy regarding God. You know how they can be sometimes. Anyway, I'm not sure whether she believes in the philosophy herself, but she told it to us in great detail."

"People are free to believe what they want. Free will, right?" I pick up a pebble and do as Rachel had just done. Watching the smooth orange rock plummet into the abyss alleviates a bit of my anxiety, oddly enough.

"Oh, yes, I'm not arguing with that! It may help if I just relay to you what she told the class."

"I'm all ears."

Rachel begins pacing the river edge, one foot over the other, slowly, methodically. "This philosophy ... it talks about how God gives us all these things, the ones I said earlier, as an act of love. That's not disputed. But then it goes on to ask the fundamental question of *why?*"

As I try to anticipate where Rachel is going with this, I'm left without a clue. Is this why she wanted to meet with me? So I could be her therapist for the week? Maybe she just needed someone to listen to her. Without saying anything, I hear her out.

"That's where things get ... disturbing." She pauses and looks with an empty stare into the sky. "My professor–she proposed that perhaps God gives us all this love and so many gifts as an illusion, so that he can ultimately exert his omnipotence upon *us*–his people. See, to the ones who believe this, they say religion is about *control*, operating under the assumption that free will is as obtainable as the wind that blows through our hair, as though our God has tricked us into subservience with love. I–I just..."

Rachel stops. Either there's nothing more to be said, or she's too hurt by the words to continue. I stand and ponder those thoughts for a moment. Though I do find them nearly as disturbing as Rachel does, I attempt to allow the words to interact critically with the beliefs I hold at my core. It's important that beliefs are tested by opposing opinions; without them, a belief can hold no water.

"What if they're right?"

Rachel turns and looks at me almost horror-stricken. "What?"

"Yeah." I scratch my head, just above my right ear. "You know, isn't that the whole point of faith? We don't know. We don't *know* what's true and what isn't, although we can *believe* whatever we wish."

"We should also protest evil," Rachel objects.

"I suppose. But faith is meant to be tested, to struggle with doubt. Maybe that's why you're struggling with this."

"I thought you were a Christian like Alexandra ... are you really siding with–with the devil?"

"I never said that," I reply calmly.

"So what are you saying?"

At this point I can tell Rachel is allowing her emotions to become far too involved. I understand it. Faith, religion, and any other fundamental opinions will have heart strings attached to them at the base. Whenever someone attempts to prod the opinion, it's only natural to respond with vehement

116

passion. However, my intention is only to provide her with a thought experiment.

To be honest, I'm thrown off guard by her uncharacteristic behavior. The Rachel I know was never one to get too emotionally involved with ... anything. Perhaps the few years that we had spent together, and the ways in which she had changed over the course of them, had clouded my memory.

"Don't dig too deep into this." I attempt to lower the tension with a snicker. "All I'm saying is that even though I may believe in the same right and wrong as you, there's no *real* way of knowing what is truly right and truly wrong. Our heart and conscience may tell us, and we can try our best to follow them. That's about it."

"Hmm," she stares at the ground. I must've made enough sense, as Rachel seems more comfortable by the second. She takes a few moments to ponder my words. The emptiness of her eyes eventually turns into a slight grin. She shakes her head. "Where did you go to get all this knowledge?"

I meet her eyes coldly, for just a moment. Then I offer a gentle smirk. "Hell and back."

Rachel, still by the water's edge, takes a seat upon the gravel and peers into the river. She disregards whatever damage she might do to her cardigan that looked nearly brand new at the beginning of the night. "I guess you're right."

I feel called upon by some higher presence to take a seat next to Rachel, so I do. The rocks are surprisingly soft on the surface, pressing gently against my jeans. Rachel sits with her arms wrapped around her knees, and I imitate her posture.

Perhaps Rachel wanted to meet tonight just to have someone to comfort her, in the same way that I had done at the restaurant when she had demonstrated clear misgivings about the future. It strikes me as a bit odd both that Rachel would *need* to find comfort in someone else, as she is well versed

117

in psychology, and also that Rachel has chosen *me* to be that someone. But there is no judgment to be had.

After a few minutes of agreed upon silence, Rachel inches closer to me, the rocks crunching quietly beneath her. She flips a few strands of hair behind her. Those insatiable blue eyes and her weakening smile render me frozen. "You know, you're supposed to be younger–less mature–than I am."

I force a half-second chuckle while Rachel continues to inch closer and closer, almost begging me to wrap a comforting arm around her shoulder. I don't have the courage to comply.

"Life's a mystery," I say.

"It sure is." Rachel looks almost inquisitively into my eyes. Although she sits close, she does not insinuate anything about the proximity of our bodies. Maybe Rachel just wants to stay warm by combining whatever slight radiation we give off in this open space.

For about an hour, Rachel and I make small talk. She asks me more fundamental questions about who I am, what makes me tick, similar to the ones she had asked before. My responses are minute, but that doesn't stop her from continuing her line of interrogation. She even goes so far as to ask about how certain things make me feel. Although they're random, I kind of enjoy the game. It's an interesting way of getting to know someone.

"Puppies."

"What's not to love?" I reply.

"Fast food."

"Gross ... but quick and easy, so I understand it."

"Airplanes."

"I prefer the ground."

After several minutes of this, Rachel concludes with a: "Hmm."

My intuition tells me not only that Rachel is doing what she can to get a better grasp of my character, but she's opening the door for me to do the same.

118

I think she *wants* me to inquire about her life, as though she has so many things to tell. She wants me to ask about every little detail.

But there is no point. I know this girl through and through. Partaking in that would be a charade and a waste of my time. Eventually, she'll get to know me just as she had before. For her, it will take time.

"You are one of a kind, Liam Crawford." Rachel studies me, as though she's looking for something. "Alexandra told me about you, but I'm not sure everything she told me is true."

"No one knows me better than she does," I say. "You should listen to her."

"Ha, you think so?"

I nod.

"Even if she's wrong? About the bad stuff, especially?"

"She's probably right. About the bad stuff, I mean. I can be pretty undesirable."

"Can't we all?" Rachel holds her intrigued eyes upon me. After a moment of apparent consideration, Rachel diverts, thankfully, from the romantic tension building between us, a tension that even I cannot deny, and she continues to uncover elements of my character, layer by layer. "You and Alexandra ... the two of you are very close. I could immediately tell, even in the brief moment when she introduced me to you. Connections like that...they're rare. I'm envious. You must know how lucky you are. I know your sister does."

It warms my heart to hear those words. Alexandra and I are close, but I never believed our relationship could mean as much to her as it does to me.

Suddenly, I feel ready, maybe even eager to reveal the most intimate parts of my life to Rachel. But why allow myself to become vulnerable? Why should I want to say anything at all? I don't talk much. I never talk much. Until now.

119

"Alexandra–she's my rock, the strongest person I've ever known," I say looking up into the sky. I can feel my face reddening, not just as a reaction to the outside air. "She says that from the moment I was introduced to the world, we were best friends, which I don't consider to be entirely true. To be honest, we didn't begin to grow close until a bit later in life, when we were old enough to start making our own decisions."

"How old was that?" Rachel asks with interest.

I think for a moment. "I guess I'm not sure. I don't really remember much from my childhood…some memories are tough to recall–others even harder to forget."

"That's okay. It was a while ago." Rachel offers her words in a way that tells me I don't have to keep going unless I want to–or need to.

"I suppose we really became inseparable as Alexandra began developing into a woman, discovering her desires. Meanwhile, I was at the age when I started learning that I might be a little different from everyone else. I was the quiet kid, the one who was interested in other things. Most guys liked football and girls–and don't get me wrong, I love both of them–" Rachel responds to my humor with a soft laugh. "–but my primary interests were held in various forms of art: painting, poetry, music. So I was bullied. Looking back, I'm not really sure which came first–the quiet or the bullying."

Rachel seems unsure what to say, so she just listens.

"Mom and Dad really didn't help the cause, either. They didn't want to accept that Alexandra might be more interested in girls than boys. To them, it was a sin nearly unforgivable. Maybe they're right. Only God knows. But I love Alexandra." My gaze falls to the tennis shoes I wear and their white laces tied tight. "And as for me, Dad could tell I was different, even before the kids in my class could. If anything, the bullying may have started with him. From being forced to do yard work far before I could lift a five-gallon bucket full of rocks, water, or tools, to not being able to watch the kids' channels, my Dad did what he could to cover me in the mold that I had already broken." My voice falters for the first time. "My sister and I … we didn't really have anyone else to lean on but each other. We were outcasts, even to the ones who were supposed to love us no matter what. So if there's one thing we could thank my parents for–I guess you could say it would be our bond."

I pause, the vision in both eyes becoming blurry. Perhaps I've said too much. This is where I should stop.

"Wow," Rachel says, the one-word response somehow encompassing my youth. She places a soft hand on my shoulder. "That was really brave of you to tell me that … thank you." Being complimented as "brave" doesn't seem right to me, but I'll accept it. "You know you have a ton of great qualities in you, Liam. You know that right? I mean you're sweet, you're funny, and you're genuine. That's rare to find in a man, especially now."

It's hard to resist meeting Rachel's beautiful blue eyes. I melt in the sapphire rings that surround the black holes of her pupils.

"Sometimes we see only what we want to see," I say solemnly.

"Humble guy," Rachel says, maintaining that inviting smirk. She looks me up and down, from head to toe until her eyes fall upon my face with curiosity. Her lips quiver. She leans her head just to the right. The hand she had placed on my shoulder creeps its way up to my neck, just below my ear.

I'm unprepared for what happens next. It seems rushed, too quick, too soon.

Rachel closes her eyes, she leans in close, and pulls me into a kiss. It is no gentle first kiss...or second first kiss. Her forceful lips press against mine. She seems to empty so much passion and desire into every moment, every heartbeat. Rachel even attempts to maneuver her tongue into it–successfully. I don't know how long she intends to uphold this moment between us, but quickly I realize she doesn't have a time limit in mind.

I'm unsure whether to reciprocate at first, robotically cooperating with her initially. I think I even have my eyes open for a few seconds. Then I allow myself to fall into the moment, to *feel* the same desire and passion with which

121

Rachel engages me. I lay my hand gently against the back of her neck. I pull her closer, inviting her in.

Intimacy can cloud judgment, particularly when it comes to word choice. The words of one lover may strike the other as odd, or inappropriate, but the two of them consensually dismiss such words for the purpose of the moment. One might even consider pleasing their partner with verbal cooperation.

Rachel caresses my face with each hand, aggressively. Backing away, she says, "Be my best friend."

I open my eyes to observe sincerity in hers. Unsure of what kind of response to provide her with, I lean in for another kiss.

Rachel pushes, creating a separation of a few inches between us. She says one more time. "Be my best friend."

She needs to hear me say it, as though action isn't enough. When it comes to love and life in general, talk is cheap. It means as much as dust in the wind or leaves caught in the rapids. Commitment is an act. It is not words. But strangely enough, we look for words to provide us comfort. We long for the right phrases, the ones we need and want to hear. For without them, gray areas persist.

Scrambling for the right words, I stutter until I say, "I'm here." When Rachel shows little reaction, searching my soul with her blue eyes, I double down. "I'm here."

After a nervous moment, Rachel bites her bottom lip as her mouth curls into a smile. Accepting my words, she pulls me close to display a newfound level of intimacy.

I thought my emotional barrier had previously been broken through, but this moment–this powerful moment–sends a typhoon into whatever barrier still remains, taking with it the bricks of betrayal and brokenness and sending them far downstream.

The barrier now gone, a wave of passionate aggression overtakes me, one by which Rachel will be taken aback–in a good way. I remove my lips from hers, place my fingers at the tips of her red collar, and unbutton the top. Rachel appears hesitant at first, but when I go toward her neck, she raises her chin just enough to grant me access.

I kiss her smooth neck, over and over again. She falls gently so that her back is lying upon the earthy pebble floor. I follow her, removing the hair that seeks to guard the skin of her neck. A few ragged breaths graze my ear, and that noise–that unique noise I hadn't heard but only in the recesses of my memory–comes from Rachel, and only Rachel. It is something of a gasp and a moan, a trigger that confirms her lover's success. The noise seems to unlock something even further within me.

Rachel and I engage in this sudden, unexpected wave of love that might have gone too far had we not been out in the elements. She reacts positively to my subtle movements, showing great surprise and perhaps slight concern at my knowledge of all her ticks, all the intimate ways in which I have always known her.

Eventually, she stops and pushes away from me. Rachel stands quickly, just a foot away. I stand opposite her. Her chest is slightly heaving, her eyes showing a hint of regret and awe, making me question whether I've done anything wrong.

"Keep your phone nearby," Rachel says. The edge of her lip curls upward in a devious smile. She leaves me with a wink. Then she whips around and jogs for the trail that we had originally come through.

Suddenly, Rachel's gone. I consider going after her, but something about the way she kissed me told me she'll be back. I may not even have to wait too long.

I'm stuck in place as Rachel buttons up her cardigan, dodging limbs and twigs until she disappears beyond the thicket. The sound of the river has been drowned out by my beating heart and shaky breath. I consider myself and my actions with surprise, utter disbelief, and–albeit–a touch of pride. I didn't think I had the courage nor the youth in me to do … whatever I just did.

The night suddenly has a profound stillness to it. Rejuvenation, emotion, and desire all resurrected by the touch of a woman, familiar yet foreign. Mist continues to rise from my nostrils, stronger and thicker than it had before.

Turning back toward the river, I look upon its crashing waves with a fresh perspective, not nearly as afraid of them as I had been before. I wouldn't say the water is inviting, but it isn't quite as fear-inducing. At the edge of the dam, the stream goes up and down until it passes by me and farther beyond, traces of my mind following suit. A few stars are bright enough that their reflection can be seen in the glossiness of the river's surface. I've seemingly been guided to a decision by God, or the universe, or something else. I'm going to ride this wave, let it take me wherever it may–whether it be to paradise or deep into a dark and forlorn grave.

IX

Coming out from under the final branch that guards the trail entrance, my tennis shoes meet the firm and flat sidewalk, noticeably different from the undulating rocks and muddy trail they had earlier traversed. I scrape the bottoms of my shoes against the concrete, leaving a small pile of brown-black mud speckled with multi-colored pebbles on the edge of the path. The steep grassy hillside across the road and the trees lining my side make for a slight wind tunnel that buffets my hair. Patting a hand on the top of my head, I press down the follicles that had been disheveled. Then I pull the hood over my ears and tug the drawstrings tight, so as to protect from the brisk howling winds that have picked up over the course of the night.

I march against the winds on the way back to the dorm, keeping my head down. My face and body are warm, perhaps even warm enough for me to discard the sweatshirt altogether. But I know how rapidly sweat can cool one's body when in the midst of a wintery breeze.

It is no later than nine o'clock. The night is still young. Without any further plans or noted indication of where I'm supposed to go, I conclude that a soft mattress wouldn't be the worst destination for the rest of the night. The thing is, I don't feel like resting. Adrenaline racks my nervous system, sending pulsing waves of energy through every fiber of my body. Only a few minutes removed from the moment I had with Rachel, neither body nor mind has abandoned its state of euphoria.

125

From what I can tell, I'm in. Despite the odds, I'm in. I doubted that I'd be able to get Rachel to fall for me all over again, wasn't sure if it's what I wanted ... but I'm in. It happened so much quicker than I could've possibly imagined, so much faster than I had ever remembered. A higher power must be part of the explanation.

Fate, whether I believe in it or not, has a way of intertwining souls–sometimes for better, other times for worse. A boy meets a lifelong friend on the playgrounds outside school. Another is born to a family with an abusive father who will prohibit him from knowledge of good in the world until he escapes his father's grasp. A girl has a chance encounter with a Fortune 500 employer who provides her with a successful career. Another is mortally injured by an intoxicated driver in a dim intersection lit by one forsaken streetlight. Or perhaps a boy like me finds a girl like Rachel, and we fall in love. It is not for anyone to decide with whom fate will entangle them. Fate is not fair. God does not administer fate. God is fair. Though God and fate are their own entities, we're all inevitably at the mercy of their hands.

Upon a branch hanging high over the sidewalk sits a lone hawk, his distant and accurate eyes scouring the pavement in search of an oblivious rodent brave or foolish enough to cross from one side to the next. Sometimes these scavengers are fortunate to find a free meal that has been flattened against the road by passing vehicles. Other times, they have to work and be diligent in order to eat and survive. And though the destiny of the hawk is uncertain, that of the rodent is clear–death.

As I walk beneath the branch outstretched at least ten feet above, I watch as the hawk's head instinctively twitches left and right in search of its prey, everywhere but down. He is seemingly ignorant to the man walking below, but with vision and hearing five times better than the average human, the hawk has to know I'm here. Either the creature doesn't perceive me to be a threat, or his courage is far mightier than his size.

126

When I pass, I hear the flap of wings behind me, procuring the constant memory of my boy: Casey. I can see him, arms spread wide, "flying" in circles in his room. I'm sure he sees himself way up in the clouds looking down upon those who are bound to the ground. He longs to fly high, and he will. I'll never prohibit him from doing so. That's what fathers do. It's what they're supposed to do.

Finding the bridge that crosses over Riverside Drive, I stagger just a touch as the structure lightly sways up and down. I've been told that this is due to proper engineering, that it's supposed to sway. Passing over its peak and onto the descending ramp, I notice a group of four individuals walking toward me in the distance. At first glance, their appearance is both frightening and intriguing. Then as they come closer, I realize my familiarity with the one on the left. He raises a hand just as we lock eyes.

"Mate! I wan't sure if we'd find you."

"Todd." I give a slight nod, acknowledging the three friendly-looking folks who accompany him in a similar fashion. They're dressed in clothing that I consider to be odd. Todd wears all black, with a makeshift cape of the same color tied around his neck. Black eye shadow circles his eyes, and upon a closer look, two fangs protrude at either side of his mouth. With his hair styled in a swoosh, he looks more like a "Twilight" vampire than Count Dracula.

"You've decided to come out with us!"

"Well, actually, I was just heading back–"

"Oh, how could I be so rude? Let me introduce you to my friends." Standing to Todd's right are a girl and two guys. The fellas have managed to find onesies in adult size–one of them a mutant ninja turtle and the other a red Power Ranger. Meanwhile, the girl is dressed in a plump bumble-bee costume with the spring-antenna hat on her blonde head and black eye shadow around her hazel eyes. She looks familiar. I feel like I should know who she is. "This is my girlfriend Julie and my main mates Frank and Thomas."

"It's really nice to meet you," Julie the bumble-bee says. Frank the turtle agrees, and Thomas the Power Ranger offers a salute.

"You as well," I smirk. I recognize Julie now. She's starting to form in my memory. "I should probably get back, though–"

"Wai'!" Todd startles me. He reaches into his pocket and fumbles with something for a second until he procures a small square object that he offers to me with an outstretched hand. I take it from him. "Some laydee just walked by and awsked if I would give this t'you. Not sure how she knew me, but ..."

Jay.

Todd and his friends look expectantly at me, as though they're also curious as to the contents of the small note. If they haven't already looked, I applaud their restraint.

The aura of wonder that surrounds this girl continues to grow. For someone who has fought so hard to keep her name and presence an elusive force, Jay has become somewhat lazy in her approach by involving my roommate Todd and his three friends.

Jay and I are connected in some inexplicably spiritual way, after all. She's the only one who knows about how I got here, how I traveled fourteen years to the past. She's the one who seems to be my guiding force. And she continues this game of cat and mouse by leaving notes behind, including the one I have in my hand.

Unfolding the paper, I hold it out before me and read it like a messenger might have done for a king.

"613 E Court @ 10." Not only is there a location given this time, but also a side note, which I decide not to read aloud. It says: *Don't mess it up.* In response to her clearly taunting reminder, out loud I say, "Thanks."

"You're welcome, mate," Todd says. "A strange coincidence, however. I din't recognize tha' laydee. I wonder how she could've known."

"Yeah, I didn't recognize her either," Frank chimes in.

128

"It is strange," Thomas confirms.

"Very," says Julie.

The four of them congregate amongst each other with investigative looks.

"What's so strange?" I ask.

"Mind if I have a peek?" Todd snatches the note from my hands. "Hmm, yes. 613 E Court. Tha' is what i' says." He shows it to the others. They also verify.

"And?"

"Tha's exa'tly where we're headin'. I don't know how she managed to ge' a hold of an invite, bu' I guess you're comin' with us!"

"Huh?"

"You've been invited to the party," Julie the blonde bumble-bee says excitedly.

"Party?"

"Bro, there's gonna be some *babes* there," Thomas the Power Ranger says.

"The house is a bit of a dump," Frank says with a shrug, "but it should be fun."

"So are you coming?" Julie's eyes twinkle.

"Come wit us," Todd coerces.

"Um," I say, looking myself up and down. Dressed in jeans and a black hoodie, I don't think I fit the bill for a Halloween setting.

"Oh, don't worry," Todd says as he grabs my shoulder. "Everyone'll be too drunk or high to care wha' you're wearing by the time we ge' there. Enough chatter, we're gonna be la'e." Todd pulls me along with him and his friends before I can protest. A party will be fun, I suppose. And according to Jay, this is where I'm meant to be.

Once more I cross the bridge over Riverside. The four of us follow Burlington East, past the campus rec center, a brilliant multi-million dollar building that stretches over half a block. It has windows that allow passersby

129

to see the rows of black and gold squat racks on the bottom floor and the elliptical machines on the floor above that. At nearly all hours of the day, this building is in use.

"I wonder if those windows make fat people want to go into the gym or if the jockeys inside scare them from entering." Thomas leans his head around us so that he can get a good view. "Frank, why don't you tell us?"

Frank the ninja turtle receives a nudge. He isn't overweight by any stretch of the imagination. However, standing next to the twigs that are Todd, Julie, and Thomas, Frank certainly appears to be heavyset. He pushes Thomas hard enough to knock him off his course but with enough restraint so that his friend doesn't completely topple over the nearby rail. "You want to go? I could take you with my pinky finger, shrimp. No wonder that Power Ranger costume is red. Shrimp color. Ha, yeah. Shrimp."

"Good one," Thomas says in a manner that indicates no fear.

"These two are always bickering," Julie informs me.

"Must get old," I say.

Todd watches as Frank and Thomas prod at each other with both verbal and physical jabs. "No' really. It can be quite entertaining."

After following Burlington for several blocks, we turn right onto a much less trafficked street until we find a lone house inserted among apartment buildings. Frank was right. It sure doesn't look like anything special, not from the outside at least. A streetlight shines upon the couple hundred square feet of yard space next to the house. That's something you won't get with an apartment.

Attached to the side of the house that faces the street, the side we approach from, is an old wooden porch from which various Halloween decorations hang. Scraps of tattered cloth hang from a miniature skeleton next to one support beam while glittery fiber pumpkins are stabled to the others. There is a roof overhead that would protect the fifteen or so partygoers packed on the porch if the night sky were to decide to rain. Judging by the old, white,

130

beat up boards that line the house, and the faded shingles up top, it's safe to assume this place has been here for a while. Similarly, the porch must also be old. I wonder what the weight limit on those old boards must be. The drunken people stomping to the beat of the music must be maxing it out.

Swerving in between many beer-holding devils, vampires, angels, and jersey-wearing football players, we make our way toward the house. Before finding the front door, Todd greets a few people he recognizes on the porch with a high-five and a bear hug, and Thomas veers off to partake in a shotgun challenge. Frank must have coordinated with a few other ninja turtles, whose names I'm not aware of, because he finds a crew who sport the same costume he wears. Soon I'm left with just Julie and Todd, a bit uncomfortable as we're stuck in the cramped swarm of dancing zombies.

This is when I consider turning back. A scene like this–crazy, dangerous, and uncomfortable–prompts my hands to shake and my heart rate to escalate. My weight shifts back and forth from one foot to the other. I keep my head down. Eyes closed.

"Don't worry," Julie says quietly to me. I look up to see her bumble-bee spring antennae wobbling a few inches from my face as we find ourselves in an unconventional mosh pit. "It should be a little less … hectic inside."

Eventually, Todd makes his way past all his buddies–too many of them to count–disappearing through the front door. Julie and I follow just behind.

Inside, the scene is just as Julie had predicted. More peaceful. However, even with fewer people inside, the claustrophobia doesn't cease. Tight hallways that are barely wide enough for one person open up to the left and right. One leads to a kitchen while the other has an ascending staircase leading to the top floor where I'm assuming a few empty rooms can be found.

The loudspeakers outside combine with the ones inside to produce violent vibrations that shake the foundation of the house. A noise complaint is guaranteed if one hasn't been raised to the police already. Then again, if you live in a college town, you probably expect at least one of your neighbors to

131

cause a Halloween raucous, and you plan accordingly–either by getting out of dodge for the weekend or buying some high-quality noise-cancelling ear muffs to drown out the incessant hoots and hollers of intoxicated individuals.

With almost nobody on the main level, I'm left wondering where the noise inside the house stems from. Then I notice the cracked door to our left, concealing more dancing fools and a boom box.

"The party continues downstairs!" Todd yells over the music.

While he leads us down the hallway toward the kitchen and around a corner to a descending staircase, Julie turns back to me once again and rests a comforting hand on my shoulder. "I think down here it will be more…your pace."

I appreciate her obvious intuition and her ability to identify my discomfort as though it were as obvious as a six-inch wasp fluttering in the room. Perhaps I'm not as great at hiding my emotions as I thought, including the confusion I convey as I look between Julie and Todd, wondering how a guy like him and a girl like her end up together. I've only known Julie for an hour or so already, but I'd like to think I'm adept at character assessment. Julie is a caring girl, sweet and good-hearted. That's not to say she is too good for Todd. It's not that Todd is a complete D-bag. He's not. I think he's a good guy. He's just young … and slightly dim-witted at times.

"Todd and I," Julie continues, apparently able to read my mind, "we're kind of opposites. That's no secret. But I think that's sort of why it works. He keeps me on my toes, and I keep him from getting into too much trouble." Todd turns the corner at the bottom of the stairs and an elated holler that could only come from him reverberates up the tight walls of the staircase. "Speaking of trouble …" Julie stumbles down the stairs slowly. She doesn't appear to be in too much of a rush. She must know there isn't much real trouble to be had.

Upon rounding the corner, we find a room that is less compact than the rest of the house. It opens up into a large rectangular space where there are no more than fifteen people casually talking amongst each other. To the right, a few individuals, maybe five or six, are congregated in an open circle, leaning against the white walls that appear blue in the blacklight, sharing a few jokes. Some wear jerseys, one wears a lab coat with goggles, and one girl who catches my eye is dressed in a vampire costume with black eye shadow that has been applied too heavily. Straight black hair falls no lower than her shoulders, but her skin is too sun-tanned for a vampire's. She looks somewhat appealing at first glance. Her smile does, at least. Every so often, the girl and those around her take sips from their beer cans. Sips. It is definitely more my pace down here.

To the left sits a large brown couch where a group of a three girls and two guys lean their heads back and pass a joint around. Above them are a few signs hanging on the wall. And I mean literal signs, probably stolen from city streets. A stop sign, a little white parking sign, and even one that says "DO NOT CROSS". I'm very much in favor of them. It's kind of a power move to display that you're an outlaw, and I respect it. That's what true country music used to be all about.

The music playing throughout the house at the moment is typical: rap mixed with dub-step and the occasional 2000's pop-rock hit. It doesn't carry so much down here, but it's still loud enough that voices have to be raised in order to be heard. Todd doesn't have a problem with that.

"Pass that joint over here, bro!" he yells once the substance makes its way to a zombie sitting in the corner. I can't tell if the zombie is wearing a costume or if he's just that baked. As Todd takes a large hit, he holds it in for a second with a face that conveys both pain and satisfaction, almost like the kind you get when you toss a sour candy in your mouth. Then he exhales, and a cloud of smoke conceals his face for a moment until it rises and disappears into the ceiling like Casper the ghost. He holds the joint out for Julie who stands at his side. "You want a hit, babe? No? Hmm...Liam!" Todd stumbles over to me, offering me a hit.

133

"No thanks." I reject the joint by slowly pushing his arm away. "I don't touch the stuff."

Todd lets out a hearty laugh, easily drowning out the sound of the music. "Mate, you must think I'm stupid. You can't convince me tha' you've changed your ways all of the sudden."

"What? No, you've got it all wrong. I don't touch the stuff, Todd. I swear."

He looks smugly at me, taking another hit. "Wha'ever you say, lad." Another puff out his mouth. "Can I a' least get you a beer?"

"Uh…sure. That sounds great."

"Alright," Todd slaps me on the back, squeezes past me, and stomps up the stairs. To the zombies' dismay, Todd takes the joint with him. He returns in less than thirty seconds, with a room-temperature can that he slaps into my palm. "There you are. Le' me know if you need anything else. I'm glad you're here." Todd rejoins the zombie couch.

"Thanks." Cracking the can, I take a sip.

Taking up the space that allows for entry and exit up or down the staircase, I subtly watch those on the couch interact with each other. They crack jokes, make small talk, and give off a vibe of unanimity, almost like they've known one another their whole lives. Those on the other side of the room have a similar bond. Fate chose to bring them together, something fate got right.

I stand alone at the moment. I don't mind. Often people see a guy at a party who chooses to isolate himself, and they react one of two ways. They either resort to immediate judgment or self-righteous empathy. It doesn't cross their mind that this might be how a lonesome soul decides to live his life. Comfort can be found in isolation for a guy like me.

Leaning against the wall, I whip out my cell phone. Scrolling through my contacts, I find Rachel's name. Then I tap on the message button. The icon blinks at me expectantly as it waits for me to type words of romance or

134

cleverness into the message bar. It's then that I remember how much Rachel always preferred not to talk over text. It was always over the phone. It had to be. I think that's because Rachel is like me, in that she despises everything in this world that isn't real. She abhors the superficial. And though text message communication can be handy at times, there is no escaping the truth that it isn't real. It's not the same as face-to-face, and therefore, in Rachel's mind, it shouldn't be used.

I stow the phone away in my front pocket. At that moment, I can feel a set of eyes boring into me from across the room. The vampire girl. I look up to meet black eye-shadow for just a second.

She holds my gaze for a long second before tipping her beer can back and rejoining her crowd. She smiles as the guy in the lab coat postures himself in an awkward stance, evidently doing an imitation. Just then, her face angles toward mine.

Look away. Now. I tap the tab on top of my can. I pretend to be interested in its design. For an awkward amount of time, I examine the label. *Is she still looking?*

I meet her eyes again. One more time, and she's going to think I'm a creep. I hate how that works. It's always the guy who's the creep, always the guy who is blamed for the awkward. I'm not saying that this logic is unwarranted. There are far more creepy guys than creepy girls in the world. Still, it's not fair to me in this moment. Who's to say she's not the creep?

Tempting fate, I glance again in her direction, and this time I'm not only met by a vampire's eyes, but also by a toothy vampire smile. She abandons her group and starts walking my way.

A wave of anxiety sends spiders down my spine. A pit in my stomach expands until I feel like I'm going to explode. The girl walks closer, closer... I begin preparing an explanation for myself. *I didn't mean to look ... uh, I'm sorry.* No, that's not going to work. She's close, within a foot. I open my mouth to speak, but she beats me to it.

"Hi," she says simply, offering up a one-second wave. Her tone is friendly, neither empathetic nor judgmental. "You know, the whole point of being at a party is to … party, with other people and everything. And the way you're milking that beer and avoiding crowds tells me someone either doesn't care to party, or he doesn't like people."

I scratch at the back of my neck. "Yes."

Placing her hands on her hips, she leans in closer as if to inspect me. "So…which is it?

"Oh, um … both, I guess. You could say I'm a little past my prime."

"Your prime?" vampire girl cries out in a moment of laughter, her hair in the black light appearing violet. "You can't be older than a freshman. This world is tough and oppressive, but dang. You must've started drinking at age four."

"Not quite."

"Relax, stiff. I'm giving you a hard time."

"I am relaxed," I protest.

I'm met with a skeptic glance.

Then vampire girl comes close, really close. Finding immediate comfort with strangers doesn't seem to be a problem for her. She puts one arm around my back and another on my chest. Her hands send a shock through me. I can't tell whether her touch calms the anxiety or exacerbates it. Just a few inches shorter than me, the top of her head rests just below my nose as she places an ear on my chest, just above her hand. She stands like this for about fifteen seconds, leaving me frozen and unsure what to do.

When she retracts her hands and steps away, she says, "Ah yes, a heart rate like *that* indicates clear relaxation." She doesn't shy away from the sarcasm. "It's okay," she says looking around the room. "I don't like crowds either."

I don't say anything, giving an awkward grin as my eyes bounce between her and the floor. From the moment she walked over here, the girl has demonstrated a level of comfort and confidence with which I am completely unfamiliar. My natural reaction to people like her is to retreat within myself. She's not repulsive. In fact, I'd say she's entertaining. But for me to partake in the entertainment, I have to step outside my comfort zone–something I'm rarely willing to do.

"What's your name?"

"I-I'm Liam."

"I'm Becca. But you can call me Bec, 'cuz it's close enough to *Bach*, or you can call me Reb as in rebel, whatever you want really."

"I like Becca."

Becca smiles. "And I like Liam, the name I mean. It's stoic." I peek at her eyes, past the black eye shadow. Even in a dark setting, I can tell her brown eyes are simple, honest. Then I look her up and down.

"The vampire costume is popular tonight."

"Oh, this isn't a costume." Becca's face is grave for a second until she takes out the plastic canines. "Except for these. And the makeup. I hate Halloween, really. Just an excuse for everyone to put on another face."

I take a final sip of my beer, and Becca does the same. Noticing we're both empty, she says, "Can I get you another one of those?"

"Oh...I can grab it."

"Nonsense, you stay here." Becca puts a hand on my shoulder to ensure that I stay put. She sneaks around me, her back against the wall, providing me with a warm smile before climbing the staircase. Her boots knock against the wood steadily.

As she disappears, I'm suddenly startled when a hand clasps my shoulder. Apparently, this is a touchy-feely Halloween party.

"Becca Knight? Mate, you are talking to Becca Knight." I turn to see Todd with a big smile plastered onto his plastered face. He and his bloodshot eyes are a bit too close for comfort. Removing his hand from my shoulder he says, "She's cute, no? I've heard she can be vola'ile, bu' she's a girl. Wha' can you expect?"

"She seems nice…well, yeah. Nice."

"Sure is." Todd gives a wink.

Julie walks over and overhears our conversation, warranting Todd a decent slap on the back of the head. Her slight grimace softens as she offers me a bit of advice. "Just be careful around her, Liam."

"Careful, why?"

"Din't I tell ya?" Todd interjects. "She's vola'ile."

"Hmm…"

"What he means is that she's rumored to be …" Julie spins her index finger in a circle up next to her head–the sign for *crazy*.

There's a word and an insinuation I really don't like. *Crazy*. When someone doesn't fit society's restrictive mold, people use that word if they determine someone to be in violation of the norm, ignoring that each and every individual on God's green Earth is uniquely insane. The word is naturally ostracizing of a human being, regardless of the validity of the accusation. It divides, and the word's *only* purpose is to divide. It doesn't matter to me if you use the words *different, interesting,* or even *odd*. But *crazy* … no.

My blood slightly boils. Any animosity I hold isn't directed at Julie, however. She's trying to look after me. Doing my best to subdue anger, I say placidly, "I appreciate your concern."

The staircase behind me creaks. Todd and Julie stiffen and seal their lips. Soon Becca arrives at my side, her tone sullen. "Looks like we're fresh out of booze."

That sounds like the end of the world.

"Isn't there a place right down the street that sells?" Julie asks.

"Yeah, the place on the corner," Todd agrees. "Expensive."

"That's okay–" I begin.

"I've got a better idea." Becca's face brightens as much as it can in a nearly-black basement. "Now hear me out … bars. Not the busy ones, just the ones where we can sit around, shoot some pool."

Julie scrunches her nose disfavorably. I'm in concurrence.

"Let's do i'!" Todd exclaims. "Just the fo' of us, eh? Leave everyone else behine, we have ourselves a time, ge' a few drinks. And by a few, I mean as many as i' takes before we're BLACKED OUT, BABY!" Julie hits him with a stern and grave stare. "Wha'? I'm only kiddin', babe." Todd mouths the words *I'm not kidding* on the other side of a hand wall he puts up between him and his girlfriend.

"Yes," Becca says. Her voice is deep and rich. "That is, as long as stiff here is willing to join us."

An elbow nudges my shoulder. As everyone's eyes turn on me, I shrug and shake my head no, much to Todd's chagrin.

"Mate, le' yourself live a little. At least come out and have one. I promise you can leave after tha'."

"Just one," Becca chides.

I try not to look directly at her. I can feel her persuading smile like the sun warming my skin.

"I don't think Liam really wants to–" Julie goes to bat for me, but as she does so, Becca steps gingerly in front of me, leaving me no choice but to acknowledge her stone-brown eyes. She ensures that she's got my full attention.

"I'm going either way, with or without you. I'm not saying you have to go…but it'd be more fun if you did."

Behind her, Todd is pumping his fists up and down, mouthing *Do it!* Julie naturally rolls her eyes.

I don't understand how or why fate brings people together. It has no rhyme or reason. Understanding fate would be to understand the future, and that only happens in the movies. Staring at the floor that's covered in sticky

139

droplets of alcohol, I feel as though my heart weighs too much within my chest, like it will collapse, bringing my rib cage and intestines down with it.

Becca tilts her head just to the right, perhaps pondering my thoughts. My silence doesn't discourage her. In fact, she maintains her aura of confidence, slightly lifting one eyebrow above the other.

I can't risk messing it up, my second chance. I *won't* mess it up, not this time around. This is what Jay warned me about. Then again, it's not up for me to decide who fate brings into my life.

"Just one," I say.

X

The transition from concrete roads and sidewalks to red-brick alleyways signifies a change in culture, a departure from the norms of highway commutes, daily walks, or midnight beggars as they meld into clinking glasses, outdoor seating, and the ever-iconic bars of a college town. When the sun escapes into the horizon and the crescent moon takes its place, the lights come on, the fools come out, and trouble becomes inevitable. Although brotherhood and family are themes held close to heart by those who inhabit this city, war does persist. These aren't mortally wounding wars, but rather the types of battles that plague the commoner. From boys wrestling one another within the beam of a streetlight in order to prove their manhood, to a couple who finds conflict in the night, much more than glasses can be broken here. Crowds are drawn to a place where "good times" are consistently thought to be achieved on a Saturday night when in reality, all that can be sought and found here is pain.

Julie and Todd lead the way, Julie on the left, Todd on the right. Becca and I follow closely behind them. The girls' heels click against the red bricks as we approach an area where loud jams escape the crowded bars and fill the night air. As we stroll by the public library and pass the playground just outside it, my discomfort grows, not just because of their poor placement near often drunk and belligerent folks. On a night like tonight the wars will be even more prominent.

Observing the playground, I notice the ladders leading up to holed hexagonal platforms where children have a wide selection of swirly slides to choose from. They have monkey bars to swing on, and if they fall, the padding will be there to cushion them. However, if Casey were one of those falling children, I'd be there long before the mat could ever halt his descent. As a father, you never risk anything hurting your children. I can see Casey sliding down one of the ramps, hands in the air, boyish screams escaping him. I smirk at the thought as we continue forward.

It's been a while since I've been in a crowd. Accustomed to standing and singing in front of them, it'll be an adjustment for me to revert to normalcy and join them instead. In some ways it'll be nice. I won't stand out in the bars around here, won't have fans who recognize me and ask for pictures or autographs. I'll be no different than the group with whom I've arrived.

On the way over, the four of us chatted. Well, I stayed mostly silent and listened to the others. Through some back and forth between Becca and Todd, I learned that Todd had previously crushed on Becca. The way he recalls it, Todd allegedly decided not to date her because he had met Julie and liked her more. Becca recalls it differently, insisting that she rejected Todd and that luckily for him, Julie came along right after. Either way, the two of them must've never been more than friends because they made it clear that there were no hard feelings between them. I was surprised that Julie didn't mind this talk, but at the same time, I realize there must be bigger fish to fry in her relationship with Todd.

Beyond the playground, there are a few benches that have been painted several times over. One bench is rainbow colored. Another has been painted with a shark head that stops at the gills and transforms into a banana. It's not only the unusual design of this bench that attracts my attention. Something else draws my eyes to it as well. Between two of the wooden boards that make up the bottom of the chair, a flapping object seems to be stuck as it's hit by the brisk, unrelenting winds. It summons me.

142

The others are currently comparing the two vampire costumes of Todd and Becca, not paying me any attention. So I walk over to the bench, the small waving object taking form as I move closer. Once I'm beside it, I do a three-sixty. Julie, Todd, and Becca are just ahead, and they still haven't noticed my disappearance. I'll be able to catch up with them. They aren't walking fast. Other than those three, there are only a few others around. What I find wedged between the boards of the bench are a ten-dollar bill and a driver's license. Picking both of them up separately, I stuff the ten in my back pocket and examine the ID. It looks like I've found my ticket into the bars tonight.

The name on the license is Paul Rosskeutz. His eye color and height are the same as mine. Coincidentally, the man's face also closely resembles my current form. The only difference is that Paul evidently has a hearing deficiency, which is no big deal. I can pretend to be deaf for a bouncer or two. I stuff the ID in my pocket next to the ten-dollar bill, concluding that Jay must have left both behind for me. I must be in the right place.

Now approaching the first and only bar I intend to walk into tonight, I catch up with the others, and we stand in a line of about twenty.

"Waits will be long tonight," Becca observes.

I was hoping not to stand out, but when you're the only one dressed in the moderate clothing of jeans and a hoodie while everyone else has chosen to dive right into their most elaborate costumes, you tend to receive plenty of disdainful looks throughout the course of a night. A blonde angel sneers, a jersey-wearing jockey jeers, and the rest of his group snickers.

So much for blending in with the crowd.

We wait patiently. I observe the crown molding that surrounds the outside glass windows of the bar. Doing this helps me avoid the eyes of strangers. I notice the wood has been painted black and gold, colors that give the place a classic feel, oddly attracting a not-so-classic crowd. This is where the freshmen and underage drinkers can typically expect to be served.

143

Normally I would advise against entering here, but I have to remember I'm no longer in my thirties. This body of mine is juvenile.

A cacophony of screaming conversations can be heard the closer we get to the entrance. Voices join together with the bumping tunes in what sounds like cheering stands at a football game. Even for an introvert like me, a scene like this gets the adrenaline pumping. It's the brain's natural reaction to loud noises and being surrounded by more people than one person could ever hope to know. The adrenaline fights with anxiety for control. I think they'll be at war all night.

The man checking ID's is dressed in a black coat that has the word "SECURITY" written over his chest in yellow. He appears to be bald, but it's hard to tell with the stocking cap covering his head. Sitting on a barstool, he guards the entrance. Though the man is formidable, his apathetic manner tells me he's not looking for anybody to bust. Nothing more than a glance at Paul Rosskeutz's license, and the man hands it back to me.

"You're good."

Todd and Julie are the first ones in, holding hands after having a pink band tied around their wrists. They don't look back to see if we're following but instead make straight for the dance floor on the far side of the bar, trotting along with the beat of the music. I'm sure I won't see them for the rest of the night, which is okay. Getting lost is easy in a downtown setting, and that's the point. To live young, wild, and free is to free yourself from any restraint, even if that restraint is the people around you.

As I place the ID into my back pocket once again, I allow a skinnier gentleman to wrap a pink band around my wrist. I enter the bar, just behind Becca. She reaches an arm out behind her, grabbing my hand in hers to ensure I don't get lost.

As can be expected, there isn't much room to move. The place has reached maximum capacity, and then some. Rainbow lights strobe and flash upon jumping bodies and bouncing heads of hair. Beer bottles, pint glasses, and plastic cups raised in the air shower overtop those who are too far gone either to notice or to care that their scalps will be a sticky mess in the morning. Conversation is a nearly impossible task. I can hardly hear myself think. It's a shock that the entire town can't hear the music that blasts from the dance-floor speakers, can't feel the rumbling of the subwoofers like the first signs of an earthquake. Maybe they can.

Merging with the sea of chaos, Becca pulls me toward the front where I can hopefully order a brandy to settle my nerves. Near a few barstools, she pulls out a twenty and waves it in the air.

The scene around me is frightening, not just in relation to the skull-painted faces that surround me or the devils that dance in some kind of ritual amongst one another. I'm frightened because it feels as though every face is here to judge me. Only me. Their belligerent behavior and incessant shouts, nothing more than an act they put on to conceal the truth behind their presence here. I find solace knowing that only God provides true judgment.

My head falls, and my eyes close. I take a few deep breaths, suddenly startled when a finger taps me on the shoulder.

"Ah!"

"Boy, you really are a stiff. Here, take this. It'll help."

Becca yells at the top of her lungs to be heard. She stands before me holding a white plastic cup close to her chest in one hand, extending another drink out with the other. Her short black hair, the makeup around her eyes, and her all-black clothing make her stand out. Becca's darkness absorbs the light that shines on her, so I don't have to focus on the others. She makes this place less daunting.

"Thanks." I grab the drink and take a sip from the straw. My face sours.

"What?" Becca asks, concerned. "You don't like it?"

"It's okay, just ... fruity."

"Ha! Were you expecting top-shelf bourbon?"

Observing the contents within the plastic cup, I watch a few ice cubes float in a reddish-pink carbonated liquid. It sure isn't brandy.

"Let me get you something else." Becca sounds apologetic.

"No, no. This is fine. Thank you."

"Sure?"

"I'm sure."

Becca wraps both hands around the plastic cup as though it were a hot cup of coffee, taking a sip from its edge. I try the drink again, hoping it tastes better the second time around. Becca moves with the beat, then stops when she sees me stuck in place. I don't dance.

"So what's your deal, stiff?"

"My deal?"

"Yeah, your deal."

"Uh..." my reaction is blank. *My deal.*

"You haven't looked at me for more than a second all night. You've got a cute face. Some girls might even go as far as saying you're *hot*. But you're shy. You could and *should* have the confidence of a stallion, but you're shy. So again I ask ... what's your deal?"

I struggle with the question. "I–I don't know."

"It's me isn't it? I'm a bit much, I know. Not everybody's cup of tea. Sometimes, I–"

"No, it's not you."

"Oh."

We both pause. Becca and I are two statues, stuck in the middle of a chaotic scene. I can almost feel my ears ringing from the loudspeakers.

"You know this is all fake, right?"

"What?" I look around at the very real people who surround us. Everything from the sweat on their skin to the smiles on their faces looks real to me. If they were fake, I'd give massive props to the artist.

146

"I'm not talking about *them*," Becca says, "although we do live in a simulation, but that's a conversation for another time. I'm talking about me."

I give her a confused look.

"*I'm* the one who is fake."

I reach out and tap her shoulder. It feels real, too. Becca's face shows both amusement and annoyance.

"I'm not made of plastic, you fool." She looks off to the side. "But I might as well be."

Why are girls so confusing?

"This bold, confident girl who I'm sure you think you see ... she's not real. She's not me, Liam. It's a face that I put on. I hate it. I hate that I'm fake. See these people all around us? Dressed up in costumes, putting on makeup for one night a year just because they can. I do that every day, all year long. I put on the same face, and I'm tired of it. *That's* why I hate Halloween."

"I see."

"But then you come along. From the moment I saw you walk in with Todd tonight, I *knew* you were different. I don't know if it's your presence or your aura. You're *real*, Liam. Granted, it might help if you were to try to put a little more skip in your step every once in a while. But the shy, coy son of a gun who lives within you is the same one who lives on the outside, and you know what I felt when I saw that? When I saw *you*?"

"Um, I don't know."

"Envy."

"Hm?" My lips wrap around the straw in my cup. I can hear Becca's voice straining under the task of competing with the music.

"I *wish* I could be like you, Liam. When you see me, you probably think you see someone who is courageous, unafraid. Right?"

"Well," I shrug. "Yeah. I guess."

"That's not true. It couldn't be farther from the truth. True courage is being who you are. *You* are courageous, Liam. *That* is your deal."

147

Suddenly, the music changes as the DJ plays a remix of "Monster Mash". A few dancers hang their hands straight out like zombies, unsettling me, so I look back toward Becca. "I appreciate that, but you don't even know me, to be fair."

"Oh, but I do. All too well, because I *am* you. You and I, we're the same. Looking at you for the first time was like looking into a mirror. On the inside, I'm just as shy as you are, just as lost in this world. The only difference between us is that I don't have the courage to *be* that in front of everyone else. Concern for the way I'm viewed traps me into a corner, and it forces me to escape. I have to pretend all the time. It's exhausting."

Her eyes wander. Some people get down on themselves just for the attention, but this isn't that.

"So don't."

She lifts an eyebrow. "Don't?"

"Yeah," I say simply. "Don't pretend."

She grunts in amusement. "You make it sound so simple. See, that's the thing. I've been pretending for so long … I don't know any other way. It wouldn't be simple for me to just … stop."

Becca averts her gaze, her head falling to the ground while I stand beside her in shock. I don't know why she's chosen to be vulnerable, least of all with me. We've only just met. My eyes dart to those around us who likely won't have heard us over the music, but I check just to be sure. Everyone continues to dance the night away, and again it frightens me.

"You're scared," I say.

Her chin rises, and her eyes follow suit. Then her voice falters. "Terrified."

"Of judgment."

She nods.

"I don't judge."

A laugh escapes Becca. "I know you don't."

148

Taking a final sip from the straw, a sucking noise erupts from my cup. I'm out. Becca shakes her cup, and all that can be heard is ice. She flips her hair to the side.

"Can I convince you to another?"

"I only agreed to the first one."

"Plans change."

Her brown eyes meet mine, and we stand in a visual embrace. No matter how much she may insist that the poise she exudes is a façade, it is still part of her character. She persuades with that creeping smile. She turns her head in just a way so that her eyes can peek up at mine. I should go, but she hasn't caused any harm yet.

"Alright, but after this I'm *done*."

"Deal."

"I'll buy this round," I say.

"Nope." Becca plucks the plastic cup from my hands, turns around, and captures a bartender's attention.

We down two more drinks. Then two more. A doctor buys a round of shots. Loose, I start to feel loose. Time starts passing too fast. Every time I check my phone, another ten minutes has gone. In the war between anxiety and adrenaline, peace seemingly becomes the victor. Neither side fighting for control, instead vanishing into the background like helpless bystanders. I'm free. The world around me vanishes with every drink. Soon, all that's before me, all that's around me is Becca.

She and I take the dance floor. While she demonstrates some crazy moves, bending this way and that, my foot taps the floor with the beat. It's about all I can manage. I don't dance, don't really know how, but I chuckle when Becca does, throw my hands in the air when she points at me, and drink too much every time our plastic cups clink together. I envision the two of us in the Cave, Becca dancing amongst everything that has been banished to that

149

small square space. Perhaps I'd sit back in the office chair and observe the fearless way she moves. The thought comforts me.

The world is spinning. A queasiness in my stomach begins, but I ignore it. I'm enjoying myself. I can *feel* the music working through me. It hasn't taken me away yet. I don't think it will. Perhaps *I* am the one in control of my *taken* world now. The tables may have turned. Maybe I'm finally on the right track, finally doing something right.

Then a shriek as loud as a battle cry sobers the moment. "COPS!"

The Cave I envision vanishes, and the chaotic swarm of gremlins, goblins, demons and all others bolt toward the exit while I'm frozen in the middle of the dance floor. Becca's eyes widen.

"We have to go."

She grabs my wrist and leads me toward the exit. Nearly everyone in the building clogs the door, fighting for their escape. Soon we make it to the entrance, but it might have been better to turn back. A hand takes my other wrist. Becca tugs one direction, but the other hand is stronger. I've been caught.

"ID."

At this point, all my brain can process is a spinning black uniform that stands like a sentry in my swirling vision, a golden badge staring me down. This is no costume-wearing drunkard. This man is real. My head lolls to the left to see that Becca has also been stopped. The two of us are a saving grace to the ones who are still fleeing. Some luck we have.

But a moment arises where both men in uniform release the tension of their grips at the same time. Becca notices it just as I do. She nods to me. I nod back. This is our chance.

We both rip our hands from the policemen. Becca darts in one direction at an amazing speed. I follow, almost losing her within the crowd. Behind me, I hear, "Hey! Get back here!", prompting me to run even faster.

150

Becca slows to take my hand. She pulls me along, and we run. We don't have to run too far before we reach another entrance. I recognize this one, but the recognition doesn't provide any solace. This is a "senior bar". There's no way for a couple of minors like us to sneak our way into this one. Becca and I are stuck here for a moment, considering our options. To our right, the cops are juking their way around those who block their path, only twenty yards away. Becca and I are both drunk and tired. There's panic in her eyes.

Suddenly, a window of opportunity opens for us when a bouncer storms out of the entrance, pushing a white-haired, Billy Joel-looking dude out into the middle of the brick-paved alley. "You're done, get out of here." He's left the entrance open.

Becca quickly pulls my arm, and we sprint through the doorway, a few people hollering at our backs telling us to stop. We don't.

The place, though crowded, opens up significantly more than the previous bar. With a countertop that follows the entire side wall, however, the space narrows and is difficult to maneuver from front to back on nights like this. Most everyone is at a standstill.

"Weew not gonna make it through." My speech is slurred, and this bar is nearly as loud as the previous, but Becca manages to comprehend as we shimmy through any gap we can find.

"Yeah, neither will they." She's referring to the cops, or maybe the bouncers. Possibly both.

Because Becca has a smaller frame, she is able to scoot past tightly compacted groups with ease. Yet she doesn't allow me to fall behind, waiting whenever she has to, increasing her chances of being caught.

"Keep going!" I yell. "I'll catch up with you."

"Shut up. Just keep moving!"

Behind us, the cops have formed an alliance with the bouncers near the entrance and have set out a search team for us. They seem to be covering ground quickly. There's only so much more room to run, only so much space to hide.

I duck to avoid being seen. Eventually, we reach a small opening of floor space near an old arcade machine where Becca and I stand close. She searches for a spot to hide, an exit sign maybe.

"There!" she says. "Follow me."

"What do you think I've been doing?"

She takes us from one side wall to the other, where we find a group of about six or seven characters dressed in either Star Wars or Star Trek outfits. I'm not really sure. I never watched either series. One wears a dark helmet that conceals his face with a red sword-thingy hanging by his belt. Another, a girl who must be freezing, wears a brown metallic-looking bikini, and two others have joined in a worm costume that takes up plenty of space. The perfect cover.

Becca and I huddle up behind the worm, and the group looks peculiarly at us.

"Cops?" one of them asks.

"Yes, do you mind if we stay here 'til they're gone?" Becca pleads for the both of us.

"Not at all," says the guy in the dark helmet. He breathes heavily after saying this, and my eyes widen with discomfort.

"Thanks," Becca smiles at them in the same delightful way she must smile at everyone.

We stay huddled between the wall and the two-person worm costume for a few minutes. My heart races, probably processing the alcohol in my system twice as fast as it regularly would. I don't want to get caught, for obvious reasons, but the chase is fun. I haven't felt excitement like this for a while.

When the guy at the mouth of the worm costume tells us that the "coast is clear", I feel relieved but also slight disappointment. The chase is over, just like that.

152

Becca and I slowly rise in unison. Sure enough, there doesn't appear to be anyone in pursuit of us. They must have given up, deciding it wasn't worth the fight. Becca turns to me with a frightened expression. Then her cheeks rise, dimples forming. Her eyes squint, and she bursts into laughter. I'm at first confused by this reaction, but quickly come to understand it and join her. This is what it's like to live young and free again, to live on the edge of exhilaration and destruction. It feels amazing. Every hour in this world brings something out of me that I hadn't even known was there. The laughter I share with Becca opens my eyes to this.

In just a few hours, I think I've met a companion, a true friend. Someone who seems to understand me, someone who *gets* me, who knows my struggles and weaknesses. I'm not one who is quick to trust, and nobody could ever earn my trust, not all of it at least. Yet here is someone who might be different. She doesn't take her eyes off me. She lets me know I exist.

We laugh to the same beat, and I wonder … aside from a few random folks like Frank and Thomas who I met earlier in the night, nearly everyone I've seen in the past few days I've recognized. I've been able to summon their image from the cobwebbed caves of my distant memory. And then there's Becca. I'm certain that tonight is the *first* time we've ever met. Not a second first time, a *real* first time. I'm certain because I couldn't have forgotten someone like her, no matter how poor my memory may be. I wonder why fate had chosen that we should meet in one life but not the other. It's possible that she could be just like the red-haired girl, someone who's been planted in this second-chance life to act as a guide.

The scenery of this bar and the upbeat mixes that the DJ has strung together contribute to a setting of harmonious beauty. An elevated wooden dance floor surrounded by rails offers an outlet to expel the stresses of the week. Barstools and high-top tables extend welcoming hands to the ones who'd rather sip on a beer and watch a ball game. Dart boards on one side of the dance floor, pool tables on the other, vintage signs hanging on the wall: everything from an old PBR can to the unique Clydesdales of Budweiser.

Becca catches me admiring the signs. Something about the tokens from days gone by makes me feel at home.

"You know their secret ingredient is rice? Most beers use corn, but Budweiser uses rice."

"I didn't know."

"And the Clydesdales? Those were a gift to commemorate the repeal of prohibition back in 1933."

"How do you know this?"

"I *love* beer."

"You love beer?"

"And useless tidbits of information that I find interesting."

"Interesting."

"Right?"

Becca looks across the room toward the bar, particularly at a boy in a backwards ball cap who stands out among the Halloweekenders even more than I do.

"You want to see me get us a couple free drinks?"

"How do you suppose you're going to do that?" I rub my chin.

"That guy. He's been looking at me all night."

"You've got an admirer," I say. "Nothing wrong with that."

"Admirer. Womanizer. Victim-maker. Potato, po-tah-toe. There's nothing good going on behind those eyes."

"You don't know that."

"I do. I've had enough experience with guys in this city to know adorning eyes from lust-filled ones."

"Okay. What are you proposing?"

"Watch this."

154

Becca strides away, making a bee-line toward the guy. He peeks at her as she approaches. She flips her hair to the side, probably offers the batting eyes, and tugs at his jacket as she stands close to him. He smiles. She smiles. Both devilish looks with similar intentions. They talk for no more than a minute before the backwards-hat admirer raises a hand to call over a bartender who places two pints on the counter after taking the guy's card. Without delay, Becca swipes the beers, tucks her chin to her shoulder, says "thanks" with a smile, and walks back across the room.

When she gets back, the guy looks on the two of us with frustration. He can't believe he's been duped. But then his eyes move on from Becca as he searches for the next target. She hands me one pint, taking a hefty gulp of her own.

"Too easy," she says.

"How'd you do it?"

"What do you mean? You watched me, didn't you?"

"Yeah, but–"

"I made him vulnerable, he thought he had a chance, so he bought a couple beers. He just didn't realize they weren't for him."

"You don't feel bad?"

"Should I?"

"I don't know … maybe."

"You're too innocent." Becca smiles.

Quickly we down our drinks, and the buzz subsequently follows. Twice more, Becca manipulates new "admirers" for our benefit, and it's not long before the world twirls around me once again. Becca brings back a couple of darker glasses this time.

"One for you," she says as she hands me a glass. "One for me."

I reach into my back pocket and pull out the ten I'd found earlier. "Take this."

"What? No." Becca's frowns.

155

"These drinks weren't free."

"*I* didn't pay for them."

"But in some ways, you did."

"Look, pal. I'm just giving a bit more balance to the scales of justice. Keep your money."

"Whatever you say!" I indulge in the darker beer, noting its rich taste. "What is this?" I say, pleased with the lager.

"Local brewery made it," Becca says casually. "Good stuff, eh? I think the guy who bought it was trying to impress."

"You sure he wasn't a good one? Usually bad ones don't go the extra mile like this."

"Oh, yeah. Had *strong* 'rich parents pay my bills; I'm better than you' vibes."

"Ah." I take another sip. "What's this called?"

"Something like the Daring Dark Chocolate brew ... I don't really know."

"Daring Dark Chocolate. I like it."

Becca's tone drops. "I like Liam."

"It's a basic name. Biblical." I find myself giggling at the way my mouth barely forms the word "biblical" as intoxication takes over, so I say it again just to hear it. But Becca's face is solemn.

"I'm not talking about the name." She lifts her chin to expose her eyes, which struck me as honest before, but now I see that there's something more within them. Fragility. I'm not sure whether it stems from pain, her past, or whatever. But there's no denying it. I've seen it in the mirror's reflection countless times before.

I can only meet her eyes for a mere second before diverting. That's when something else catches my eye at the far end of the bar. I squint and do a double take, then frown. In the midst of a group of plaid-jacket lumberjacks is a head of blonde hair dressed in black. That's all I can see, all I can make out

156

at the moment, since the girl faces the opposite direction. Still, she looks familiar.

Rachel?

"I didn't mean to make you uncomfortable ... sorry." Becca grits her teeth apologetically.

"No, no. You didn't." It's not my intention to ignore Becca, but I find myself glued to the girl in the distance. Every so often, her head turns. I think it's her–Rachel. I don't know why she'd be here. I thought she had somewhere else to be, judging by the way she stormed off when she left me earlier in the night. My curiosity is replaced with something else. I'm filled with a boyish excitement, one that urges me to go tap her on the shoulder and yell "Hi, it's me!"

Placing a hand on Becca's shoulder, I say, "Sorry, will you stay here for a minute? I'll be right back."

"Uh, sure. I–"

I weave my way between the masses of partying drunkards, careful not to spill my drink. Though my vision is still blurred and spinning, I force myself to focus. With every step, I come closer to the girl, now in the middle of it all. But it's still too hard to tell whether it's Rachel. I need to get closer.

She stands like Rachel does, with one leg planted straight while the other crosses over. I think that's her hair color, too. It's tougher to recognize in a ponytail. It wasn't tied up like that earlier. Closer, closer.

"There he is!" I feel a hand firmly grasp my bicep. "Hey, bub. It's time for you to leave."

A guy in a red shirt who looks way too sober to be in a bar stands tall at my side. He snatches the beer from my hand and sets it on a nearby table. Then I realize just who has a hold of me.

"Wait, no I–"

He jerks me in the opposite direction, and the crowds part to form an alley toward the exit. He takes me further and further away from Rachel.

157

"My girlfriend is back there!" I plead.

"Your girlfriend? She just doesn't know it yet, right? Yeah, yeah. Heard that before."

"No, I'm serious. Rachel!" I yell, hoping she'll come to my rescue. "Rach!"

She doesn't hear me.

"Hey! Let him go!" Becca's voice rises above the noise. I look back to see she's not far behind, climbing her way through a human wall.

"There's the other one!" Another red shirt emerges from the crowd and rushes toward Becca. She doesn't even try to escape his grasp.

I wrestle with the one who's got my arm until another red shirt grabs my other. In a belittling way, they lift me off the ground to stop me from resisting. Three guys take Becca and I out the front door. I squirm in their hands and accidentally elbow one of them hard in the face. I feel bad until the two of them toss me to the ground like I'm nothing more than a garbage bag. What bothers me most is that they do the same with Becca. She hits the paved bricks hard. A cry escapes her.

I rise quickly to my feet.

"What the hell's wrong with you? She's a girl!"

"She's a *minor*," the one with curly brown hair says to justify his cruelty. He turns to the others to chortle.

That's it.

I throw a haymaker at curly-hair, my fist meeting him square in the face, knocking him to the ground.

"Liam, don't!" Becca desperately cries.

The next one comes charging at me. He's bigger, much bigger. With liquid encouragement and drunken pride, I stand my ground. When he approaches, I hit him in the gut. It doesn't seem to faze him at all. This is when regret starts to kick in–when it's too late.

158

Grabbing me by the chest, the man lifts me off the ground. Becca screams. While in the man's hands, I meet her eyes for a split second. There's horror in them as she stands and covers her mouth. Then I'm thrown like a rag doll toward a landscaped area surrounded by elevated bricks.

My knee scrapes the ground first. A shriek splits the night. My head snaps downward, hitting something sharp. Then the world goes dark.

XI

The desperate cries of both woman and child are contained in the walls, fighting to be heard. The same walls continue to close, close in as the clock tick, tick, tick's. The shimmering light flickers upon the path laid before me. A doorway. The cries suddenly subside, or are perhaps drowned out by the quiet noises. The hum and the beat.

Thump thump.

One step forward.

Thump thump.

The light shuts off. Total darkness surrounds. I feel the presence of someone else. No, not someone. Something. It's sinister. I know its intentions. It aims to rip away the flesh of my chest with its long claw-like appendages, reach in past the cage that guards my heart, and tear my life to shreds. It's too horrific to look at, though it can't be seen. Too unavoidable to look away. Step back to avoid it. Hide. STEP BACK!

Thump thump.

"Liam, are you in there?"

The light reemerges, constant now. It shines upon the path, upon the rim of the entrance, and upon everything inside. A glass door, a mirror, a sink or fountain for washing sin, a trash can.

Thump thump.

Though the light is on, I don't see it. But I know it's here.

The door. I step through. The hard floor crushes the bottoms of my feet. I rub a hand on white granite. The ceiling falls slowly. Walls still closing in.

"Liam, are you in there?"

160

The cries shatter back into existence, ringing through the surface of the mirror. Half of a worn bearded face reflects off its edge.

"STEP BACK!" the half-face screams, one bloodshot eye wide with terror.

I turn, but the door has shut behind me. There is no escape.

"Liam, please. Say something!"

Thump thump.

My eyes flutter open to a scene of white. It's blinding at first. Everything is blurry. Distant white ceiling squares, soft white sheets, white marble flooring, white crown molding around the window that lets in bright white light. This must be what Heaven looks like.

A blurry figure stands at the bed to my right in blue, peaking his head just over the edge.

Casey.

Blinking a few times and wiping the crust from my eyes allows me to inspect my surroundings in higher definition. What I had thought to be my son is really a small empty desk, standing tall beside me. I sigh longingly.

A black television hangs from the ceiling at the far end of the room. It's turned off. A couple light blue visitor chairs lay empty near the window, a lowered wooden table topped with fresh magazines tucked between them.

A quick and almost comforting beeping noise rings once in my ear. It stops. Then it rings again. I notice the white-gray pulse reader attached to my left index finger. The beeping noise goes off again.

I shut my eyes and take a deep breath. Resting the back of my head against a stack of white bed pillows, I feel a pain both throbbing in my brain and sharp against my skull. Breathe. Smoothing my hair, I inch a couple fingers toward the back of my head just above my right ear until...

"Ow!"

161

Instinctively, my arm jolts after my fingers react instinctively to the cold flat metal heads jutting from my scalp, and my cranium rings with a stinging sensation. I grimace, shaking my feet at the end of the bed in hopes that the sting might weaken by dispersing itself throughout my body. After a minute, the pain subsides, lessening with each second. I reach for the spot on my head once more, this time much more carefully. I barely brush a finger over it, resulting in more anguish. But it's bearable.

Suddenly the door near the far left corner of the bed begins to creak open. A tall figure in pink polka-dot scrubs presses her back against the door as she smiles at someone out of sight. Her smile is warm. Perfect teeth. Straight black hair tied in a bun. Once she's swung the door completely open, she ushers someone else into the room.

I hear the slight jingle of either a purse or a set of keys coming from the hallway. When someone turns the corner in white jeans and a navy top, I smirk.

"Ugh, thank *God* you're okay!" Alexandra opens her arms as she walks swiftly toward me, hugging me so tightly that a few cracking noises escape my back. Backing away, she holds both my shoulders. "I've been waiting all night. They told me you'd be okay, and that's when I knew they were lying. I told them, 'My little brother is *never* okay.'"

"Yet here I am, feeling like a million bucks."

"You don't look like a million bucks. You look like ten."

"Thanks."

"Always." Alexandra scans my eyes, as if she needs to know that the person on the inside isn't as hurt as the one she sees on the outside. She grabs my forearm. "Let's get you out of here, get you into clean clothes and a shower."

"Ahem," the nurse peeps. "Actually ... he should really stay here. Your brother suffered some severe head trauma resulting in a mild concussion. He's lucky it wasn't any worse than that, but he won't receive better care anywhere else …" She pauses to look at Alexandra. "No offense."

"None taken."

"No," I say, calling Alexandra's attention. "Alex, I'd rather leave."

"Are you feeling up to it?"

"I am."

"If he thinks he's good to go," the nurse says coyly, "I guess I can't stop him. But he *should* stay."

Alexandra looks back at me for confirmation.

"I'm okay to go." I nod.

"You heard him," she shrugs. "As stubborn as a Crawford ever was."

The nurse scratches at the back of her bun. "If you insist."

"Alright." Alexandra shifts toward me again. As the nurse exits, she asks for the door to be shut behind us. Alexandra pats my leg twice. "Spill the beans. They said you got into a fight, but I know you too well. You don't fight. So what happened?"

"I got into a fight."

Alexandra gasps.

"With a bouncer. Knocked one of them out, the other evidently knocked me out." I point to my injury.

"Who are you, and what have you done with Liam?"

"The guy threw my friend to the ground. She looked hurt."

"Wait … *she*? Oh, now you've really got to spill. Is she cute?" Alexandra puts an elbow on the edge of the bed, resting her chin in her palm.

"Alex–"

"What's her name?"

"I-it's Becca, but it's not like that–"

"You haven't said whether she's cute or not."

I sigh.

"Sorry … go ahead."

163

"I met Becca last night at–" I grimace as my pounding headache makes it hard to recall. "I think it was at a house. Yeah, it was. With Todd and his girlfriend. The four of us got split up when we went downtown. After that, I don't remember much. I think I was really drunk."

"They said you threw up several times in the ambulance on the way over."

"Couldn't tell ya."

Alexandra takes a sip from a bottle of water she procures from her purse. When she sees me eyeing it like a hawk, she screws the cap back on and tips it toward me. "Mm?"

"Please," I say, finishing the bottle in a couple gulps.

"So ... this Becca girl. You say she's just a friend?"

"Yes."

Alexandra's mouth curls into a grin. She's prying.

"She's cute, all right. Are you happy?"

Alexandra covers her mouth but not before a yelp of excitement escapes her.

"But *just* a friend."

She slumps.

Then I frown in both confusion and slight disappointment.

Rachel.

Alexandra inquires about Becca as though she doesn't know about Rachel and I, which I suppose is possible. Maybe the two of them haven't seen each other in a while. College does that sometimes. It can leave you with little time for anyone besides yourself. But with modern technology, it takes a matter of seconds for a girl to send a text saying, "Hey, I'm dating your brother." Plus, girls tell each other *everything.*

"What's wrong?" Alexandra asks.

I meet her eyes. I open my mouth to speak but freeze.

164

What will her reaction be when I say that I'm dating her best friend? Maybe I should keep it a secret until Rachel lets the cat out of the bag. Come to think of it, I can't remember what Alexandra thought when I told her the first time around. Was she happy for me? Upset? Angry?

Alexandra looks expectantly upon me. She's my best friend, and nobody could ever change that. The two of us have been to hell and back with each other, never leaving one another's side. Fights, grief, and name-calling have entered our relationship on several counts ... but never secrets or lies. Secrets and lies are one and the same, originating from the intention of deception. Yet something compels me to keep this one secret–cowardice maybe. One lie couldn't hurt anything, right? No ... I can't. I have to tell her.

"Alex, um ... this is tough to say. Wow."

"What is it?" Her eyelids droop like she's had too much to deal with in the past twenty-four hours. I guess when it rains, it pours.

I hesitate again, my mind going back and forth. But I'm too deep now. I have to go for it. "Rachel and I are together ... we're a thing, I guess."

Alexandra's face becomes sullen. Her eyes drop to the floor as she takes a small step away from the edge of the bed. She rolls a lock of hair behind one ear. "Oh."

"I'm sorry. I know this puts you in a tough place."

She examines the floor with a concentrated frown, clearly trying to process the news.

I sit more upright. "Look, it kind of just ... happened. I wasn't expecting it, either. Didn't know if I should be the one to tell you, but I thought you should know."

"Rachel told me," Alexandra blurts. Then she says quietly, almost as if to herself, "I just ... wasn't sure if it was true."

"Oh," I say. I shift my gaze toward the window where a beaming light still streams through the panes, shining upon my sister. "I hope you're not upset."

165

She doesn't respond at first, perhaps unsure what to say. Alexandra scratches her temple. "No. I'm not upset."

"Alex, it's okay if you are. And if it bothers you enough, I–I'll drop the whole thing. I'll stop seeing her. I–"

"I'm happy for you, Liam." Alexandra puts on a clearly fabricated smile. "I'm happy."

Her reaction makes my heart drop to my stomach. It puts an immeasurable weight on my tear ducts. The last thing I'd ever want is to hurt her. I start to twiddle my thumbs and look back toward the window as my vision becomes blurred. Alexandra clears her throat.

"We should go home."

"Alright," I force a grin. "Let's go home."

After changing back into the clothes I had been wearing the previous night–still smelling like alcohol–we check out of the hospital and hop in Alexandra's car. She takes me no more than half a mile back to my dorm, without a word shared. Pressing the little red button that turns her hazards on, she stops outside the glass doors marking the front entrance.

With my fingers lightly on the door handle, I pause.

"Can I ask you something?"

"Sure." Alexandra faces forward, her hands still gripping the wheel.

"Last night, Rachel and I were together for a little while. Then she left like she had somewhere to go. I'm pretty sure I saw her at one of the bars later on. It's not a big deal. Just confused why she wouldn't tell me."

Alexandra looks interested for a moment. "Was she with anyone?"

"I mean, there were a group of guys in plaid shirts. I think they were supposed to be dressed as lumberjacks or something, I–I don't really know. It looked like her with them, but–"

"It wasn't," she says.

"Oh ... how come?"

166

"Hm?"

I cock my head to the side. "How come? What makes you think the girl I saw wasn't Rachel?"

"Oh, yeah. I forgot she was studying last night. She texted me."

"But ... you asked if she was with anyone."

Alexandra finally turns to me with a smile. "Mental lapse. I just forgot."

"Hm." I nod and look out the front windshield, a path of desolate gray cement leading to the road beyond.

"I should get going," Alexandra says, tapping her thumbs on the wheel.

"Yeah. Yes. You're probably busy."

She presses her lips together into a grin.

"Love you," I say.

"Yes, have a good day!"

Hopping out of the car, I wave to Alexandra and slowly shut the door. She speeds off down the road a second later. Her car turns the corner, leaving me alone in the cold. I have to squint due to the bright sun reflecting off the ground. The wind aims to make my eyes water, too.

Have a good day? She didn't even say "I love you" back.

I didn't realize she'd take the news so hard. Oh well. Give her some time, and she'll come to acceptance just like she did the first time.

Through the glass doors, up the elevator, and down the hall. That's where I find my room empty. I assume Todd must be with Julie because he surely isn't in class. I take off my dirty clothes, throw them in the hamper, and shuffle through my drawers until I find a pair of sweats and a t-shirt. Wrapping a towel around my waste, I cross the hall, entering an open bathroom stall.

The door clicks behind me as I lock it, the little white tile squares feeling like a massage against my feet when I walk over to the towel rack. Dropping my clothes on the floor and hanging my towel next to the shower, I look at the mirror's reflection.

"Whoah."

167

It's the first time I've been able to get a good look at myself since last night. My eyes are bloodshot, skin pale around them. My brown hair is disheveled and greasy. Then there's an ovular patch of mussed hair where a small row of staples are surprisingly well-hidden–well, as hidden as you could expect. Both hands part the hair around the staples for me to get a better look in the mirror. I have to angle my head to the side and peek out the corner of my eye, but there it is: a spot that will undoubtedly be a scar. I spend a solid minute examining the spot before facing the mirror straight on.

A water stain on the glass starts at my head until it streaks down the center of my body. One arm falls to my side, the other lays across my smooth, muscular chest, rubbing. Even after a couple days of settling into this younger body, it's a pleasant surprise to be greeted by something other than a pudgy frame and messy beard every time I look in the mirror. A little five-o'clock stubble has broken through my skin, but that's an easy fix with a few glides of a razor.

Letting out a huff, I spin around.

"Hi, there."

"HOLY SH–!" I stumble back, reaching for the towel rack but miss. Falling back against the wall, I cover my lower extremities with one hand, while bonking the uninjured side of my head on the rack bolted next to the mirror. "Ow! Son of a ..."

A leather jacket stands near the shower, where the curtain has been opened slightly. Above the jacket is a head of vibrant red hair sitting upon a scrunched-nose face. She covers her eyes with one hand while the other holds a towel extended toward me. "Would you mind covering yourself? I don't want to see that."

"Well then don't barge into an *occupied* bathroom! Privacy! Ever heard of it?" I rip the towel from her grasp and scramble to tie it around my waist. "What are you doing here? How'd you get in?" I tie the towel securely, then hold it with one hand to ensure it doesn't fall.

168

"I have something to tell you." Jay paces back and forth in the small cubic room, attempting to look elegant in doing so. However, her manner just makes me more uncomfortable. The metronomic heel-clicking against the tiles doesn't help, either.

"You couldn't have chosen a better time?"

"No better time than the present, Liam. Now hush."

I roll my eyes, placing a hand on my neck. The expression on my face says, *Go on.*

"How are you coming along?"

I cock my head in confusion.

She stops. "I asked you a question."

"You just told me to hush."

"I did, didn't I? Never mind that."

I close my eyes and grumble. "Um, I'm doing well, I guess. I don't know, you tell me. Have I been following your notes closely enough?"

"I'd say so."

"So...?"

"Well done." She stops mid-pace to give me a couple claps. Then she keeps walking. Back and forth. Back and forth. "You've quickly made some close friends. Todd, Julie, Becca ... Rachel." Jay talks in more of an interrogative way, making it hard to understand what she's getting at–good to see nothing's changed. "I've come to let you know that this is the last time you'll see me ... for a while at least."

"So I don't have to worry about my privacy being invaded anymore? Great!"

"You sound ungrateful. Have I not led you through this journey thus far?"

Biting my tongue, I stand in silence. She's right. I do have her to thank for setting all the pieces up in the right places.

169

"That's what I thought." She continues pacing again while I wait eagerly for her to explain herself and leave. "You have an important decision to make, Liam. One that has the potential to change the course of your life."

I continue to stand in silence, waiting for her to clarify. After ten seconds, her pacing prompts me to speak. "That's it?"

"What do you mean, 'that's it'?"

"I mean ... that's it? That's all you've come to tell me? You thought it was necessary to barge into my bathroom stall to tell me I've got a decision to make." I place my hands on my hips. "Enlighten me. What's this so-called 'important decision'?"

"Firstly, drop the attitude, mister. And if I told you why the decision was important, wouldn't that take the fun out of it?"

"Isn't this clue, note, advice–whatever you're giving me–pointless if I have no idea what it means?"

Jay wanders over to the shower. She turns the dial until the water comes out with steam rising off the white-washed plastic walls. Majestically twirling her hand through the multiple streams, she says, "You know what it means. In your heart, you know. If not now, you will soon."

Two beads of water trace down her palm, flowing beneath the hard black sleeve of her jacket. Taking her hand out of the path of the showerhead, she folds her fingers into her palm one-by-one. The water glistens off them. She looks down toward my towel, then up into my eyes.

"Don't even think about it," I say.

She gestures toward the shower curtain.

I heave a sigh, step in the shower, just before the circle of falling water, and close the curtain so that she can't see me unwrapping the towel from my waist. With one arm, I reach out and hang the towel on the rack once more, pulling the curtain close to my body with the other.

Before stepping into the steaming hot torrent hitting the walls of the shower, I watch Jay slide over to the towel. Her hand disappears within the folds of the gray cloth as she looks onward toward the sink and the mirror above it. She wipes her hand on the towel for much longer than necessary. One minute passes by, then two. Instinct urges me to yell at her, to kick her out, but something about her jarringly silent and slow manner begs my attention, leaving me looking upon her in a trance.

When she finally moves away from the towel, she takes one seemingly cautious step toward the sink, then another, almost as if she's afraid the drain might suck her into another dimension. She plants two hands on either side of the white porcelain and stops.

Splashing water pounds the shower walls behind me. Steam rises up and out, floating upon air until it clings to the mirror, obscuring Jay's reflection within it. Her index finger slowly rises, twitching almost, until it touches the glass. She pauses again.

I close my eyes. Backing up, my skin burns with the initial shock of a boiling sensation, but my body quickly acclimates to it and finds comfort within the waterfall that clings to my body, snaking down my chest, past my thighs, through the webs of my toes, and into the stainless steel drain. I pull the curtain tautly shut.

A few moments later, I hear a *click* beyond the curtain–the sound of the door swinging open, and the hiss of it slowly shutting.

I twist the knob sticking out of the shower wall. The water stops, save for small droplets dripping from the head onto the shower floor with tiny thuds. I toss the curtain aside, plucking the towel from the rack. I shake it back and forth across my scalp, my hair follicles drying slowly beneath the friction, careful not to aggravate my injury. Next I wipe my face, scrub my chest, and then–

That's when I see it.

I freeze. It stares at me obviously. My next and possibly final clue. Written in an almost horrific squiggly pattern and in all caps across the mirror is the message:

Knowing this girl, Jay, it was probably her intent to add a bit of dramatic flair to the clue. Admittedly, it might've worked. The lettering sends a wave of tingling chills down my spine. I can't really place my finger on why.

I walk keenly to the mirror, reading the message once more before swiping my towel across it. That's now the second clue she's given me that has departed from the norm of a location and time.

Find the truth.

It now accompanies *"Listen carefully"* as the only clues that are just words–vague words at that. The two phrases run over and over in my head.

Listen carefully. Find the truth.

I dry myself off, jump in the sweat pants and t-shirt I left on the floor, and turn toward the door. Without thinking, I twist the handle, but the door doesn't budge. It's locked.

I twist the lock open, walk through the door, and find my room across the hall.

The clock on my desk reads 3:00p.m. A yawn opens my mouth wide and forces me to stretch to the ceiling.

Rung by rung, I climb up the side of the bunk until I get to the top, falling face first into the pillows at the other end. Immediately, I've become immobile. I rest against the soft pillows without covering myself with a blanket, legs splayed and arms resting at each side. The comfort of my own bed reminds me of home.

I miss Casey. I miss his adorable laugh, a laugh that will certainly deepen with age. I miss the way he looks up at me like I matter. It's been tough living without him, even if just for a few days. I miss the Cave and my guitar collection that hangs from its walls. I miss playing music for my son.

This new start has been wonderful, but I start to fear that if I change my past too drastically, my future might also change more than I'd hope. What if Casey doesn't exist in my new future? What if I have to choose between a successful relationship with the woman I love or the existence of my wonderful son? Or worse, what if the fate Rachel and I have is unchangeable, that we're destined for failure and I lose Casey anyway? Negative thoughts are a disease to the mind. I have to stay positive. I have to stay the course and fight for the life I want. If Casey were here, he'd probably say something cute and mildly inspiring like "Don't give up, Daddy." I have to do everything in my power to ensure that I see him again. I *will* see him again and raise him into the man he's meant to be. That's what fathers do.

Find the truth.

My brain is spinning but will soon find another avenue to process my thoughts as the rest of my body shuts down. My eyelids flutter before closing. My mind is slowly taken elsewhere. The voices of characters in my head begin to speak ... until something interrupts my slumber.

Bzzzz Bzzzz.

Lethargically I lift myself to peer over the edge of the bunk. My sight has already gone blurry, and it hastens to focus. Below, a phone screen is lit upon the surface of my wooden desk.

Bzzzz Bzzzz.

It vibrates too loudly to ignore, though I do my best to do just that. After a while, it stops. The room falls quiet. I rest my head against the pillow but only for another moment until the buzzing begins again. With a groan I peer once more over the edge of the bunk, the name on the screen becoming clearer each second. When my brain eventually registers, exhaustion is wiped from my body.

Jumping out of the bed, I rush over to the desk, picking up the phone just in time. Fighting to hide my heavy breathing, I gulp.

"Hey, Rach."

173

XII

"Shhhh!"

"I'm being quiet. You *shhh!*"

In the pitch black hallway, too dark to tell how far and wide it stretches, Rachel and I snicker together. She covers her mouth with her hand and fights the urge to burst out laughing.

"Are you not allowed to have boys over or something?"

"If we were at the sorority house, I'd never even *think* of trying something like this."

"But this is your apartment … your roommates are asleep, right?"

"Exactly. I don't want to wake them up. Plus, I'd never hear the end of it if they found out I had a boy with me so late at night. So would you just hush already? A few more feet and we'll be in my room. You can feel free to ask questions there."

Both frightened and amused by her derisive response, I zip my mouth shut. Two silhouettes in the night, we step carefully as we can on the wood flooring, doing our best to avoid causing any creaking or groaning. In front of me, she reaches into an open space with one arm, flips a light switch, and yanks me in behind her.

Gently closing the door behind us, Rachel shuts the lights off immediately after, encasing us in another sheet of darkness. My eyes had been blinded by the light and struggle to readjust to the dark. I stand still. That's when she pulls me close into a kiss. Evidently she'd been eager to pick up where we left off.

"You couldn't wait more than a day to see me, could you?"

"Just shut up, and kiss me."

Bumping into a mini fridge, running into the hanging shirts and dresses of an open closet, and finally falling onto a soft, wide mattress, Rachel pins me down upon the bed and sits on my lap. My head rests against the pillow. Gracefully, she removes her shirt to reveal the smooth skin beneath. She leans down, ripping mine off my chest as well.

In between breaths, I say, "You don't think this is moving too fast?"

"Sure it is," she says, "but we're young and dumb, so who cares?"

Fair enough, I think to myself.

She undoes the hook of her bra, pressing her breasts against my body as she kisses my cheek and moves to my lips. The intimate touch of another is wonderful. When it's someone you care about, it's even better. And when it's the woman of your dreams, it's incomparable to any other feeling this world has to give. Yet I feel uneasy. Though this isn't *my* first time with her, it is Rachel's first time with me, technically speaking.

Lightly grabbing her shoulders, I stop for a moment. "Don't you think this won't be the best foundation for a relationship?"

As she kisses my chest and neck area, she says, "Maybe. Maybe not. Only time will tell. If you don't want to do this, just say so." She unties the laces of my sweatpants.

"I just … don't want to mess this up."

Rachel pauses. "If something goes wrong, we'll fix it."

Within my head, I think of her words. Eventually, I accept them and nod. "Okay."

She smiles, pulling my pants off my legs, taking my boxers along with them. Rachel then plops down at my side, lying on her back to shed her last layers.

Into the night we make love quietly. We toss and turn until she lies below me. Rachel's neck strains. Her moans do not escape the folds of her hand as she covers her mouth. I missed this. My lips are drawn to her neck. I can't resist. I know just what she likes.

That's when the sound escapes her again, the sound I live for: her tattered breaths complimented by the moans that are only triggered in this moment. I tug at her hair to lift her chin and grant me more access. She complies, I go for her neck, and that unique noise escapes once again.

I can't help but grin. Her satisfaction is mine. Now her passion has increased. She digs her nails into my back, just above my waistline, pulling me into her once more.

"Oh, Liam."

I love you, Rachel. I love you. Oh, how I love you …

"Becca!"

Pulling away, I feel the euphoric state. My eyes shut, my chest heaves, and a relaxed grin strikes me. A few chuckles escape. Beads of sweat trickle down my forehead that warrant a towel. I smooth my hair back with a few fingers. That's when I open my eyes to see Rachel's face, perturbed with an unknown horror.

"Rach, what's wrong?"

She backs away, sitting with her elbows as her supports. "What's wrong? What's wrong!"

"Yes! What's the matter?"

"Who's Becca?" She says the name like it's garbage against her tongue.

"Huh?"

"You heard me. *Who* is Becca?" She pushes me off her, scrambling for her underwear, then hooking the bra around her chest while she sits on edge.

"She–she's a girl I met at a house party with Todd and his girlfriend last night. I don't understand?"

Her frown and piercing eyes bore into me, her mouth hanging slightly ajar. "*You* don't understand? Have you been fantasizing about climaxing on top of Becca? Or maybe *that's* what you were up to last night! Is that why you yelled her name?"

What? I didn't realize until now the monumental mistake I made. Why would I do that? I love Rachel, not Becca. Becca's just a friend.

"Rach, wait." She gets up to put the rest of her clothes on. "Rachel, I don't know why I said that. I–it was an honest mistake. She's just a friend, I promise."

Facing the door, her head has fallen to the ground, her voice trembling. She talks quietly to her chest. "Alexandra told me you met a girl. I can't believe this. I can't believe this."

"Rach." I hop off the bed, snag my boxers and hop around to get them on. Then I walk behind her and put a comforting hand on her shoulder.

"*Don't* touch me."

I quickly retract my hand. I don't know what to say. I'm not sure there's a way to explain myself. Dread and guilt rack my insides, the pit in my stomach rapidly becoming unbearable. There's no way I could have messed this up already. There's no way. How could I do this?

Don't give up. I hear Casey's voice ringing in my head. I can't give up, *won't* give up.

Suddenly my brain begins to throb. It starts off as a gentle beating pain and quickly turns into a burning sensation where the staples have been born into my scalp.

"Ah, ow. Son of a ..." I shut my eyes, drop to the bed, and place a hand on my temple.

"Oh, that's rich. Are you five?" Rachel scolds.

I try not to grimace, but the pain quickly becomes unbearable. Stop hurting. Stop hurting. But my head pounds. "Ah!" I place my eyes into my palms. The injury burns even more. It feels as though a rubber mallet is beating my brain.

"I'm not falling for this."

177

I grit my teeth. My body teeters back and forth. It grows and grows, getting worse by the second.

"Liam, stop."

With both thumbs, I plug my ears. I can't take noise. No noise. Even the wonderful sound of Rachel's voice exacerbates the problem.

"Liam."

I don't think I can take it anymore. It hurts. Oh, it hurts. Then just as suddenly as it came, the pain is washed away. A dull and aching throb is left in its wake. I breathe heavily, my eyes watering. My chest heaves even more violently than before. Naturally, I fall back onto the bed.

"Liam ..." Rachel says softly. "Are–are you okay?" She sits at an angle on the edge of the bed, keeping a foot or two between us.

"I'm sorry. My head." I point to the injury. "The nurse said this might happen if I didn't take time to rest."

"Let me get you some water." Rachel moves over to her mini fridge, pulls out a miniature plastic bottle and unscrews the cap for me.

Sitting upright, I take it and with one gulp, it goes down. "Thank you."

The two of us sit next to each other without a word. I can't think of anything to say, and Rachel appears too stunned to speak.

That's when she sighs, not meeting my eyes. "Tell me why you said her name."

"Rachel I ... I honestly don't know." The remnants of the sudden migraine make it hard to concentrate. I keep one hand on my forehead, hoping that it'll ease the pain.

Find the truth. The phrase repeats in my head. I can't lie. I've never liked lying and don't really know how to do it ... successfully, at least. I don't *want* to lie, anyway. Not with Rachel. So I have to find the truth. The truth is my only chance.

"What I do know is that she is just a friend, nothing more. I could never see her as anything more."

178

Rachel peeks out of the corner of her eyes. She doesn't say anything but waits for me to continue. I know she's listening.

"They said I had a mild concussion at the hospital. Besides the fact that it hurts now and again, I think it can affect the brain in other ways, too. From messing up thoughts, to short-term memory loss ... stuff like that, I guess. That's the only logical way I can explain this. I know that's not what you want to hear. It's not what you *need* to hear." I pause, meeting Rachel's eyes. They're intent. Lifting Rachel's chin with a finger, I continue. "You are the only woman I have eyes for. I love you."

The last three words slipped. This girl has known me for a few days. She'll think I'm insane for saying that I love her. Of course, I do. That *is* the truth. But it's too soon to tell her. I start to panic but am slowly relieved when I catch a glimpse of a smile.

I hope that I'm not seeing only what I want to see when Rachel's eyes subsequently melt with compassion. She struggles to fight it for a moment. I know she wants to stay upset. It's easier to let the anger take control. But she lifts herself into a grin. "You promise?"

"A million times," I say with relief.

"And this Becca girl ..."

"She might as well be one of the guys."

"You won't see her again?"

I cock my head to the side and pull back an inch or two. "Huh?"

"You're not going to see Becca again, right?"

"You don't trust me? You don't think I'm telling you the truth?"

"I didn't say that, I–"

"She is a friend, Rachel."

She sits in silence for a moment. Then she starts to nod her head. "You're right." She nods more and says again, "You're right. I'm sorry, it's just ... I'm slow to trust. I've been in love like this before. I'm hesitant to accept it this

179

time around." Rachel gulps, wiping at the corners of her eyes. "He cheated on me. I can't … just can't go through that again."

"Rachel," I say in a soft tone, doing my best to comfort her in the moment. In the way she says the words and the way she obviously shows her pain, I feel for her. I thought I knew everything there was to know about this girl, but I didn't know she'd been cheated on before. I now understand her concern more than ever. "I'd never do anything to hurt you, especially not that. I could never cheat on you."

Rachel wipes a tear slowly falling below her eye. She faces me, shutting her eyes. Pressing her lips together, she says in a whisper, "I know."

Slipping into her bed, she pulls the covers over her body and nestles her head into a pillow. She shuffles for a short time while I sit at the edge. I'm unsure what to do and can't decipher her body language. I sit like a statue awaiting her voice.

That's when she lifts her head off the pillow. "Come here," she commands, lifting the covers and tossing her undergarments to the floor.

My mouth curls into a smile.

XIII

A few weeks pass, generating a rhythm and pattern for me to follow. Play guitar, sneak into Rachel's once a week–sneak out just as successfully–, and spend time with Todd, Julie, and Becca. The four of us have oddly formed a strong union. I think it's because everyone brings something new to the table, making our relationships with one another something special and unique. Julie has always been the voice of reason, Todd brings the charisma, Becca seconds that, and I'm a willful bystander. It works.

We've done everything from conduct weekly Texas Hold 'Em nights to heading out to the movies, axe throwing, driving around the city, and getting drunk on the weekends–doing those last two separately, of course. Becca and I can only be seen together when Todd or Julie are around. It's a promise I made to Rachel. Nothing intimate could ever come to fruition between Becca and myself, no matter how close our friendship has gotten. I know that. Still, to provide a protective layer of comfort to Rachel, I agreed to her conditions. Relationships are all about compromise, after all.

As for Rachel and I, we've grown closer than I could have imagined. It's all happened so quickly, but that's life. I'm just taking it as it comes. We don't get to see each other much, but our time is well spent. Because her schedule became so hectic at the end of the semester, she's only ever had time to see me late at night, usually just once a week. It's always at her place. I don't mind. I can understand why she wouldn't want to be caught dead in a dorm-style bunk. Her bedroom is bigger, anyway. So I sneak in, and before the sun rises, I leave. Not every night do we make love, either. We've reached a middle ground to ensure a healthy relationship. Granted, Rachel tends to struggle with

181

keeping up her end of the bargain. If we've designated a night to watch movies, or even play board games, she often gets ... distracted. Even on the nights where we try to sit down and talk, things can often lead elsewhere. At least we can say we try.

Before I knew it, winter break had arrived. I figured this would give me more time to spend with Rachel, but she was evidently preoccupied with her research position. So we maintained our once-a-week dates throughout the entire month. This left Alexandra and I plenty of time to spend together. Since the dorm closed over break, Alexandra allowed me to stay with her. Typically, we spent our days watching different TV series. This gave Alexandra some time to decompress before her final semester, and it gave me more time with my sister.

The red-haired mystery girl Jay has yet to be seen. While my life has become more peaceful, I almost enjoyed the challenges she presented to me. The notes she left provided an odd source of adventure. But now she really is gone. I'm not saying I miss her popping up at random. But it was fun.

Thoughts and memories of my boy Casey remain as consistently present as ever. I miss him. Oddly enough, even with Todd around, I have a union with the little man that no guy could replace. That's what it's like to be a father. For now, I await his reappearance with a longing passion.

All in all, my life has been restructuring itself very similarly to the way it had been before everything took a turn for the worse. Except this time, things will work out the way they're supposed to, I can feel it.

Now winter break has come and gone, opening a new year and a new chapter in life. With the snap of a finger, I find myself alone inside my dorm room...

Arpeggio chords. Strumming a combination of the strings one at a time, accentuating the beauty of each individual note. A minor, C, G, D minor. Somber tones create intense, captivating verses that inherently create tension as the song builds, builds, and builds to a chorus of G, B flat, F, and C. These ring with definition, although just an experiment. My soul weaves and flows into every movement along the neck, every strum, leaving no time to see or feel anything else from the world around me as it dissolves into the background.

"Liam!" *Rap, rap, rap.*

Sucked back into the room, the soul of my body and the soul of the guitar are suddenly ripped apart by a woman's voice. I growl. It's rude to interrupt art.

Dust motes hang peacefully within the shallow beams of light shining through the window pane, a sign of the sun's attempt to reheat the Earth by melting the mounds of white piled onto street corners outside, by reviving the trees and swelling their buds, ultimately bringing new life and new color to the world. Sadly, its attempts are futile for the moment. Spring is at least another couple months away.

I look down upon a neatly-made bed resting against the opposite wall with the Australian flag quilted on its top. My bunk reaches higher, also making it a pain to get down. With my back pressed lightly against the wall and the guitar sitting between my legs, I have no more than a few inches to spare before my head touches the white ceiling.

Laying the neck of the guitar down on the head pillow, I bite the pick and awkwardly maneuver down the ladder. Walking over to the door, I toss the pick on top of my desk. It ricochets off the lamp but stays on the wooden surface.

The lock feels cold against my sweaty hands as I twist it open with a *click.*

"Mate." A red-cheek smile and a disheveled flame of brown hair greet me. Snowflakes are scattered across his puffy tan jacket. Clapping hands, we bring each other into an embrace, and Todd says. "Forgo' my key here."

183

I hold the door open for him as he waddles inside with a large bag strapped around his chest, a backpack on his back, a duffel bag hanging from one hand and the handle of a suitcase in the other. Lifting my chin, I squint across the room at his desk by the window. Sure enough, his key sits atop it, reflecting tiny beams of golden light.

I stick my head out the door. "Where's Julie?"

A bag hits the floor, followed by a fatigued exhale. "Oh, she doesn't ge' in until tonigh'."

"Hm, thought I heard a girl's voice when you knocked on the door."

"Real funny, you are."

"No, I'm serious."

Todd eyes me pretentiously. "You're no' back on the stuff again, are ya?" He taps his nose twice.

My eyes roll back into my head, and I let the door hiss shut. "I was never on 'the stuff', and you know it."

Todd snorts. As I saunter back to my bunk, he bends over to let the rest of his bags fall to the ground, each one of them nearly exploding from being over-packed. Clothes are literally sprouting out of his suitcase, ripping the zippers farther and farther apart.

"Far out. Mind lending a hand, lad?" Todd sheds his outer jacket, tossing it to the floor by his desk.

"Sorry, *mate*," I sneer at him as I reach the top rung of the ladder. "I think I might be a little too *high* for that right now." I tap my nose mockingly.

"Oh, you dir'y lit'le …"

Resting on the pillow is my beautiful cherry-wood guitar, just as I had left it. I take the neck in one hand and begin strumming, picking up right where I left off. Perched atop my bunk, I feel like a bird singing his morning song to the humans bound to reality below. Todd tosses a stack of clothes onto his quilt, then another. He rubs his neck, frustrated. It gives me a devilish idea.

A low riff begins the song. My vision flickers with each note.. "*I hear the train a-comin'; it's rollin' 'round the bend, and I ain't seen the sunshine since I don't know when ...*"

"'Folsom Prison Blues' by Johnny Cash ... you really ough'a be a comedian, mate." Todd shakes his head as he turns to look up at me, but even he can't hide the smirk that creeps across his face.

I stop playing for a second. "How about this one?"

Todd begins folding his shirts in two lazy swipes and throwing them in the top drawer of his dresser immediately after. I don't even make it through the opening riff of the next tune before he says, "Tha's 'Home'. Oh, this just gets bettuh and bettuh. I swear ... if you put a country spin on tha' one, I'll come up there righ' now."

Transitioning to another song, my fingers strum until Todd can guess it. I continue with as many songs as I can play. Todd names each tune as he works on unpacking the rest of his bags. I think it helps the time pass for the both of us. By the time I make it through at least fifty songs, Todd finishes folding his last pair of pants, promptly slamming the bottom drawer of his dresser after tossing them in with a victory screech.

"Wooh!" He throws his arms up in the air.

"Done?" I ask.

Turning, he points a finger up at me. "You're pretty good a' tha' now. I'm impressed."

"This?" The guitar rests in my palms.

"Yeah. Keep i' up, and you could slay some major–"

"Alright, enough of that." Placing the pick between my teeth, I carefully climb down the ladder, holding the guitar out with one hand so as not to put any scratches on the body.

"Speaking of, did you and Becca ... hangou' ova break?" Todd's eyebrows slant with insinuation.

"No, Todd. We did not." I set the guitar underneath the bunk.

185

"Why no'?" he asks rather theatrically.

"You know why."

"Remind me."

I stumble over to the gray office chair by my desk. Todd hops onto his bed. I plop down in the chair after flipping it around to face him.

"You're not going to convince me to break up with Rachel, so stop. You haven't even met her."

"Pish posh. I don't have to mee' her to know that nobody looks a' you the way Becca does."

"Stop it with that. You've been on this since Halloween." I rub my scalp, right where the injury used to be. In its place is a small bump where hair has grown over. Just like most scars in life, nobody can see this one.

"Look," Todd says, leaning forward. "I'm not saying you have to break up with Rachel. I'm not saying tha' at awll! Wha' I am suggesting is maybe you should—I don' want to say 'take advantage of the situation at hand'–but *Carpe Diem*. Seize the Day!"

I frown. "I hope I'm misunderstanding you."

He gets up and begins pacing. With a finger on his chin, he says, "You have to stop being closed-minded. Wha' if you din't have to make a choice between the two of them—Rachel and Becca?"

"I'd still choose Rachel," I say frankly. But Todd ignores me.

"Wha' if you could have *both*?"

I don't know what it is about him that doesn't allow me to take the Aussie seriously, but I do my best to convey a disturbed tone when I say, "You're one sick son of a–"

"Come *on*, Liam! You could be going off like a frog in a sock. Just think," Todd rushes over to wrap an arm around my shoulders. With his free hand, he arcs a rainbow. "You'd have the best of both worlds. Keep your Rachel. Do wha'ever i' is that the two of you do. *Annnnd* to entertain me, at least kiss Becca, and you can lie to me and tell me that you din't bloody enjoy it."

I shake his arm off. "Todd, if you don't can that shit, you'll be in your casket wearing my guitar around your neck."

"She's right, you know." He sighs, loping over to his bed. "Becca. Calling you a stiff all the time. Just consider i'."

I shake my head, folding my hands together. If I had to guess, I'd say Todd is trying to live his darkest desires vicariously through me. If that's the case, it's making me really reconsider our friendship. Then again, that's just who Todd is. No matter the circumstance, his advice is often meant to be ignored. But part of me wonders if there isn't some reason to be found in it. After all, in this world of chaos, it would serve as poetic justice if chaotic words still had some truth to them. But even I know better than that in this case.

My eyes wander around the room until they land on the gaming system next to the television under my bunk.

"What I will consider," I say, "is kicking your ass in Call of Duty."

Todd's face brightens. "You're as dead as a dingo."

In a bout of furious clicks and jolts, Todd's forehead glows with sweat as the final rays of the orange sun shine through the window pane upon the two of us. He smashes buttons with gusto, mirrors the man on screen by dodging and diving along with him, and exhales violently after inadvertently holding his breath for too long. Meanwhile, I sit calmly in the chair next to him while he takes a commanding lead. We played a few times before break, and our matches were never too close. But Todd must have worked on his skill while at home just to further prove his dominance in the virtual realm.

"Aha! Take tha'. Sixty-two to twelve. You're get'ing rusty, lad."

"I suppose I am," I say, entertained.

A few more rounds commence, and Todd takes care of me similarly each time, with far too much pride in that beaming smile. Yet the fatigue written on the folds of his face is evident. Eventually, we have to switch to game modes that aren't quite as ... intense, for Todd's sake.

"Must be je' lag," he says, wiping the corners of his eyes.

"Must be."

For the first time in a couple hours, Todd implements the back rest of his chair. He releases his tense grip on the gaming controller, setting his forearms on either thigh.

"So tell me abou' this Rachel girl. I haven't heard much more than a peep abou' her."

My eyes fall to the controller in my hands. "We aren't the type to kiss and tell. Rachel, especially."

"That's wha' everyone says. Go on."

I look up to the underside of the bunk, wondering where to begin. "Well ... Rachel has one more semester of undergrad before graduating in Psychology. She–"

"Whoah, whoah, whoah. Hold i' righ' there." Todd pauses the game. He sets his controller on the ground and rests an elbow on his knee. Facing me, he says, "*Gradua'ing*. Did you say *gradua'ing*? As in ... she's a–"

"Senior. Yeah."

Todd's eyebrows raise. He says in a low voice, "You really are a dir'y lad." He gives me a clap on the back. "Wha' else?"

"I don't know," I shrug. "I mean, she's beautiful. Really pretty eyes. They're like some of the darkest blue you'll see. You know, they pop in the sunlight like you can't believe. It's–"

"Oy! Spare me the BS," Todd scoffs.

My mouth twitches as I frown at Todd's rude interruption, but he looks as though he's ready to explain.

188

"I said tell me abou' *her*. I don't care what she looks like–well, I do–but wha' makes you *like* her?"

"Um, well …" I shift in my seat.

Just then, there's a knock on the door. My head twists, but I look at Todd to make sure he heard it too.

"You gonna get that?" he asks with the slightest twitch of a smile.

"You're closer to the door."

Another knock.

"I don' care. Go grab i'!"

"Then get out of my way!"

I duck to ensure I don't bump my head on the bottom of the bunk and scramble around Todd.

Another gentle *tap, tap, tap* on the door.

The room has turned dark, so I flip the light switch. I twist the lock open, press down on the handle, and pull.

"Stiff!"

Pulled into a hug, I almost lose my balance. She pulls away with a smile, dressed in clothes as dark as the night that has fallen upon the city. Black boots, black leggings, a black coat with a furry hood, short black hair and a face too tan for the season.

"Becca …" I say with half excitement, half confusion. There's something different about her. "Glasses?" Now she has black glasses with large square lenses to match the rest of her scheme.

"Do you like them?" She tips them down just below her eyes and then adjusts them back into place.

I tip my head to either side. "I have to admit they're cute."

Her perfect white teeth are exposed when she smiles and enters the room, carrying a small white sack. "I brought ice cream! Did you guys know it takes an average of fifty licks to consume a scoop of ice cream? And that chocolate was invented before vanilla? Probably because it's better."

189

"Fridge is over there," I say between laughter.

She shuts the top door. "Toddster!"

"Becca." Todd stands straight as Becca approaches. His face flushes as Becca wraps her arms around him. After several conversations with Todd, I know he's as committed to being with Julie as anything. Yet it's obvious to me that no matter how hard he may try, subduing his so-called "subconscious desire" for Becca isn't going as well as he'd like me to think.

"How–um, what are you doing here?" I ask.

"Todd invited me!" A sparkle reflects off Becca's eyes.

I sigh to myself. *Of course he did.*

Becca claps her hands together, scanning the room. "So what are we doing tonight? Where's Julie?"

Todd raises his cell phone in the air. "She just go' in."

"Great! When will she be here?"

"Abou' that..." Todd inhales through gritted teeth. "She's go' lots of baggage tha' needs to be unpacked ... asked if I'd help her out."

Sure, Becca comes in. Todd goes out, leaving the two of us inevitably together ... alone.

My eyes narrow as I direct an obvious glare toward Todd. He looks away.

Becca clears her throat. "Okay...we can all go together. What do you think, Liam?"

"Hm?" I blink twice at her like I'd been staring into the light for a minute straight.

"I don't mind helping Julie unpack. I miss her."

"Uh, well. I suppose–"

"I'm unfortunately gonna have to stop you righ' there." Todd offers a tone of fabricated disappointment. Squeezing between Becca and I, he wanders over to the closet, plucking a large winter jacket from a hanger. As he slips his arms through the sleeves, he says to us–more to Becca than myself–

190

"The two of us–Julie and I–would *love* your help. We would, lad and lady. *But* we've also go' something planned, you know, just for us."

Before his hands can gesture toward something immature and inappropriate, I cut him off. "You've got your car. Could you at least give Becca a ride back?"

Her eyes flicker back and forth between myself and Todd.

"Ope!" Todd looks at a message on his phone that I'm not convinced is truly there. "Got'a run, mate! Sorry, loves!"

"Todd–" I begin, but he's already disappeared in a flurry out the door. I tilt my head back, close my eyelids tight, and sigh. My fingers grab multiple tufts of hair on the back of my head and hold tight. I give Becca a sorrowful look. She knows just as well as I do. She can't be here.

"Becca, I'm sorry, I–"

"I know ..." her head drops to the floor. "Rachel."

I pull out my smartphone and fiddle with it, quickly searching the college's transportation sites. "I'll find you a bus, and you can hop on one of those–"

"Buses aren't running, not 'til tomorrow."

"Oh." I take a step closer to the desk and slowly lower myself into the chair. "How'd you get here?"

"I walked." Becca flips her hair to the side, looking at me intently through her glasses, standing still as ever. I have to look away.

"Shoot." I bite my lip, trying to come up with a solution. "Was it cold?"

"Yes, it was fucking cold! It's the end of January."

"Shoot."

"Yeah ... shoot." Becca starts bouncing in anticipation. I can feel her eyes boring a hole in my skull. She walked all the way across the river, in the freezing cold elements, the dead of winter just to get to us. It wouldn't be right to make her walk all the way back by herself, especially now that night has fallen.

191

I sit still, chewing the inside of my cheek while my eyes swing back and forth like a pendulum, considering the only two options I can imagine. I can choose the asshole option, and I kick someone out who's been nothing but a great friend since we've met. Or I choose the other asshole option by allowing her to stay, thereby breaking Rachel's trust. Either way, I'm an asshole.

Then I come up with an idea that meets somewhere in the middle of the two, but not before Becca offers one.

"Play me your guitar." She nods to the instrument sitting in the corner. "I've never heard you play, despite the *countless* instances I've asked you to do so." Gingerly, she rests her back side against Todd's bed, crossing her arms and planting her feet firmly against the carpet.

From the opposite side of the room, I ponder her suggestion for no more than a second. "I was thinking I could walk you back to your dorm, just so you're not alone."

"Not before you play me a song," she says indignantly.

"Becca, no. I–"

"Liam, can the BS," she points at my guitar, "and pick it up. Then you can walk me back."

At this point, I know better than to argue with Becca. She's as stubborn as anyone I've ever met, maybe even more stubborn than myself. It's one of the things I like about her.

I stumble to my instrument, keeping my head down to avoid the satisfaction that has inevitably swept across Becca's face. Sitting back down in my gray office chair, I say, "One song."

"One song," she confirms.

"Just one." I hold my index finger up and stare at Becca to ensure she and I are both at the same understanding of the word *one*.

"We don't have all night, stiff."

The notch in the body rests softly upon my leg. I inhale deeply, hold it in for a second, then exhale slowly.

192

When playing any instrument, it's vital to release tension. Tension doesn't create music, it ruins it. In fact, you could even say that music with tension isn't really music at all. It's an imposter's version of it, because it takes away half of art's true components. Real music, real art, and real melodies aren't found in different chords or notes alone. They can only be found when emotion, heart, and soul work in unison with notes and chords to form something immaculate, something collaborative with life itself.

Becca bites her lip anticipatively, arms crossed, one eyebrow hanging slightly above the other. Usually this is the part where I find my *taken* world. I make the reality around me disappear so that I can be alone, so that I can conjure the heart and soul necessary to craft true music.

But that isn't the case now. For some reason, I don't need a *taken* world at the moment. I see Becca. She sees me. I can acknowledge her presence, she can acknowledge mine. There's nothing prohibiting me from playing something spectacular.

I close my eyes, focus.

A series of slow, quiet strums begins the song. Already I can feel the emotion of the guitar and the soul of my heart intertwining like they do, almost like invisible tendrils of fabric wrapping around each other, becoming separable only by the termination of the melody. My eyes remain shut, not purposefully. It's just … necessary.

The song picks up speed with quicker strums, faster transitions, and intense progressions. That's when I open my eyes. Becca's testy look has vanished, replaced by something foreign to me. Enjoyment? Recognition? Perhaps it's admiration. It distracts me for just a second but does not take me away from what's truly important–the bond I have with the guitar is something no human could ever replace.

Finally the song reaches a section where chords strum loudly, then softly, then loudly again, where the buildup of the beginning pays off with the climax of the end. Naturally, I smile.

193

Again, I look up, but what I see this time horrifies me. Becca's black outfit is slowly morphing into white. Like a winter disease rapidly creeping across a blacktop area, white fabric replaces the black starting at her chest, working its way down, down, down. I try to stop playing, but the music continues. I've been trapped as the music grows louder, louder until it's ringing in my ears. The noise doesn't seem to bother Becca. Her look of admiration remains until, along with her black clothes, it transforms into something white.

Becca stands straight on the opposite side of the room in a white gown, a white headdress suddenly appearing above her forehead. Her face has aged five, maybe ten years, noticeable only by the slight wrinkles that have formed at her brow. My heart pounds, a look of horror undoubtedly upon me. Yet the music continues to grow louder, louder.

I can hardly take it. I want out. I want to stop, but my hands have entered into a contract with the strings of the guitar, flowing up and down the neck in a bid with the devil. Becca takes a step closer to me, the world around her fading, until in a tunnel of darkness she approaches. Her long white gown flows swiftly behind her. Another step.

Stay back.

Suddenly, in her arms, a baby in blue materializes. Becca rocks him back and forth.

Stay back!

Closer. She comes closer, closer. The music intensifies, sounding more like a blaring organ than a guitar.

STAY BACK!

Becca stops a foot before me. The baby in her arms isn't crying. I can't see its face, but I know it's a little boy. Becca rocks, rocks the baby. Then with a loving warmth, she offers the boy up to me. She reaches her arms out, and the baby I see is unquestionably ...

"CASEY!"

194

The music stops abruptly with the stark sound of snapping strings and shattered wood. Becca is sucked backward through the dark tunnel. Her white gown vanishes, seemingly pulling the darkness into it until she's dressed in all black once again, and the bright world around her returns.

Becca stands against Todd's bed with admiration pasted back onto her face.

"Liam, that was amazing."

Lying on the ground before me is a guitar that has been absolutely decimated. The neck has been split from the body. A few strings wiggle as they're held only by the turning pegs. Wood has splintered and fallen in scattered pieces around what is left of the instrument.

My breathing is heavy, tattered. I can feel sweat at my brow.

With an odd smile, almost as though she doesn't see what's happened before her, Becca says, "You're really talented."

I look upon her with utter confusion. But when I look down again, the guitar is resting perfectly on my lap, completely intact. I stand quickly, grabbing the guitar by the neck, thanking God that it's still smooth as it used to be. I set it beneath the bunk, shut my eyes, a tear forming in one of them.

"You have to go," I say, my lip quivering.

"What?" I hear Becca's voice behind me and a soft chuckle.

"You have to *go*," I say with more conviction.

"Wait, you're serious?"

I flip around. "Go, Becca! Get out of here!"

She bats her eyes in shock. She readjusts her glasses, standing straight as a sentry. "Did I say something wrong?"

"Just ... *leave*."

Hesitantly, Becca turns toward the door. She begins walking and turns back. "Liam, I–"

"Becca, please ..."

She purses her lips. Her head falls, not as far as her eyes. "Okay."

I lead her to the door. I open it, and she walks out alone. She offers one last glance filled with hurt before I let the door shut between us.

Once it clicks, I lay my back against the door. I heave a sigh. My heart pounds as I stare at the floor.

I don't know what happened. I'm unsure of what I've done. Maybe panic overtook me, and I allowed it to do so. But I couldn't fight it. It's almost like it had something to tell me. What I saw … Casey as a baby, Becca holding my child like it was hers–I had no way to escape but through panic.

The back of my head hits the door softly. Flipping the light switch, I stand in darkness. The light is too much. It shows too much. I don't want to see anything, not right now. I try to breathe, just breathe. In. Out. In. Out.

The darkness does comfort me. It hides the shape of my guitar propped against the bunk, making the pattern of the carpet indecipherable and the remaining objects in the room silhouettes. However, the curtains have been left open on the window across the room, allowing some light to sneak through, likely from one of the streetlights below.

What I see beyond the window is frightening. Small objects go in and out of view as they become visible at the top portion of the window pane, disappearing at the bottom. They look like falling ashes, likely covering the ground with morbidity. However, upon a closer look, I discover that the falling objects are just white snowflakes, slowly falling down, down until they come to rest on the covered street below.

Although the scene outside looks peaceful from a warm and comforting setting, I know how brutal winter nights can be. When the wind picks up, as it appears to be doing now, sending snowflakes diagonally across the sky, the outside world grows bleak and uninviting. It'd be awful to be out there alone right now…

Suddenly the harshness of what I've done dawns upon me. I forced her out, left her on her own. Why did I do that? What's wrong with me?

No time for questions.

I bolt to the closet, grab a winter jacket and a stocking cap, and run out the door. Before taking more than a couple steps, I stop. My eyes flicker back and forth. I re-enter the room just as the door is shutting. There's something I forgot.

I find it, slamming the top door of the refrigerator as the sack in my hand rustles with each stride.

"Becca!"

Winds of at least twenty miles an hour blow falling snow sideways. The small white crystals amalgamate, latching onto the sides of buildings, the tops of leafless trees, the curving and bending streets, and the sidewalks that accompany them, turning the city into a dangerously beautiful winter wonderland.

Holding an arm above my brow, I shield my eyes and face as much as I can with the thick navy blue sleeves of my winter jacket. Delving further into the storm, with every step I plant my feet firmly upon the snow-covered sidewalk so as not to slip and fall.

The sidewalk leads toward a bridge overhanging desolate roads below. The red and green traffic lights have nothing to signal to, nothing to communicate with but the freezing air. At the peak of the bridge is a lone figure, a silhouette trudging through the night, getting farther and farther away.

"Becca!" I shout again. I stop, squinting as a few flakes hit my eyelashes.

The figure keeps moving, and for a moment I think I see a flash of red.

"Becca?"

I climb the shallow incline of the bridge, struggling to keep my footing. Sharp winds pester the sack in my hands as it flaps violently. After making it to the peak, I see the figure not much farther away, now hitting the spiral that leads down to the Burlington Bridge. This time the flash of red behind her is more evident.

"Hey. Hey, you!" It appears she doesn't hear me, so I yell louder. "Jay!"

197

This prompts the girl to twist around but not until she's stepped off the bridge. From the bottom of the spiral, she looks up toward me. She says nothing. There's a hood obscuring her face.

Grabbing the rail, I push myself forward, sliding down the curling bridge until I meet her at the bottom. But my foot catches something about ten feet before the end of the bridge, and I fall forward, losing the sack in my hands in the process.

"Whoah!" I catch myself just enough before my face takes a mouthful of snow. My cheeks had already felt frost-bitten and cold enough. The snow packed against them certainly doesn't help.

"Liam?"

I groan.

The girl grabs my hand and helps me to my feet. I brush the snow from my legs, off my chest, and wipe my eyes.

"The last thing you need is another head injury …. Did you call me Jay?"

I cock my head to see pink cheeks, short black hair, and fog-smeared glasses, behind which small tear-sized droplets of snow surround dark brown eyes. When Becca sees me noticing them, she looks away, swiping a finger beneath her lenses.

"Uh, no. I just said 'hey'," I lie. "I was trying to get your attention." The snow and wind relentlessly batter our shivering bodies. I look at the ground around me. Toppled sideways on the snow is a pint of ice cream, its cap lying a few inches from it. Apparently the sack was swept away in the wind. Carefully I bend over to pick up the frost-covered pint, wiping away the flakes that have stuck to the outside, then popping the cap back on. "I–uh, I brought your ice cream."

Becca struggles to meet my eyes, but she accepts it when I hand it to her. "Thanks."

I nod with a grin.

The two of us stand near each other, awkwardly. Becca stows the pint in one of the larger pockets of her jacket, zipping it shut after. My jaw falls as I try to say something, but words fail me. I gulp, scratch the back of my neck, rocking on the balls of my feet.

Becca's eyes are plastered to the ground for a minute. Then they bounce to me. She sighs, flipping her hair out of her glasses and behind her ear. Pursing her lips, as if struggling to summon the right words, she closes her eyes. When she opens them after a long pause, she looks at me with a confronting frown. Her words express more hurt than anger.

"What was that, Liam? Back there."

"There must have been a patch of concrete between all the snow. It caught my foot–"

"No, not that. Why'd you kick me out? You exploded ... like I've never seen before."

I look off to the side. Embarrassment floods my cheeks, probably making them even redder than they had been before. I don't know if I have a sufficient response to give. But she needs an explanation.

"I'm sorry, I–I don't know. Something took over me, thought I saw stuff that wasn't really there." Becca shows no judgment, more concern than anything. I shrug. "I was scared."

Batting her eyelashes rapidly, as more snow has come to rest on them, she asks, "What were you scared of?"

My gaze falls off to the distance. I shake my head. "I don't know."

Becca steps closer to me. She tilts her head to the side, as if she can examine exactly what's going on in my head. Then unexpectedly she inserts her hands softly between my arms, pulling me into a hug. Once she pulls back, she keeps both hands on my shoulders.

"You don't have to be scared to show me your dark side, Liam. We all have one."

I soak up her words. They comfort me. Suddenly the snow seems to be falling slower, the winds dying down as well.

Becca continues, "Next time, just talk to me ... okay? Instead of kicking me out into–" she waves around, looking up at the sky, "–all this, let me know what's really going on. Maybe I can help."

I nod, finally meeting her eyes. Her smile pulls a grin from me.

The only person I've ever felt truly comfortable around is Alexandra, my sister. Particularly when it comes to revealing whatever bothers me, I've always gone to her. Even Rachel struggles to pry into my brain, despite the fact that she frequently asks me to "tell her how I feel". Maybe I'm afraid of judgment. I've never wanted Rachel to see me for who I truly am, never wanted to expose my issues to her. I thought I'd lose her if I did. But I suppose that might've been the reason *why* I lost her in the first place. Maybe that's why Becca is here. She's showing me how to be open, how to trust. It might be working.

Though the winds have settled down, even the slightest breeze in the air feels like a thousand tiny blades simultaneously pricking our ears and cheeks. If we stand out here much longer, we'll freeze to the sidewalk along with the snow.

With hands in her pockets and her head tucked into a shrug, Becca shivers.

"I should walk you home."

She shakes her head up and down, whether in a nod or as a natural shivering reaction I cannot tell.

Upon crossing the Burlington Bridge, I look backward as we walk side-by-side beneath scattered streetlights. My brow furrows as I cock my head to the side.

"We're going the long way."

Becca clears her throat. "We are? Hm, I guess we are."

200

"On a night like tonight, that's not very smart."

Becca continues her stride, not uttering a single word. She took the long way on purpose.

"Why?"

"Why what?"

I stop in my tracks. Becca does the same.

"Oh come on, don't play those games with me," I say, almost laughing. "Don't be me. Don't shut down."

"Haven't we discussed this? We're the same."

I look at her expectantly with a long pause. "Becca."

Rearing her head back, she sighs. She purses her lips, debating whether she wants to say anything. Then finally she says, "The long way is harder, more painful."

"Seems like a reason *not* to take the long way."

"No, no. That *is* the reason to take the long way, Liam. What's the old saying? Doing what's right isn't easy, and doing what's easy isn't right."

I look at her, unconvinced. The night we met, she told me how she takes the easy way out on a daily basis, giving in to outside pressures by conforming to societal norms, not being herself. She'd spend more time being herself if she truly preferred the hard way. There's something more to it, so I wait for her to explain. Often silence is more powerful than words.

"Okay, okay," she says. She looks down. "You hurt me ... kicking me out like that. We're supposed to be friends."

I maintain my silence, sure that there's more to be told. Sure enough, it cracks her open like a can.

"It's not just you," she admits. Then she takes a seat on the freezing snow below, pulling her legs close. Apparently, she has a lot to say. "My family ... my parents recently split."

"I'm so sorry," I say, genuinely heartbroken by it. I'm more familiar with divorce than she could possibly understand.

201

"Don't be." Becca begins slightly shaking again. Something tells me it's not just the cold causing it. "The part that hurts is that it took so long for them to do it. Nineteen years. Nineteen years too many."

Becca's tone grows sullen, and it hurts me. I want to tell her she doesn't have to continue, but she's been holding this in for far too long. I can tell.

"Dad was a drunkard–the stereotypical 'constant five o'clock shadow' type. Mom hated him for it, but she had her vices, too. Just like everyone else. Cheating, sneaking out …. They were always fighting, growing up. Screaming, yelling, throwing things. Ever since I can remember, I wanted out. They were just so–" she scrunches her hands into claws, her body growing tense, "–abusive. Mostly to each other.

"Then finally this past year, the papers went through, and it was over. I thought things would be better, my life would be more peaceful. I was wrong. Two Christmases this year–every kid's dream, right? Not when you're being told that all the problems in the world are *your* fault, not just once a holiday season, but twice." She chuckles sarcastically. "You know, they almost did deserve each other."

"But you deserved none of that," I insert.

Becca says nothing.

"You didn't. And *none* of that is your fault."

"I know. I know that." Her voice shakes. "Still, when you're told something repeatedly, you start to believe it after a while."

"I know what that's like."

She looks up at me, another drop of melted snow falling down her red cheek and into the corner of her shaky grin. "I know you do. We're the same."

She likes to say that a lot. I don't believe it to be completely accurate. The way I see it, Becca and I are two unique people, molded and characterized by two very different lives. One of our obvious differences is that she's a woman, and I'm a man. A man can never fully understand a woman, and a woman could never understand a man. Perhaps that's why many people spend

202

their lives in pursuit of a partner of the opposite sex. They're drawn to the challenge of uncovering the secrets that make up the elaborate mind of their partner. Secondly, I eat a lot of meat, and Becca is a vegetarian. Well–sometimes. Occasionally, she caves when we order chicken tenders from the local fast food chain. The point is that we're different.

Our lives have been filled with diverse struggles and unique pains, bringing us close to one another. It's almost as if the types and levels of pain you experience in life don't matter. It's just pain, and it hurts everyone the same. Some experience it early, some late. I think that's why Becca believes we're "the same", as she likes to put it. We've both spent more time in the "pain" department than we'd like to admit.

Becca looks back across the frosty road and the footprints along the longer path back home.

"When I'm hurt, I tend to surround myself with things that hurt. The longer I'm out here, the more hurt I'll find." She shrugs and shakes her head. "I guess it justifies the pain, right? Like … if the outside hurts, it's okay for the inside to hurt, too."

Becca hugs her knees. The long black sleeves of her coat jacket cover her arms. Suddenly it dawns on me that I've never seen her wear a short-sleeve shirt. Granted, we met in late October, and it's only gotten colder since. But even then, it makes me wonder … what does she have to hide under those sleeves?

She notices me staring, and pulls at her jacket before continuing.

"You think your problems will disappear when you move off to college. But they just follow you no matter where you go. There's no escape. You learn that all along you were just a fool and that finding peace was a simple-minded fantasy. At the end of the rainbow is just a big dumpster fire of shit called life."

My foot taps the cold ground, both anxiously and purposefully in order to heat my body. This is the part where I'm supposed to comfort her, tell her that she's being pessimistic and her words aren't true. But I can't. As far as I know, she's right.

She hops onto her feet, swiping snow off her behind. "That's why I asked Todd if I could come over tonight."

"I thought you said Todd invited you?"

"No. I lied ... I needed to see you guys." There's a pause, then, "I had to see *you*."

"Me? Why me?"

Becca sarcastically rolls her eyes, as if to say I've asked a stupid question.

"Oh, right ... because we're the same."

A myriad snowflakes, every one of them unique, have fallen. All of them are minute in scale, and grand in effect. We continue our stroll through the city, the eerie feeling of desolation starting to take hold. The roads are empty. The sidewalks are too, save for the snow relentlessly falling on its surface and the two sets of feet that become imprinted there.

It's amazing how people often believe themselves to be so firmly in control of their lives. They have a schedule, and they follow the schedule. They have an exact space in time to fill, and they don't think twice about filling it. But suddenly, a storm passes through, placing everyone's lives on hold. Then nobody thinks twice about *not* filling their space in time. With a gentle shrug, they toss their keys on the counter, whip up a cup of joe, turn on their favorite show, and waste away into the night. They cancel all plans, yet they *still* believe themselves to be in control, when the sky clearly demonstrated the authority it holds over life, completely wrinkling their spaces in time with the natural flow of winter precipitation. Oppositely, I like to think that I have a solid understanding and respect for the lack of control I have.

Seven or eight blocks down, Becca and I approach a tiny brick house facing one of the busiest streets in and out of town. Of course, tonight it remains quiet.

"This is me." Becca jingles her keys.

"Great ... sorry you walked all the way over in the first place."

She pauses for a while, flipping between her keys. She flips and flips through them. That's when I notice there aren't more than three keys on her chain. I swallow, ready for her quiet tone. "What is it about me, Liam?"

I want to pretend like I don't know what she's asking, that I misheard her, or that the stillness of her voice doesn't suddenly cause goosebumps to flare up my arms. But I know exactly what this is about.

"Becca ... we talked about this."

"Answer my question. Don't stammer, and don't bullshit me like you did last time."

I sigh, pinching the corners of my eyes.

"What is it about me that just isn't good enough for you? Am I too short? Not good looking enough? Not blonde? Is it because I've been 'used' too many times–"

"Whoah! Hold up. None of that is even remotely acc–"

"–I told you about my past with guys because I felt comfortable confiding in you. I didn't think you'd use it to judge me."

"I'm not judging. I'm just ... not a cheater. I would never cheat on Rachel–that's not what I'm about."

She looks up, and her eyes bore into mine. "I never asked you to cheat."

"Right," I say. "Just break up with the love of my life. You've been listening to Todd too much."

This forces a laugh from Becca, her eyes tracing the road as it disappears over a hill. "Love of your life..."

"What?" I scoff.

"She's not the love of your life."

"How dare you–"

"The love of your life doesn't make time for you *once* a week."

"Grad school," I shrug. "Keeps her occupied."

"I'm sure the football players do, too."

"Becca." I grit my teeth, and a subtle rage in my voice creates a wall between us, which she knocks down almost immediately.

"I can't help that I love you, Liam ... happy? I *love* you."

I'm literally taken aback by her words, taking a step back with a frown. My jaw opens, nothing coming out. I stammer.

Becca bites her lips down. She leans a shoulder up against the front door of her house, flipping her hair to the side. Facing the road still, she adjusts her glasses but moves them back into the same spot they had already been sitting.

Finally, I say, "Becca I–"

"Don't, stiff. I shouldn't have said that ... I'm sorry." She shoulders closer to her door.

That's when I ease toward her to provide my friend any comfort or consolation I can. I wipe at my running nose. "Rejection is hard, both to give and get. I know."

She sniffles, still looking off to the distance. She starts making tiny snow angels on her front step by swinging her shoes outward, pivoting on her heels.

"You're a great girl. It's why we're so close ... but I'm not the guy for you. I can't be. That doesn't mean you won't find someone. And I'll always be here for you. I promise."

The snowfall stops. The remaining oak tree leaves rustle in the wind. My face has grown numb to the bitter cold. My body shudders.

Becca leans away from her door. She asks timidly, her voice shaky, "Can I have a hug?"

"Hm?"

"A hug. Please ... I need one."

"Um, yeah ... sure."

Unexpectedly, Becca falls heavily into my arms. She lays her head against my chest and sobs. She holds me tighter than I've been held by anyone before. At first, I gently hug back, not realizing that I needed this, too. But then I hold her tight. Becca is a girl I care about. She's one of my best friends, and my spine tingles uncomfortably when I see her sad on my account. If I could give myself to more than one person, I'd give myself to her, just to see her as happy as she deserves to be. But that is not reality. That is why decisions that affect other people are the most vital ones we can make.

When Becca finally releases her grip, she takes a small step back, looking up into my eyes. What I see in hers is what I used to see in the mirror: self-doubt, a desire for reassurance, but above all a desire to be sought after by someone who offers unrequited affection. Maybe she's right. We are the same.

That's when she makes a sudden movement. She stands on the tips of her toes, closing her eyes, leaning her head to the right. She grabs my neck and pulls me into her kiss. I'm too shocked to pull back at first and find myself kissing her too.

What am I doing!

I push her away, just firmly enough to create space between us. As she steps away with a gentle smirk, I stand in wide-eyed shock. So many emotions flood through me, like never before. Anger, surprise, anxiety, and ... something else.

"What the–"

"Goodnight, stiff." She winks.

While I ramble maddeningly, Becca pays me no attention, simply turning to unlock her door, disappearing behind it a moment later.

"...you didn't listen to a word I said. What were you thinking? You could have ruined our friendship, ruined my relationship. Are you MAD?" My words echo off the surface of the white door and vanish into the air, falling upon no one's ears but my own.

She's as stubborn as I am, as unwilling to listen to reason. Every fiber of my body tenses.

Have I just made a huge mistake?

No, I can't be held responsible for what happened. She kissed *me.*

"That girl ..." Staring at the door, I shake my head slowly. I clench my fists, whipping around to take the same path back home, the hard one. Now my heart is beating furiously. I can feel my face redden with rage, so I start running.

It's one of those moments that run through your head constantly, like a country song on repeat. She kissed me, didn't even ask. I couldn't have seen it coming. It can't be my fault. It's not my fault. God, it could be my fault.

Don't mess it up.

"Shut up," I say to the snow that crunches beneath my feet.

The more the moment replays in my head, the more my nails dig into my palms. I'm breathing heavily, vapor rising from my nose and into the sky.

Betrayed by a kiss ... Judas.

It isn't the kiss alone. It could be her stubbornness, her maddening ability to discard all common sense, or it could be Todd. The next time I see him, I'll be sure to give him a piece of my mind. Furthermore, I'm going to have to lie and say I "didn't bloody well enjoy it." That *really* frustrates me.

Just then I feel a buzzing against my thigh, so I pause in the middle of the white-capped street.

"Hello," I say into the phone.

"Liam, where the hell are you? The show's about to start in ten minutes. You told us you'd be here."

I pull the phone from my ear to check the time. "Shit. My bad, sis. I totally forgot."

"Hurry. Rachel and I are waiting here for you."

Alexandra ends the call.

Tonight there is a performance at the campus auditorium that Alexandra repeatedly insisted I attend. Somehow it completely slipped my mind.

I shiver in the middle of the road. Out of habit, I look both ways–left then right. No headlights are coming from either direction. Moonlight reflects off the green street signs, allowing me to gage my position. Hancher auditorium, where the performance is about to take place in fifteen—now fourteen—minutes, is regularly a twenty to twenty-five minute walk from here. If I run, I might be able to cut that in half.

I inhale deeply, feeling the cold air fill my lungs, and inexplicably a boost of energy runs down my back and into my legs as I bound carefully over slick pavement.

XIV

Art and theatre are illustrative of class and culture. They're meant to be accepted with an open mind and open heart so that their interpretation might be received by both. Therefore, silence and elegance are typical attributes of those who gather within Hancher's walls to observe inspirational performances. High-class attire like gowns and tuxedos are standard. Slow and polite are those who greet one another in the lobby before flowing to the auditorium and coming to rest in their respective seats. The majority of the building is white upon entry–the floors, walls, pillars, tables, and stairs. For a building that offers art, one might consider it to be a lifeless setting, even with brilliant lights that shine upon the inside like a thousand stars. One might expect vibrant colors to be thrown marvelously against the walls, or strewn randomly upon the floors, not white. However, the selection of an all-white setting *is* in itself a work of art. A building can only add so much color to a space, anyway. Ultimately, it's up to the *people* to fill it with color.

I barge through the front doors in my jeans and winter jacket. Chest heaving, sweat on my brow, I address the two fashionable young guests near the entrance with a gentle nod. They offer curt smiles before turning toward the white elevated staircase just ahead.

I skirt around them. "Excuse me. Sorry."

Scurrying up the stairs, my hand grabs the rail to keep me from slipping. The gravelly brown snow that has accumulated on my shoes falls off as my feet pound each step, which I regretfully regard with gritted teeth. Another flight of stairs leads me to the entrance to the upper balcony. That's where Alexandra said she'd be … I think.

210

Gosh, my memory sucks.

Just beyond the doors, I hear a faint drumroll and perhaps a number of violins. I open the doors as quietly as I can so as not to disturb anybody. In doing so, the music quickly hits my ears with gusto. The couple nearest the entry gives glances of contempt and condescension as they study me for no more than a second before resting their eyes upon the opening curtains down below.

I scan the rows of the upper balcony quickly, unable to spot either Alexandra or Rachel. I start to wonder if perhaps I'm supposed to be at the lower balcony. One more run-through with my eyes when suddenly I see a hand pop up and down quickly. My eyes dart to it.

Alexandra, sitting in the middle of the center section, nods her head as if to say, *Get over here.* Meanwhile, Rachel is facing forward, adamantly observing the stage.

In the section closest to the door, multiple sets of impatient eyes are fixed on me: that one guy who always has to be late. Ducking as low as I can, I offer my apologies to these folks with a quick wave of my hand. Climbing the stairs, I find the correct row and scoot past many disgruntled guests until I find the open seat next to Alexandra.

I give her a gentle hug.

"Sorry I'm late," I whisper. There are a couple shushes immediately sniped at us.

"It's okay. Now we're even," Alexandra says lowly.

Rachel sits on the other side of my sister in a stunning black dress that makes her curly blonde hair pop brightly. As per usual, her makeup is done perfectly. She looks beautiful.

Just then, a wave of hot guilt washes over me, prompting me to remove my jacket.

Becca.

Suddenly the kiss begins replaying in my head, over and over again. My chest gets tight, heart beating quickly. Have I made a grave mistake? I allowed for it to happen. I *allowed* Becca to kiss me. If Rachel finds out, it could be the end of us.

Jay's words ring. *Don't mess it up. Don't mess it up.*

I lean over, wave and whisper "hello".

Rachel smiles wide, leans in close, and grabs the top of my hand. "Hi, Liam! It's so good to see you. I'm glad you came to be with your sister."

My head cocks sideways at Rachel's tone. It's higher, much brighter than usual. So is her smile. And her eyes … they seem blank.

"Uh … yeah. And to see you."

Another round of shushes are aimed at us. I'm afraid it's three strikes and you're out here, so Rachel politely puts a finger up to her lips and then points to the stage.

Her behavior quickly strikes me as odd. I understand the necessity for short interaction in a moment like this, but something seems noticeably different in her. Reclining in my seat, I shake the idea from my head. Sometimes my mind can be my own worst enemy.

I notice Alexandra's attire–black pants, a collared shirt and tie, and a slim-fitting white jacket. It's an interesting and artistic combination … especially for Alexandra. She usually dresses in colors like gray, blue, and black. Her mind is always so business-oriented. Facts, numbers, equations. That's what she loves, what she believes in, so that's how she expresses herself through clothing. Yet here she is, at a theatre performance, clearly soaking up its beauty by participating in the beauty herself.

I risk a third strike by whispering in her ear. "You look wonderful, sis."

At first her glance questions whether there's sarcasm in the statement, but only sincerity can be detected. Alexandra gives a humble grin before focusing once again on the performance that is now beginning. So I focus on it as well.

212

Not all forms of art suit everyone. Some people are interested in film. Others prefer novels. Some like music or painting or woodwork or theatre. Most everyone likes a unique combination of those. There's nothing wrong with it. Everyone has their own tastes.

I am among those who, for instance, would much rather listen to music, indulge in a film, or lose myself crafting with wood, rope, etc. than look at words all day. You'll never find me sitting down with a novel in hand. As a singer/songwriter I understand the importance of words, but novels are far too long and often too boring for me. Many are fantastical, others simply unreal. And then you have the ones that are *too* real. Those are truly problematic. Find me a novel that's just real enough, illustrating real world consequences with a few theatrical scenes, and perhaps it'll pique my interest for a while.

I'm discovering tonight that theatre may need to be added to both the favorable and unfavorable categories. The music is tremendous. Throughout the First and Second Acts, I'm not sure a single musician makes even the tiniest of mistakes. And the voices ... they're wonderful. I thought I'd always been able to appreciate good singing. I love George Strait and his silky honest voice, Dolly Parton and her classic twang, and Johnny Cash with his low thrumming tunes. But those performing tonight on stage put every one of those icons to shame. Their ranges dive deep through the wooden floors upon which they twirl and leap, and in a quick transition their voices rise all the way to the artful ceiling with interestingly-shaped light fixtures. Their faces, upon which blinding bright lights shine—so bright I'm sure they can't even see the packed house for whom they're performing—mimic every emotion so convincingly. Crying when it hurts, laughing through triumph, and solemnity in conversation all while simultaneously belting out the most complex combinations of lyric and note. It's a spectacle worth seeing and hearing.

With that said, every additional progression through the story procures an uneasiness within me. Each act feels like another large chunk of cement being thrown on my lap, trapping me in position while also crushing me and laboring

213

my breath. The worst part is that I can't really tell why it makes me feel this way. Perhaps all the others are experiencing something similar. The weight of the story is inescapable.

Before the Final Act commences, I glance at Alexandra and Rachel who both appear to be relaxed, snickering at each other's quiet comments. I don't know how they can detach themselves from the story so quickly at each intermission. How don't they feel trapped like me? Suddenly, they quiet. The lights dim, and the curtains are opening for one last time.

Unsettling music begins quietly, with occasional and sudden bursts of intensity. The scene that is revealed immediately repulses me. I don't know if I can stay here. But I must.

At center stage, angled just enough so the crowd can see his face, is a jester in an orange and blue suit. He's bent over, hands tied behind his back with rope, head jutting through a wooden hole, and a basket below his face. The jester breathes heavily, sobbing.

"No, wait! You have to let me go, my queen!"

On the right side of the stage stands a tall woman with a white face in a blackish-gray gown that poofs outward at her hips and falls lavishly to the ground. Her dark black hair is tied in a bun on her head. Behind the queen are a group of men, their chests covered in armor, who subtly tap their feet with the beat of the music. Every one of their faces is stone cold.

"You know what the punishment is for treason, do you not?" The queen speaks with undeniable elegance, a beautiful voice indeed. It's what makes her so dangerous.

At that moment, fog starts creeping lowly across the stage, originating from both left and right. It crawls around bodies, working its way gradually to the center.

In between breaths, the jester says, "I swear to you, my loyalty has never wavered! Your shoes I have shined with delight on my face, my soul has been

214

thrust into the dances I've performed for you. My queen, surely you mustn't question my loyalty."

Dramatic irony is the term for when an audience has knowledge of the story that some of the characters do not. It's often why someone might yell, "Don't go in there!" at a horror movie. At a theater, that type of behavior is acceptable. In a place like this, it is considered to be an egregious assault on the integrity of the performance.

Currently, it's taking every fiber of my body not to scream at the jester from the upper balcony. Surely he must see it–the evil in her eyes, the ways in which she has been deceiving him this whole time. How can he be so blind?

"Oh, but my jester ... you know *exactly* where you've gone wrong." The queen's low voice pierces the room, along with the heightened sound of violins.

At that moment, the stage lights shift left where a woman with the awful name of Gertrude appears on the opposite side of the stage. A female jester in red and white, she sings high and proud.

"My sweet love, do not listen to her. Snakes live in her mouth."

But the jester cannot hear her, as an evil spell has been cast over him–one that does not allow voices of true love to be heard.

My leg starts shaking. I grip the armrests tightly, feeling a shaking coming on in my hands as well. Both Alexandra and Rachel watch intently. Rachel's face shows a hint of a smile, while Alexandra must share my feelings. The horror on her face is evident.

"I assure you, my queen. Wherever you believe me to have gone wrong, I can make up for it! I will. I will, indeed."

"Hmm." From the other end of the stage, the queen observes him with snake-like eyes. "And how do you suppose to do that?"

"For the rest of my life, I will serve you." The jester's words are nearly choked out of him. The weight of his body has been resting on his neck in a wooden trap for too long. He must be suffocating.

215

I feel the need to warn him. He has to know. He has to *know.*

Gertrude puts her hands up to her face, singing loudly. *"My sweet love, do not listen to her! Snakes live in her moouuuuuuth!"*

The music intensifies again, filling the auditorium with sound. The knighted men behind the queen start stomping their feet. My vision begins to waver. In the back of my mind, I can hear a voice.

Liam, are you in there?

For a long pause, the queen measures the jester with her eyes, perhaps wondering of all the ways in which she can abuse and manipulate the poor man down on his knees. The fog reaches the center where everyone has converged besides Gertrude. The gravity of the moment grows and grows with the volume of the orchestra. My eyelids falter.

"Liam, are you in there!" a woman who sounds like Alexandra yells.

When I look to my left, my sister sits on edge, as still as can be.

"A lifetime of service," the queen ponders. "Sounds wonderful."

While the jester bursts into tears of joy and laughter, the music falls, getting softer and softer. Gertrude sings quietly, desperation in her voice. *"My sweet love ... please, do not listen to her. Snakes live in her heaaarrrrrrt."*

The music ceases. The knights tap their feet softly on the stage. Then they stop, too. Deafening silence envelopes the auditorium. Everyone in the audience holds their breath.

"So you'll release me," the jester says with a relieved laugh.

The queen responds, "Indeed I will."

Her stillness unsettles me. Then she takes one provoking step toward the jester, the tap of her heal the only audible sound. And another. The knights follow one-by-one, forming a half-circle around the guillotine as the queen places a gentle hand on the jester's cheek. She says nothing.

"My queen." Concern fills the man's voice. He must finally see what lies beneath those eyes. "No, my queen!"

216

The knights close in, stomping in unison as their circle closes around the jester, concealing every part of him. It's almost like he's no longer there. Then armor clinks as they take a knee. The queen stands tall in the middle of them, her hand on a rope. The upper half of the guillotine is the only other object that can be seen, along with the sharp blade at the top. Gertrude sobs in the left corner of the stage. A low drumroll begins.

No.

Violins, trombones, all working together to gradually rise in volume.

NO!

The queen wraps her hand securely around the rope.

"Liam, are you in there?"

NO, NO, NO!

In a quick flash, the blade drops at the speed of gravity, undoubtedly slicing the jester's head clean off with a loud *thunk.*

"NO!"

A tear forms at my eye. I struggle to breathe. Without realizing I'd risen to my feet, I look around uncomfortably, receiving intense glares in return. There are grunts of annoyance aimed at me, sounds of concern as well. Alexandra looks up to meet my eyes, still seated. She shows understanding. Grabbing my arm, she slowly pulls me back down into my seat.

The queen looks directly up at me with a smile on her face, her arms outstretched, as the massive red curtains shut. A roar of applause ensues.

"You're sure you're okay?" Alexandra gently rubs a hand on my arm, that same look of understanding filling her eyes. We've been together forever, side-by-side. There's nothing I could hide from her, but that doesn't stop me from trying.

"Yeah, yeah. I'm good." The outside of the building shines nearly as brightly as the inside, with its sharp edges and the large glass panes that

217

release light onto the surrounding concrete paths. I turn around to give it one last glance. "The performance was so good ... *so* good. Don't you think?"

"Yeah, it was." Alexandra appears dejected.

"Sorry, I didn't mean to yell."

"Meh, whatever," she chuckles. "Some people thought you were an artistic addition to the act."

Rachel stands just behind my sister, hands folded together in front of her. Her purse dangles back and forth as she gently rocks on her heels. She observes each of the guests departing the auditorium. She's been uncharacteristically shy tonight.

"Rach, um. What are you up to after this?"

Her head snaps to me, those blue eyes still as blank as they were earlier. Checking her wristwatch, she looks up at me and says, "It's already past my bedtime, so I hope I can get my full eight hours in!"

"I could really use a talk right now." I do my best to hide the smirk creeping across my face. *Talk*, at this point, is practically a euphemism for another four-letter word.

Next to Rachel, Alexandra's face quickly shows discomfort, except rather than a disgusted look, she expresses something reminiscent of sorrow. Oddly enough, Rachel mimics her.

"Is everything okay?" Rachel asks, an abundance of concern filling her voice.

"Uh, yeah ... everything is okay. I just figured, you know, we could–"

"Well, if everything is alright, we'll wait 'til Wednesday night, okay?"

Wednesday is always our date night, the only night she has any sort of free time to spend alone with me.

I look down and off to the side. Scratching the area behind my ear, I say, "Sure, yeah. Of course!"

Rachel shivers, nose and ears red. "Brr, Alexandra. It's cold, we should head back."

218

"Agreed." Alexandra rubs her hands together and breathes vapor into them. Her white jacket is camouflaged in the surrounding snow. She approaches me, giving me a hug. Rachel, in her black dress, is right behind her. Alexandra lets go. Rachel's next. For a split second, I can't decide whether I should give her a kiss on the lips or on the cheek. As Rachel approaches, my mind flip-flops between the options. Then with a big smile, she makes the decision for me.

"So good to see you." Rachel gives me a half-second hug, adding, "This semester will be wonderful, even better than the last. I can just tell."

Caught off guard, I stammer in an attempt to reply. Yet I stand speechless. I look to Alexandra. She looks ready to be home and out of the cold.

Before she and Rachel start down the opposite path, Alexandra points to me and says, "Liam, we're running tomorrow. Don't forget. I'm holding you to that New Year's resolution."

I nod with a fabricated smile. "Goodnight, you two."

Alexandra offers a wave, and Rachel has already gone too far to hear me. She must be really cold.

XV

Standing uncomfortably before a set of double doors, I'm rooted like a tree while gym clothes, backpacks, and shaker bottles funnel in and out before me. I'm reminded of what one of Todd's friends said Halloween night. *I wonder if those windows make fat people want to go into the gym or if the jockeys inside scare them from entering.* To be honest, it's not the jockeys in particular who scare me. It's not the fit young women working on their physique, either. Nor is it the ones who are starting fresh on their New Year's resolutions only to give up in two more weeks. It's the uncomfortable truths waiting to spill out of me that inhibit me from entering. But Alexandra needs to know. And quite frankly, those uncomfortable truths are the only reason I'm here. I hate running.

After stretching my neck, I start forward. Meandering through the double doors, I walk a little farther to display a small yellow ID card at the front desk.

"Thanks, enjoy your workout."

I hardly hear the polite young lady over my own thoughts. It's not my intention to ignore her when I walk inside. It just happens.

Upon passing through the spinning chrome gate, my eyes take a moment to marvel at what is nothing short of an architectural masterpiece. I'd forgotten how amazing this facility was–the rec center. I suppose that's because I hardly ever utilized it when I was here the first time. Concrete pillars support the massive levels of the building. There's a smoothie bar to the right, at least twenty filled squat racks extending beyond it by the windows overlooking the nearby street, a pool to the left, then a rock wall stretching all the way up to the ceiling windows of the third floor, and a large gray staircase in the middle.

220

On the second floor, I find elliptical machines, stair-steppers, and treadmills all the same lined up against more windows. The amount of natural light that fills the place really must keep the electrical bill down. At the far end next to a window, brown hair tied in a ponytail bounces above a white shirt. I make my way toward her.

"Thought you weren't going to make it," Alexandra says exasperatedly once I find my way over.

"Almost wish I wouldn't have," I mutter beneath my breath. I turn the machine up a few notches to start at a jogging pace. The sun rising just above the city skyline in the distance is awfully bright. I shield my eyes. "Not the greatest spot for an early-morning run."

"Nobody else … comes to this spot … just how I prefer it."

Keeping an arm up to provide shade to my eyes, I say, "They probably prefer not to be blinded. Running is painful enough as it is."

"The sun … gives me … something to chase," Alexandra says in between breaths.

I tilt my head to the side. "Fair enough."

Increasing my pace, my heart begins racing, but not as much as my mind. I have to make this short, sweet, and to the point. I have to say it. I need it off my chest. Somebody has to know besides me.

I hesitate. Conjuring up the right words has always been a weakness of mine. For several long minutes, Alexandra and I run side-by-side. Although she runs at a much quicker, much steadier pace than I, we remain right next to each other. She's on my right. I'm on her left. Treadmills are frightening in that way. No matter how hard or how fast you run, you end up in exactly the same position as where you began. I look out the window at the streets below. If I were running outside, skirting the tall black streetlights and the masses of early-morning individuals with coffees in hand, I'd be covering more ground, discovering new corners of the city … eluding the truths that aim to sneak up from behind. On the treadmill I feel those truths lurking in the background,

221

crawling on the floor, getting closer, closer. I turn up the treadmill another notch. My heart rate increases, the steady *thumping* like a drum line. Sweat drenches my face. Breathing becomes more difficult. The truths choke me ... or perhaps they aim to relieve.

That's when I blurt in between shaky breaths, "I kissed Becca ... last night ... before I came to Hancher."

Alexandra's head snaps to me. Immediately, she turns off her machine. "What?"

"Technically ... she kissed me ... but I sort of let it happen ... she said she "loves me" ... it was a fiasco ... I've been thinking about it all the time ... had to tell someone ... I feel so bad ... it's–"

"Whoah, whoah, hold it." Alexandra wipes her face with a towel, setting it back on the arm of the treadmill. "That's more words than you've said in your life. Slow down."

As hard as it is revealing my colossal mistake to my own sister, it's even harder to look her in the eye when doing so. I boost my speed up another notch, face forward. "That girl I told you about ... the one who was with me on Halloween ... she's one of my best friends ... you know ... Becca?"

"Right! Her, I remember."

For some reason, I sense a hint of excitement coming from Alexandra. "Stop running!" She reaches over me and presses the red button on my machine. When it slowly comes to a stop, I turn to her, chest heaving, sweat clinging to the gray shirt I not-so-intelligently chose to wear this morning. Inexplicably, Alexandra's face depicts an awfully bright smile, the kind I haven't seen from her in a while–not exactly the type of reaction you expect to get when telling your sister that you practically cheated on her best friend. She says, "Tell me about her."

My brow furrows. "What? No, I don't want to talk about her. I feel awful, I can't stop thinking about it."

"Do you like her?"

222

Perturbed by the question, I repeat, "Do I *like* her?"

"Yeah, do you like Becca?"

I stutter. "Um–uh, sure … as a *friend*."

"That's sweet." Alexandra smirks.

"Alright, enough of the jokes. I'm lost, Alexandra. I don't know what to do, and Rachel … she was acting weird last night. There's no way she could've known, right?"

"I didn't think Rachel was acting weird. Weird, how?"

"You know, like being shy, especially when I talked to her. That's not usually how it goes when we're alone."

Alexandra nods left and right. "Hmm, I think she's dealing with a lot right now."

"Great," I say. "And now she has a cheating boyfriend on top of it all. It would crush her if she found out."

Alexandra struggles to meet my eyes. The constant pounding of nearby treadmills sends small pulses through the ground that feel almost like miniature earthquakes.

"What do I do?" I ask, making my remorse sound as obvious as possible.

Eyes darting back and forth across the ground, Alexandra puts a finger on her chin. Her other hand rests on her hip against her yoga pants. "You said this Becca girl told you that she 'loves you'?"

"Yeah, it was totally uncalled for."

"But you're sure that's what she said?"

"Yes, but Alexandra–"

"I think you should tell Rachel."

I give her a blank stare. Surely I need to find some q-tips to clean out my ears.

"Yeah, you tell her," she repeats after reconsidering her words.

"Are you crazy?" I blurt.

"No, Liam! Honesty is always the best policy. You tell her, and you might be shocked at what she says! I think she'll understand." At this point, Alexandra wears another grin. It's almost like she's doing her best to hide it, but the excitement is overwhelming her. I'm unsure what to make of it.

"I tell her."

"Yes."

"Like, next month, just after school is really underway? No. That's a bad time. Midterms would be even worse. Right before graduation? I can't dump that on her *then*–"

"You do it as soon as possible."

"What do you mean?" I ask.

"I mean as soon as possible! Tonight, even. You should tell Rachel tonight. You can call me after if you need someone to talk to, but I imagine you'll be okay."

The optimism, along with that unwavering smile, I find extremely unsettling. For the first time in my life, I feel as though Alexandra is hiding something from me. There has to be something she isn't saying. I try to look past her eyes, but they're nearly as obscuring and blank as Rachel's had been last night. Although I don't exactly know what "normal" looks like, I can say with complete certainty that this interaction has *not* been that.

"Um ... you're sure." It's a statement more than a question.

"Absolutely. You know I'm here for you." Alexandra leans close to me as if for a hug, considers the sweat on my body, then steps back with a smile. "Ugh, I'm so glad you talked to me about this. We should do this more often."

Yeah ... no, my mind says. But my mouth goes, "Okayyyy."

Alexandra gives me a tap on the shoulder before snagging her towel and jogging toward the staircase with it slung around her neck. She turns the corner, flying down the stairs like it's the beginning of another run. She vanishes out of sight.

Treadmill belts keep zipping around and around beneath nearby feet, elliptical machines spinning, and stair-steppers still going. The world evidently doesn't have time to stop for me.

Frozen on the still treadmill, I put my hands on my hips. "What in the absolute *fuck* was that ..."

A pair of offended eyes glares at me from the elliptical machine just ahead.

"Sorry," I mutter.

XVI

"Mate," is Todd's response when I tell him everything.

Pacing back and forth from the window to the door, both mind and heart run at a million miles an hour while Todd lounges comfortably upon his Australian flag quilt. At first I questioned whether I should confide in him at all. His advice has always been ignorable at best. But as far as guy friends, he's really all I have.

"Wipe that smug look off your face. I already know what you're going to say."

The red bag of potato chips at his side crunches every time he reaches into it.

"Loo'," he says in between bites, "this in't as bad as you think."

I stop and arch my brow at him.

"Alrigh', maybe i' is, but–"

"Exactly, Todd! I'm up a creek without a paddle." I continue pacing.

"Wha'?"

"It means I'm screwed."

"Hmm," Todd munches on more chips. I can see him contemplating something. It can't be anything good, which in all honesty could still be helpful; his suggestions tell me what *not* to do. A devious smile starts, and I don't think it's because he loves potato chips. "You loved i', din't ya?"

I shut my eyes, placing my hand on my temple. I can already feel the headache forming.

226

"Holy shi', you did." He crinkles his bag of chips shut, rolling the top down with a satisfied grin. From his bed, he tosses the bag carelessly into the trash like it's a three-pointer.

"I don't need this right now, Todd. I need to know what I should do."

"Well," he grunts as he hops off his bed. "Julie's picking me up righ' outside, so I'm afraid I can't offa any help, mate. Sorey. You're on you' own for this one." He walks over to the door and begins slipping a pair of shoes onto his feet, then adds, "If I was you, I'd go after Becca, but that's just me."

I stop by the window, watching the sun shine relentlessly upon countless crystals of snow on the sidewalks below. A few flakes are blown sideways, floating across the streets. I turn to Todd as he slips into a thick winter jacket.

"You and Julie … what do you guys do when you're struggling? When you do something wrong, how do you make it right?"

"Shoo'," Todd slides a hand through his messy brown hair and exhales. "I can't say I've eva kissed anotha girl while dating someone, so…"

"Todd," I abandon my post at the window and take a few pleading steps toward him. "Please."

His eyes wander around the room, appearing helpless. Then suddenly he seems to recall something. "Your sis said to tell this Rachel girl, righ'?"

"Yes, but–"

Todd interrupts me with a shrug. "That's wha' you do." Before I can protest, he says, "Got'a run. Good luck!"

The door opens and shuts, and Todd is gone.

I'm left staring at the oily fingerprints left on the wooden frame of the door. I guess the only hand being offered to me now is my own.

Night falls over the town early in the wintertime. Five o'clock, and the world is pitch black. In the hours leading up to this, I continue my subconscious pacing, fiddle frustratingly with my guitar only to produce some of the worst sounds I've heard, and watch the sky's blue color melt to orange

227

and later succumb to darkness. In between all that, I stare at the name on my phone on several occasions just to shut it off and toss it back onto my desk.

Now I sit anxiously on my uncomfortable gray desk chair, chewing at my nails, contemplating the cell phone that sits within the lamp's still beam. The pattern of the wood flows like a river, leading inevitably to the device.

For the past several hours, Jay's unbearably rich voice has been bouncing off the edges of my brain, procuring a headache that feels one step short of a concussion–and I know what those feel like. *Don't mess it up. Don't mess it up.*

What awful advice to give. I can't imagine how I'd do if a man were to come up to me before a performance, slap me on the back side, and say, "There are a lot of people watching. Don't bomb on stage!" *Don't mess it up.* Words of "encouragement" like these almost always ensure failure.

The lamp flickers, enveloping the phone in darkness for a fraction of a moment. A quick look out the window reveals yet another snowstorm. It won't be long, and multiple areas of the city will lose power. Time is running out.

Rocking on the edge of my seat, I lace my fingers at the back of my head. *I have to do it.*

Only a few clicks are necessary, and the phone starts ringing. After a couple tones, the call is terminated. I frown, staring at the screen for a second. Then I try again. Three tones this time before the automated voice comes through. So I try once more…

"Liam, what's up?"

"Rach, we need to talk."

A sigh comes through. "Liam, Wednesday is like two days away. You know how busy I am."

"Yes, yes, I know. But listen, there's something I have to tell you. It's been bothering me all day, and–"

"This can't wait?"

"No."

228

Rachel pauses. She must be able to hear the urgency in my voice. After another sigh, Rachel says softly, "Okay. Meet me beneath the railroad tracks by the library. I'll wait for you there."

"I'll be there right awa–" but before I can finish, the call has been ended. I look curiously at the device resting in my palm. I start to wonder if Alexandra hasn't given Rachel a "heads up", but the thought doesn't dwell for long. Rachel must already be on her way.

In a dash, I throw on a pair of boots, a hoodie, and a jacket overtop to stay warm. Without locking the door behind me, I sprint down the hall.

When winter breezes are absent, snowfall is actually quite beautiful as it turns the city into something from a Hallmark Christmas movie. Traffic is dismal yet again. Crossing the bridge, the only sound I hear is the irregular cracking of ice on the river far below. I realize as I'm admiring nature that time is wasting. Rachel is likely standing beneath the tracks already. She doesn't have time to wait.

I begin tracking across the snow-covered sidewalk with little regard for safety. I need to get there quickly. Between the water-processing plant and another building, there is an alley-wide shortcut. Zipping through it, I find myself on the far end of a massive parking lot, the icy river off to the left, the library on the right beyond the tracks. My eyes follow the railroad tracks that are barely visible in the distance until I see a figure standing patiently beneath the bridge.

Rachel.

I jog across the lot, my footprints interrupting the smooth surface of the snow. Under the railroad, two wide and short tunnels open. Rachel stands in the tunnel on the right. When I'm fifty yards away, she looks up. My chest tightens, my headache returns, and my body begins to freeze. Even from this distance, I can see the apprehension in her eyes. Wearing a white jacket with a large black belt below her sternum, Rachel's hair falls naturally over her hood. She does a double-take, surveying the area around her.

My breath is short once I stand eye-to-eye with her.

"Liam, what's going on?" She sounds more like a general at a debriefing than my girlfriend.

I've been running this scenario through my mind all day. I repeated over and over the words I was going to say to her once the time came. Now that it's here, my mind has gone blank. My pathetic memory has struck again.

"Uh, well ..." After a few stutters, Rachel eyes me uneasily. I look over my shoulder at my footprints being slowly covered by new white flakes. It's too late to turn back now. "Look," I say, meeting her eyes. "There's something important I have to tell you, and it's really tough."

Rachel nods, looking me up and down. Then she turns to look behind her quickly before turning back to me.

"You know I love you."

Rachel remains patient, but she won't be for much longer. I have to get on with it.

"Ugh!" I groan. "This is hard. I just have to say it. I need to say–"

"Liam, what is it?" she says curtly.

"I kissed Becca," I blurt. My hands cover my mouth, frozen along with the rest of my body as I react to my own bluntness with shock. Immediately, I see Rachel's eyes process the hurt and betrayal. She closes them, turning off to the side. "Rachel, I'm so sorry. I was walking her home last night in the storm. She leaned in to me. I wasn't expecting it. I'm still so upset."

She puts up a finger, indicating that I should stop. I swallow, standing up straight. When she opens her eyes, she scans me up and down. Then she looks off to the side, and I can see her contemplating. We stand in mutual silence for a while. I wait for her to speak before saying another word.

"You were with Becca before you met up with Alexandra and I?"

"She wanted to hangout with Todd and I, but–"

230

"Yes ... or no."

I sigh sorrowfully. "Yes."

When it appears that Rachel has no words for me, I try to explain. "I–I talked with Alexandra about it this morning. It was so weird ... it was almost like she–" I frown, trying to capture Rachel's attention. I know she's listening. I just have to keep going. "–she was *glad* I kissed Becca. She said that I should tell you and that ... you'd understand."

Rachel leans against the white wall of the tunnel, shaking her head. She looks at me as though she has something she wants to say ... that she *needs* to say. But she must think better of it, shaking the thought and looking the other way. She looks down at her feet. I can see a tear forming in her eye as her voice wavers.

She mutters something inaudibly, then I hear, "... fault."

"This is my fault, I know." I take a small step closer.

Rachel offers me a confused glance at first. Then after apparently pondering my words as if she's just gained an idea, she wipes the tear from her eye. After a long pause, she evidently comes to a conclusion.

"You have to stop seeing her."

I back up. "What?"

Rachel stands straight. "Becca. I don't *ever* want you to see her again."

"Rachel," my voice pleads. "We discussed this before."

"Yeah, that was when you so eloquently assured me that she was just a *friend*."

"She is! Becca, uh–" I stammer.

"That girl is clearly a problem, Liam!" The anger in Rachel's eyes as she approaches frightens me. I've never seen it before.

"No, Rachel. You don't understand."

"You like her, don't you?"

"No!" my voice cracks. My eyes bounce left and right before a timid response. "No, of course not." I take another small step back.

231

Rachel's eyes bore into my skull for a long and uncomfortable minute. She doesn't appear to be convinced. "You do."

"Listen, Rachel. Becca will not be a problem. I've already scolded her for her intolerable behavior. You have to trust me."

But Rachel is obstinate. "I want you to forget her. Wipe her from your memory. She's nothing but trouble. Forget that you've ever known her, otherwise I'm gone."

"Rachel, no."

"You have a choice to make, Liam." *The exact words Jay used.* "It's either her ... or me."

Don't mess it up.

"Rach, let's talk about this–"

"*Her ... or me.*"

This must be it. This is the decision Jay warned about. I don't know why, but when she said it would be *important*, it didn't cross my mind that the decision would be this hard. Either I abandon Rachel to maintain one of the most unique friendships I've ever formed, or I make things right with the love of my life by completely cutting Becca off. My mind jogs between the options, but not for long. I know the reason I've been given a second chance. I know why I'm here, and I *know* what choice I have to make.

Snow begins falling harder, but it's painfully peaceful. Each flake doesn't make a sound as it comes to rest. I'd almost prefer pounding rain, something loud ... something that would allow me to shout, to scream. But the night is still–I must be also.

I look into Rachel's eyes. In them I see the future. I see Casey's eyes, identical to his mother's. Softly, I say to her, "You're my best friend. I love you."

Rachel stands like a sentry, awaiting my response.

I stare at the white floor of the earth. The words are getting stuck in my throat. My heart feels like a brick in my chest. The most important decisions in life are the hard ones. Once again, I look up at Rachel, the blue rings of her eyes as alluring as ever.

Finally, I say, "You have to let me talk to her … one last time."

With that, Rachel's mouth curls slowly upward. She doesn't say a word, instead looking behind her again before turning back to me. She grabs my jacket, pulling me into a long, passionate kiss.

I'm hesitant to indulge at first, but the power her touch has over me is undeniable. I push her up against the white wall of the tunnel. I kiss her lips, her cheek, moving down to her neck. Inevitably, the unique moan escapes her. It's her tick, one she can't help. In the same way, she is mine. Helplessly I'm drawn to her and forever will be.

Rachel pushes me an inch away, locking me in a visual embrace. "You're my best friend," she says.

Delight fills my voice as I say, "And I choose you."

We kiss some more before Rachel makes another rapid escape, running back in the direction of the library, but not before leaving me with an inviting wink and an air kiss. Both fill me with even more desire.

My smile is short-lived, however, as quickly my delight is replaced with sorrow. I stand beneath the tunnel for another moment, then lean against the wall and sit, cradling my knees. What I have to do won't be easy. Like a band-aid, it'll hurt less the faster I tear it off. But I deserve to hurt. I deserve to feel as awful as I do. I messed up, so I have to make things right.

I shed my jacket, the cold night air immediately attacking everything above my torso. With only a hoodie to protect me, my body will hurt in this weather–justifiably. But I will survive.

Whipping my phone out of my pocket, I dial a number. A woman's low voice answers.

"Hello."

"Becca."

"Yes, Liam."

233

"Meet me under the railroad tracks by the library ... we need to talk."
Before she can ask questions, I terminate the call.

The snow does not quit, and a slight breeze picks up. Off in the distance, mini white tornadoes swirl above the frozen river.

I start rocking back and forth, holding my knees close. My winter jacket quickly accumulates more snow as it sits just beyond the protection that the bridge provides. I take off my gloves, tossing them on top. My body shudders as an aching arises within my bones.

I know Becca. She will be here as soon as possible, but it'd be alright if she waited a while.

XVII

"Stiff, oh my gosh, you look freezing."

Becca Knight approaches carefully from the library side of the tunnel, wearing all black as per usual. The makeup on her face appears as though it's just been done, and her jet-black hair falls straight at her shoulders, just like it had the night we met. That Halloween was unforgettable, filled with memories I'm sure I'll have for the rest of my life. Becca's smile reminds me of the true friend I've met. Anguish in my gut arises, knowing what must be done.

Instead of responding, I continue to rock slowly, facing forward, arms holding my knees tight. I try to focus. I'm at the point where remorse and obligation meet. Looking up, I observe Becca's smile, weakening with every second. She recognizes my silence.

"This is about last night, isn't it?"

I nod.

"I figured." She nods solemnly. Wandering within the protection that the tunnel provides, she begins, "I'll say my life has been filled with regret. Falling for the wrong boys, drug addiction, being born with awful parents … but last night," Becca huffs in amusement, then pauses. "I don't regret that. I'm not making an apology, I hope you know."

"I know." My body aches with the effort it takes to stand after sitting in a hunched position for so long. "But I am."

I expect a sullen response, but Becca's voice rings with subtle glee. "You've come to your senses then."

I tap my foot habitually upon the frozen cement. Without a word, Becca takes an enthusiastic step forward, but what I have to say erects an iron gate

235

between the two of us that will never be taken down. "I don't want to see you anymore."

Her face flattens like she's run into a brick wall. "What?" She quivers, whether because of circumstance or the freezing air I am unable to tell.

Her brown eyes are too innocent, too familiar with pain. I can't look into them any longer, afraid to see further damage. A stiff breeze whirls through the tunnel, causing me to shake. I cross my arms.

"I can't see you. Not anymore."

Becca stands patient and confused, perhaps waiting for me to tell her that this is all an early and somewhat demented April Fool's joke. The truth hits her quickly, however. Wiping the area just below her eye, Becca gives a sarcastic laugh. "You can't? Or you don't want to? Those are two very different things."

My gaze falls. I don't answer her question.

"So, what …" Becca raises her hands on either side before slapping her thighs. "We just pretend not to see each other the next time Todd and Julie want to get together?"

I'd already considered the consequences of ending my friendship with Becca. When you cut ties with one, naturally another one falls in its wake. There will be no more Todd, Julie, Becca, and Liam, a difficult reality to accept. Sometimes in life you have to make important sacrifices to get what you want, and Rachel and Casey mean more to me than any combination of friends, no matter how close they are.

"No pretending. We just won't be seeing each other." My nose has started running. On several occasions I have considered resurrecting my snow-covered jacket and providing warmth to my body once again, but I can't. Not yet. I need to feel the air like a frosty knife cutting at my skin.

At that moment, Becca looks past me, and her eye catches the small black corner of my jacket sticking out of the snow. She eyes me curiously as I stand, shaking. Once more, her eyes bounce to the jacket, back to me, and understanding washes over her.

"She's making you do it, isn't she?"

"No." I say defensively. "It's my choice."

"Uh-huh."

I grit my teeth while my foot keeps tapping.

"And how does that choice make you feel, Liam?" Becca asks testily as she closes the gap between us.

I respond, "It has to be done."

Becca steps away, rubbing two fingers on her temple. She shakes her head. "I'd love to say I don't understand, but I do. Trust me, I do. We *are* the same, after all."

"Stop saying that."

"Saying what?"

"That we're the same."

"Ho, ho!" Becca's hearty laugh echoes off the tunnel as the snow falls harder behind her. "Does it make you uncomfortable? That we're both afraid? We're both cowards? Boy, your cowardice is on full display tonight. Have you ever fought for *anything* in your life? Just once? You know, for a stiff, your spine is *weak*."

"Fuck. You."

Becca cups her ear. "Sorry, what was that?"

"I said ..." but I shake my head defiantly, zipping my mouth shut. I haven't come searching for a feud. I didn't want this to be a confrontation. Coming to this decision was hard enough in itself.

"Exactly," she says satisfactorily. She points an accusing finger at me. "You have nothing to say. You know I'm right, and that bitch is controlling you!"

I bite my lips together, staring at the ground. If I said anything else, it would just add fuel to the fire.

237

The shock in Becca's voice is obvious. "You know what? Fine." Becca slaps her legs finally. "I genuinely hope you're happy with her. Despite all this, you *deserve* to be happy, Liam. I mean that."

The shaking doesn't cease. My foot taps the ground methodically. Remaining silent, and through watery eyes, I offer my best stone-cold expression. Behind Becca, beyond the far side of the tunnel, a little white object bounces along the ground. It catches my eye, so I tilt my head to the side to get a better look.

Is that a ... no, wait.

After mistaking the object for a headdress tumbling through the wind, I blink to realize that a white rabbit instead is hopping along, probably searching hopelessly for a new home somewhere in this concrete jungle.

"What are you looking at? The least you could do is look me in the fucking eye."

Becca's anger has taken over, but I know that there isn't an ounce of true anger in her body. It's the façade she puts on, the mask she wears to hide the turmoil beneath the surface. She's hurt. Her voice is thick with it. And I know all this because she's partially right. We are indeed...

"...the same," she says, her voice shaking. "You'll always be the same."

Before she allows the ensuing tears to be seen, Becca shakes her head in disbelief. Naturally, a desire to comfort her arises within me. I know the pain she feels. I know the sting of rejection all too well. But before I'm given the chance, she whips around, heading back in the direction from which she came.

My heart longs to call out, to ask her to come back for just another moment. But the words are caught in my throat. Soon she's nothing more than a black speck disappearing into a white wintery night.

I lean against the tunnel wall one last time, wrapping myself in the embrace I need.

This isn't how things were supposed to end. It's not how my night was supposed to go. I didn't even get to say ...

"Goodbye," I whisper to myself as the wind settles, and the snowfall quits, leaving me alone with just the cold air, my thoughts, and one forgettable night.

***

XVIII

Black, starless skies are always to blame for sucking the life out of the world below, when in reality, it is the city lights–created by us nonetheless– that obscure the sky's beauty. Only out in the country, where the deer leap and bound across endless grassy fields, where the toads and frogs sing their summer tunes near the water's edge, and where the earth has not yet been trampled by the human foot that the sky can be seen in its true, wonderful form. Strolling the sidewalks tonight, I'm pleased to look up and see anything but small white flecks floating down toward me, even if the constellations are hidden.

Preparing for Spring weather in the Midwest is about as possible as predicting the PowerBall. The average week experiences fluctuations of temperature of up to forty to fifty degrees. Tonight, Mother Nature must have chosen to reward us for braving the frosty elements she'd been casting over the state all winter long, the reward being a still night with temps just above forty. The suit and tie I've donned tonight are enough to keep me comfortable.

Although higher temperatures have arrived, and summer weather is nearly on the brink, a few remnants of the winter season remain. Large muddy piles of snow and leaves sit despairingly in the corners of every parking lot, melting in liquid tendrils that flow down with gravity to the sewers. The white substance is like splotchy acne dotting home lawns and fields, soon to be dispelled by the sun's heat.

On this starless night, my dress shoes click against the sidewalk as I pass a yard where a figure stands within the shadows, frightening me with a start. However, upon a second look, I see that the figure is nothing more than a stack

240

of three large snowballs. What was likely once a tall and proud snowman has now faded and will soon disappear. The pebbles that once formed a smile are falling into a frown, and its stick arms now droop at the snowman's side as it slumps in defeat. It reminds me of a sad memory, sending a pang of guilt through my gut. But soon, much like the snow, the memory will have melted away.

I keep walking. Rachel's place is just a few more blocks down the road.

Not long after messaging Rachel to let her know I've arrived at her apartment complex, she rushes down the stairs, lets me in, and sneaks me back up to her room. This is our ritual, our Wednesday night tradition. Well, every *other* Wednesday now. With graduation fast approaching, Rachel has been consumed with schoolwork and miscellaneous tasks that she assures me are necessary for her to wear the cap and gown in just over a month's time. I remember what it was like to graduate, and I also remember how stressful the time was, so I've more than happily awarded Rachel her space. That's what you do when you love someone.

Rachel's bed sits in the corner, the bright blue comforter on top of it left with a few wrinkles. The mini fridge she keeps near her bed provides a low hum, only heard when the room falls completely quiet.

As the door shuts quietly behind me, Rachel kills the lights. I freeze as the room goes completely black. I can feel her slowly creeping up behind me, the beginning of the game she so often enjoys playing. For an instant, nothing can be heard except the refrigerator. Then her arms sneak between mine. Rachel presses her hands flat against my chest as her chin comes to rest on my shoulder.

"My boy decided to play dress-up tonight," Rachel says, using her low and seductive voice. Each word flows from her mouth like violet–smooth and slow. "How about we play *my* favorite game instead?"

"Mmm, and what would that be?" I inquire.

241

Rachel twists my body around to face her. My eyes have not yet adjusted. All I see is her silhouette, but I can feel her body pressed up against mine. Then her fingers crawl across my chest, unbuttoning my suit jacket.

"Let's play dress down," she says before pulling my blazer off my body. It lands somewhere in the room with a small *thump*. Wrapping her arms around my neck, she jumps, expecting me to catch her, but her feet hit the ground the next second. She pretends it doesn't happen, as we often do when something goes wrong. She presses her lips against mine, but the kisses she offers aren't well reciprocated. Usually, when I show hesitation, Rachel keeps trying until I give in. But tonight is different. Eventually, she pauses, saying softly, "Babe, what's wrong?"

I shrug, attempting to peer into her eyes, but the room is far too dark. Slowly pulling her arms away, I say, "Oh, it's nothing, I–um … can you turn on the lights?"

I feel Rachel's body slip away. A second later, the room comes to life, Rachel standing near the switch. Her brow furrows with concern. "What's wrong?"

"Nothing. Nothing is wrong," I say. My blazer lies awkwardly against the edge of Rachel's bed. Bending over, I pick it up, wiping the wrinkles off before slinging it over my shoulders. "It's just … we kind of tend to do this every Wednesday."

"So …" The confusion has yet to leave her face. "You don't want to do this anymore?"

"It's not that. I–" Looking down at my suit, I look up to Rachel, who wears the same white night gown that she typically wears to bed, and I note the contrast in our apparel. "I have a surprise for you … but we have to go somewhere."

I can already see the hesitation in her face. Rachel and I are far too similar. We're both introverted, don't enjoy risks, and leaving the comfort and warmth of the indoors for even a moment is a risk we both prefer not to take.

242

We would much rather stay in and enjoy one another's company. But tonight I need to get out. I've spent too much time, sitting alone in my room, pondering what my friends have been up to for the past couple of months–the friends I had to abandon. I have to get away.

"Liam, I–" Rachel shakes her head, but I interrupt her first.

"Before you say no, just know it'll be super special."

She gives a skeptical shrug. "I don't know …"

I walk slowly over to her, grabbing her hands in mine. "Please. For me."

"Where are we going?"

"It's a secret," I say, holding back a grin.

"No, Liam. Where do you want to take me?"

"You'll want to dress nice, just for fun. That's all I can say."

Rachel studies my face contemplatively, reluctance undoubtedly ever present. She appears to be considering her options. My heart drops as I see her preparing to let me down easy, say "maybe another time" or something like that. Then with a sigh and forced smile, she says, "Alright."

"Yes?"

"I'll go."

I kiss her joyfully.

"Give me ten minutes, and I'll be ready."

I lay a pleased smirk on her as she shuffles through her closet, searching for the perfect outfit. Not paying me any attention, she sheds her gown, and hops into a spotless pair of khaki jeans and a denim jacket. The tiny mirror hanging on her wall soaks up the perfect reflection of her face as she does her makeup.

After a couple more minutes of bouncing around her room, Rachel turns to me and says nervously, "I think I'm ready."

Rachel's face pales when, from the bottom of the hotel, her eyes climb to the top to gaze uneasily upon green and yellow lights refracted through glass windows.

"I've been told the rooftop is great ... thought I'd take you here."

Rachel does a three-sixty. "Liam I–I don't know."

Taking her hand in mine, I sense a tension within her, evident in the way she shades her eyes. Car tires toss water droplets sideways as they pass.

"What's the matter?"

"Maybe we should go," she says looking off in the direction from which we came, where the streetlights are less frequent and the traffic isn't so heavy.

"Rach," I say gently, while gripping her hand.

"You said you were taking me somewhere special," she protests. "I didn't think you meant *this*."

"It'll be great," I say persistently.

After some coaxing, I manage to convince her that the view from the top of the city skyline is something she cannot miss. I'd always known Rachel was afraid of heights. Getting too high induces the fear of falling, no matter how secure you may be. That's just it. Nobody is truly afraid of heights. They fear falling.

With a quiet *ding*, we reach the top. The doors slide open before us, and we're escorted to a table in the center of the room and away from windows, where the hard and frightening concrete far, far below can't be seen. The ambiance is something truly special. Everything from the dimmed overhead lights to the quiet clinking glasses and even the unblemished white table clothes creates a classic setting. This is what true romance looks like.

Menus are placed before us, and the prices must really worry Rachel. She starts rubbing her thumb with her index finger, something I've noticed she does when she's anxious.

"Babe, don't worry. I've got this."

244

"Hm?" Her eyes dart around the room. Men in suits, silver and gold watches tied around their wrists, drink whiskey, wine, and champagne casually, smiling at their dates across the table who blush and laugh convincingly at their jokes. Perhaps Rachel didn't hear me over their slight murmurs that merge into an inaudible concoction of conversation.

"Don't look at the price," I say.

Rachel nods. Then, while looking uneasily around the room, Rachel rubs her thumb even more quickly. Perhaps she feels intimidated. I've known her to avoid crowds like I do, but I've never seen her like this before.

"What's wrong?" I reach across the table for Rachel's hand, but she pulls back rapidly as I do so. I frown at first, until I notice the ringing cell phone she pulls from her purse.

For a moment she studies the screen. Her eyes bounce up to me, then back to her phone. "I'm sorry, I've really got to take this." Although she phrased it as a statement, Rachel waits awkwardly at the edge of her seat for me to give the "ok".

I offer a wry smile and a nod.

"Thanks," she says, rushing off in the direction of the restrooms, skirting between tables until she disappears from view.

A few pairs of wandering eyes reach curiously across the room, likely hoping to retrieve the scenario from my face. At one of the tables Rachel passed, a woman in a gold sparkling dress turns around in her chair to look excitedly toward me, but when she notices my face isn't riddled with some kind of disappointment, she loses interest and picks at her meal with a fork.

Alone at the table, I feel the constricting tightness of the tie around my neck. I adjust it to perhaps allow for some breathing room. Just then, a waiter with a white towel hanging from his arm approaches. His black hair is gelled back, and his eyes squint beneath his glasses.

"Can I get you a drink, sir?"

I look pointlessly at the menu for a second, already knowing what I need.

245

"Bourbon on the rocks."

"Mmm, alright."

"And for the lady, red wine. Doesn't matter what kind. She's not picky."

"Lady?"

"Yes, she's taking a call."

"Of course," he says politely. "I'll be back."

The smirk on the waiter's face as he turns around tells me I probably should've been more specific. The most expensive alcohol is coming my way. It's okay. I couldn't be less concerned with money, anyway. Money isn't real. It may be perhaps the most disturbing truth of our universe, however. People spend all their lives chasing money, wealth, and fame, all of which are unfulfilling and pointless. And above all they aren't *real*. *Discard all lies this world has to offer, and find the truth.* A voice rings in my head, but I can't remember whose it is.

Find the truth.

I'm reminded of the last note Jay gave me before she disappeared. I haven't seen her in a couple of months now. Can I conclude from her absence that I've already succeeded, or that I'm well on my way to fixing the mistakes I made the first time around? Perhaps she thinks I don't need help anymore. After all, I've got everything I could want.

"For the lady," the waiter pours ruby liquid that swirls into a wine glass until it's a quarter full. "And for the gentleman." A half-full glass of bourbon and ice is then set before me. *Half-full or half-empty?* I suppose the night will decide for me.

"Should I wait for your date to come back before ordering or ...?" the waiter's voice is apprehensive.

"Yes," I say, "but you won't have to wait long. She'll be right back."

The waiter's already-squinty eyes shut completely when he offers a smile. "Alright," he says before working his way to the next table.

246

I stare at the clear brown liquid in which three cubes float seamlessly around the glass, as if my drink were a carousel. It'd be a sin if I were to allow my first sip to be watered down. I take the glass in my hand, swirling the liquid around once more. With it just below my nose, I watch it form a funnel before testing. *Smooth ... definitely expensive.*

A few more minutes pass, and the chair across from me remains empty, the contents in the wine glass as still as ever. An unlit candle in the center of the table has not yet fulfilled its potential to shine bright. My eyes wander subtly around the room, so as not to attract any unwanted attention to myself. I notice that every other table–even the two or three empty ones–all have a lit candle. Granted, some of them are no more than an hour or two from needing a replacement, but at least they're lit. I look once more at my candle, the wax filling the glass halfway but no light to melt it down. Why did they forget mine?

Another sip of bourbon burns down my throat. I love the burn.

"May I ask, sir," a voice appears to my left, "is your lady well?"

The waiter stands patiently with one arm behind his back, the same smile on his squinty face.

"The candle." I point to it. "It needs to be lit."

His eyes grow wide. "Oh, my. I'll be right back."

I wash another taste of bourbon down my throat. Holding the glass up at eye level, I notice it's only a quarter full now–three quarters empty. Each sip leaves me wanting–no–*needing* more.

My head swivels again around the room, observing the content couples who sit joyfully in the presence of one another. A man cuts through his steak as effortlessly as if it were a twelve-ounce slab of butter, but his eyes peek out the corner. He must notice me watching.

So my eyes flutter invariably to the next table, where a woman snaps a crab leg with a deafening *crack*. Before dipping the meat into a small cup of butter, her body freezes. She peeks me out of the corner of her eye. At the next table, no more than a second after looking there, a pair of wide eyes in a suit jacket stare me down as a piece of dripping white meat is suspended in the air by the man's two large fingers. I'm repulsed but can't look away. That's when I notice the terrifying collection of eyes that are set unwaveringly upon me at every God-forsaken table in the room.

Another swig of bourbon empties my glass. The ice cubes rattle inside as I set it firmly on the table, where a small flame now burns at the center.

The waiter's appearance at my side nearly startles me, especially considering the smile that has left his face to be replaced with something grim.

"I'll have another," I say, tapping the empty glass twice with my index finger.

"Sir, I–"

The waiter cuts himself off as a head of curly blonde hair and a denim jacket approaches from the far end of the room. She weaves through the assortment of tables, her head hanging slightly with dismay as though the night has been tampered. Before the waiter says anything, Rachel cautiously approaches her chair, gritting her teeth like she has no intention of sitting.

"Rach–"

"I'm so sorry, I have to go. An emergency came up." Rachel gingerly plucks the purse from her seat, accidentally knocking the table with it as she does so, causing the glass of red wine to stir. But it doesn't fall.

I back my chair up to stand, and the waiter retreats, moving swiftly toward the bar area. I frown in his direction for a moment but then turn back to Rachel as I hop to my feet. She's already started for the door.

"Rach, wait." Rounding the table, I jog lightly to catch up to her. Though I have my sights on the woman fleeing, I can feel the undeniable presence of stares aimed at me, judging. "Rachel." I grab her shoulder, her denim jacket rough against my hand.

She turns around, but begins walking backward, hunched with regret, "I'm sorry, Liam. I just really have to go." Her eyes bounce back and forth across the room, and her growing anxiety is made evident in the way her face reddens.

"Babe, what's going on?"

Instead of answering, she eludes me as she makes for the elevator, pressing the down arrow twice for good measure. She looks anxiously for the light above the steel doors to flash on. Meanwhile, I'm frozen ten feet away, considering whether I should follow or not.

Find the truth. Jay's advice suddenly rings in my head. What does it mean?

A *ding* rattles in my ears, calling me toward the elevator that Rachel has just entered. While the doors begin to shut, I see her crossed arms as she leans against the back wall, her eyes scanning the ceiling. Those blue eyes are the same ones my son will have. A quick impulse forces me to act, so I sprint through the doors right before they close.

"What are you doing?" Rachel asks, appalled.

"I can't just let you go by yourself. Tell me what's up so I can help."

She shakes her head. "This doesn't concern you. I just–I have to go help someone."

"So let me come with you! This is our date night. You know, the one that comes around every other week?"

The elevator begins its rapid descent to the bottom, where we'll find the street. It's a tight space in here, plenty of room for two people, but Rachel looks as though she's suffocating from claustrophobia. Closing her eyes, one leg bounces anxiously. Rachel takes a deep breath and turns to me with a half-hearted smile. "Look, you're just going to have to trust me on this one."

I feel dismay wash over me. "Are you sure I can't at least walk you back to your place?"

"I'll be fine!" Rachel rests a hand on my shoulder. Then with one final *ding* the elevator doors open, our cue to exit. As we walk out side by side, we approach the sidewalk where the two of us stop to face each other. Rachel says, "You head back home. I'm sorry our night had to be cut short."

Before I can say anything, Rachel begins speed-walking in the opposite direction, leaving me frozen in shock. The sound of every step slowly disappears into the night until she turns the corner at the next block. Everything happened so abruptly. I have no idea what to think. A troubling thought arises in my head, but I push it off to the side.

Just then I feel a light tap on my shoulder, which I mistake for a raindrop until I feel the tap again, twice. Perhaps somebody is mistaking me for a rich man based on the suit I'm wearing. I turn around, but no beggar stands at my side. To be honest, I'm not sure why I expected anyone else but...

"Jay."

"Hello, Liam." Her black leather jacket is pulled tightly across her chest, her brilliant red hair falling to her shoulders, but it appears to be more disheveled than usual, with tiny strands sticking out in either direction that would be unnoticeable if she weren't standing so close to me.

"What, uh ... what are you doing here?" I take a small step back to create some space between us.

"Was Rachel just here?" Her sharp eyebrows arch as she pokes her head off to the side. I start to explain that something came up when Jay interrupts me. "Ah, yes. She was just here. Important, important..."

I begin looking uneasily at the vibrant woman before me, biting the inside of my lip. Something seems off about her, even more so than usual. Her blank eyes seem to look past me, through me even. Above that, I have so many questions to ask. It's been months since I've seen her, meaning it's been months since I've been given any notes.

"Where have you been?" I ask.

"Here," she responds placidly.

"Here?" I look at the tall gray building across the street, the hotel to my right. "I've walked down this sidewalk hundreds of times in the past months, and not once have I seen you standing here."

"No, silly. I've been here with you."

The discomfort in me grows exponentially. What is she talking about?

"Always watching, listening," she says as though it isn't creepy. Then she diverts back to Rachel. "The girl … something seems funny." Jay starts to pace in a circle with a finger at her chin. Then she stops, tipping the same finger in my direction. "Don't you think?"

I stare at the ground before her, my face falling into an angry grimace. What is she getting at? Is she trying to mess with my head?

"And Alexandra, too," she continues, "…hiding, hiding something, right? They are, the two of them. Don't you think?"

Mom taught me better than to cuss, except sometimes it's necessary. "What the fuck is wrong with you, Jay?"

Her head cocks. "Wrong? With me?" She bursts into a bout of laughter, but her face hardens a second later. "My problem is you, Liam."

"Me." I roll my eyes, and she starts walking slowly around me.

"So blind to the world around you … so tremendously in denial of the truth. FIND THE TRUTH!" she screams from behind. But I'm stuck in place as she circles me. "Looking back is interesting, important–oh, so important when you *listen carefully*. But you don't listen to the world. Liam listens to you. You listen to Liam."

"Get to the point," I say sternly. Jay stops once she's facing me. She points behind me.

"You don't think something's up?"

"I do. It's your time." I brush past her, softly laying my shoulder into hers as I make for the street corner.

"Why don't you check it out?" she calls just before I cross the street.

251

I stop, closing my eyes as I stand in place, fists clenched, gritting my teeth. I should ignore her, head back, get a good night's rest. She has nothing to offer me. *She's messing with my head!*

A moment from my childhood is called to mind. Our little white house in the country with a one-acre backyard guarded by trees and a maintenance shed pops into my brain. It was summer. I was little. While Dad was working on neighbors' cars in the shed, I would sneak out to a little nook in the back where leaves piled up, and old wooden boards were tossed to decay. The area was surrounded by trees. It was my own little hideout–well, mine and the family of rabbits I fostered there. "Rabbits are scoundrels, runts, pests," my dad would say before he knew about this. "They damage your mother's garden. You know what happens to pests around here, LJ?" James is my middle name, so Dad often called me LJ. "They die," I said. But when I saw those baby rabbits huddled in the corner of that shed, instinct called me to protect them, not hurt them. Eventually, late one summer day, my dad finished his work in the shed early. I didn't know. When he noticed I wasn't in the house, he came looking for me, and not only did he stumble upon his son, but also the *runts* he demanded we dispose. I cried when he smashed the bodies of all those babies; the crunches and squeals they made were nearly unbearable. "Inevitably drawn to conflict," my dad scolded as he dragged me and my tear-soaked face back to the house. "When will you learn?"

He was right. I *am* drawn to conflict … especially when I know the consequences have great and dire potential.

"Check what out?" I turn around to scowl at Jay.

A pleased smirk crosses her face as she takes slow, but confident steps toward me. "You don't think you should at least make sure Rachel is okay? Isn't that your duty? Isn't that the promise you made to her when you said '…in sickness, and in health…forever and ever'?"

"I trust her."

"I've never questioned your trust, Liam ..." her eyes flash with something unfamiliar to me. She says, "–but neither have you."

At this moment, I feel a migraine coming quickly. So many voices telling me what to do, pulling this way and that. *Go home! No, follow her. Listen carefully. FIND THE TRUTH!* Rubbing my temple, I close my eyes. I stare deeply into the blackness they provide, hoping some kind of vision will guide me. But the voices keep yelling over each other. A few deep breaths should quiet them. After a minute of quick meditation, the migraine subsides. The voices quiet. Breathing in, then out, I open my eyes.

"Jay?" I ask uncertainly. My head swivels. "Jay?" I call again, but my voice falls upon nobody's ears, instead echoing off the buildings to my left and right. She's gone.

A car honks in the distance, and tires whir upon the moistened streets as a mist begins falling from the sky. I look up. The water droplets are imperceptible, except when falling within the constant beam of corner streetlights–and when they land directly in my eyes. However, even though the annoying precipitation pesters me as I gaze at the sky, something remarkable appears off in the distance that holds my head up for just a moment longer–a star. Without surrounding stars for reference, I can't confirm whether this is the North Star, Mars, Venus, or just an unidentified ball of gas and light somewhere in the universe. Regardless, it aims to tell me something, I'm sure of it. I ponder what it could be, staring at the ground as a few beads of water drip from the top of my head all the way to the sidewalk below–all without a sound.

I think of the times Alexandra and I used to go star-gazing when we were kids. It was so easy when we lived far away from bright lights and loud noises. Living in the country, the sky was always open. There wasn't anything to get in its way–no skyscrapers, no bright neon signs, nothing. My sister and I used to play this game where she would have me close my eyes and count to twenty, and she would run and hide somewhere on our property. But before

253

she hid, she would leave me with a clue, like "The Big Dipper" or "Orion's Belt" or any other constellation. This is how she taught them to me. After counting to fifteen, not twenty, I would search madly across the sky, and when I found the collection of stars I was looking for, I'd bolt in that direction. Sure enough, Alexandra would sit somewhere below the stars, usually on the other side of a tree. I'd laugh joyfully when I found her, but I was nearly brought to tears when I didn't.

Then it dawns on me. I look up once more to view the single shining orb hanging midway in the sky. I get it. I now understand. The star appears to be shining directly above Rachel's apartment.

XIX

Crawling anxiously ever closer to the door, I feel dirty, the stain of guilt marring my conscience. Trust is hard to come by in this world because by nature, its existence is fleeting. An entire lifetime can be dedicated to building and earning one's trust, perhaps with little to no success, but all it takes is one moment—one single instant—to decimate the foundation of that trust, thereby toppling every laborious building block of a relationship in the process.

Yet here I am, standing beneath the red cloth awning that covers the entrance to Rachel's apartment ... risking Rachel's trust. She told me to go home, to leave her alone, but to me that was the same as giving up, something I'll never do—not again. *Inevitably drawn to conflict.* That I am.

Rainwater falls off the awning's corners, slapping the cement below. The entrance to the apartment is locked from the inside. The only way in is with a key or by having someone open the door, neither of which are available to me at the moment. I've rung Rachel's cell at least three, maybe four times—each one taking me directly to voicemail: "Hi, this is Rachel! Sorry I couldn't answer your call, just leave me one at the ding!" Groaning, I rest my back against the building and watch the falling rain pound the streets, forming puddles that flow along the curbs. Maybe I should have gone home. I should have listened to her. Rachel knows what's best.

I think of the relationship she and I have built together. From our first meeting at The Pub, to our first kiss by the river, to our first time in bed, and all other first's we've experienced with each other. It's been incredible to relive these wonderful moments. Trust, something Rachel has repeatedly asked me to give. It's not something that comes easily to me, but I've given her all that I can. Then I recall what Jay said—"I've never questioned your trust … but neither have you." What did she mean by that? Her riddles frustrate me.

Just then, a rattling noise draws my attention. As the front door opens, a frail old woman walks out, descending the stairs with caution. My hand catches the handle just before it closes, and I rush inside.

Up two flights of stairs, I turn a corner. The musky smell contained within the walls of the building hits me pleasantly every time, primarily due to the memories attached to it. Otherwise, I'd find the scent bothersome. At the end of a short hallway with two doors on each side is a golden number "12" screwed unevenly into Rachel's door, the tan welcome mat on the floor recently soaked.

Hesitantly my knuckles approach the thin wood. I question whether I should be here or turn around, but I remind myself that Rachel could be in trouble. She needs me right now. After two solid knocks but no answer, I turn the knob, expecting it to be locked. Miraculously, it's open. Swinging the door slowly on its hinges, my first cautious step produces a small *thud* on the hardwood floor, followed by a creaking noise. All lights are turned off in the living space to the right, only the feeble beam under the microwave to the left providing the room with illumination. More cautious steps lead me forward, past the kitchen. *Thud, creak. Thud, creak.* The television is off, the couches empty. Nobody dines at the table.

"Damn," I mutter to myself. The place is empty.

Frustrated, I walk over to the sink, bowing my head and brushing off the droplets of water that have clung to my hair. *Where could she have gone?* I wonder. I remember she told me that there was an emergency. Was someone else in trouble? Could they be hurt? She said it was an emergency. My mind wanders until it falls upon … *Alexandra*. My heart sinks.

Scrambling to pull the phone from my damp pocket, I wipe off the screen with a dish towel, frantically dialing my sister's number. Each ring buzzes in my ear, increasing the tension in my fingers. Then, on the last ring, I hear …

"Hello?"

"Alexandra, where are you?"

The urgency in my voice prompts her to hesitate. "Um ... home studying. Why?"

"Are you okay?"

"Yes, I'm okay ... are you?"

"I'm great. You–you're not in trouble?"

"I'm fine, Liam," she exhales with a laugh.

"Oh," the weight in my chest disappears. I apologize to Alexandra and say, "I just had to make sure you were alright."

"I am alright. How's your night with Rachel going?"

"Well ..." I trail off.

"What's wrong?"

"I don't really know where she is. I'm at her apartment right now, but–"

"She's not there?"

"Nobody's here."

"How did you get in?" Alexandra wonders.

At that moment, I hear a faint noise coming from the hallway past the kitchen.

"Liam, are you there?"

"Yeah, sorry, sis. I've got to go." Hanging up the phone, I stow it immediately back in my pocket. Frozen in a trance, I wait to hear the noise again. It almost sounded like a scream, a call for help. Suddenly, I hear it once more.

Definitely a scream.

Inching closer to the hallway that is currently nothing but a black abyss just a few feet before me, I listen with a newfound level of intent, but all I hear are my slow and steady footsteps. *Thud ... creak. Thud ... creak.* That's when a bone-chilling *bang* hits a wall, followed by a much louder scream that undoubtedly comes from Rachel.

My eyes widen. "She's in trouble."

I start for the hallway where her room can be found, but quickly it dawns on me that I have nothing with which to protect myself, meaning also that I have nothing with which to protect Rachel. My eyes move quickly, scanning the kitchen area. Hanging pots and pans … *no, those won't work.*

Another *bang* and a scream penetrates the walls, sending chills down my spine. I have to act quickly. My heart races, and I search the kitchen area faster, opening drawers and raiding cabinets when a large wooden block secluded in a dark corner catches my eye.

Knives.

I stare tentatively at the large meat-cutter. Violence is something I've always avoided. God never intended men to use violence, yet he gave us the necessary ability to use it in order to affect justice. Someone is hurting my Rachel, my love. There has been no better time than now for violence.

I yank the knife from the set.

Bang. "Ow, God!"

The scream comes even louder. I dart to the sound, into the hallway, all the way down until I find Rachel's door–locked. I rattle the knob a few times, but to no avail. I lean my ear close to the door. I can hear her struggling. She needs me, *now.*

Bang. "Oh!" Rachel gives a subtle cry.

My grip on the knife handle tightens. I close my eyes, take a few breaths, and with all the courage I can muster, I kick the door, smashing the lock in the process.

Rushing in, I yell, "Let her go!" But the scene is nothing like what I expected. It's much more horrifying. I freeze. "Rachel?"

Perched on top of another body, Rachel covers her breasts in shock, her blonde hair a crazy mess on her head. Two sets of familiar eyes stare at me, not as though I'm a hero, but rather a monster. The combative, athletic stance I entered with slowly disappears until I stand straight, dropping the knife on the floor. It clatters and comes to rest a second later.

"Liam, what are you doing here? I told you we weren't meeting tonight!"

My eyes bounce from Rachel to the dark and naked man lying on the bed beneath her. I recognize him. I know this man all too well. My lips don't have the courage to speak what my mind is thinking. *Marcus?*

Rachel scrambles for the comforter to cover herself. "Liam, get out of here!"

For another second, I stare in shock and horror. *Marcus?* I ask myself again. Another uncomfortable moment passes until I back away slowly, taking one last look at reality. I scoff internally, thinking I must be hallucinating. I didn't think I drank *that* much tonight. Helplessly, I stare at the couple: Marcus and Rachel, both naked.

"Liam, get *out!*"

I give one last glance at Rachel before I bolt out the door, down the hallway, sprinting down the stairs, and out into the pouring rain. My feet pound firmly against the ground, hoping the Earth's floor might give way and send me into the fiery furnace of Hell. That's the type of pain I might find justifiable.

I run into the middle of the street, the storm coming down harder than before, soaking my clothes.

"NO! *Why!*" I scream at the sky. My eyes search to find the gleaming star that betrayed me, but the rain is coming down too hard and fast. So I run. Aimlessly, I sprint through the streets, searching for somewhere to numb the pain, to drown myself in misery.

Inevitably drawn to conflict.

Cars swerve around me, honking madly. But I don't care. I can only hope that one of these times a pair of headlights meet me head on, taking me to a different life where pain isn't my only destiny and where happiness can finally be found.

I keep running and running, desperate to escape somehow. As I slow onto the Burlington bridge, the awful image of Rachel on top of Marcus flashes in my eyes. It's far too much for my heart and mind to take. I fight the tears, knowing that grown men don't cry. That's what Dad always told me. But the pain is too much, it's unbearable. Besides, the rain will obscure the truth.

"Oh, God." Letting out a sob, I stop and bend over on top of a white stripe in the middle of Burlington. "Why do you hate me? Why do you do this to me?"

Lightning strikes in the clouds above, giving me hope. Maybe a flash of a hundred thousand volts can fulfill me with enough hurt to justify this life. Then another flash, the following thunder like a distant pounding.

Honking car horns speed past me, but even their deafening blows cannot drown out the voices in my head. *Liam, what are you doing here? I told you we weren't meeting tonight!* Rachel's voice bounces around in my head, and I can't avoid it. *Get out of here!*

In this second life, I didn't think I'd need a *taken* world. My life was supposed to work out just the way I had planned. Yet now more than ever, I need to escape, to go somewhere else. I open my eyes to the distant sight of red taillights, blurred by the pouring rain. Another lightning strike makes the world bright for a split second, the thunder this time sounding off in three distinct *booms*.

Liam are you in there?

Taking a deep breath, I slow time down. I feel the humid air filling my lungs. *Breath in ... out.* I ignore the showering sky. Shutting my eyes, I summon the environment I need. I imagine myself on stage, a guitar in my hands, bright lights on my body. Suddenly the horns dissipate, and the thunder quiets until my breathing is all I hear. A low hum should do. The words are sung in my head and suppressed in my throat before they gain power and are then thrown outward by my trembling voice.

260

Though the sun may rise upon this town,
A broken man don't feel no joy.
As Conway Twitty, I used to 'Lay You Down',
"But without you, girl, I remain…
A Mourning Cowboy."

"I didn't think cowboys dressed in suits and ties." The low feminine voice in the distance sucks me back into the pouring rain. Thunder knocks three times, reverberating through the clouds.

"You." I growl, staring at the head of red hair near the edge of the bridge. She leans casually against the rail under a flickering light. At the sight of the woman, an intolerable anger blossoms in my chest. *It'd be a shame if she were to fall down, down, down into the river.*

I stand slowly, scowling. With no concern for oncoming traffic, I prowl to the other side, regarding Jay with cold eyes. Lightning flashes. *Boom, boom, boom.*

Vaulting over the three foot wall separating the road from the sidewalk, I stand menacingly before Jay's smug face, my hands balled into fists at my side.

"This … is all. Your. Fault."

She appears to ponder my words as though they're entertaining, saying, "Debatable."

Through gritted teeth, I say, "If I was a lesser man, I'd–"

"You'd what?" Jay challenges.

My body tenses for a moment, but I shake my head and let my chin fall to my chest. I can only cover up my hurt with anger for so long. Water drips relentlessly off my head and down my neck. I blink a few tears from my eyes.

261

Jay walks over, placing a hand on my shoulder. She says nothing. Though her presence irritates me, I'm surprisingly glad I'm not alone. Then her voice breaks the silence.

"Say it."

I look up to meet her eyes. The green I see in them is nearly as brilliant as the scarlet in her hair. Wiping just below my nose, I look off to the right, watching the banks of the muddy river rise quickly. I can see the current picking up as small and large branches alike are swept up.

"What am I supposed to say?" I ask, my eyes intent on the waves.

"You're not *supposed* to say anything." She pauses. "Tell me what you *need* to say."

I struggle to look at her, my breath shaky, my vision blurred. "You set me up," I say with as much conviction as I can muster. I expect a defensive response, but Jay appears to be patiently awaiting a barrage of insult and accusation. So I continue, "From your ivory tower, you've been watching me run a little rat race through which you, the conductor, have led me. With your little notes, you made sure I'd end up exactly where I am now–exactly where I was before. You didn't want me to succeed! No, you received a sick pleasure from watching me struggle. That's what this is." I think back to the opera night with my sister and Rachel, the way Rachel acted at the restaurant tonight, and how she's been asking for more space. "Rachel ... she's been acting weird for a while. That's because of you, isn't it? I–I knew something was up, but I couldn't accept it. I wouldn't. And Alexandra–my own sister–she's in on it isn't she? My *own* sister! You managed to corrupt her, you disturbing witch, you, you–"

"That's enough," Jay says calmly. Though I can tell she senses the obvious rage in my voice, she measures me with a soft expression, wiping a raindrop from my cheek. "Do you think that's true, that I haven't been here to help you?"

"It has to be, it's the only explanation. I–"

"Liam." Her still voice is confronting. "Is it the truth?"

I try to maintain my posture, holding my ground. I need somewhere to place the blame. If it's not on her, then it's on …

"No," my head falls. "That's not the truth." I wipe my eyes with both hands. I shake my head and pause for a moment. "But I don't know what *is*."

Lighting strikes once more, and in the ensuing thunder–coming again in three *boom*s–I hear a voice.

Liam, are you in there?

I look up, but the rain stings. Once again, I close my eyes.

However, as I do so, I'm pulled fiercely into a hug. It's a strange embrace, coming from Jay, but she offers the comfort I need. So I shut my eyes, resting my chin on her shoulder.

"I know how bad this hurts," she says, "and I hate to see you like this …"

Suddenly, she abandons the hug, and I feel a tug on my suit jacket. Looking down, I see Jay's hands grasping me firmly. I witness an odd determination in her eyes as she pulls me close, seemingly for leverage.

"… but maybe it's time for you to–" she grunts, lifting me off the ground, and in one swift motion tossing me over the edge of the bridge. "*–find* the truth."

I fall toward the current in slow motion, my arms flailing above me as Jay observes me from the bridge far above. I'm too shocked to scream, too stunned to move or cry or pray, instead just falling inevitably to a watery grave.

They say that when you die your life is supposed to flash before your eyes. But all that flashes before me are massive pulses of electricity shooting across the sky, rainwater falling alongside me, and a woman leaning over a bridge. Next to her, I think I see a little boy in blue, then …

SMACK.

My body hits the water, and I'm immediately pulled down by the current. I struggle to swim to the surface. What feels like two hands tugging at my ankles keeps me down. I fight and fight for my life, thrashing underwater for as long as I can when suddenly I ask myself, *What's the point?* My body grows still. I'm not sure whether I'm looking left or right, up or down. No matter, a sea of darkness infiltrates my eyes, literally. I have no more tears to cry, no more breath to hold, and no more life to live. With closed eyes, I accept my fate and allow the muddy water to fill my lungs as I descend into a dark and suffocating oblivion.

XX

The door has just slammed shut. The bearded half-face in the mirror warned me. He said, "Step back!", but I wasn't quick enough. The cries, the hum, they've both been hushed, perhaps blocked by the wooden surface. The enclosed space keeps closing in, the ceiling dropping, the walls moving in faster. It's eerily quiet.

My eyes search frantically. The vent, the drain, both spaces too tight for an exit. My hands grasp the corners of the white granite. I want to bend over and vomit, but the bearded face, now full, stares back at me with wild eyes.

"FIND THE TRUTH!" he says, almost as though a time bomb will continue to tick unless I heed his commands. "It's your only escape."

"Where is it? What do I do?" But suddenly the bearded man disappears, a look of horror the last image to leave the mirror. "Dammit!" A fist slams the center, sending a spider web across the surface, dark red liquid oddly flowing horizontally toward the right edge, not down with gravity.

Then the lights cut off. The only sound to be heard is the delayed thumping that erupts from my chest. I stand still in the darkness, half expecting to be consumed by it. I know it's here. It wants to destroy me. But where is it?

Suddenly, a small flashing red light rides up the wall just to the right. It blinks, unsettling me, its source coming from near the ground. I lean over to discover that whatever is producing the flashing light is sitting at the base of a small canister, hidden beneath tissues and crumpled papers. My foot doesn't make a sound as I step over to the canister and sit on my haunches to examine the light closer.

"This must be it," I say, watching the red light penetrate the white tissues. "The truth."

Plucking the tissues one-by-one, I pitch them behind me. My heart begins to race. Thump, thump. *The closer I get to the light, the more I hear the hum, and the cries ring back into existence, too. I hear them more clearly this time: a mother and a baby. Why do they cry?*

"Don't cry," I say.

In spite of my plea, the cries grow in intensity, bouncing off the walls and shaking the Earth's foundation. Somewhere to my left and right, metal objects rattle. Though they are loud, they cannot distract me.

Pulling the last obstruction from the canister—a bloody tissue—the flashing object is revealed to me. My eyes don't recognize it ... or maybe they don't want to. Either way, I need a closer look.

A trembling hand reaches in for the object. It's small, about the length of a pen but wider, more rectangular, with a tiny centimeter-long screen. I lift it before my eyes and notice that the light isn't red at all ... it's pink. I squint. Rather, two pink lights.

"My God."

Then, as if the cries were being absorbed by the pounding in my chest, the voices of mother and child vanish and become silent. The world shakes violently, growing more intense with every second. The lights flicker on and off, and I stand wide, bracing for anything. I can feel this world on the brink of collapse when suddenly the shaking stops. The low hum disappears, and the beating in my chest can no longer be heard. The walls retreat, the ceiling rises, the mirror repairs itself, and the lights flash on as though they had never failed. This feeling is uncomfortable, like my intestines are being ripped out as I'm thrown inevitably into ... reality.

Standing before the mirror with the object resting in both hands, I look upon the blonde-bearded face before me. It's mine. My eyes are red, bloodshot. Distantly in the reflection, there is an open doorway, where a thirty-year old blonde woman faces me, teary-eyed and panicked.

"What is this?" I turn, the stern words leaving my mouth as I hold up the object.

"It's nothing," she says, wiping the corner of her eye. She wanders away from the door.

"It doesn't look like nothing." Taking a step closer to my wife, I feel the weight of the ring on my left hand, heavier now than ever before.

Her lips seal; she appears distraught.

"When were you planning on telling me?"

The woman, with a palm across her forehead and a hand on her hip, walks to the bed and comes to rest on the edge. "Oh my God." She plugs her face in her hands, muffling the following words. "How did I let it get this far?"

"Rachel." I step closer to her, and her voice bursts with intensity.

"Liam, it's *nothing*!"

I step back, surprised. Rarely does Rachel raise her voice like that. Warily, I say, "You're pregnant, Rachel ... *we're* pregnant."

"You're not listening," she says.

My brow furrows. "What are you talking about?"

I don't know where the memory comes from, but it rolls through my mind anyway. A dark image enters where I feel Rachel's body on mine. Tucked beneath the covers, we made love. It was after our wedding. I suddenly remember that we had eloped. That's what Rachel wanted. Nobody was there but us, not even a priest. The marriage was performed by us, for us, and the promise we made to God and each other was forever. It was an evening wedding, I think on a Wednesday, at home: our apartment. But it doesn't matter. All days and all places are the same. We're all under God's roof.

Glancing at the two pink lines once more, I realize this must have been the result of that night.

"How long have you known?"

She shrugs, turning around to look out the window, even though it's night and the sky is dark.

I say, "This is no time to watch birds fly, Rachel. *Talk* to me."

Her blue eyes struggle to meet mine. "I've known for a while, but Liam–"

"Stop, stop." I pause, taking a deep breath. This is no time to be confrontational. I move slowly toward the bed to take a seat beside Rachel. She sniffles, staring at the ground. Taking her hand in mine, I say, "Rach … no matter what it is, we do it together. Remember?" Her eyes move silently across the floor, so I continue. "This is nothing to be ashamed of; this is wonderful. I'm happy for us–"

Rachel shakes off my hand, getting up and moving toward the wall, her chin falling to her chest. She sniffles again. "You don't listen, Liam."

"Then talk to me!" I stand but keep my distance. For some reason, it appears that Rachel doesn't want me near her right now. Perhaps she's embarrassed. I stare at her back for a long moment, but she says nothing. Exhaling through my nose, I shake my head. "What are we going to do?"

She mumbles something that I can't hear.

"What?"

"I said I took *care* of it already." Rachel whips around to face me, mascara trailing down her face.

"You took care of it? What does that mean?"

"It means *that*," she points at the test in my hands, "is *nothing*, like I said."

I try unsuccessfully to understand her cryptic stare. Why doesn't she just tell me what she's trying to say instead of beating around the bush? Is the truth too hard for her?

Then a look of awful understanding sweeps over me. *It's nothing.* My eyes rise from the ground to meet Rachel's hoping she might deny what I already know to be true, but instead the grimness of her posture confirms it. "Rachel, you don't mean ..."

She nods slowly.

"My God." My hands roll through my hair, an exasperated sigh escaping me. I groan, staring at the ceiling. "My *God*." I scrunch my body overtop the bed, suddenly feeling the urge to retch. I grasp the small object tightly. Lifting my head sideways, I look her in the eyes. "Rachel you didn't, y-you wouldn't!"

At this point, tears are streaming madly down her face. With her sleeve, she wipes at her nose, and her eyes hesitate to fall upon me. She seems to stare mournfully upon the object in my hand. After a minute of standing there, she shakes her head and bolts out the bedroom door.

"Rach, wait!"

Her footsteps on the stained-wood floor are rapid and powerful. When I turn the corner, I see her struggling to slip a shoe onto her right foot, probably unable to see through the tears obscuring her sight.

"Where are you going?"

Her hair falls to the side as she faces me for a long, uncomfortable moment. The pain in her eyes hurts me, but I can't wipe the horror off my face. I can't believe she's done this. There's no way she could've killed our child, not our baby! *What's going on?* I ask myself. It appears as though Rachel is attempting to answer, but with one last sob she flies out the door, slamming it behind her.

I take a step after her with an outstretched arm when I'm stopped suddenly by a voice behind me.

"Don't."

I freeze, eyes wandering the floor before me. I look to one of the framed pictures hanging on the wall and notice a figure in its glossy reflection. Slowly, I turn around.

269

Leaning comfortably against the island countertop is a woman with her feet crossed, her elbows supporting her as her fingers lace together. "Everything you need is right here," she says in a calm and low voice. "No need to chase."

I cock my head confusedly at the woman, but a flurry of memories suddenly wash over me. *The bridge.* My right hand pats my chest, suddenly recalling the river that had invaded my lungs. Looking up to the woman, my voice turns cold. "You have some nerve to show up at *my* home after throwing me off a fucking bridge."

"Look around," she says, ignoring me. "It's all here before you, Liam."

"For once, could you speak like a normal person?" I say defiantly, yet curiously looking around. *It's here before me ... what? Where?*

"Come on," she laughs heartily. "College, your friends, Becca, Rachel, and now this ... don't you see it? You must understand by now." She studies my face, and her smile fades. "By God, you don't understand."

"Just tell me what the hell is happening!" I shout. "I'm tired of the mind games."

This summons another bellow from the red-haired woman. "The mind games," she says as her heels click against the floor, taking two steps toward me, "are the only reason you're here. But not for long. It's about time you let them go."

Just then, three raps on the door capture my attention. My first instinct tells me Rachel must have come back to talk it out, but I look back to Jay who nods toward the sound with a satisfied grin. She mouths the words *listen carefully.*

"Liam ... Liam, are you in there?"

I start toward the front door but freeze after one step. The voice I hear isn't Rachel's at all. Rather it's ...

"...Alexandra," comes the sobbing voice of my sister from beyond the door. "Brother, if you can hear me, I love you. We're worried about you.

270

Please, please tell me you're okay. I need to hear your voice ..." she trails off with another cry. "Please, God."

I look expectantly at Jay. Again, I pat my own chest. It's not as tight and muscular as it had been–clearly no longer the body of a teen. "What is she talking about? I'm fine. I'm right here."

Jay measures me with sudden compassion, swallowing, almost like she knows her next words will be hard to bare. "I've been trying to tell you ..."

"Tell me what?" I swallow. "Tell me what?"

"Liam ..." comes another desperate call before Alexandra's voice fades into the background.

"All of this–" Jay motions to nothing in particular, pointing vaguely at the room around us, "–you have to let it go."

I shift my weight uncomfortably, letting out a stutter. "I–I don't understand."

Jay walks over to a photo of Rachel and I sitting on the counter. She picks it up and examines it. "For too long, you've put your energy into ignoring the past, denying it even. Yet now, it's caught up with you, Liam." She pauses for a moment. "At some point, you have to live in the present. You cannot let your past own you. You have to let it go."

Those words sound familiar. Staring blankly upon the floor, I whisper to myself, "I've heard that before."

"Liam, please ..."

Jay sets the photo back down. "You can hear her. Don't ignore your sister."

"I'm not!"

"Then go to her," Jay commands.

I go to turn toward the door, but suddenly I find myself paralyzed. The world seems to spin around me, and I feel my body forced into a squat. Sitting in a gray office chair in the center of the room, I have no bounds rendering me

271

immobile, but I cannot move. I have no idea how the chair got here or how I ended up in it.

"Wh–what's going on?"

Jay moves gracefully closer to me. "Do you think you can change the past?"

I grunt in an attempt to escape the chair. "Let me out of this! Ugh!"

"Answer my question," she says with a blank face.

I struggle for a moment more before conceding to her. With a sigh, I say, "I–I don't know where you're going with this."

Leaning close to my face, Jay whispers, "Then let me explain." She backs away and paces like she does. "First, let me ask why you think you're here, and–" she points to herself, "–why you think I'm here."

My head falls back against the headrest. "Here we go."

"Liam," she says sternly. "Answer me."

I blink twice. "We've talked about this. I've been given a second chance at life, which *you*, not to mention, have so generously ruined."

Bemused, Jay says, "So you *do* think you can change the past."

"What are you talking about?"

What happens next catches me completely off guard. Jay rears back with an open hand and swings at my face. I flinch before impact, waiting for my cheek to sting with pain, but nothing happens. When I open my eyes, the hand Jay swung is now across her body, her face stricken with a beaming smile. She missed, why would she be smiling? Or maybe she hadn't missed at all.

"This isn't *real*, Liam!" she yells. "None of it is real! It's all in your head."

I look around me. The white walls are solid and vertical, the picture frames are sitting firmly atop hard surfaces, some hanging around the room, and the office chair I'm on is hard as brick … it all *feels* pretty real to me.

Then suddenly I hear the *rap, rap, rap* against the door, along with Alexandra's pleading voice. "Liam, please…"

That's when I notice it. Every time her voice comes into view, the world around me blurs, my vision becomes static. I look to Jay when this happens.

"Wait ... I *am* dead?"

"No." She smiles, pulling a chair from the dining table and sitting across from me. "You're still very much alive ... just not present. Not yet anyway. Right now you're ... elsewhere." Maintaining her smile, she looks up to the ceiling. "I will say your imagination is very impressive. The vibrant colors you see, the settings you can procure, and the people you conjure ... brilliant. Your mind is beautiful."

"Um ... thanks?"

Observing her cryptic smile, I struggle to understand. *The people I conjure ...*

"Don't you see?" she asks. "I am just a part of the illusion, another figment of your colorful imagination. My purpose has been to show you the truth, to nudge you toward it. And now you've found it! You might not know it, but you have." Her head tilts to the side as she gazes toward me with what appears to be compassion. "I've always been present, not only in your mind, but also your heart."

Scoffing, I say, "Not gonna lie, you feel like migraines and cholesterol."

She laughs hard. "The truth often does. That's why so many people avoid it ... like you." She pauses, shifting in her chair. "Who do you think I am?" she asks again.

"Uh ... Jay?" I say placidly.

She huffs in amusement. Without a word, she stands from her chair, pushes it back into the table exactly how it sat before.

Another three knocks on the door, my vision blurs, and I hear Alexandra, "Oh, God. Liam, are you in there ..."

Jay walks over to the square of light shining brightly through a window on the far side of the space. She lets the light hit her skin, twirling her hand in it as though the warmth of the sun gives her power. The smile she wears hasn't left.

Alexandra bangs on the door once more. Simultaneously, Jay appears to offer one final glance before saying, "It's time for me to go."

My eyes are drawn to her smooth face. Confusion and perturb strike me, however, as it starts to change. Jay's young and angled features begin to wrinkle, slowly at first, and then more quickly with every second. Her cheeks start to droop, her eyelids too, and as they do so recognition washes over me. Jay's red hair, instead of growing, recedes and curls as its vibrancy fades into short and curled streaks of ginger and white atop her head. Finally, her tall, skinny frame shrinks and becomes plump, removing all doubt. *The leather jacket ...*

"Oh my gosh," I say, "Jay ... your name. You didn't actually mean Jay, as in blue Jay. You meant *J*, as in the letter ... You're–"

Rap, rap, rap. "Liam!"

In the still beam of light, an elderly Jay begins to fade, the world around me shakes.

"No! Don't go! I still need you!"

But Jay vanishes with a *bang* like that of shattering wood, and at that moment my eyes are opened.

XXI

In the sturdy chair, I shift my weight to either side, feeling my world materialize around me. Though I am no longer held down by invisible bonds, I voluntarily remain seated simply because I don't have the urge to stand. As I blink away the blur from my eyes like the waking moments after a dream, I find myself staring blankly upon a small monitor. Its colors are vibrant: the tall green pines in the background, the cloud-spotted sky above, and in the foreground angled on a pot-holed patch of mud is an old blue Ford with a rust patch just above the rear tire, steam rising slowly from the crumpled hood as it nearly wraps itself around the base of a tree. The sound of radio music lightly emanates from the monitor, as well. My left hand clutches the black and yellow steering wheel attached to the table while my right hand falls at my side, held down by the weight of something cold and heavy. I blink twice more to remove the gloss from my eyes, looking at the object I'm holding while a smoky scent rises up my nose. Gently I set the gun against the floor. Afterward, my head swivels to observe this familiar room.

My mouth falls into a befuddled frown.

The scene of the Cave is almost always tidy. Everything sits in its place, and that's where it belongs. The guitars hang on the wall just above the stage, the treadmill sits in the corner, and the shelves against the wall are organized alphabetically with all its items evenly spaced apart. But the Cave before me looks much, much different, almost like it's been ravaged by a burglar.

Up and to the left, a small bullet-sized hole drops dust from the ceiling. The treadmill in the corner is lit up as though it was just in use; it's supposed to be turned off. Scattered all across the floor are small squares of notebook paper that appear to have little inscriptions on them. Perhaps the strangest combination of items rests beside the monitor: a nearly-empty bottle of bourbon and a pint glass. *Who drinks bourbon in a pint glass?* Then resting by my feet is a tear-inducing sight. Bending over to rub my hand across the cherry wood, my heart wrenches. Strings dangle off a Mitchell MX430 guitar that has been snapped clean at the neck and seemingly tossed to the floor. *Who would commit such a heinous act?*

A shattering sound erupts from behind me, but I sit still, unaffected. I don't really have the energy to move right now, anyway.

"Oh my God. Liam. Oh, thank God you're okay." A pair of soft hands are laid against my face as Alexandra kisses my forehead. The sleeves of her gray suit are stained with thin, wet streaks, and I wonder why. In her teary eyes both relief and anger can be found. "I was worried sick about you. Why didn't you answer me? I called your name a hundred times." She looks me up and down. Again she asks, "Why didn't you answer?"

I don't have the courage for words right now. All I can muster is sorrowful eyes that I hope she can see.

Alexandra waits desperately for a response. After a silent moment, she looks to someone behind me, motioning them over. A moment later, a familiar head of blonde hair comes into view. After rushing to turn the monitor off, thereby cutting the music out, she flips around.

"Liam, talk to me. I'm right here."

My lips tremble. "Ra–Rach."

Her eyes are blank and emotionless, almost like she's just finished a business matter–or she's about to deal with one. Still hunched with hands on her knees, Rachel looks up to Alexandra, who now stands at her side. "I called as soon as I heard the shot." At that moment, she gently grabs my wrist, and her face goes still with focus.

I look down at the hand gripping my wrist, then up at Rachel. In a swift motion, I pull away from her. "Let go of me."

This action plasters shock onto her face, as though she were expecting lamblike docility instead. To Rachel's right, I watch Alexandra's eyes look curiously around the Cave. It's at this moment that I notice the slight age on the faces of the women before me, no longer as young and innocent in appearance. I'd say they're the same age as they were *before* I …

My eyes dart to the gun resting on the floor. "Wh–what…" I attempt to speak, but words still come with difficulty.

"I really busted that door," a deep male voice says pridefully from behind.

"Marcus, will you go upstairs, please?" Rachel asks lightly.

"Yup."

Now both Rachel and Alexandra study the contents of the floor like criminalists analyzing a scene. I can see their minds turning, deducting the cause and culprit of my broken guitar and the notes riddled all over. There's a slight horror written on their faces.

Rachel bends over to pick up one of the notes in her hand. She flips it over once, twice, and sets it back down. Apprehension fills her eyes as she glances in Alexandra's direction.

My sister's voice is stern. "We have to tell him."

Rachel peeks at me from the corner of her eye for a split second. "I–I don't think we should."

"Rachel … it's time he knows."

"We've tried before."

"It'll work this time. Trust me."

Rachel's head falls, and her eyes close. She pauses for a long moment, perhaps saying a prayer of some sort. She flips another separate note before she turns, studies my face, and sighs. "Okay."

In the upstairs living room is where the women decide it would be best to "sit me down". First, Alexandra notes my pale complexion and determines that

277

we can't start until I've had, as she would call it, a proper meal. Helping me to the couch, she holds my hand like I'm a frail cancer patient and observes me worriedly until I'm firmly seated on the middle cushion. Then she strolls to the kitchen.

I'm not sure what time it is, but judging by the chirping of the birds and the orange light coming through the open window at my back, I'd say it's almost dusk. It's hard to describe how I feel in the moment. The state I'm in is not lucid, dreamlike still, but every passing second grounds me further into the present. *It's time he knows the truth.* Alexandra's voice bounds through my head. *What truth?* Suddenly my stomach growls, reminding me how famished I am.

Upon the short and wide glass table sits a colorful magazine. I move to the edge of the couch so that I can thumb through it. On the other side of the table are two white cloth chairs angled inward. Rachel sits on one, and the other will be Alexandra's. Marcus, standing a couple of feet behind Rachel, crosses his arms as his eyes wander aimlessly around the room. He looks more like a guard than a husband, in my opinion.

Then a ham sandwich on white is placed before me, along with a cup of coffee and two pills. I'm not sure what the pills are for, but Alexandra usually knows what's best for me, so I don't object. With a sip, they go down the hatch.

Alexandra sits gingerly on the edge of the open chair, rolling up the sleeves of her shirt and sharing a glance with Rachel. They watch intently as I devour the sandwich and set the plate back onto the table. Wiping my hands, I look expectantly upon the women across from me.

Innocuously, Alexandra sets her cell phone face down onto the glass while Rachel procures a small notebook and a pen. She holds them almost like a reporter would. Once more, the two of them exchange looks like they haven't yet decided who should speak first.

"How are you feeling?" Alexandra starts.

I pick a few crumbs from my chest, tossing them to the ground. "Fine."

"Does your head ache?" Rachel asks. I struggle to look at her, but I respond anyway.

"So-so." I gesture with my hand. She jots something down.

Alexandra nods, and the room falls silent once again. I can tell the two of them are hesitant to continue. *We've tried before.* My sister, rubbing her temple like she does when fighting back tears, looks to Rachel for help.

Rachel clears her throat. "Liam."

"Yes?"

She sighs. "What were you doing down in the Cave for so long?"

"The Cave?" I frown. "I showed up right when you did."

Another shared look of concern. After a few more scribbles, Rachel says, "Right … I guess I should ask what you were doing before then."

I recall the months I spent at college. Jay, Todd, Julie … Becca. Time, doing what it does, passed far too quickly for me to grasp it. Looking back, the months felt like days, now no more than a flashing memory. But despite the good times and new friendships, my mind focuses more prominently on–and summarizes my "rebirth", you could call it, as–one word: failure. Even in a second life, knowing the mistakes I could not repeat, I couldn't get it right. I still wasn't good enough for Rachel, which leaves me wondering … *What's happening right now?*

With index and thumb, I massage my brow. Then the images of the bathroom, the blinking red–no–the blinking pink lines, and Rachel's mascara streaming down her cheeks all resurface like floating corpses that the river's waves couldn't keep down. I shudder at the thought.

"Please answer her, Liam," Alexandra insists solemnly.

Meeting Alexandra's eyes, I respond after a pause, "If I told you, you wouldn't believe me."

Rachel interjects, "Try us."

279

Instinct urges me to respond sourly. *Why do you care, anyway?* But instead, I attempt at an honest answer. "I–I was elsewhere."

"Hmm," Rachel writes something else down. "And what were you doing before you went, as you would call it, *elsewhere?*"

I huff in amusement. What am I supposed to say? *Yeah, well I shot myself ... in the head.* But suddenly I recall what I was doing even before that. "I was in my truck ... driving. Um, and then I turned the radio on."

The two women share a familiar nod. "So you were listening to music," Rachel says.

I move my head steadily up and down.

"And..." Rachel uses her hands to summon her thoughts into words, "then you went *elsewhere?* Where exactly was that?"

My eyes bounce between the women before me and then up to Marcus, who seems to be equally as intrigued with the ceiling's delicate pattern as he is with the conversation. I put a finger up to my lips as I think. I don't know if I should tell them. What will they think of me? But Alexandra gives a nod of encouragement, prompting me to begin.

"Well," I start, "I–I was at college."

"Mhmm," Rachel nods. She flips to another page. "What happened at college?"

I look longingly upon the eyes that browse the small notebook paper before they rise and I look away. It's strange. When I look at her, I feel nothing. To be honest, I don't really feel much in general right now. My soul, once again, feels hollowed out, almost empty.

Alexandra, still on the edge of her seat, sits patiently, but her face is eager.

"Uh, well ... I–" I struggle for the right words, but my head falls in defeat.

I expect them to keep pushing, but to my good fortune, Rachel decides to revert back to something else. Not taking her eyes off the notepad, she says, "So you were in your truck … listening to music. Then you drove to college?"

I shake my head no.

"How did you get there?" she asks, but something in her voice tells me she might already know. "Did it have anything to do with the gun?"

I look warily to each of them, afraid of being judged, but there is no judgment to be found. All I can detect in both their faces is a simple desire for truth.

I nod.

My sister's head falls dramatically to the floor, followed by a stifled peep.

"Liam, can I talk with Alexandra for a second?"

"Uh … sure," I reply hesitantly, wondering why she would ask my permission.

Reaching over to place a comforting hand on Alexandra's back, Rachel leans in with a hushed tone. I hear only a few words: "*shot … triggered … world.*"

Shifting uncomfortably on the couch, I scratch at my ear. Rachel writes on her pad while Alexandra appears to be composing herself, blinking excessively and wiping at the corners of her eyes. It appears that Marcus is now taking more interest in us, as his eyes are mostly intent upon his wife.

"So, Liam," Rachel summarizes, "is this the first time that your *taken* world, as we refer to it, has brought you to college?"

"Wha–" my body jolts in bewilderment. How does Rachel know about my *taken* world? I never told her. Alexandra was supposed to be the only one who knows. "How?"

"It's interesting …" Rachel bites the pen. "Your *taken* world has brought you to the past before … bullies at school, the rabbit story, your grandmother

281

standing up for you and scolding your dad–that one comes up quite a bit–, but I don't recall college coming up before."

"Whoah, whoah, whoah," my mind flutters between the thousands of questions I have, but I toss them to the side. I have to set the record straight first. "This one wasn't my *taken* world. I–it was ... different. I know it was." My voice raises ever so slightly. "How did you know about that?" My mind focuses on what Rachel insists to have been my *taken* world. I can still see it so clearly: her and Alexandra, both acting out of the ordinary as a couple of young college women. If that really *was* my *taken* world the whole time, why did I end up in college? And what could it be trying to tell me? "Something's up," I say. "Something's *been* up. Tell me what's really going on here!"

"Liam, that's what we're trying to do," Alexandra jumps in somberly.

"So get on with it!"

Rachel breathes deeply. She looks to Alexandra for confirmation. My sister nods.

"Alright," Rachel begins. "we'll get on with it."

"It started in college ..." Alexandra says. "You were just a freshman. You probably don't remember much."

I sit in silence, attentive on the two of them as they go back and forth, sharing the burden of explanation.

"After your first couple months, you hadn't made many friends. That's when your sister Alexandra told me about you."

"I said you'd been struggling."

"She did," Rachel nods. "Long story short, I thought I could help. So after some coaxing, your sister introduced the two of us. That's when it began."

You don't have to remind me, I think to myself. That's where our relationship started, where my rise and fall was instituted. I think of the pub where we had our first meal.

"Each week, the two of us met, and almost immediately, you showed unprecedented signs of improvement, the likes of which I haven't seen since."

"It was incredible," Alexandra beams. "You made a few friends."

"You started playing guitar!" Rachel adds. "A God-given skill, no doubt."

"You even met a girl." Alexandra smiles at the ground in recollection.

My face contorts with confusion as my head turns to Rachel. "Uh, yeah … I did. I'm looking at her."

This seems to wipe the smiles right off their faces.

"Right …" Rachel says, followed by a long pause where she and Alexandra struggle to abandon their nervous stares. "That's where I was headed next." Alexandra clears her throat, but she doesn't speak, instead waiting for Rachel to continue. "Let's retrace our steps for just a second. Your struggle to make friends …"

"When I told Rachel about it–"

"–your sister was hesitant to accept my help, not sure that therapy would be the solution to your problems. However, I told her that *my* kind of therapy would be different. Instead of the 'tell me how you feel' mumbo-jumbo–which we also did occasionally–I insisted that what you really needed was a friend. See, the problem often with, well, people like yourself is that society ostracizes you, considers you to be an outcast, different than everyone else. The isolation that results often exacerbates the problem. Having a friend to combat the loneliness, in combination with well-known therapeutic methods, would be just what you needed … so I offered to be that!"

"Okay," I grumble. "And then we became more than that, got married, had a kid, and got divorced, and we all lived happily never after."

Rachel grits her teeth and rubs her scalp. She looks contemplatively at the table, closing her notepad and setting it lightly upon the glass. "This is always the hardest part."

"What part? What do you mean?"

283

After a deep breath, Rachel says, "Your illusions … this is also where they began–or rather, got worse."

"Illusions? What are you saying?"

Alexandra jumps in emphatically, holding my gaze. "Liam, please. Just let her explain. If you have questions after, we'll tell you *everything*."

Gruffly, I say, "Okay." Then I sit back in the couch, crossing my arms.

Rachel nods in thanks to my sister before looking in my direction. "As I said before, 'therapy' is what we started. We'd get together, usually at my place, play board games, watch movies–you know, the basic friend stuff. I'd ask about your days, how school was going, et cetera. Then … your illusions." She pauses, biting her pen again. "Somehow, you started getting the impression that you and I were … together. Several times over, I informed you that we were nothing more than friends, and by the end of our meetings, you'd come to acceptance with that truth. Then the following session would come, and at the beginning of each one, I could tell the illusion of you and I, no matter how persistent my denial, was progressing in your mind throughout the course of each week. I had to tell your sister."

"And I said," Alexandra offers, "that we should stop it right in its tracks."

"I agreed," Rachel says. "We couldn't let it go any further."

"But …" Alexandra stares at the table.

"But …" Rachel concurs. "You were making so much progress in the other aspects of your life–your friends, your musical talent, the girl you met. Every time we terminated our sessions, your progress would subsequently halt. You would immediately seclude yourself from the outside world."

"So we decided that it was for your ultimate good to have you keep meeting with Rachel. We thought that eventually we'd convince you to chase– oh, what was her name–Becca! And in doing so, we hoped you might forget about Rachel."

Rachel's tone quiets. "But your feelings for me kept intensifying, and along with them, so too did your illusions. Eventually in your insistent 'love' for me, you dropped the girl. Your mental health started taking a *real* hit after that."

"No, that's not—" *true*, I wanted to say, but Alexandra's stern gaze kept me quiet.

"So we thought," Alexandra picks up, "ending the sessions *then* would be best."

"However," Rachel declares, "we'd seen you make progress before. Our thought process was: why couldn't you do it again? Besides," she clutches her heart, "it hurt me too much to see you struggling. I couldn't let your mental health fall without a fight."

"I wasn't sure about continuing, but I trusted Rachel. She knew more about your mind than even I did at this point."

"So we continued. And once again, you were showing signs of progress, but it would ebb and flow, ebb and flow for years. I continued to be that steady friend in your life, encouraging you to take risks, get out there and meet someone. But after some time, your sister and I could no longer deny that the more time you spent with me, the worse the illusions were getting. From the idea that you and I were intimate partners, then to married lovers, and finally parents to a child, it had gotten to the point about three years ago that I had to end all contact with you."

"And your mind processed Rachel's sudden disappearance from your life as a 'divorce'."

Rachel finishes, displaying her best impression of remorse. "The entire time, all I wanted to do was help. I thought that my assistance would end your illusions, cure them maybe, but they only got worse. I promise you, with every fiber of my being, that it was not my intent for any of this to happen. I know this doesn't mean anything. Still, I–I'm truly sorry."

This is where they pause, perhaps noting the horror on my face. My mouth hangs agape, and I'm nearly too stunned to speak. I spend a few moments recapturing all the information they had just laid out. Marcus stands

285

firmly behind Rachel now, and the pieces start assembling themselves in my brain. Supposedly Rachel and I were never together ... she was just a friend ... and it was all for the benefit of my mental health.

"Are you insane?" I blurt.

"Liam–" the women try at the same time, but I don't give them a chance.

Leaning on the edge of the couch, I rest my chin in one hand. In a mocking tone, I let them have it. "Let's pretend that everything you're saying is true."

"It *is*, Liam," Alexandra starts, but by offering her my best glare, she hushes herself.

"So ... basically you want me to believe that my relationship, marriage, and divorce with Rachel were never real, and judging by the way in which Marcus is suddenly now invested in this drama, my assumption is that you were supposedly married to him the whole time?"

I stop to observe three feeble nods. Utter confusion rattles me. Not only do I struggle to comprehend their complex story, but I'm conflicted by their resolve in convincing me of its validity. Do they really think I'm dumb enough to believe all this? Besides, I've already thought of one key detail that they forget to mention: the jenga piece I can pull that will topple the entire tower of fabrication.

"And Casey?" I question. "Are you going to have me believe that I had him with another woman? Or that he was born to Marcus and Rachel, because–no offense, Marcus–my boy's skin isn't exactly dark enough for you to sell that one."

Her hands in steeple position, Rachel purses her lips and sighs. I can tell her reluctance to say anything else is genuine, but why? Then she looks to Alexandra for help. After a sigh, my sister says timidly, "Liam ... Casey isn't real."

286

The words hit me like a sledgehammer. I stare in shock at the three sullen faces before me. "W-wha–? That's impossible. I–" I stammer for a moment when Rachel silences me with one powerful word.

"Schizophrenia."

I shake, whether with anxiety or rage, I cannot tell.

Rachel looks me dead in the eyes, and I see that hers are still blank, perhaps concealing something. I try to look away, but I can't. From beside her comes Alexandra's soft tone. "You've struggled with schizophrenia your whole life."

"No ..." I can barely utter the word.

"Hereditary," Alexandra continues in a matter-of-fact way, but she doesn't have the courage to say it directly to my face. "Grandpa struggled with it, until he ..." she trails off. "I didn't want you to end up like him."

"I'm so sorry, Liam," Rachel says. "We–no ... *I* should have never let it get as far as it did."

Silence befalls the room. My mind works through everything like a mathematician analyzing an algebraic equation, except that I cannot balance the two sides. One side is right, and one side is wrong. There is the side of truth and the side of lies. *But what if there is gray area?*

My eyes dart from Rachel, to Alexandra, to Marcus, and back again. Compulsively, I shake my head in denial. *No*, I tell myself. *No, they're wrong. I'll show them!*

An idea pops in my head. Without explanation, I stand and bolt to the stairs, sprinting to the top where I find a plain white door. I burst through it. Inside, the lights are shut off, but there's still enough sunlight coming in through the shades for me to see. My eyes search frantically from left to right. The twin bed is empty. The action figures lay motionless upon the ground. I check the closet. Nothing.

Adamantly, I search the rest of the house, eventually coming to an awful conclusion. Casey is gone.

287

I find myself back where we started: the living room, unable to avoid the tears in Alexandra's eyes. The sorrowful looks I receive from husband and wife … too much to take in. I cannot hold the waves back on my own.

"No!" I fall to my knees and sob. "No, no, no."

Tears stream down my face, getting caught in my beard. It's tough to breathe, which is alright. I'm not sure I want to breathe anymore, anyway.

After living a lie for so long, the truth becomes too much to bare, making it easier to keep on lying and lying and lying until, brick by brick, the wall is erected that not only separates fact from fiction, but also emotion from apathy. But now that wall has come down–truly this time.

My tears fall to the hardwood below, only the sound of my cries filling the room. I'm sure Alexandra wants to comfort me, perhaps Rachel and Marcus too, but there's nothing more they can say or do. It'd be easy to blame them for everything, but it would do me no good. *I* am responsible, no one else.

Yet I can feel a tugging at the back of my mind, like my brain is holding onto something too important to let go. Wiping my eyes, I compose myself to the best of my ability. I lope to the couch and sit right where I had been before. Facing the floor, I look to no one when I say, "I want to talk with Rachel."

"Anything," she responds.

"Alone."

A low, apprehensive groan stems from Marcus. "I don't know if that's the best idea," he begins.

Alexandra agrees, but Rachel says. "Okay. Alone, just the two of us."

"What?" Marcus's voice fills with astonishment. "Aren't you–" his tone quiets, "–*scared*?"

"Listen, babe," Rachel rises from her chair and places a soft, reassuring hand on Marcus's stubble-filled cheek. "You're my best friend … I'll be okay."

288

"Wait, Rachel. Are you sure?" Alexandra chimes in. "I'd be happy to stay here with you."

"I want to talk with her alone," I say firmly. Addressing their concerns, I add, "I'm not going to hurt her."

Marcus watches me warily, but Rachel's confidence is strong. "It's okay. I'm sure there are questions he has for me–and only me. Go."

His hesitation is evident, but after a kiss from his wife, he moves slowly to the front door, holding it open for Alexandra who is right behind him.

Before my sister gets to it, I notice her cell on the table. It had probably been recording this whole time. "Alex, your phone."

Turning around, she pretends not to have left it on purpose. "Right," she smiles wanly. "Thanks." She plucks her phone from the table, and a moment later she, in her suit, and Marcus, in his usual plaid shirt, exit through the front door, leaving Rachel and I to each other, only a glass table between us.

After the front door clicks shut, I stumble to the kitchen to grab a glass of water, offering one to Rachel as well. She accepts.

"So," she says as I place the glass before her. "I–I know this must be a lot to take in, and I'm sure it doesn't really make sense to you right now. I'd be happy to answer any questions you have."

Taking my seat on the couch, I sip from the glass. Without a word, I set it onto the table. After her eyes wander to avoid the tension, Rachel interprets my silence as an invitation to continue.

"Maybe you could tell me what happened in this previous trip to your *taken* state?" she says while inspecting a bowl-of-fruit painting on the far wall. "I've usually found that this aids me in determining the root of deeper issues."

Again I say nothing.

Instead I examine the woman across from me. She's unable to meet my eyes. Her discomfort is evident. Instinct told me I needed Rachel alone, that I needed to hear the story from *her*, without the comfort and reassurance of two helping voices. I think of Alexandra and Marcus exiting that door, surprised by

289

my evidently stellar performance. Rather convincingly in my opinion, I made it appear as though I believed their story, that I trusted their word. I knew it was the only way Alexandra and Marcus would allow themselves to leave Rachel's side. But it was simply an act.

I'll say my stomach turns at the thought that I could be capable of lying, particularly to Alexandra. Lies are fake, and I can't stand the superficial. Some evils, however, are necessary.

To some extent, I really do believe what they've said. I trust that Alexandra wouldn't lie to me. Although painful, the truth of Casey's false existence is undeniable. A part of me always knew but couldn't accept it. And schizophrenia. Though the word itself sounds like a disease, mostly in part due to its stigmatization, it characterizes me rather accurately. It hurts, and I've already processed the irony. Almost like a fisherman who gets seasick, or a musician who hates loud noises, I'm a schizophrenic who abhors the unreal. Still, something in my gut knows there's more to be said. I've already uncovered *some* truth. But I'm close to uncovering the *whole* truth.

Rachel's brow eventually furrows. "What's this about? Are you okay?"

"Tell me what really happened."

"Pardon?" Rachel leans forward.

"No more 'I care about you bullshit'. What's the truth?"

"Liam," she gasps. "I *do* care about you."

I respond with a grunt of amusement.

Rachel doubles down. "I'll even admit that I love you. I do. As a friend. We've spent so much time together, and you really are someone special. I hate to say it, but everything I've told you is absolutely the truth." She pauses, rubbing her forehead contemplatively. "The methods I used to help you ... unconventional, sure. But everything they taught us in school was so wrong, so rigid. It was all a step-by-step guide to 'fixing' the malfunctioning human brain, as though people are, and have always been, nothing more than machines.

"When Alexandra explained your problems to me, I considered it an opportunity. I could show everyone in the field of psychology that there are other ways to help those in need. By breaking their molds, we can discover even greater, more *genuine* methods of psychiatric care." Finally she meets my eyes, and slowly I see the veil that had previously covered them being lifted. "I truly thought I could do it. I don't want to say *cure* you, because that implies that there was something wrong with you in the first place. No, I'll say I just wanted to relieve you of your burdens. I tried so hard, and I continued to do so for so long. It just … it didn't exactly work in my favor, or yours for that matter."

Rachel sits back in her chair, appearing truly dejected. I can't let her posture persuade me.

"No, no, no." I wave my hands. "I heard you the first time. But there's something you're not telling me. I can *feel* it."

"Liam," she says adamantly, holding my gaze. "Haven't you ever wondered about your Nashville career?"

"Huh?"

"When you play at Tootsies, or Legends, or Honkytonk, who comes to see you? Who watches you?"

I scoff. "I have plenty of fans, even one who comes to see me every night."

Rachel leans forward, her eyes intent. "What's her name?"

Her? How does she know it's a woman? "Uh … Josephine?" I say hesitantly.

"Okay, we'll get to her later. First, what do you think of Nashville? Me personally, I don't care for the drive. Eight and a half hours is a bit too long to sit in a vehicle for my liking."

I frown. *Eight and a half hours? It's no more a twenty minute drive …*

"I'll spell it out. You don't live in Nashville, Liam. You're still in Iowa, where you've always been. Your Nashville career has never been anything

291

more than a figment of your imagination. Again, I'll say you're really quite talented, maybe even talented enough to play in Music City for real someday. But up to this point, your only gig has been down there." She points to the stairs. "In the Cave."

"No, tha–"

She doesn't allow me to finish. "In a few of our first sessions, we discovered the origination of your *taken* state. That's the name we gave it. Whenever you leave the world of reality, you are *taken*. The way in which you get there? Truly remarkable."

"Look, I don't know where you're going with this."

"Music, Liam. Music is one of the catalysts that takes you both to and from this state. It's the most powerful one, I've noticed. Many musicians talk about escaping through music, but you're *really* able to do that." She diverts her gaze. "Sometimes I really wish I could, too."

"Now wait," I begin to object but fall into silence a moment later. The Cave pops into my mind. The computer and monitor, with the steering wheel mounted on the table. "My truck," I realize. My old blue Ford I've always used to "drive" to Nashville. "It was never a real truck. It's in the video game."

"Right," Rachel nods. "Your performances–often we'll watch. You start by sitting in that chair. Once you turn the radio on in the game, it only takes a few moments–"

"And I'm *taken*," I finish the sentence for her.

"Straight to Nashville, or as we know it: the stage in the Cave."

I think of all my performances, the "trick" I've used to avoid the crowds. I always thought I was escaping to the Cave, but ..."When I play guitar, it takes me back to reality, doesn't it? It combats the 'radio' in the truck."

Rachel offers a pleased smile. "You're getting it." Apparently taking advantage of my willingness to accept her words, she wastes no time. "The woman you see–Josephine. Who is she?" Rachel phrases the question in a way

292

that indicates she might know the answer better than I do, so I let her inform me. "She's your grandmother."

"What?"

"In fact, she often arrives in your *taken* state, I think mostly because of the way she used to stand up for you when no one else was there to do it. Alexandra told me that Josephine would attempt to teach your parents to be more ... understanding. After all, she knew better than anyone how to help someone with schizophrenia, marrying your grandfather and all."

I stare heavily at the ground, unable to speak.

"The way your parents used to treat you and Alexandra–I've heard the stories. I'm so sorry." Rachel takes a moment of silence before continuing. "Due to their abuse, in addition to underlying heredity, you've essentially spent your whole life using this *taken* state as an avenue to run from the truth, from multiple truths, rather."

Run from it, or run to it? I wonder. Now I sit with the slightest bit of contentment. It makes sense. It all makes sense. But something else just doesn't add up.

"I don't want to talk to you about Nashville, anymore."

"Okay," Rachel says lightly. "What do you prefer we talk about?"

"Us." I meet her eyes firmly.

"Us? What about us?"

"You mean to tell me that in every one of our 'sessions', or whatever, we were never intimate? I know my memory is bad, but for some reason those memories are always the most vivid."

Taking a deep breath, she lets it out in a huff. "Your *taken* state can be truly convincing for you. I'm just awfully sorry that it tried to convince you the two of us were–" she shrugs, but she doesn't have to say it.

Putting my scruffy chin into my hand, I allow my mind to wander. *I'm close ... what am I searching for?* "You're sure?"

"I'm sure."

293

Rachel looks once more upon the bowl-of-fruit painting. I wonder why she's so intrigued by it. Only an orange, a pear, and an apple sit in the streaky woven bowl. She scratches at her ear, and when her hand drops, I notice it. I know what I have to do.

"You're right," I say. "It all makes sense."

Rachel drops her tone. "I can't apologize enough ... for everything."

I nod slowly. "It's alright."

She appears content, hands on her thighs, maybe preparing to call Alexandra and Marcus back in. As she stands, she begins to speak, but I interrupt.

"Is there any way I could have a hug?" I ask despondently.

"A hug?" she looks apprehensive.

Not looking directly at her, I nod my head.

She appears to consider my proposal, and to my luck, she determines that I'm harmless–which I am.

"Okay. A hug."

We both stand, and Rachel extends her arms, which I, just as uneasily as her, accept. She must be able to feel my heart pounding against my chest, against hers, probably misdiagnosing its cause as unrequited love or innocent anxiety.

In my arms, I hold Rachel. Her body feels just the way I remembered. After a few seconds, Rachel lets go ... but I don't. I hold her gently. This is where I expect her to become tense, maybe even ask me to unwrap my arms from around her. But something prompts her to reciprocate my embrace once more. This time, she holds me tightly, resting her chin on my shoulder. It's the perfect time to act.

In a response to the call of destiny, my lips fall to Rachel's neck, kissing with the passion I've held within me for three years–ever since the moment she left. She doesn't fight back, not at first. But then she says ...

"Liam, no, Li–" but her voice quickly falls into a moan; her breath shakes–just like it used to.

That's when I know ... I've found the truth.

My lips retreat. With my left arm still curled around her back my right quickly rises and covers Rachel's mouth, which she reacts to with shock. If she makes anything more than a peep, Alexandra and Marcus will be through the front door in a matter of seconds. Looking into Rachel's blue eyes, I see the past. I see all the memories, all the intimate moments we shared ... the pregnancy test in the bathroom, and it all finally comes together.

"I knew it," I say coldly.

Rachel attempts to speak.

"Shut it," I demand, fighting the urge to scream. But right now, I have to be discreet. "You're a good liar," I whisper. "I can tell you've become even better–perfecting your craft, I see." I nod to the door. "I see the way you lie to him, too."

Rachel shuffles, but I hold her steady. The terror in her wide eyes is evident. No longer are they concealed. I can see into her soul, and the fear within her stems not from a fear of being hurt or wounded. She knows I'd never hurt another human being, especially not her. No, Rachel is terrified that I've finally seen through all her wonderful lies.

"God knows why I trusted you. Meeting once a week in college, you disappearing in the morning when we–no I–used to live in that apartment. I was such a fool to think you really loved me. I thought we were *married*, for God's sake! The entire time you had me convinced. Meanwhile, you were fulfilling whatever sick desires you had with me–the schizo boy, knowing nobody, *nobody* would take my word over yours. You even went to desperate lengths to ensure my love never reached anyone but you, forcing me to forget Becca and vow my endless love. Forcing me to forget the time I caught you with Marcus. You kept the 'illusion' theory running with everyone else while spinning my brain into a muddled web of lies until even *I* could not tell what was true and what wasn't." My eyes narrow. "But eventually you left … why?"

Hesitant to remove my hand, Rachel's words luckily come out in a whisper. She shakes her head. "Liam, no. It's not–"

I cover her mouth once more. "Spare me with the bullshit. Give it to me straight."

Frantically searching, she says through tears, "I'm a good person."

Dismissing her desperate response, I roll my eyes and place the muzzle of my hand on her face. "And that's not even the worst of it. *You* messed up. You got pregnant with *my* child. Lord knows you couldn't have word of that getting out." This is where the truth becomes nearly too horrific to accept. My throat tightens, and the words become choked, but I still utter them with the same restraint. With a confronting gaze into her eyes, I say quietly, yet sparing no ounce of passion, "Y-you killed our baby–*my* baby, my Casey. My boy! I could have given him the life *my* dad never did, but no … no. You destroyed my life, and you knew there was no turning back. Too much damage had already been done. Like a teenage boy, you threw me away as though I was never anything more than a tissue that caught your disturbing mess, over and over again."

My eyes crowd with a watery blur while tears stream down Rachel's face and into my hand. We're closer now than we've ever been before. Despite the moments of intimacy, the fabricated series of so-called friendship, Rachel and I are closer now than ever, finally united in truth.

"My problems were never that bad," I continue. "I used my *taken* world as an escape … and after you met me, so did you." Fighting back the tears, I say finally, "Fuck you. You ruined me, Rachel. *You* did. And every day you have to live with that, knowing you fucked up your own life more than you did mine."

A sudden stabbing pain hits my hand, and I realize she's bitten me.

"HELP!" she shrieks as instinctively I pull away. "Marcus, help!"

Bursting immediately through the door are a burly black man and a skinny white woman: Marcus and Alexandra, both with anxiety-ridden faces.

Rachel backs away from me and cowers in a corner, gripping her shoulders and sobbing relentlessly. "He's crazy!" she points to me. "He's fucking crazy."

I'm sure with the maniacal eyes I have, her claims appear to be valid, but as Alexandra comes over to hold me in place, I stand still in no attempt to go after Rachel. I'd never hurt her. With sincerity, I grasp my sister's attention. "She's lying, Alexandra. She's been lying the whole time."

"Yeah, Liam," she says dismissively, firmly gripping my arms, pushing me further away from Rachel.

"No, Alex, I'm serious … you have to believe me."

Marcus, after inspecting Rachel for bruises, barges toward me with glaring eyes.

"You psychotic fuck, I'll kill you!"

"Marcus, no! Don't touch him!" Alexandra puts a hand up to stop him. "Just leave. The two of you … just *leave*. I'll handle this."

Fists clenched, looking nearly as crazy as he believes me to be, Marcus with wide, furious eyes turns around with a disappointed grunt. "Come on, baby. We're getting the fuck out of here." Taking Rachel carefully by the arm, he escorts her out the front door, slamming it shut.

Alexandra turns to me, one hand still grasping me by the arm. Her grip is tight. "Liam, what the hell did you do to her?"

"Nothing," I say, looking deep into my sister's eyes. "She did it to herself."

Appearing hurt, Alexandra lets go of me. She begins walking around the living area, one hand on hip, the other on her brow. I hear her muttering to herself. "–he was right. They were right. Mom, Dad. Oh my God."

"Sis," I say gently, staying right where I am. "What are you talking about?"

297

"Dad!" Alexandra whips around, fury in her voice. "He wants to send you to a goddamn institution! He thinks you're insane, as he always has, but *I* stood up for you." She goes back to pacing around the room. She says quietly into one palm, "He might've been right."

"Alex–" I try, taking a step forward.

"No, Liam! Don't say a goddamn word. Just … go downstairs while I figure this all out."

My heart longs to explain myself. I know the truth now. Surely Alexandra will believe me. She has to. But right now is not the time. Straight-faced, I lope around her and descend the stairs.

Slowly I take them down. When I reach the bottom, I turn right to enter the Cave, looking knowingly upon all the notes on the floor, the steering wheel, and the broken guitar while Alexandra's tormented, self-insulting cries reach me from upstairs. She continues with this for a number of minutes until she quiets, and the front door slams moments later.

Once more, I find myself in isolation, accompanied only by the broken and unused objects abandoned to the Cave.

After a few hours and the arrival of nightfall, I hear the front door open and shut once again, more gently this time. What I presume to be Alexandra's footsteps are bounding across the hardwood, sounding through the ceiling of the basement. While she was gone for a few hours, probably consulting with Rachel and Marcus at their place across the street, I took it upon myself to clean up the mess I made in the Cave. I tossed the notepad papers in the trash, thinking about the notes I came across in my *taken* state–all from Jay, or so I believed. Then I rearranged the shelves, placing the gun back in its case. Before I latched the small hard-case shut, I laid thankful eyes upon the weapon lying gently on the bumpy gray foam–thankful to God for protecting me and showing me the truth. I presume it was the gun shot, as Rachel indicated, that triggered the memories that I had unknowingly abandoned, and by accessing

298

and interacting with those same memories in my *taken* world, I was able to "FIND THE TRUTH". Obviously, my brain had taken a few creative liberties, but for the most part, what I saw and experienced was accurate. I snapped the case shut.

Of course, I then mourned the loss of my first guitar until I came upon the grand idea of attempting to fix it. Though it's split at the neck and the body has considerable damage, an application of glue and a bit of effort should repair the instrument. It's my first one, after all, and it's worth more to me than its weight in wood. Lots of memories are attached to it.

When I had finished cleaning, I set the guitar aside. Tonight is not the night for anything to be mended. To fix an instrument, the mind needs to be clear. Focus is essential when dealing with an object as delicate as a six-string.

A mind clearer, I think to myself. *That's what I need.* My eyes roam the basement until they land on an area in the far corner. *And I know just where to find it.*

Our in-home bar rests on a pad of linoleum by the staircase. The only illumination in the basement is provided by blue lights that overhang our wide selection of liquor. They're dimmed, giving the space an eerie and dark feel. Somehow, I'm comforted by it.

From the cabinet beneath the countertop, I find a small glass. When you pour bourbon just right, it swirls around the edge, creating a funnel in the center until the brown liquid flattens and comes to rest. After the initial reality-checking sip, I realize my exhaustion.

Lounging in the large black leather couch, I point the remote at the screen, and an Australian guy in tight khaki apparel appears. He seems to be explaining the evolutionary features of different reptiles by holding them in his hands. I can't really tell because the volume is on its lowest setting. I sit back and chuckle at the animated man, however, reminded of my past roommate Todd. Odd though he may have been, he was a good guy with a good heart. I suppose that's all you can really ask of your fellow man.

Suddenly my eyes abandon the lizards, snakes, and alligators on the projector screen to view a regretful-looking Alexandra prudently descending the stairs on the far side of the room. She's abandoned the outer layer of her suit, along with her tie, unbuttoned the top of her collared shirt and rolled back the sleeves. Her brunette hair is disheveled, falling over her shoulders. The blood that had been rushing through her face earlier seems to have receded.

"Hey," she says coyly as she approaches.

I press mute on the remote. "Hey."

Alexandra flips a couple of lights on. She then sits at my side. "This guy's entertaining," she says, nodding to the screen. "But nobody will be better than Steve."

"Mr. Irwin *was* the best."

"He was," she says absently.

While I'm slumped against the back cushion, Alexandra contradicts me by sitting on edge, apparently wondering how to ease into the unavoidable conversation. I help her out by turning off the projector. Though she had been staring at the screen, she hardly seems to notice when the colors fade to black.

Eventually, she says, "I spoke with Marcus and Rachel." She scratches at the back of her head. "They're leaving."

"Leaving?" I say.

Alexandra says to the floor, "Rachel was pretty shaken up. I don't think I've ever seen her like that before."

"Hm."

"She believes distance is probably best for you."

Best for me ... or for her?

"I agreed. Um ... as for what I said about Dad," she rests a hand on my knee, "I didn't mean that." She turns to face me. "I'd never let him do that to you. You and I stick together, like always."

I offer a wan smile, haunted by the thought of being sent to a mental institution.

"But," she says obstinately, "we have to get you some help. *Real* help. Not for my sake–for yours."

"Alex," I lean forward.

"No." She puts a hand up. "That is my condition, and you'd be best to follow through with it."

"Okay, fine. But please, *please* hear me out."

Pursing her lips, she heaves a sigh. Before she can shake her head no, I give a pleading gaze that changes her mind. "Alright."

I can tell she's none too interested in what I have to say. But she's the best sister in the world. Even if she believes it will do no good for me to explain myself, she'll always listen. Now more than ever, I need that.

"What I'm about to say is a lot to take in. I just need you to trust me." I stare into her brown eyes, finding the same companionship I've always found, along with a hint of uncertainty. "Can you do that?"

She nods slightly, which will have to do for now.

"Alright." I think for a moment, ordering my thoughts and wondering the most effective way to say what needs to be said. This isn't about my truth or Rachel's truth. This is about *the* truth–the one and only. That's all there ever is and all that ever will be.

I begin recounting the events I experienced in my *taken* world, which Alexandra must be able to recall from her own memory. Placing them as specifically in time as I can, I quickly engage my sister's attention. After giving detailed accounts of the progression of my relationship with Rachel– everything from our first meeting to the day she left–my sister's amazement at the sudden accuracy of my memory is paired with my own. She remains silent the entire time, allowing me to spill everything that's been bottled up for so long.

When I reach the end–the part where I explain Casey's origin–Alexandra looks past me blankly, her eyes jogging back and forth between scenarios. "Rachel wasn't just lying to me the entire time," I explain. "She had everyone

301

else, including you, operating under the pretense that she was some kind of "Good Samaritan" helping a boy in need. I don't mean to accuse. Obviously I fell under her spell, too."

This is where Alexandra finally interrupts. Frowning, she says, "On several occasions, I spent time with both you and Rachel. Each night the three of us were together, she treated you just as she always had–like a friend." She pauses. "I heard you when you said you loved Rachel. I believed it. Hell, I saw it with my own eyes how much you truly loved her. You told me she loved you back. I wanted to believe you, it's just … when I saw it for myself–"

"That's the thing!" I say with perhaps too much excitement. Alexandra is taken aback, so I dial it down a few notches. "I–I didn't see it back then, but I do now. Every time I was with her and you, or if Rachel and I were in public, she always acted … different. I shrugged it off in each and every instance. But I see it clearly now, I promise!"

Alexandra leans forward, her elbows on her knees, hands folded together. She looks longingly at the floor. I can see her mind spinning. A couple times she makes an objecting peep, followed by a hushed "Well, no" or "No, wait", immediately quieting herself and resuming her process of deep thought.

I reach for her hand after several minutes of silence. Taking it in mine, I lock her in a visual embrace. I can almost see the same horror in her eyes that must have been in mine when I learned the truth. Earnestly, I say, "I know you believe me." When she makes no hint at either a yes or no, I repeat. "You believe me, don't you, sis?"

Alexandra's lips quiver, and I can feel her hand start to shake. Her eyes fill with sorrow that eventually lead to tears; she's let too many of them fall already. Pulling her hand from me, she stands and moves toward the bar, but she has no intention of pouring herself a drink. Instead she stops, her back turned to me. Like a child afraid of the dark, or rather what could be lurking within it, Alexandra refuses to look at me when, with pain in her voice, she says, "No, Liam. I don't."

302

Helplessly, I sit on the edge of the couch. I want to reach out to her, to somehow let her know my words are true. I pray to God, hoping he might reveal himself just for this moment. I need Him to let her know. If my own sister, the one who's never left my side, cannot trust me ... who will?

"Alex–" I attempt, but she cuts me off.

"I'm going to find you help," she says, her back still turned. "I'll find help." Then, after a deep breath she climbs the stairs one-by-one, leaving me behind without even saying "goodnight".

Feeling like a prisoner with his feet bolted to the ground and his voice trapped inside, I reach my hand out, but nobody is there to take it. I've faced my struggles the same way all my life: alone. In isolation I've always found comfort, living with a perpetual fear of others, a fear of what they might think. But in the back of my mind, I always knew–or thought–I wasn't truly alone. Alexandra has always been there. I've always been able to rely on her to catch me, to save me. But now, with not even her in my court, I'm tasting *true* isolation, and I never thought I could abhor it so much. The taste instills a desire to double over and retch. Knowledge may have been what I needed, but the accompanied pain arguably may not be worth it. I guess this is what they meant when they said 'Ignorance is bliss.'

XXII

Routines. They're all that anybody truly longs for. Waking up at five, heading off to work, and looking forward to binging four episodes of your favorite show at the end of the day, even though you promised yourself you'd go to bed after one. Staying out until three, living it up with the boys, the girls, or in solitude just to stumble home and wake the next morning with a splitting headache and a faint or suppressed memory of the fool you were ten hours ago. These are the two stakes that mark each end of a spectrum of routines. Nobody's to say which routines are superior, though I suppose it depends on one's definition of success to decide. Still, it is not the content of the routine that matters, only that there is one. After all, routines are the roots of reality.

Pouring the same Costa Rican blend into a black mug, just as I had done the previous day, I begin my routine. Typically this is the part where Alexandra ambles into the kitchen, drops an ounce of cream into her mug, and mixes it with coffee. But it's the weekend. She has no reason to be up at six, unless she were interested in listening to the birds beckoning the sun's arrival, which she is not. Or so I thought.

As I pull up a chair next to the island, methodical, unhurried steps descend the staircase. For a second, fear paralyzes me. I start to wonder whether an apparition of a little boy in blue pajama pants will swing around the corner just to light up my morning with his smile. A sigh of relief escapes me, however, when Alexandra's lifeless form saunters to the coffee pot without a word. If I didn't know better, I'd guess she spent all night tousling her hair, but even in Alexandra's deepest sleep, she tosses and turns uncontrollably, which produces the brown flame on her head like the one she dons now.

The caffeinated drink escalates its pitch as it rises to the brim of her mug. In a sluggish motion, Alexandra slurps once, twice, then turns to set the mug on the island, her head drooping in the process.

Rough night? I want to ask, but obviously I know the answer. It was a rough night for the both of us. Instead I settle for:

"You're up early."

She groans, and for an instant, I wonder if that's her response. Then she says, "Didn't get much sleep."

"Ah." I take another sip. *Me neither.*

In fact I hadn't gotten any sleep at all. Last night, I stared absently at the ceiling mostly, completely caught in my own head. I wasn't *taken*, though it might have been easier if I had been. No, my mind was shuffling through potential solutions to my problem. How could I get Alexandra to understand? How could I regain her trust? I thought about the way I told her my truth–no– *the* truth. Perhaps I hadn't been articulate enough. Maybe I left out a few bits and pieces. I wondered if telling her everything once more, but attempting to do so from a more neutral perspective, would finally convince her. But no, the way she reacted tells me that she would have no interest.

I'm sure it's been a dilemma she's faced for a while. Does she trust her best friend since college, or her schizophrenic brother, who is practically her other half? Doubting what I say must be like doubting herself, and I know how hard that can be.

Then I thought that maybe I could get Rachel to tell Alexandra for herself. At face level, it sounds improbable, likely impossible, as she has repeatedly demonstrated tendencies of a pathological liar. Why give up the grand lie now, after so many years of stringing it along? But then I remembered Rachel's eyes. I remembered the way they had been so blank. I wondered the reason. Then it hit me. Rachel's true form is hidden behind the

305

great wall of deception she's built. She might even be trapped. Somewhere inside of her, there's an honest, pure woman suppressed by an evil outer shell screaming that she wants a way out–that way out of course being, as it is for everyone, the truth.

But neither Marcus nor Alexandra would let me within a hundred yards of that woman, so that solution regretfully had to be thrown out. For at least another hour in the dark, my mind couldn't procure any other ways to persuade my sister. I'm sure that from her end, I sound insane, and I even consider the possibility myself. I've pondered that this truth I've found *could* be yet another "illusion", as Rachel called them. But something inside me *knows* otherwise.

Finally, I realized that I had two options, two roads to travel: the easy or the hard. *Nothing worth doing is easy*, I reflected. After some thought, I knew what had to happen, and I knew that it would hurt more than any truth ever could. That's why I came up for coffee. I thought it might burn a little.

Alexandra clears her throat. "I spent most of the night looking at the best psychiatric doctors around, and after some digging, I think I found one."

"Interesting," I say. Then I swallow, attempting to conceal my eyes as successfully as Rachel had. *It's just another performance*, I tell myself. "Have you been looking at therapy for a while? Or do you think a doctor can use their *psychic powers* to predict future market trends?"

Slowly, Alexandra's head swivels from her cup of coffee, focusing her eyes on me.

Choke down the pain, I tell myself. *It's only temporary.*

"What?" she asks shyly.

"I'm not sure why you'd need someone like that. You're the strongest person I know. But I hope you start feeling better." Not once does my tone waver. *I hate this. I don't want to lie ... but there's no other way.*

There are many unbearable noises in this suburban area. It's not the barking dog, not the chirping birds, not that lifted Duramax that drives by. It's

306

not even the house across the street. The worst of them all now is the insufferable nagging of my own necessary fraudulence.

Befuddlement first strikes Alexandra's face as her eyes narrow when suddenly, they widen. And I think she's come to the exact conclusion I was hoping to lead her toward. She mouths the word *no*, like someone who's just discovered their dog's cancer has relapsed.

Before she can say anything, I divert my gaze as they start to fill with tears. *Fight it.* Pretending to check my phone for the time, I say, "I should practice some before my gig at HonkyTonk tonight. Josephine said she can't wait to see me." My voice cracks at the end, and I hope Alexandra doesn't notice. I don't even take the time to check. Swiping my coffee off the island, I head downstairs with a bleeding heart that's just been ripped in half.

Sometimes, for the greater good, sacrifices must be made. When one individual's truth contradicts the world's, perhaps it is better to lower the spear and simulate the act of assimilation. Surely there will be no lies in the next life, anyway.

Into the Cave I go. The broken door hangs off one hinge and closes awkwardly behind me. I take a heavy swig of coffee, and it burns down my throat just as I hoped it would.

I suppose I'd better hop on the stage. In doing so, I view my collection of hanging guitars with intense anxiety. My *taken* world has always been a source of profound comfort. It's always been my escape. But there's something I now find unsettling about it. Regardless, it will forever be a part of me. I might as well embrace it.

Delicately, I hold the Gibson Les Paul in my hands, the classic sunrise gloss of the body almost immediately warming me. It plugs into the amp with a slight crack. It strums like a beauty. I close my eyes, working through ballads that reflect exactly how I feel. Minor chords are typically the sad ones, but they need to be paired with powerful happy chords to be truly effective.

I'm afraid to open my eyes. The way the music interacts with my soul … I can feel myself slowly being *taken* far, far away.

The opposite of a wink, I quickly open my right eye and shut it. What I see shocks me. Maybe I hadn't opened my eye for long enough. So I do it again.

By God.

Inexplicably, the Cave remains in sight, despite the chords, despite the chaos they usually usher in, I'm here. I'm present. Until something flashes before me in a streak of white and black, startling me to the point that I nearly fall off the stool. Reactively, I stop playing, breathing heavily.

What was that?

Then my eyes fall upon the monitor, and an idea presented to me by God arrives. I unplug the guitar, setting it back on its hook. My feet clop down the steps of the stage as I rush to the computer.

I grab the mouse firmly. Intent eyes search the screen. A few clicks later, I have what I need.

I pull out my phone, dialing the ten-digit number. I wait a moment, building up the courage to hit the call button by implementing the one method that usually works to calm the nerves. Closing my eyes, taking a few deep breaths, my thumb instinctively twitches. Moments later, I hear the ringing in my ear.

Oh my gosh, please pick up. Wait, no. Don't pick up, I'm nervous. What am I going to say?

It becomes too late to bail when a deep and alluring female voice calmly picks up on the other end.

"Hello?"

"Hi, um … hi."

"Who is this?"

I wipe the drop of sweat trickling down my forehead. "This is–um–I'm Liam Crawford." There's a long moment of silence between the two of us. My heart pounds furiously in the seconds it takes me work up the necessary courage to ask, "Is this Becca Knight?"

Made in the USA
Middletown, DE
26 March 2022

63214466R00176